2 5 JUL 2022

Born and raised on the Wirral Peninsula in England, **Charlotte Hawkes** is mum to two intrepid boys who love her to play building block games with them, and who object loudly to the amount of time she spends on the computer. When she isn't writing—or building with blocks—she is company director for a small Anglo/French construction firm. Charlotte loves to hear from readers, and you can contact her at her website: charlotte-hawkes.com.

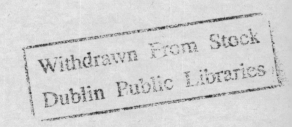

Also by Charlotte Hawkes

Falling for the Single Dad Surgeon
The Doctor's One Night to Remember
The Bodyguard's Christmas Proposal
Reunited with His Long-Lost Nurse
Tempted by Her Convenient Husband

Reunited on the Front Line miniseries

Second Chance with His Army Doc
Reawakened by Her Army Major

Discover more at millsandboon.co.uk.

SHOCK BABY FOR THE DOCTOR

CHARLOTTE HAWKES

FORBIDDEN NIGHTS WITH THE SURGEON

CHARLOTTE HAWKES

MILLS & BOON

First Published in Great Britain 2022
by Mills & Boon, an imprint of HarperCollins*Publishers* Ltd,
1 London Bridge Street, London, SE1 9GF

www.harpercollins.co.uk

HarperCollins*Publishers*
1st Floor, Watermarque Building,
Ringsend Road, Dublin 4, Ireland

Shock Baby for the Doctor © 2022 Charlotte Hawkes

Forbidden Nights with the Surgeon © 2022 Charlotte Hawkes

ISBN: 978-0-263-30123-6

04/22

MIX
Paper from
responsible sources
FSC® C007454

SHOCK BABY
FOR THE DOCTOR

CHARLOTTE HAWKES

MILLS & BOON

Mum & Dad

It's nice to be nice…
wait, what the heck do you think you're doing?!

CHAPTER ONE

BASILIUS JANSEN WASN'T merely aware of his reputation as the incorrigible playboy surgeon of the Thorncroft Royal Infirmary, he actively revelled in his notoriety.

At least, he usually did.

Even now, as he strode purposefully through the corridors towards the resus department, he dipped his head and automatically flashed his trademark killer smile at the usual chorus of flirtatious greetings that rang around every turn.

'Hello, Bas, your surgery last night was amazing.' Hairtwirl.

'Hey, Dr Jansen, have you just been working out?' Sashay.

'Hi, Bas, see you at the Jansen Ball tonight.' Eyelashflutter.

Smile. Grin. Wink.

But his heart wasn't in it.

It hadn't been for some months now—and these days his greetings were more of a baring of teeth than his usual infamous, wolfish charm. Actually taking any of them up on their overt hints held even less appeal.

He growled under his breath. It made no sense.

Boundary-pushing surgeries, stunning women, and expensive liquor had long been his three favourite activities—in that order. And whilst the latter two had never, *never*, impacted on his medical focus, the phrase 'work hard, party harder' might as well have been coined exclusively for him. And he'd been more than happy with that.

He could blame the letter that lay, even now, crumpled and unread in the bottom of the wastepaper basket—to his mind, sullying the luxuriously appointed corner suite on the coveted twelfth storey of the hospital, which boasted a dual aspect over the verdant green landscape that was Thorncroft Park, and for which he'd worked insanely hard.

It had been the last of three letters that he'd received over the past five months, and though he'd hated himself for even opening it, Bas hadn't been able to stop himself from traitorously skimming the contents.

Henrik—the brother who he hadn't heard from in almost thirty years and would have been happy not to hear from for another thirty years. The brother whose one, all too easily dropped lie had caused their mother to eject Bas from the family home, and turn her back on him, never once responding to a single letter or phone call, from a desperate seven-year-old son.

Learning that Henrik was now a surgeon like him had been galling. Worse, that the man who remained his brother in name only was apparently, not only in Britain, but even now on his way to Thorncroft, already stirring up hateful memories that Bas had thought he'd long-since entombed.

Enkindled, incinerated, and entombed.

And now, apparently, resurrected.

Old, hateful memories rose up shamefully inside him. And Bas hated himself for such weakness. For the fact that a trio of unwanted letters could strip away the happy, shiny life he'd built for himself, and hurtle him straight back in time to his vicious past. Making him wish he were anyone else but himself.

Ludicrous.

Surely he was built to bask in who he was? And revel in his Scandinavian heritage?

From his six-foot-three broad-shouldered frame to his shock of light blond hair, and from the dash of stubble that enhanced his strong, square jawline to his eyes, which were the iciest-blue of the fjords themselves, Bas knew he was heart-stoppingly arresting. Or so women loved to tell him—and who was he to tell them any different?

Yet, as if basking in such heritage wasn't enough, Bas also gloried in his reputation as one of the country's rising plastic surgeons. His name—and indeed that of his even more of a playboy plastic surgeon father—was above the entrance to the *Jansen wing* and it was no coincidence that this ultra-modern, staggeringly hi-tech, private medical suite in Thorncroft Royal Infirmary was one of the most sought-after medical care facilities in the country.

Between his father's high-profile reputation as cosmetic surgeon to the deliriously rich and achingly famous, and his own growing name for plastic surgical trauma, surgeons around the world were fighting for a rotation within one of their three UK-based Jansen facilities.

And now, it seemed, Henrik was to be one of them.

Surely that was reason enough for his own uncharacteristically dour mood?

Yet still, deep down, Bas fought the odd notion that it wasn't just the letter that had got under his skin.

Rather, he was finding it hard to explain the growing sense of disillusionment that had been building inside him for several months now.

Bas couldn't explain it. Or perhaps it was more that he didn't care to. Not for the first time, a memory of the last gala night drifted towards him before he thrust it aside, the way he'd been doing for months.

But sometimes, on nights where sleep eluded him, he caught the distant sound of a big band playing. And he saw a shimmer of emerald, heard the ghost of a sweet laugh, and took in the hint of a delicate scent.

Logic told him the memory wasn't sticking so much because of the woman herself, but more because she'd been a welcome distraction—along with the fact that he'd uncharacteristically tried to drown himself in a bottle of the most expensive brandy he could get his hands on—after receiving Henrik's first letter. But still, his skull pounded with the effort of keeping the memory at bay.

Bas emitted another low growl and flung the thoughts from his head as he stabbed the buttons to access the main hospital's resus department.

'Someone paged me for a consult?' he announced, striding over to the ward sister, who was standing at the central computer station. 'An eight-year-old who landed face first off a swing?'

'Hey, Bas.' The sister nodded, making a point of flicking her long ponytail as she changed her pose. 'I didn't know you were on call. Lucky us.'

'I could say the same.' He flashed his killer smile again, and she didn't seem to notice how robotic he sounded. Or maybe it was only in his head. 'Which bay did you say?'

She flicked her tongue out over her lower lip—deliberately probably—and lifted her hand to point across the room.

'Bay five.'

Dipping his head in acknowledgement, Bas swivelled on the spot and began to make his way across the floor, relieved to be away though he couldn't explain that, either. Stepping around the curtain to the bay, he took in the sight of an older doctor, Val, who he knew well, smiling at her charge as she carried out her examination.

'I just want a quick feel of your neck, Bradley, can you turn your head for me?'

'Which way?' the kid asked, his voice clearly thick with tears.

'Whichever way you like. That's perfect. Good man.'

Bas watched as Val gently felt the head and neck.

'What have we got?' he murmured to no one in particular, his eyes still on the patient.

'Eight-year-old kid. Bradley,' someone answered. 'He was brought in by paramedics a few hours ago.'

He watched as Val continued to check the kid's head and

neck, telling him he was doing great, and asking him to turn his head to the other side.

'Any more details?' Bas pressed, his eyes still not leaving the boy.

'He was playing a game of dare with his friends, trying to see who could swing the highest and then jump off. Bradley fell. We think he landed face first.'

'You only *think* he landed face first?' Bas checked, when they didn't continue.

He turned his head to look, only to find the nurse in question staring at him and blushing bright red.

Great—not what his patient needed.

'Anybody?' he gritted out, barely casting a cursory look at who else was in the bay, waiting to get called on to help Val.

There was another beat of hesitation and then a reluctant voice piped up.

'It seems there were no actual witnesses to the fall. Apparently the other kids had all been distracted when a police car had driven by on the road below the woods, with its blues and twos.'

That voice.

Something walloped into Bas—like being struck by a bullet from a forty-four. Only the impact of this strike was mental as well as physical. He was aware of his head swivelling around though he couldn't have said how he managed to move it.

The flash of green, the laughter, the music, all swirled around his head as he stared at the woman. This time, there was no batting her away from his brain.

Naomi Fox.

The woman who'd been haunting his dreams ever since that night of the gala. Longer, in fact. Because the truth was that he'd noticed her first day she'd worked on the resus floor—what red-blooded male wouldn't?—but he'd warned himself to stay away.

There had been something about her, something he couldn't quite put his finger on, that had warned him that Naomi Fox was not a woman with whom he could ever share just a simple, single night of harmless fun.

Striking and tall—almost Amazonian—with a halo of shiny black curls that was almost angelic, and a body that was nothing short of sinfully wicked, she was any man's X-rated dream. And even from that one, single case he'd worked on with her, he'd known she prided herself on being serious and professional. Any man chasing her would have to be equally serious.

Which had made her totally off-limits to someone like him. So why was he still staring like some lost puppy?

And still he stared as Naomi blinked, swallowed, and then, inconceivably, carried on. As if she didn't want to acknowledge anything had ever happened between the two of them.

'From what the ambulance crew were able to piece together at the scene, we believe Bradley suffered initial loss of consciousness for a few minutes,' she hurried on. 'He complained of pain to his neck and right side as well as blurred vision when he was admitted. Significant lacerations near the right eye, on the forehead, and to the right side of his upper lip.'

It should feel like a relief that she was pretending to ignore the electricity that positively crackled and arced between them. But it didn't. Not when a myriad questions were tumbling through his traitorous brain, and not when his body was reacting as though he were some kind of excitable adolescent.

Get your head back in the game.

'Do we know what the ground material was?' mused Bas, irritated by how much effort it took him to revert his gaze to the young patient. To concentrate on peering at the boy's facial injuries, and the blood-soaked clothing.

'Possibly a bonded resin rubber mulch.'

'You've taken bloods? Carried out a CT scan?'

Naomi reached to her side and picked up a tablet, walking towards him calmly. Majestically. And he wondered if she knew he'd spotted that faint tremor in her hands.

'Bloodwork was clear, and we did a full body CT.' She handed him the tablet with a set of results. 'It cleared him on any neck or spinal damage, so Val's just taking off the collar to do a final check for where the pain is located. However, scan did show a fracture to the eye socket.'

Hence why he had been called. He watched Val with the boy.

'Great, Bradley, last thing now, can you lift your head off the bed for me, sweetheart?' the doctor was saying. 'Nice. Great work.'

'No internal injuries?' Bas mused.

'We thought possible damaged spleen at first, but that's also come back clear. It's coming down to lacerations to his face, the orbital fracture and the blurred vision.'

'Okay.' He nodded, his eyes still on the scan, before swiping through the rest of the notes. 'I just need a closer look.'

Handing back the tablet, he moved across the space to where Val was finishing up. It should feel like such a relief to step away from Naomi. But it didn't. Not even when it calmed his body down—if only a fraction.

She shouldn't matter to him at all.

'Mind if I take a look, Val?'

'No, of course not.' She blinked at him in surprise. 'Good grief, if it isn't young Basilius.'

They'd known each other so long that it was as if the older woman had released a much-needed pressure valve from the spectre of Naomi, and he cast the older woman a genuine grin.

'Are you ever going to simply call me Bas?'

Val shot him a pointed glance, which had the effect of further helping to ground him. She'd been at Thorncroft for over three decades—a former army nurse who had become a doctor later in life, and whose skills were legendary. But more than that, she was the one new doctors turned to.

She was also the one who had first looked after him when he'd wandered the hospital corridors as a heartbroken child. A desperately confused, lost kid who'd just been foisted onto a father who had never wanted him and who had been—and still was—even more of a Lothario surgeon than Bas.

After twelve months of his being shoved from proverbial pillar to post, his eight-year-old spirit hadn't just been crushed by what had happened with Henrik and their mother, and then his deeply resentful father, it had been utterly decimated.

But then Val had come along, plucking him from whatever unused consultation room or quiet sluice room he'd been hiding in—so that no one could see quite how unwanted he was—and marching him determinedly towards the canteen to feed him up. And it was Val who had told—instructed—the unapproachable Magnus Jansen that he was going to pay for the refurbishment and redecoration of the small storeroom next to her department, so that Bas would always have a safe space of his own when he was hauled along to the hospital.

Having her there had been better than any babysitter his father could have paid handsomely to employ.

Val had almost been the mother he'd never had.

'I prefer Basilius,' she replied archly, the way she always did. Though the corners of her mouth tugged upwards. 'It is your name, after all, correct? Or perhaps you would prefer the nickname I gave you when you were a boy?'

'No, ma'am.' He laughed. But still, he was entirely too aware of Naomi watching them.

He couldn't shake the feeling that she saw too much. Worse, that he didn't *mind* it.

With a jolt, he turned his attention back to the patient and for the next few minutes Bas busied himself with checking the boy's lacerations, paying particular attention to the right eye socket.

'Good lad, you did well,' he praised the boy at last as he stepped back to where Val was still standing.

But before he could start to speak, she summoned Naomi over. Clearly she was taking the younger nurse under her wing, which meant she thought that Naomi was good. He knew the older woman too well, and it meant she was hoping her young charge would be able to take advantage of the new rules allowing capable nurses to train up as doctors within a matter of a few years.

He tried not to file that away as a point of interest.

'Given the CT results, the location of the fracture, and from what I can see of young Bradley himself, it doesn't look as though he has done damage to the eye itself, or the tear ducts,' he told his old friend.

'That's as I thought.' Val nodded before turning to Naomi. 'But you understand why we paged Plastics rather than suturing ourselves?'

'I do.' To her credit, Naomi looked right at him, even though her voice was quieter than he thought it ought to be. Bas didn't care to examine quite the effect that had on his body. 'Given the complexity of the human face, and Bradley being so young, any doctor who sutures him would need to fully understand the structure beneath, since facial trauma could have such a deleterious effect on the development and growth of facial bones.'

'Good,' Val approved. 'If there was any misalignment of the underlying tissue when they did the suturing, it could result in a malformation, which would likely on become more pronounced as the boy grows up.'

He was about to answer when Naomi started speaking again. More confidently again, this time.

'The fact that the lacerations are in such complex places—around the eye, on the lip across the vermillion, and on the forehead—means that particular care will need to be taken to carry out careful debridement, ensuring no foreign bodies remained, as well as the suturing itself.'

Clearly, she wanted to learn and he couldn't help but feel a little impressed. She was like he imagined a determined young Val to have been.

Only hotter, of course.

And incredibly dangerous to his libido.

'I'm confident I can treat the kid whilst guaranteeing little to no scarring,' he heard himself say.

As if he wanted to impress her, too.

He didn't dare glance at Val, and was almost relieved when a doctor from another bay popped his head around the curtain and asked if he had a moment.

But then—with Bradley now occupied by his mother— it was just him and Naomi, and he wasn't sure he cared for how much he liked that.

'Okay,' he bit out. 'So, I'll want to carry out a more detailed test in my own department once Val's happy to release him but, as I said, at this point it looks like a minor eye-socket fracture. No suggestion of damage to the tear ducts or eye muscle itself. Most of the time, fractures like this go away on their own, with application of an icepack, rest, and pain relief.'

She nodded, then bit her lip and he wondered how he knew she wanted to ask him a question.

'Go ahead,' he prompted, just as the low buzz of Bradley's mother grew quiet.

So when Naomi murmured quietly, he couldn't quite hear.

He turned to his patient, but the woman was merely kissing her son's forehead, engrossed in pushing the damp, bloodied hair away from his face, even though Val had already ensured it was done.

Still, when Bas turned back he instinctively took a step closer to Naomi, a waft of coconut-scented shampoo assailing his senses.

And this time, the wallop was a hard punch to his gut.

A split-second image of her curls tumbling down onto his chest as she bent her head to kiss a scorching trail along the ridges of the six-pack he was so famous for.

The punch sucked the air from his very lungs.

He'd slept with more than his fair share of women, over the years. But now, looking at Naomi, it was impossible for him to even recall any other name. Or face.

'We considered getting someone from Ophthalmology,' she muttered, and he actually had to fight the urge not to sway closer so that her lips might graze his cheek. 'For the blurred vision.'

Bas hesitated. His throat was suddenly so parched that he could barely breathe. What the heck was happening to him? He enjoyed women, certainly, but they didn't *affect* him. Certainly not like this.

He had no idea how he managed to respond.

'I'll take a closer look upstairs but, at this level, even that often goes away without the need for further treatment,' he ground out. 'I have a case to get back to, but have him sent through when you're finished up.'

'Okay.' Naomi nodded, and something about it sent a whole lot more fragments of memory spiralling through his head.

'Thank you, Basilius.' Val came up behind him.

Bas grunted something akin to a reply as he turned to leave the department. The sooner he got out of here and back to the relative sanctuary of his private wing, the better. He was definitely not accustomed to this sensation of feeling turned inside out.

'Do me a favour, Basilius.' Val stopped him. 'When I send one of my nurses up, don't…shall we say…*keep* her like you did last week.'

Bas turned back, raked his hand through his hair with uncharacteristic irritation. Only Val could get away with addressing him that way, and normally he might have made a joke of it. He was never embarrassed, *ever*, but right now he couldn't even bring himself to look at Naomi.

'Then don't send that nurse again. She seemed to have practically glued her hands to the wheelchair and ended up cluttering up my department for an hour, claiming she needed to wait with the patient. I ended up having to order her out of the wing.'

She had also flirted with him incessantly. Or tried to. He was accustomed to the odd flirtation—or ten—behind the scenes, but this woman had been particularly unprofessional in front of the patient. Something Bas had never tolerated, for all his playboy reputation.

The older woman sniffed tellingly.

'Well, if you didn't play up to that reputation of yours…'

'Val…'

'Fine, I'll have Naomi take him to you.'

'Naomi?' The name rolled around his tongue as if he couldn't help but sample it. Taste it. *Again.*

'Naomi,' Val repeated impatiently, gesturing to his emerald goddess and clearly misinterpreting his hesitation.

Which was preferable to her realising the truth.

'Does she suit your taste better?' she asked, oblivious to the salacious thoughts that promptly raced around his brain. 'She's quiet and professional, keeps herself to herself most of the time, so I can't imagine she'd be the type to be inclined to…*clutter* anywhere up.'

'I'm standing right here,' Naomi spoke up unexpectedly, eliciting a chuckle from Val.

'She also isn't afraid to speak her mind,' Val noted appreciatively. 'Which is why I told your father that he'd better grant her one of your darned prestigious Jansen Bursaries, or I'd want to know why.'

Without knowing he meant to, Bas swung his head back around to peer at Naomi.

'You're a JB recipient?'

'You didn't know?' She narrowed her eyes at him and, too late, he realised he'd almost revealed too much.

Like the fact that, for all that the public reputation of the Jansen brand was that he and Magnus shared a close father-son surgeon connection, the reality was that his father was a prideful, jealous egotist who only acknowledged his own son's achievements because it enhanced the Jansen name and reputation. And, by extension, meant more money flowing in.

The only reason his father offered a handful of bursaries around the country each year, to retrain some of the most promising nurses as doctors, wasn't out of the goodness of his heart, but because the man hoped something so charitable would result in some kind of official honours. Maybe an MBE, or an OBE, but most likely, knowing the ruthless Magnus Jansen as Bas did, he was probably after a knighthood.

Still, less than altruistic motives aside, the Jansen Bursaries were worth their proverbial weight. Usually awarded to kids who had never had the same opportunities to go to university to train as doctors, but who showed particular medical aptitude in whichever medical profession they had chosen instead.

And Naomi Fox was apparently one of them.

'I didn't pay that close attention to who the recipients were,' Bas lied easily, grateful that Val was called away by another doctor just at that moment, and couldn't put her tuppence worth in.

'Of course you didn't,' Naomi clipped out. And there was no reason at all for her disapproval to cut through him the way it did. 'Well, for the record, it was awarded to me a couple of years ago.'

All he could think was that if she'd been awarded the JB a couple of years ago, then she was already part way through her training. So where had she been training up until her move to Thorncroft?

Bas frowned, thinking back to the sparse memos he'd read.

'I thought the new trainee doctor coming to Thorncroft had been an army nurse?'

'That's right,' she confirmed, her tone carefully neutral.

He should have paid more heed to it.

'You?'

Naomi's jaw locked tightly, almost imperceptibly. But Bas didn't miss it. Just as he didn't miss the vaguely defiant tilt of her head. A hint that his magnificent Amazon queen still stalked beneath that calm outer skin.

That image of her, dressed spectacularly in a shimmering emerald sort of metallic dress, hurtled through his mind. And then—more mouth-wateringly—that same dress pooling on the floor of a hotel room, and long, deep brown legs, her feet clad in the sexiest of green heels, stepping seductively out.

And now he found out that his glorious green goddess had been in the army? How deliciously apt.

'You don't think an army nurse could be female?' she gritted out. 'How disappointingly medieval of you.'

'Is it?' he asked, almost cheerfully.

She either didn't know that Val also used to be an army nurse, or she didn't know that *he* knew it. Or perhaps she didn't think he cared enough about his old friend to remember. But instead of setting Naomi right, Bas found himself deliberately goading her and he couldn't seem to help himself. It had to be some twisted reward that when her eyebrows shot up into high, disdainful arches, he found it so utterly fascinating.

'You do know that women have been a part of the British army for centuries, whether it was legal or not?' she demanded.

'Have they really?' He deliberately notched his eyebrows a fraction higher as she glowered at him.

He was getting under her skin and making that professional edge of hers slip—even if only a little. And what did it say about him that he relished the concept?

'Yes. They have,' she hissed. 'In fact, during the British Civil Wars in the mid-seventeenth century, so many women disguised themselves as male soldiers that Charles I issued a proclamation banning women from wearing men's military uniforms.'

And now he knew he was in even more trouble than he'd first feared. Because, as irrational as it was, he found her waspish attitude all the more thrilling.

It was certainly better than her pretending she didn't know him, that they hadn't spent nowhere near enough glorious hours exploring every single inch of each other's bodies. Indulging in their most carnal needs.

The quiet, almost meek Naomi of before was not the version of her that he wanted to remember.

'Thank you for the impromptu history lesson.' He flashed his most wolfish grin at her. As if he were about to bite her—and probably in the most carnal way—and he revelled in the punch of triumph as she didn't quite suppress a shiver. 'But I'm not entirely ignorant.'

She made a noise that wasn't a grunt precisely, but suggested that she was graciously biting her tongue from verbally expressing her scepticism. No doubt she wouldn't have been so restrained had Val not still been there, though it was getting harder and harder not to forget about the older woman's presence.

'I am fully aware there are plenty of female military nurses, and female military doctors, and, indeed, female frontline combat soldiers,' he told her, his tone deliberately leisurely. 'Val here was also an army nurse, so my surprise was not about females in general—I'm not a philistine—but about *you* in particular.'

'Right.'

She didn't sound as if she remotely believed him, and an

inexplicably crazy urge to get under her skin charged through him. He ratcheted his grin up to lethal.

'Especially given that, the night of the gala, you didn't mention being in the military at all. Then again, I don't recall us doing much talking. Do you?'

She made something of a strangled sound, her rich eyes—already the colour of his favourite deep, hickory-infused brandy—darkening to almost black, and her breathing becoming suddenly shallower and more rapid. Clearly their not-even-one-night stand wasn't far from Naomi's mind either.

He didn't know why he should find that so deeply satisfying. Bas grinned.

'I *do* recall asking you to dance, only for you to tell me that my reputation as Thorncroft's playboy of the decade preceded me, and that I should keep on walking.'

Though it hadn't deterred him. Their mutual attraction had been undeniable, and she hadn't tried much to resist him after that. She'd certainly been waiting for him around a quiet corner in the hotel lobby as he'd instructed, when he'd emerged from the gala after her.

'Which is why she's unlikely to be daft enough to fall for your particular brand of welcome party,' Val cut in, reappearing without warning and catching the back end of their conversation as she turned to Naomi. 'You're due off duty in ten minutes anyway, so if you take Bradley up, you won't get collared onto a new case and you might even get home on time, for once.'

If looks could have killed, Bas was fairly sure Val would have been flat out on the floor. Naomi didn't even attempt to conceal her dismay, though he didn't miss the telltale kick of her pulse in her neck.

Right where he was sure he had sampled with great satisfaction, more than once.

It certainly cost him far more than it should have done to bob his head in some semblance of normality as he turned back to the older doctor and forced his suddenly deadweight legs to move again.

'Fine, send her,' he managed, astonished that his voice actually sounded normal. 'She seems perfect.'

Which was not at all what he'd meant to say.

CHAPTER TWO

THIS WAS A NIGHTMARE.

Worse.

Watching a surgeon of Bas's skill suture young Bradley's face with such precision and care deserved to be appreciated. It was like an artform in itself—especially since she'd been interested in this particular speciality ever since she'd been an army nurse and seen the soldiers who could benefit from good plastic surgery.

Certainly, the trainee doctor inside her tried to appreciate Bas's skill. Just as much as the woman inside her tried *not* to appreciate the movement of those muscled biceps, or the defined shoulder blades, as he worked.

She really was losing the plot.

Fighting to stop her hands from moving to her belly in what could too easily be a revealing gesture, Naomi contented herself with scowling around the impressively hi-tech Jansen suite. As though her displeasure could somehow remedy this entire ghastly situation.

How did you tell a one-night stand—not even that long, if she were to be accurate—that you were now expecting his baby?

More significantly, how did you justify *not* telling him?

Obviously, she hadn't expected to be able to stay out of Bas Jansen's way for ever. To the contrary, she'd known she had to tell him the truth sooner or later. Or, more pertinently, sooner rather than later. It was the right thing to do. The *moral* thing to do. And when he tried to pay her off and buy her silence—which men like him were universally famous for doing—she could tell him quite loftily that she didn't want his money. She didn't want anything from him.

She'd simply be doing the right thing.

There were three problems with that, however. Problem number one was that she had absolutely no idea how she was to begin to go about doing the so-called right thing and telling him the truth.

Especially since—problem number two—to her utter shame she hadn't realised quite how drunk Bas had been until after they'd actually been…intimate. He certainly hadn't shown any…physical signs of liquor-induced impairment—far from it.

And problem number three was that, after looking after herself, her kid sister, and—to a lesser degree—her grandmother ever since she was about fourteen, Naomi was used to dealing with situations all on her own. From cobbling together some kind of dinner—usually a butterless ham or cheese sandwich and a piece of any fruit that Leila might possibly be convinced to eat—when their grandmother was still out at her second job, to racing to her sister's school to try to smooth things over with the irate headteacher when Leila had tried yet another of her pranks.

Naomi had done it all on her own. She simply wasn't accustomed to opening up her life to other people. She wasn't used to baring her heart and *sharing*.

But this was different. This was a baby. And Bas was the father.

And she'd almost told him.

Twice.

The first time had happened the day after she'd spent half the night on the edge of the bath in her tiny, cold apartment bathroom, staring in shock at the white stick in her hand which—for such a little thing—wielded such life-changing power. Bas had stepped into the hospital lift she'd been in. Even though it had been crowded, and even though she'd been half hidden at the back, she'd kept expecting Bas to realise she was there.

But he hadn't.

The second time she'd been throwing herself into her work, grateful for the organised chaos of the resus department to distract her racing thoughts, when, just like today, Bas had strode onto the floor as one of the plastic surgeons on call.

She'd been with a different patient from him but, nonetheless, a part of her had kept expecting him to see her. To stop. To say something. But he'd been wholly focussed on the emergency in front of him, and he hadn't even looked up.

And when he hadn't, it had felt like *fate* lending her a hand and offering her some much-needed space to decide on the best way to proceed, and how she was going to go explaining it all to Bas.

In fact, it had been a shock. She'd known Bas would be in the private Jansen wing where he was paid obscene sums of money for his admittedly formidable skill as a surgeon, but it had come as a shock to realise that he also gave his time to be on call to the main hospital.

It told a story about him that she didn't want to have to factor in to the image of him that she was trying to keep in her head. The image that would make this little pickle she'd got herself into seem easier to bear.

But now, without warning, she found that the sand had run out of her mental hourglass. Bas was right here, in front of her, and there was no way—not morally, anyway—that she could avoid talking to him any longer.

What a mess.

Accepting the Jansen Bursary was supposed to have been a fresh start—that proverbial clean slate. It was her chance to prove to herself, more than anyone else, that she was worthy of first place. That she would never be anybody's second choice, ever again.

And choosing to do this part of her retraining back at Thorncroft—the place where she'd grown up and was, for all intents and purposes, *home*—was her way of proving to herself that she'd moved on from her less than enjoyable childhood here.

Most of all, retraining as a doctor was supposed to give her the professional life she'd always dreamed of having, but had never thought was for her. Especially not, having effectively taken care of her kid sister, Leila, as well as her grandmother, for most of her life.

It was not, she scowled to herself, supposed to be about falling into bed with the hospital's resident playboy.

And yet, wasn't that pretty much the first thing she'd done?

'Nearly there, Bradley,' she managed to murmur to her young charge, more for something to occupy her mind than out of need.

Bas was doing a flawless job of suturing his patient and talking enough to keep the young boy's mind distracted. He'd even taken the time, whilst anaesthetising the area, to discover his young patient's interests, so that he could keep his conversation light and relevant.

He wasn't just an impressive surgeon, he actually cared about his patients, too.

Damn Bas Jansen and the stupid bursary. Did she really believe that she might lose her one chance at becoming a doctor if he found out her secret? Had she really feared that he might take her bursary away as some sort of revenge?

Or was it more that she feared her own reactions? And the fact that losing her prized bursary would be another reason to look at herself as second-rate.

Certainly, the most incriminating part about the unexpected earlier encounter was that heat, that awareness, still simmered between them.

The *need*.

And not for someone stable, and kind, and potential partner material, but for the kind of playboy male that she'd sworn she would never be foolish enough to fall for. If she'd learned anything from her absent mother, surely it had been that much?

She waited until he finished up, with more words of praise for his patient before turning to her.

'Wait here with young Bradley whilst I go and speak to his parents,' he instructed as he peeled off his surgical gloves.

Without waiting for an answer, he was gone and finally, *finally*, Naomi felt as though she could breathe.

'Well done, Bradley, you did really well.' She smiled brightly as she crossed the room to him. 'Dr Jansen just wants a quick word with your parents and then they'll be in here to sit with you a little longer, whilst we discharge you.'

Which meant she could get back downstairs, out of the private wing that was Bas's territory, and to the relative safety of the main hospital. And if that made her a coward, then so be it.

Still, she wasn't entirely prepared when the door opened a few minutes later as Bas held it open for the parents to enter and signalled her out, making her stomach lurch horribly.

At least, she told herself it was 'horribly'. It couldn't possibly be in anticipation.

'I should accompany the family out,' she managed as he closed the door behind them, leaving the two of them alone in the sleek corridor.

'Give them a bit of time to catch their collective breaths.' Bas strode down the hallway, leaving her standing outside the door.

Without stopping, he half turned to call over his shoulder. 'Let's go, Fox.'

What did it say that her legs followed, almost of their own volition?

'Don't call me that,' she muttered as she caught up to him.

'What? *Fox?*' She didn't need to see his face to hear that grin of his. The one that was all straight white teeth, which she could practically feel against her skin. 'It's your name, isn't it?'

She couldn't bring herself to answer. At least it was better than *älskling*. He'd called her that that night. It had sounded far too intimate, and made her feel things she ought not to have felt.

'Isn't that how you guys address each other in the army?' he challenged, his cheerful tone mercifully dragging her back to the present.

'Sometimes.' She gritted her teeth, and tried to shoot him a dirty look. 'But you are not them.'

Not least because no one else could infuse it with quite the same sense of wicked delight as Bas could.

Or perhaps that said more about her than she wanted to admit right now.

And still, she was obediently following him through the pristine wide corridors, without demanding where he was leading her.

'I hadn't expected to see you in the main hospital,' she managed, at last.

'Indeed?'

'I figured you spent all your days up here, in the Jansen wing.'

He stopped and eyed her.

'You mean in my ivory tower that is a private suite?' he asked, a little too perceptively.

She wrinkled her nose, not liking how easily he seemed to be able to read her. Again.

'Perhaps I would have stayed up here.' He lifted his hand in a gesture that might well have been a shrug. 'But you paged me.'

He had a point. More accurately, though, Bas hadn't been on call. The moment Val had realised that the plastics surgeon who was on call was already with an emergency, she'd told Naomi to page up to the private suite. She'd known Bas would send someone if he could.

Actually, the older doctor had offered quite a few surprisingly complimentary insights into Bas, the surgeon. Not that Naomi was about to mention any of them.

'I did not page...*you*,' she emphasised instead. 'I paged someone from your department. I thought you might send someone else. Someone more junior.'

'Then it was your lucky day, or rather your patient's lucky day, since I was free.' He levelled his gaze at her. 'Or would your patient have preferred someone more...junior?'

Naomi cast him another dirty look, and he didn't care to evaluate what it meant that he got a kick out of getting a rise out of her.

'Obviously not,' she gritted out, before emphasising, 'My *patient* will be better with the best he can get.'

'I'm flattered.' He laughed.

She scrunched up her nose.

'Don't be.'

But apparently he wanted to needle her some more.

'Perhaps you should refrain from calling me the next time some kid inconveniently falls from a playground swing and smashes his face. I would, of course, far rather be in the ivory tower than down here in the dirt.'

Heat bloomed in her cheeks. Still, she wasn't about to apologise outright, it seemed.

'All right, no need to be facetious,' she muttered. 'I now know you're a dedicated surgeon, especially for patients who really need your help, whether they're private patients or not.'

'How very magnanimous of you,' he remarked dryly.

But, as his eyes locked with hers, another jolt of electricity arced between them, and she couldn't respond. With one look, he'd sent her mind spinning, and spinning, and threatening to upend everything she knew to be logical.

What was she thinking, goading this particular man? Not

just a fellow colleague to whom she ought to show respect, for his surgical ability if no other reason. Not simply a member of the hospital board who could have her fired for talking to him in such a way, if he so chose—not that she thought he would. But as the man who was, for better or for worse, the father of the unborn baby she was currently carrying.

A result of the one and only one-night stand she'd ever had in her entire life.

She was almost surprised he hadn't noticed. The bump wasn't huge, but it was clearly there. Then again, the flowing tops she'd taken to wearing recently helped. Along with the fact that she had become adept at keeping the patient between her and other staff, and if not the patient themselves, then a piece of medical equipment. The bed, the monitoring equipment, a computer, it didn't matter what.

Anything to keep off the hospital grapevine for as long as she possibly could. The last thing she wanted was to be the gossip of the whole of Thorncroft Royal Infirmary. Hadn't she had enough of that throughout her entire childhood?

She'd grown up standing out from the crowd. With people staring at her. Talking about her. Because of her family situation, with both parents absent, her height, making her eight-year-old self look like a twelve-year-old, and her skin colour, which didn't match her own mother or grandmother, let alone anyone else on the estate.

She didn't know how long they stood there. Perhaps a few seconds, perhaps a few lifetimes. There were mere inches separating them, though it might as well have been a gaping chasm, and yet at some point, she realised, she'd clenched her fists in her pockets. Presumably in some desperate attempt to stop herself from reaching out. Reaching *for* him.

It didn't help that he was staring back at her with such an expression tugging at his unaccountably striking features. As though he was reliving the same memories. As though he still wanted her, too. Every bit as badly as she wanted him.

But that couldn't be right.

The entire hospital knew that Bas Jansen didn't do revisits. She was simply projecting her own silly fantasies onto him.

And she still needed to tell him the truth. Now. Before she bottled out yet again.

It wasn't as though she needed him to respond. In truth, she doubted he would be remotely pleased to hear what she had to say, and he'd be more than happy to hear that she didn't expect him to play any kind of active role.

But still, she had to do the honourable thing and at least… *tell* him the truth. She might have spent the past few months telling herself that *not* telling him was the right thing to do— the honourable one.

Now, she feared, it had just been the cowardly thing to do. And she was nothing if not a person who owned her mistakes.

'Bas…' she choked his name out '… I have to talk to…'

'Not here,' he rumbled, his voice low.

Without warning, he lifted his finger and pressed it gently to her lips. A jolt of electricity fired through her in an instant, leaving her body tingling crazily whilst her brain turned to mush.

She might have thought it embarrassing had she been able to think at all.

A thousand warning sirens going off in her head at once. Accompanied by a thousand brightly lit fireworks. The part of herself that wanted him—so very badly—warring with the part of herself that hated such weakness.

And so, her eyes were riveted on him. Then, abruptly, Bas spun away and resumed his striding through the corridors, leaving her hurrying to keep up.

Or be left behind altogether.

'Where are we going?' she muttered as she raced after him, his long, muscled legs eating up the long, pristine corridors.

'Patience,' he told her airily. Or perhaps it was *patients*.

She couldn't stop herself from asking him.

'Both, *älskling.*'

And there was that endearment again.

She panicked as he flashed her his trademark grin—the one that usually had an assortment of women falling over themselves.

All she could do was roll her eyes. It was that, or swoon. And she refused to let him see her do the latter.

But Bas didn't notice. He was already a few feet ahead of her.

She'd never felt so glad to be able to keep up with him without needing to break into a run; odd, since she'd spent most of her life hating being tall—yet another difference making her stand out from most other girls.

Being a nurse in the army had been somewhat better. Her colleagues and senior officers had been more interested in whether she could help save lives or not. Coming back to Thorncroft had only happened because her sister had started playing up again. This time more rebellious than ever. And her grandmother was getting too old to control an ever more wilful teenager.

Still, it had shocked them all when it had worked. With her sister back around, Leila had knuckled down and had just secured a place on a fashion course at the college just outside Thorncroft. And her sister was like a different girl, the happiest and most settled that Naomi thought she'd ever seen her. So, in that respect, opting to give up her career in the army had been worth it.

By contrast, ending up pregnant with the child of her benefactor's son certainly hadn't been part of Naomi's big plan. Not least because she'd never wanted to emulate the mother she'd barely ever known.

She'd thought it couldn't get much worse...until Bas had walked into Bradley's bay in the resus department, and it had been as though her entire body had ignited all at the same time.

There had been no denying it, even in that first moment that he'd rounded the curtain. The chemistry from that night had been there, swirling around the vast space and shrinking it to a tenth of its size.

Smaller, even.

When he'd turned to look at her, she'd feared the closeness might suffocate her. Or perhaps it had been more like the memory that had clawed through her. The *need*.

With every hair on her arms, her neck, standing to attention.

She'd known seeing him again wouldn't be easy, but she'd never imagined it would be *this* hard. And that was without even telling him that she was expecting his baby.

Naomi's stomach lurched horribly.

However many times she'd run through the scenario in her head these past few months, she still hadn't worked out the best way to give a person that kind of news. It was the excuse she'd been giving herself for not having sought him out before now. It had been hard enough to work out how to approach it, and that had been before it had become apparent that the chemistry still fizzed.

But now he was here, scant inches away. And she couldn't fake any more excuses. She *had* to tell him.

'Bas—'

'Ready?' he cut her off cheerfully.

'Ready for what? No, wait…'

But it was too late, he was already opening the door and stepping inside. All she could do was follow.

'Hey, Jimi, Heather, how are you doing this afternoon?'

A young boy, perhaps mid-teens, looked up from the comic book he was reading, a genuine smile brightening what had been a rather sullen expression.

'Hi, Bas.'

It was echoed by a woman, clearly his mother, who was sitting in a chair across the room, also reading quietly. The woman looked tired but welcoming, and Naomi shot her an easy smile, before joining Bas at the young boy's bedside.

'This is Naomi Fox—I mentioned her before, you remember? She's a junior doctor who is interested in my field of work.'

'Hi, Jimi.' Naomi smiled softly, stepping forward to shake the boy's hand. But thoughts were racing through her head at a hundred miles per hour.

When had Bas talked to this boy? Presumably when he'd left the resus department ahead of her. And had he really remembered that she'd been interested in his specialism? It was something she'd mentioned briefly, the night of the gala, but Bas had been more interested in other things than conversation that night.

Then again, so had she.

'Hi,' the boy managed tightly, barely looking her in the eye. He pulled the bed covers up over his chest awkwardly.

'Nice name, huh?' Bas stage-whispered.

'Nice,' Jimi mumbled, flushing a deep scarlet, though it was clear to Naomi that he delighted in the camaraderie with Bas.

'I've been telling him that you were a nurse in the army.' Bas turned to her, before swinging back to his patient. 'Jimi is hoping to join as a vet, one day. Right, buddy?'

'Yeah.' The boy wrinkled his nose and forced himself to relax his white-knuckle grip on the fabric. 'As long as the doc here can fix me.'

Naomi glanced at Bas, smoothing her uncertainty into a mask.

'Jimi, can I carry on? And remember, if you've changed your mind about talking to Naomi, that's fine.'

The boy pulled a pained face, but shook his head.

'No, I...want to.' His fingers moved to his pyjama shirt. 'Should I...?'

'If you're ready, buddy.' Bas nodded, turning back to Naomi, his voice deliberately professional. 'Jimi came to me about a year ago suffering from idiopathic unilateral gynaecomastia as a result of pubertal development.'

Naomi watched as Jimi finished unbuttoning his shirt and, after a quick glance at his mother for reassurance, he opened it for her to see.

One side presented as a flat, boy's chest, the other presented like a clear female breast.

'So, then, there's no way to know why this has happened?'

'The major cause of gynaecomastia is considered to be an imbalance between oestrogen and androgen effects, largely as a result of an over-increase in oestrogen production. But in cases like Jimi's, where it only affects one side, that provides an additional layer of complication.'

'Right.' She bobbed her head in understanding. She had so many more questions, but not all of them would be suitable to ask in front of the patient himself.

'As you can see, it's quite large,' Bas noted. 'And although in Jimi's case the mass is benign, it has understandably had a significant negative impact on his self-esteem, affecting all aspects of his life, not least his schooling.'

'I can't do PE in school, or go swimming,' Jimi muttered. 'I get laughed at, or called Jemima instead of Jimi. They tell me to show them my...'

He tailed off, clearly embarrassed, and Naomi's heart went out to him.

'His schoolwork began to suffer and it began to really damage his relationship with his mum, because of their frequent rows over missing school, or playing truant.'

'Constant rows,' Heather offered sadly. 'Though I can't imagine how it was for Jimi, putting up with those boys. And girls, too, sometimes.'

'Kids can be horribly cruel,' Naomi agreed. Wishing she knew the right thing to say. 'I can sympathise, Jimi, I had my own share of idiot bullies, too. I admire how brave and mature you clearly are, Jimi.'

He glanced at her almost hopefully.

'You think so?'

'I do.' She nodded, relieved.

'Hey, buddy,' Bas teased gently. 'Your mum and I have been telling you that for months, and you didn't believe us? But when a pretty doc tells you, you believe her?'

The boy grinned and flushed scarlet again.

And as crazy as it was, and as much as she knew Bas had simply been using her to strengthen his connection with the young boy, when Bas lifted his head to share a warm glance with her, Naomi had to fight to pretend that her own body wasn't sluiced with heat.

'So.' Bas turned his focus back to his patient. 'Jimi has been through both physical and psychological evaluations to ensure that surgery is for him—I think it's fair to say quite a few psychological evaluations, wouldn't you, Heather?'

'A ton of them,' the mother agreed emotionally. 'Though I'm grateful for every single one of them now that they've finally brought us to this point.'

'But Monday's the big day, right, Bas?' Jimi looked simultaneously eager and emotional.

'It is indeed.' Bas lifted his arm for a fist bump, which the young boy was only too happy to provide.

It was impossible not to smile.

Her own worries seemed so insignificant compared to what this boy was going through. And it was clear that none of the claims she'd heard—that the gifted Bas genuinely cared for his patients—were exaggerated.

All of which might not erase the concerns she had about telling him the truth about her own current situation, but at least they reinforced her belief that telling him was the right thing to do.

Whatever he chose to do—or not to do—about it.

'Thank you so much for trusting me enough to show me, Jimi.' She focussed on the young boy with a positive smile.

'After Monday, I won't have anything to show anyone any more.'

'It's important to remember that, although I'll use every trick I know to minimise the scarring, there will still be some,' Bas noted carefully, and Naomi knew he was ensuring he managed the boy's expectations.

'I know.' Jimi nodded at once. 'But a scar will be sick. Like a battle wound. Not like—'

'Everyone will say how cool it will be,' Heather jumped in.

Jimi rolled his eyes.

'*Sick*, Mum,' he groaned. 'It'll be sick. Not cool.'

'Yeah, buddy, you'll be sick.' Bas grinned. 'Okay, I'm going to leave you to educate your mum on current vernacular.'

'Okay, see you, Bas.'

'Bye, Jimi. Heather,' Naomi added as she followed Bas out of the door.

She waited until they were in the hallway before talking again.

'He must have been getting a really hard time with other kids.'

'I think it's safe to say that the last few years have been hell for him,' Bas agreed. 'Plastic surgery for kids can be quite controversial but I've performed thousands of similar operations—though not all gynaecomastia—over the years, and it never fails to get me, how much difference it makes to their lives.'

'Do the other kids really let them forget it?' she couldn't help asking.

'Definitely. There's always one kid who wants to keep it

alive, but it's incredible how quickly most other kids forget, and life goes back to normal for my patient, once all traces of the disfigurement are gone. I thought you might like to see it for yourself, given your interest.'

She bit her lip, weighing up whether to refer to that night together, or not. She almost didn't, but she was going to have to mention it at some point, so why not in this context?

'I was surprised you remembered our conversation. I didn't think… I thought you hadn't really been interested.' She stopped awkwardly.

'Remembered what conversation?' And it had to be her imagination that made it seem as though he was staring at her with such an intensity. 'I read it in your application file.'

She swallowed once. Twice.

'Bas, I…'

'Wait,' he instructed in a low voice, before turning back up the corridor and summoning her to follow.

He had a point. As quiet as these private wing hallways seemed to be, there could easily be someone around the corner, standing by an open door.

Sucking in a breath, Naomi tucked her hands into her pockets and concentrated on keeping pace with him. Again. She just had to hold her nerve a little longer, but it wasn't easy when, with every step, she felt as though the knot inside her were pulling tighter and tighter.

The memories.

The last time they'd been stalking halls together, it had been in a hotel rather than a hospital. Her hand had been enveloped in his and they'd been hurrying towards a luxury suite, having escaped the gala as it had been in full flow several floors below.

And she had to wonder what it was about Bas Jensen that had her obeying in a way she never would have obeyed any other man.

What was it about Bas that seemed to wind its way right through her—and, given her current situation, how was she ever to break the effect?

CHAPTER THREE

THE WORST THING about it all, Naomi decided a few moments later, was that Bas had a way of making everything feel so thrilling and dangerous, and yet so much fun.

Even now, the thrall that she remembered from the night of the gala spiralled up inside her again, and that familiar heat threatened to spill out of her. Enough to make her keep overlooking the uncomfortable truth that she should have told him a few months ago.

But having the full attention of Bas Jansen was a heady experience, and everything about him that night had been raw, and edgy. And now, just like then, her thoughts were fuzzy in her brain as he had her feeling white-hot and so, so bright, like nothing she'd ever known before. As if she were molten everywhere.

Everywhere.

She could remember her heels sinking so deep into the plush pile of the hotel corridor. And the way her dress—a pretty enough green thing that she'd found in a charity shop, but which Leila had taken and worked her incredible magic on—had moulded itself so lovingly to her body, making her actually feel sexy as she'd hurried along.

Now she was in trainers and scrubs. But somehow that same thrill—that same anticipation—seemed to be winding its way through her.

It was insane.

But she wasn't the same woman she'd been a few months ago—four and a half months, if she was going to be precise—and that was a fact she simply had to hold on to.

'In here,' Bas gritted out, stopping so suddenly that she practically turned ninety degrees on the spot to obey without cannoning into him.

And then she followed him into his office.

It was the view that struck her initially. An incredible view of Thorncroft through two stunning windows set perpendicular to each other, giving the impression that the viewer was master of it all. And perhaps, in Bas's case, that was true.

The Jansen name was more than just *well known* in these parts. It was positively lauded. And it was a reminder that she didn't run in remotely the same circles as Basilius Jansen.

But still, she couldn't stop herself.

'Wow.' She exhaled deeply, her legs moving her across the room, until she was right in front of that incredible view, her hands braced on the thin edge of metal that offered an internal barrier. 'People would pay good money for this view.'

'I didn't bring you here to look at the view, *älskling*.'

His voice rolled through her like another crack of thunder, reminding her that this wasn't the reason she had come here, either. Slowly, almost against her will, she turned around.

Then wished she hadn't as every single thought poured out of her head, as she became acutely aware that they were entirely alone for the first time since the gala night. And Bas was advancing on her. As if she'd brought him her dues and he'd come to collect.

Naomi wasn't sure she was still breathing.

His eyes were almost black with desire, foolishly daring her to believe that perhaps that gave her some power in this little scenario, even when her brain was telling her it knew better. Whilst all she could do was simply stand there, her heart unable to decide whether it was lurching or stuttering, as though she was *waiting* for him.

And then he was bending his head to brush her lips with his, but even though she lifted her hands to his chest to push him away, she found instead that they shamelessly flattened themselves in surrender against the hard wall of muscles that she could still remember tasting.

Instantly, Bas closed the rest of the gap and skilfully

claimed her mouth with his own. And, just like that fateful night, it was enough to turn her inside out, tumbling and twisting as she plummeted right back into his particular brand of rabbit hole.

She certainly wasn't prepared for him to jerk back from her, his eyes searching hers as though looking for some kind of answer. Or for him to mutter so low under his breath that she couldn't quite make out the words, which sounded like, 'It's all come back to me, now.'

For an achingly long moment, neither of them moved. And then Bas took a step backwards.

'I thought you might like to join me for Jimi's operation,' he murmured, as though it was the most seductive offer in the word. And, in a way, it was. 'Watch it. Learn from it.'

She ought to accept. It was an incredible offer; would-be surgeons fought tooth and nail for such an opportunity. So who cared if he was giving her the opportunity because of this wild chemistry, fizzing between them?

Who cared what had just happened—and not happened— between them?

She ought to be leaping at the chance, but instead her own secret weighed on her too heavily. Naomi opened her mouth only to find she couldn't even speak.

He cocked his head as though assessing her thoughtfully. And he shifted, as if mentally moving past whatever had just struck him a moment ago. Back to the cool controlled Bas for whom Thorncroft was so famous.

'Suddenly coy, Naomi?' he demanded. 'I don't recall you having any such qualms the night of the gala. Wasn't that the bargain you drove with me? I asked for a dance, and you said you'd only agree if I promised to walk you through one of my patient cases? That my field of expertise was what had originally attracted you to medicine. Though you cleverly failed to add that you were retraining as a doctor. And certainly not that you were a recipient of my father's Jansen Bursary.'

'I'm surprised you remember,' she quipped, before she could help herself.

The truth was, she had barely recalled that conversation herself. She hadn't felt like herself from the moment he'd begun to weave his very unique variety of magic.

He laughed, and she felt it. Intimately.

'Most women want something else from me than letting them in on a medical case.'

'I'd have thought there were so many women in your life that you couldn't really keep track.'

'Is that really what you think?' he challenged, in a surprisingly cheerful tone, all things considered. 'Only that hardly reflects well on you either, if that's your opinion of me.'

Her mouth seemed terribly parched, all of a sudden.

'Why, because I slept with you?'

And when he grinned at her like that—his teeth bared so sharply that she could practically feel them against her bare flesh—it only sent another delicious, if uninvited, shiver skimming down her spine.

God, how was it possible that she still wanted him so badly?

No, *craved* him.

And then he spoke and made it ten times worse.

'I don't recall much *sleeping* going on.'

No. Neither did she, if she was truly honest. Though that hour with Bas had been the most reckless, most thrilling, hour of her life.

It had also been the most life-changing, which only made her hate herself even more for showing such weakness as to fall for it again now.

Just like her mother with any one of the scores of insanely beautiful, but utterly unreliable men in her life.

Naomi shook her head as if hoping that could dislodge the unwelcome thought.

'No?' he asked, apparently deciding the head-shake was for him.

What did she say now? A thousand thoughts chased through her.

'*No* as in you agree not much sleeping went on? Or *no* as in you're claiming you don't remember?'

'*No* as in I don't remember.' She seized on the excuse instantly, realising too late that was exactly what he'd expected her to do.

He hadn't been throwing her a lifeline. He'd been laying a trap.

And she'd stumbled straight into it.

'How disappointing.' His eyes gleamed wickedly. 'Then, allow me to remind you.'

Before she could react, he had closed the gap again, and even as she backed up she managed less than a foot before the wall stopped her. There was nowhere to go.

And a part of her thrilled at the notion.

Tilting her head up, her body no longer remembering to even breathe, Naomi felt her traitorous eyelids flutter closed as her lips parted in anticipation. She didn't need to see him to know Bas's head was inching lower, then lower again. And this time, she had time to think how his breath skimmed her cheek, warm and minty—a far cry from the rich, smoky brandy taste of his mouth from that first night—but then... he stopped.

Again.

He was still there. She was so aware of him, she could sense exactly how he loomed over her—making her palms literally itch with the effort of not reaching out and laying them on that impressive chest of his. Not reacquainting herself with every mouth-watering millimetre of the granite wall.

It took her far too long to realise that the kiss hadn't happened. And even longer to sluggishly open her eyes.

He drew his head back slowly, his mouth spreading into

yet another broad smile, and his head cocked at a jaunty angle. The bastard was teasing her.

'What,' she managed, 'was that about?'

'I was giving you chance to object,' he told her cheerily. 'To tell me that you didn't want reminding. I find it interesting how remarkably silent you were on the matter, however.'

She fought to regroup, though she noted that neither of them moved.

He was right. She hadn't said a word because she wanted this. She wanted him to kiss her again. Just one more precious memory to lock away—as pathetic as that was—before she told him the truth, and then watched him run for the hills. Or, more aptly, ejected her from his private, hi-tech Jansen suite.

'I didn't see the point in objecting,' she told him primly— or what she'd intended to sound prim. 'You're Basilius Jansen. You do exactly as you please.'

'Not like that, I don't.' He didn't sound offended, exactly. More…firm. 'Not if the woman doesn't want it, too.'

Yet before she could register what was happening, he'd taken a step back. And what did it say about her that every last inch of her body decried the loss?

'Do you get many women who don't want to?' she heard herself ask, in a voice that was too sharp for her liking. 'To that end, do you get *any*?'

He lifted one sculpted shoulder, which his shirt and tailored waistcoat did nothing to disguise—quite the opposite.

'All the more reason for me not to do exactly as I please.'

He didn't say anything more. He didn't need to. Eventually, she gritted her teeth and blew out a deep breath.

'All right; not like that,' she agreed. 'Why would you need to, when you've got practically half the hospital—half the county—falling over their feet for the chance to spend a night with you?'

'A mild exaggeration.' He arched an eyebrow, but at least

he didn't seem so stern. 'I seem to recall that you chose not to remain the whole night in my hotel room.'

She hadn't thought she could.

'You sneaked out when I was in the shower,' he continued. 'When you could have joined me instead and continued our exploration of each other.'

'I didn't…'

Naomi tailed off. She hadn't realised that was an option, and whilst the logical part of her wanted to say she would have left anyway, the foolish side of her brain couldn't help feeling that she'd somehow short-changed herself.

Another weakness to hate herself for.

'Besides,' Bas cut in mildly, 'I'm not interested in the rest of the hospital, right now. I'm interested in you.'

'Interested?' she heard herself echo weakly.

It struck her that she so desperately wanted to believe him. But she had to keep focussed on those two telltale words he'd uttered…that he wasn't interested in anyone else *right now*.

And she still hadn't told him what she ought to have.

She snaked out a tongue to moisten her suddenly parched lips, only realising her mistake when his eyes dropped to watch the movement.

'I can read women, Naomi.' His voice was too gravelly for her to think straight.

Almost as if he was fighting himself just as much as she was fighting herself.

'You can?' she managed.

'Oh, I can,' he assured her. 'And I know you want this, too. But if you want to pretend that you don't…then I'm definitely not about to force you to admit the truth.'

To her shame, she felt as if she had to fight her body not to simply offer itself up to him to do with exactly as he pleased.

'I… I thought you didn't sleep with the same woman twice?' She barely recognised her own voice. It sounded too thready, and wanton.

But she wasn't here for this. She was here to tell him...
what was she here to tell him, again?

'I don't,' he growled. 'But then, I hardly count that brief
interlude between us as a full experience, as good as the sex
was. My dates usually stay the entire night, at least. As a result, I find my appetite for you has been whetted...but by no
means satisfied.'

His words thrilled and prodded her in equal measure. He
might want a fuller experience, but it was somewhat embarrassing to admit that the so-called 'brief interlude' with Bas
had been the most incredible, intense sex she'd ever had.

She didn't know she'd meant to move until she'd taken a
step towards him.

'The rumours...' she began, trailing off as he stretched his
arms out until his hands were clamped around her shoulders.

But instead of pulling her in, he held her there. Until the
urge to topple against him almost overwhelmed her.

'I can't say I've ever really cared for rumours,' he grated
out. 'But maybe there is some truth in them.'

'Oh,' she managed, flicking her tongue out again.

He watched that, too.

'Though, since you're here—' how was it possible for a
voice to scrape through her with such longing whilst simultaneously demanding of her? '—perhaps I can make an exception. For you.'

Later, much later, she would think it was that last part that
ultimately undid her. The idea that he was going against his
own unspoken rules just because it was her.

It was a spell that proved too bewitching to undo.

'Unless there is any reason you can think why we
shouldn't?' he prompted, his voice still low, now sending
her heart into a reckless thumping.

There is a reason, a part of her brain roared at her. But
as though from behind inches-thick glass. Too muffled to
make out properly.

'No reason,' she heard herself whisper. 'But...'

'I like the first part of that answer best,' he growled. 'So either walk out of here now, or accept the consequences.'

Another warning bell went off in the back of her mind, but she just couldn't focus.

Everything was spinning too fast, and she couldn't find anything to reach out and grab, in an effort to steady herself. To say something. Anything.

Then, before she could think any more, Bas's mouth slammed into hers, claiming her, and everything went too bright. It was as if a part of her had been lost ever since the morning she'd left his hotel suite.

And this time, mercifully, she didn't think he was going to stop it.

There have to be a hundred reasons not to do this, Bas thought dimly as he claimed Naomi's mouth with his for the second time. But for the life of him—as she moulded her body to his as though she had been handcrafted to fit him— he couldn't think of a single one.

It was as though this moment had been inevitable, right from the moment she'd come up to the Jansen wing. From the moment he'd walked onto that resus floor. From even before that.

There was a good reason for his reputation for never revisiting previous lovers. He had never even been remotely tempted to break that rule. Until *her.*

But the difference was, he hadn't even remembered her until today—though he didn't know how the hell that was even possible. How he could have forgotten a woman like Naomi, even for an instant.

He'd remembered the dress. And the sound of her laugh. Even the scent of her shampoo. But he hadn't remembered *her*. Not the way she deserved to be remembered. *Revered.*

But one kiss—one simple brush of his lips over hers—and

it all come crashing back. His memory, like the swell of a wave forming behind him, and then breaking over him. He'd been drinking far too much that night—trying to send the letter from Henrik into oblivion—and then she'd appeared at the bar beside him.

Even her sensual, slightly husky voice asking the bartender for a simple spritzer had slid into his head, and then down to his sex. As provocative as if she'd just stroked right along its length.

When had any woman ever made him feel so winded? As though he'd been burning straight through for her, and the longer they'd fought each other, the higher the flames had licked.

And there had been far too many other things he would rather have been licking, right then.

Just as he would now.

Because as fast as he was losing his fight to resist Naomi Fox, his consolation was that she was losing her battle to resist him, even faster.

He could certainly use the fact that she wanted him—*this*—to his advantage. Anything to make him feel less... *savage*.

Angry at her for walking out of his hotel room that night, instead of staying. Even angrier at himself for having let her. If he hadn't been dashing for the shower in an attempt to clear the uncharacteristic fuzziness from his head—purely so that he could appreciate her properly—then he surely wouldn't have been so stupid as to leave her alone. To leave her in any doubt that he wanted her to join him.

It was true what he'd said to her earlier about that brief interlude having whetted his appetite but not satisfied it. Surely that was the reason she'd been haunting his head these past months.

Naomi Fox was the reason why he'd recently lost his stomach for women and drink. The reason that only surgeries seemed to hold his attention these days.

He was still hungry for her, and once he'd sated that need—once he had taken a long, indulgent night getting to know every inch of her glorious body—he could shake off this odd melancholy that had taken hold of him, and he could get back to his easy life, be his playboy surgeon self.

Business as usual. Simple.

Bas ignored the niggling voice in his head that contemplated otherwise.

He wasn't interested in arguments, or deep thought. He was only interested in the here and now. In the way that Naomi was pressed so tightly against him—every inch of their bodies craving the contact. He wasn't quite sure when his hands had managed to sneak under the tunic of her uniform, but somehow they were splayed widely over her stomach and waist. If he was to inch them a fraction higher, they would skim the curve under her breast, and he knew from experience how she would react.

He didn't know how he held himself back from doing so.

All he could concentrate on was the feel of her mouth under his lips. The way her indecently sensual lips parted so sweetly, opening up to him. Inviting him in. And all he could do was kiss her, again and again, as if he couldn't get enough. As if he'd never be able to get enough.

For the first time, he was beginning to know what it must feel like to be addicted to something. To feel that helpless, yet that invigorated, all at once. Everything about her seemed to enslave him.

He didn't care to analyse what shot through him at that.

Instead, Bas busied himself with kissing her. Sampling her. Over and over again. He moved one hand to cup her cheek, his fingers sliding through that abundance of thick, bouncy curls, tilting her head to the side and angling her mouth for a tighter fit.

It was a revelation, the way her tongue swept against his. How had he forgotten the thrill that had given him, that first night together? How had he forgotten the thrill that was Naomi?

He'd thought he'd remembered. He'd thought he'd replayed every last second of it—despite his attempts to censor his brain—innumerable times over the past few months. But not one of his thrilling vivid recollections had come close to capturing every last detail of being with her.

That fact alone should strike fear into his very core.

Sliding his hands over her velvet-soft skin, both exploring and reacquainting, Bas cupped her pert backside and lifted, revelling in the way she instinctively wrapped her legs around his hips and looped her arms around his neck, enabling him to carry her wherever it pleased him to go.

And it definitely pleased him.

It was like a roar inside him, and the longer they'd been talking, the louder it had grown. And if sleeping with her again was the only way to silence it, then he didn't care how many of his self-imposed rules he needed to break, he intended to silence it.

He had to. Because, whether it was merely physical or not, this driving need for her was beginning to cloud every other thought in his head. And that couldn't be allowed.

Unless, of course, he used it to his advantage.

As the idea began to take root, Bas found himself nurturing it. Cultivating it. If he could have her long enough, indulge in this inexplicable greed he felt when he thought of her, then surely he would be able to sate this irrational need he had for her.

And then, perhaps, he could finally get back to the life that had been just fine—more than just fine—for him, right up until a few months ago.

Crossing the room, he set her gently on the edge of his desk, his hands still holding her tightly. Still keeping her against him. Her heat against the hardest part of him, making him burn.

Lord, how he burned.

Like staring into the fiery pit of a volcano, only to then hurl himself off the rim and into the swirling orange and white depths.

He'd never felt anything like it in his life before—this need to have her that was, incomprehensibly, even more urgent than the need that had poured through him the night of the gala.

He was halfway to going mad and he didn't seem to care. Just as long as he got to taste every last millimetre of her silken skin, all over again. He didn't realise he'd murmured his intentions aloud until she moaned softly.

'We…shouldn't…'

'I told you…' He heard his voice but didn't recognise it. 'These are your consequences. Your punishment for skipping out on the lesson too early.'

'I feel appropriately disciplined,' she muttered against his mouth.

And he didn't care to examine what bolted through him at that. Instead, he trailed his hands down her sides, using his knuckles to graze the indent of her waist before allowing his fingers to spread out and his palms to cup the silken skin of her backside. And still he wanted more.

Much more. He needed to slow himself down.

'Do you know how much I like that smart mouth of yours?' he muttered, laying gentle kisses first on one corner, then the other, then back again.

Each time moving in a fraction.

'You do?' Naomi murmured softly, letting him do as he pleased.

Which, in itself, was a turn-on.

'Very much.' He repeated the action again. 'Not least when you aren't using it to take a swipe at me.'

Before she could come back with some inevitable retort, he drew back, his eyes locked with hers as he slowly, deliberately, unbuttoned the first few buttons of her tunic top, to reveal her lacy bra.

Burgundy velvet, like wine against her dark, silken skin. Flowers that cupped the bottom and adorned the top. And between the two, a sheer lace that did nothing to hide the pert, hard nipples that he now knew had haunted his dreams with their vivid, perfect detail.

He hooked one cup down to expose her.

'Bas…' she breathed on a choppy breath.

He didn't bother to answer. Instead, he simply lowered his head to capture it in his mouth, and was rewarded with a soft, raw sound from Naomi as she laced her hand through his hair and arched into him.

It was enough to make the blood pound even harder through him. Making his sex so hard that he wasn't sure how much longer he could keep taking things slowly.

But he had to. This time, this moment, was for her.

Over and over, he used his mouth, his tongue, to lavish attention on her, drawing whorls before taking her deeper into his mouth. Vaguely, he considered that she seemed even more sensitive than she had last time.

As though something was somehow…different. Though he wasn't sure that it made any sense, and he didn't care to waste time analysing it further.

Pushing it from his mind, Bas allowed his free hand to wander down her obliques, feeling her shiver as his fingers skimmed her. Then lower. Until he was sliding it under her waistband and between her legs, into the hot, wet heat that he remembered all too well.

The low, ragged sounds she made tore through him. They made him feel wild, and jagged, from the inside out. His body ached for her so badly that it was almost painful, and it cost him far more than it should have done to keep his rhythm slow. To build up a pace the way he would normally have done without even thinking twice.

It had been like this that one night, too. As if his thirst for her would never be sated. No other woman had ever made him feel quite so primitive. Obviously, it was simply a matter of chemistry, of biology, and it would wear off at some point even if it took slightly longer than usual. And even though, logically, Bas knew this, it didn't seem to help now, when he was finally alone with her again, and she was arching that magnificent body of hers against him, so wet and so hot in the palm of his hand.

Everything about Naomi had him hard and ready. As if he wanted her too much. As if he was barely in control of himself when he was around her.

And then, without warning, she grabbed his wrist and yanked it away, with a low moan as though the action had cost her far more than it cost him.

'Bas…' Her voice was strangled as she fought to pull her clothes back into place. 'I'm sorry, I can't…this can't…'

He was barely about to think over the roaring of his blood but somehow he made himself take a step back.

More than anything else, though, it was the utter shock on her face that felt like the physical slap that he surely deserved.

'This will never happen again,' he managed. 'You have my word.'

'You don't understand…' she began, but he didn't want to hear it.

Clearly, he'd misjudged the situation horribly. He, who was infamous for reading women.

'I apologise,' he bit out. 'Whole-heartedly. Unreservedly…'

'I'm pregnant.' She shook her head as if she couldn't believe what she'd just said. 'I'm sorry…this wasn't the way I wanted it to come out but…there it is.'

Bas stopped talking.

He wanted to sit down. Grab something to steady himself. Something. But, right in this moment, he couldn't see anywhere to do it. So he made himself stand straight. Maybe if he acted in control, it would make it so.

'You're pregnant?'

But he certainly didn't expect to sound so redundant.

How had he failed to notice it? To *feel* it?

Had he been that caught up in banishing the ghosts of that night that he'd failed to spot the blindingly obvious? What was it about this woman that had him acting so completely out of character?

But, of course, it wasn't about Naomi at all, was it? It was about the fact that the first time he'd met her he'd been reeling from the shock of the first damned letter.

And, right now, he was still processing the contents of the latest letter.

Of course, that was it. It made sense.

So why wasn't he as convinced as he should have been?

In front of him, Naomi was nodding slowly.

'I'm pregnant,' she confirmed, more firmly this time.

And then there was only one other question rampaging through his head.

'How far along are you, Naomi?'

CHAPTER FOUR

IT WAS THE expression on his face that thudded through Naomi the hardest—somewhere between fury and despair. It left her with the oddest impression that her confession had left him scraped hollow. Raw. Tricked.

But could she blame him—the way she'd blurted it out? What happened to any of the multitude of dignified, eloquent speeches she'd rehearsed these past months? Even now, her brain scrabbled around for words as though she were struggling to speak in some bizarre alien language.

Then again, discussing her baby with Bas certainly felt rather alien.

'It wasn't planned,' she managed, struggling to process the simple question as her heart hammered so hard in her chest that she was afraid it was going to break out any moment.

She had never shied away from difficult conversations. Whether it was delivering difficult news to a patient's family or challenging her chief of staff at the hospital, she always seemed to have just the knack for turning the conversation so that they somehow ended up thanking her for telling them the thing they hadn't wanted to hear.

'How far along are you?' he repeated, his voice barely recognisable.

No, she'd never feared awkward conversations...but right now, if she could have avoided the one she needed to have with a certain Basilius Jansen, then she would happily have turned around and walked away.

Fled, if she was going to be honest.

Fleeing, however, wasn't exactly an option. She slowed her breathing and tried to control her racing heart.

'Twenty weeks.'

She waited a beat, her eyes not leaving Bas's face.

'Twenty weeks?' He eyed her cynically. 'You don't look twenty weeks. You don't look any weeks.'

'The tunic hides a small bump.' She shrugged as casually as she could, though it felt awkward. Wooden. 'Apparently, I'm what's called "very neat". My mother was, too. Both when she was pregnant with me, and with my sister. According to my grandmother, no one even suspected she was pregnant either time, until she was over six months gone.'

'How...convenient.'

'Not really.' Another shrug. 'It's just a fact. One study showed that one in around two and half thousand pregnant women don't know they're pregnant until they're actually in labour. Do you know that makes it three times more likely to happen than having triplets?'

'You're throwing facts around like they change anything,' he bit out, silencing her slightly manic rambling—for which she was grateful. 'The simple fact is that you're pregnant and you were prepared to let this...*thing* happen between us.'

Her heart picked up a beat.

'Why do you think I stopped you?' Her voice cracked but she pushed on. 'Why do you think I told you?'

He glowered at her harder.

'Twenty weeks ago was the week of the gala.'

'Yes.'

'You were already pregnant when you slept with me.' His low voice rumbled around her. Through her.

She could barely contain her horror.

'*No!* It happened...at the gala, of course.'

'After you were with me?' he growled, as though daring her to say otherwise.

Shock made her curt.

'Are you seriously suggesting that I slept with someone else the same night?'

He eyed her harder, but this time she refused to look away.

'All right, maybe not the same night,' he answered at last. Darkly. 'But maybe within the couple of days of the gala.'

'No.'

'You're sure?'

'I can count a calendar, thank you very much.' Her voice was much too clipped, but there was nothing she could do about that. She'd been dreading this conversation ever since she'd learned the news herself.

'I'm absolutely certain.'

Still, she couldn't drag her eyes from him as she watched something she couldn't quite identify chase across his features.

'Of course you are,' he told her thickly. 'Jansen money would tend to make a woman "absolutely certain" of the timings that would work best.'

Was he actually saying…?

'You're accusing me of getting pregnant with someone else and pinning it on you?' Indignation sent her voice higher pitched than she could have imagined.

Bas, however, remained unmoved.

'Are you?'

Her stomach tilted and churned.

'I understand that the Jansen name is a draw…' She fought to bring her voice back down to something resembling normal. 'But that would be pretty desperate.'

It was an appeal to his sense of decency, but the expression on his face didn't change. If anything, the one thing that flitted across it was so bleak that it made her breath catch.

'People can be desperate. Sometimes, their lies work— for a time. But when the truth comes out, the baby is the one who ultimately pays the price.'

She didn't know how to answer, and so she didn't. And as the clock on the wall ticked the time away, the silence pressed in on her—close, and stifling. She found herself licking her lips, hating herself for the moment of weakness.

'I'm not lying.'

'No.' His voice was dangerously even. 'Because, as you said, you're "absolutely certain".'

Naomi drew in another breath as decades of self-preservation kicked in. She lifted her head and forced herself to meet his eye. She would not cower. She would not make apologies.

'Because you're the only person I've slept with in a year.'

Bas's eyes bored into her for what felt like an age.

'Repeat that,' he demanded, at last.

At least he sounded as unbalanced as she felt. Still, it had taken all she had to say it once, so how was she supposed to say it again?

'I'm the only person you've slept with?' he answered for her, when she didn't speak.

'In a year,' she managed quietly. 'Yes.'

She'd had a couple of boyfriends in the past, so he wasn't the only man with whom she'd ever had a sexual relationship.

But he was the only one who had shown her that it could be that intense, incredible thing that she'd only ever seen in the movies Leila loved to watch. And still, he couldn't have looked any more winded if she'd landed a sucker punch right in his gut.

To his credit, he recovered swiftly.

Of course he did—because Basilius Jansen wasn't just the King of Smooth, he was the damned Emperor of it. Notorious for both his charm and his smooth tongue.

Though perhaps best not to think about the latter too closely. Naomi suppressed a thrilling shiver of awareness.

'Okay.' He folded his arms over his chest, which did little to alleviate the churning ocean that was rushing inside her. 'So you're claiming that this baby is mine?'

'I'm not *claiming*. I'm stating. It's a fact.' This was even harder than she'd anticipated. 'Run a paternity test if you like—the non-invasive prenatal paternity can be done after eight weeks. In case you still doubt me, let me remind you that I'm twenty weeks along.'

It was the nightmare that she'd feared facing yet, at the same time, at least she was finally telling him. Fifteen weeks for her to get used to the idea herself. And fifteen weeks of batting back and forth in her mind: did she tell him, or didn't she? Naomi felt an overwhelming sense of relief that she was finally doing what she believed was the right thing. Whatever the outcome.

She couldn't back out now.

'Insisting isn't going to make me suddenly believe.'

'Then do the damned test, Bas,' she cried, her impatience running out without warning.

And if her voice sounded thicker than usual, then she was probably the only one of the two of them who knew it.

'They'll take a sample of my blood containing foetal DNA, and yours, then employ parallel sequencing and analysing over two and a half thousand genetic markers. It's about as accurate as you can get—ninety-nine point nine-nine per cent, if you want the figures.'

'I know what NIPP is, Naomi,' he bit out oddly. As though he were speaking to her from much further away than the other side of the room.

An inappropriate gurgle of amusement made its way up her chest. Nerves. Not that knowing that helped her in that moment. Bas looked as though he were the one who had just been hit by a car, rather than her.

And not just a car—more like a ruddy great freight train.

'What is it that you hope to gain from this?' he demanded abruptly, making her feel rooted to the pristine floor.

Vulnerable.

She hated that part the most.

'I don't hope to gain anything from you.' The words tumbled out. '*We* don't hope to gain anything.'

'Then you've decided to keep it.'

'I have,' she confirmed. 'I know there are other choices, especially for a single mum who is supposed to be retraining to become a doctor. I know the hours would have been long enough without a baby to have to juggle, too. I could have terminated. Or I could put him up for adoption. But... this is my choice.'

Even if it hadn't been part of any plan.

In truth, up until she'd been sitting in her cramped bathroom, in the flat she'd bought for herself, and her grandmother, and her kid sister, Naomi hadn't even been sure she'd ever wanted children.

She knew how to raise a kid, sure—she'd been more of a mother to her sister than a sibling. But then, she'd had to be. Her own mother wasn't much of an example, and her grandmother was too soft. And too busy working two jobs, even into her sixties.

From the moment she'd found out she was pregnant, she'd flip-flopped from one option to another, to another, then back again. Until now she was here, twenty weeks in and finally telling her baby's father the news.

Apparently, she'd made her decision.

'And you're telling me about it out of the goodness of your heart?' Bas demanded curtly.

Warily, she thought.

Naomi shook her head.

'I'm telling you because it's the right thing to do.'

'But you don't want anything.

It wasn't a question. It was a cynical statement. One that told her that Bas didn't believe a word she was saying.

'Not a thing. I can take care of myself.' Then, before she could stop herself, 'I've been doing it for long enough.'

There was a flash of something in his eyes at that, and she could have kicked herself for the slip-up. Since when did she share with anyone about her private life?

'That's as may be.' He glowered at her. 'But I'm willing to bet you aren't used to taking care of yourself whilst pregnant.'

Naomi took another breath.

'So you believe it's your baby.'

He cast her a sceptical look.

'I believe you're pregnant,' Bas clarified. 'Whether or not it's my baby remains to be seen.'

She swallowed back a snarky response.

'It's yours. There was no one else.'

'So you keep saying.'

'Fine. Then I won't say it any more. The fact is that I told you. I knew you wouldn't be interested but I told you anyway. There. That's it. I've done my moral duty.'

She wasn't sure how, but somehow Naomi managed to turn around and make her way to the door. But as she reached for the handle his voice cracked through the air like thunder, though he barely even raised it.

'Don't even think about opening that door.'

She froze as the air tightened in the room.

Slowly, slowly, she turned.

'I can't imagine there's anything more you could possibly say,' she choked out. 'Nothing civil, at any rate.'

'Believe me, I haven't yet even started with what I have to say.'

She twisted her arm and cast a pointed glance at her watch.

'Then you'd better hurry up. There's another gala tonight. And maybe another lucky woman waiting for you to knock her up.'

She didn't need the steel in the air to know that she'd gone too far. But the whole situation was so stressful, was it really any surprise the moment had got to her?

'I'm sorry… I didn't mean…'

Bas didn't answer. Instead he watched her a moment longer, then pulled his mobile out of his pocket and punched in a couple of keys.

'Who are you calling?' She frowned, craning her neck and hating herself for not biting her question back.

He put the phone to his ear and cast her a black look.

'When was the last time you had a scan?'

'A scan?' Naomi frowned at him. 'About a month ago. Why?'

'I'd like to see it.'

She heard the phone ring, and then the sound of a robotic answerphone voice as Bas rang off irritably.

'By "it" I presume you mean the baby. Why?' She eyed him suspiciously. 'Because you think I'm lying?'

'You know what they say about a picture painting a thousand words,' he clipped out instead.

Her glower was nothing short of murderous, but he seemed frustratingly immune to it.

'I offered to take a paternity test,' she pointed out.

'I find I wish to see a scan.'

'No.'

'No?' he repeated slowly, his head snapping up.

It seemed the short refusal had caught him off-guard, but Naomi refused to feel guilty.

'A paternity test can be carried out relatively anonymously. It can be sent away to people who don't know either of us. But if you came to a scan with me, people would see us.

'Do you really think you'll be able to keep your pregnancy a secret indefinitely? Perhaps I should explain a few things about the pregnancy process.'

'Don't be so condescending.' Naomi sniffed at him.

He cast her a strange look and she got the impression that no one ever sniffed at him. She doubted anyone dared.

'People *will* find out, Naomi. Eventually.'

'I know people are going to find out eventually,' she pressed on. 'And I'll be talked about as the new trainee doctor who fell pregnant her first month here. But I don't need to be the new trainee doctor who fell pregnant her first week here, and the father is Thorncroft's very own Lothario Basilius Jansen.'

'Except that's exactly the scenario,' he commented cheerily. 'Might as well face up to it now.'

'No,' she ground out again. 'Though perhaps I should be grateful you're no longer accusing me of sleeping with anyone else the same night I was with you.'

'Don't push it, Naomi,' Bas growled. 'At this point, I'm not ruling anything out.

'So you'd rather no one here knew you were pregnant? Or just that there's no father?'

'I'd rather people minded their own business,' she corrected. 'But, in the event that I choose to explain further, I'll just tell them that he's someone from before I moved back here.'

Anything but admit it was him, clearly. A sharp expression clouded Bas's face and Naomi tried to look marginally apologetic.

'The point is, it would cause too much of a stir if you attended a scan with me. Practically the whole hospital would know about it, and for what? It isn't as though you're going to even be a part of its life.'

'You have to tell people at some point,' he pointed out, scathingly. 'What about Thorncroft as your employer? Or us, as the benefactors of your Jansen Bursary? I'm certain there's a legal obligation.'

'Not precisely, since I had no intention of taking time off work, even for maternity leave.' Not so much through choice, more through necessity, though he didn't need to know that. 'But if I *had* wanted statutory maternity leave then I'd have to inform the hospital by the fifteenth week before my due date. That means around week twenty-five. I still have a month to decide what I'm going to do.'

'You're not putting my child—*my* child—up for adoption. He or she will not grow up feeling as though they weren't wanted.'

She blinked. He couldn't possibly have known just how close to the knuckle that felt.

He wasn't the one who had grown up feeling as if they weren't good enough. Not dainty enough, or pretty enough. Not *enough*. He couldn't know what it felt like to be second-best. Second choice. However hard her grandmother had worked to try to ensure neither her nor Leila felt that way.

Naomi squared her shoulders, pushing past the familiar stabbing feeling.

'I thought you hadn't yet accepted that you're the father?'

To her shock, Bas stopped moving. As if he himself hadn't realised what he'd said.

'Let's just say that I've yet to be convinced,' he ground out, regrouping at last. 'But if that baby is indeed mine, then you won't be discarding them like the bins you put out on rubbish day.'

The ferocity in his words caught Naomi off guard. And she didn't know what it was about them, but they riled her instantly.

'I would never *discard* my baby,' she hissed. 'I'm talking about putting my child's needs ahead of my own. We can't all be the son of some famous surgeon, living some charmed life.'

'I'd advise you to stop there, Naomi,' Bas warned.

And any other time she might have heeded the strange note to his voice. But she was too full of indignation.

'My mother kept me and my sister—half-sister, if we're going to be pedantic—but she wasn't in a position to look after either of us. She certainly couldn't love us. But she insisted on keeping us. Right up until she couldn't cope any longer and my grandmother had to take over. And, as much as my grandmother provided for us, and loved us, she was old, and tired, and she wasn't our mother. And didn't every other kid in school remind us of that fact?'

'At least you had someone who wanted to do what was morally right and be there for you,' Bas replied, his stilted voice gouging at her. 'And at least, as you said, she loved you.'

'What's that supposed to mean?'

But whatever he'd been thinking, he'd shut it down now, and he shook his head. Punching the keys on his phone again, he turned to her, his voice even but inflexible.

'I want to see a scan, Naomi. And I intend for you to get one. But, for what it's worth, we'll be discreet.

'There's no such thing as discreet in this place,' she scorned. 'I don't want the whole hospital gossiping about me. Worse, someone might remember seeing us leave the gala around the same time and put two and two together.'

He eyed her sharply.

'Plenty of women would revel in being pregnant with my baby. They wouldn't hesitate in letting the entire hospital know.'

'I'm not "plenty of women",' she harrumphed.

'No,' he stated—somewhat cryptically in Naomi's opinion. 'You are not.'

She practically had to bite her tongue not to ask him exactly what he mean by that. It didn't matter much anyway. He was already talking to someone on his mobile.

'Grace? Call me back as soon as you get this. It's urgent.'

Not *someone*, then. But that robotic answerphone voice. Still, for a notoriously single man, Naomi couldn't help but wonder who the woman was.

Not that she was jealous, of course, she reminded herself hastily. She and Bas had enjoyed a one-night stand—not even that long. No strings, and all that. She knew the drill—even if she wasn't exactly practised in it.

Who was she kidding? She'd never had one before—not

even once—it was something Leila had scorned her for many times. *Prim, uptight Naomi.*

And now look at her. Pregnant the first time she'd tried to cut loose. She was a walking cliché, so the last thing she intended to do was compound it by acting like some jealous stalker.

She tried to sound casual. Or neutral, at the very least.

'Who's Grace?'

He eyed her, almost disparagingly.

'A friend.'

Naomi wrinkled her nose.

'That's hardly helpful,' she pointed out. 'Or do you make a habit of placing random calls when women tell you they're pregnant?'

'Women don't customarily tell me they're pregnant.'

He lifted his shoulders in what could be considered to be a shrug, but was so overtly masculine it made her body clench tightly.

'At least, a few have tried it but they've disappeared satisfyingly quickly when asked to provide evidence of their claim. Especially since I am always very careful to take... precautions.'

Naomi suppressed a delicious shiver.

Yes, she remembered his precautions. She'd even tried to roll it on for him. She could only presume that, in her haste and inexperience, she'd snagged it with the stick-on nails that her sister had insisted on her wearing for the ball.

Not long, or gaudy—quite pretty, actually—but not ideal for sliding on bits of delicate rubber.

And she really needed to stop picturing the image, or she was going to heat up so much that she might set the hospital sprinkler system off. And then she might have a different problem, because the image of Bas in a wet suit as it clung to his muscles was a whole other minefield.

She licked her lips.

'Is that your way of saying you want a paternity test?'

This was the moment she'd been expecting. Waiting for. In many ways, she was almost shocked he hadn't ejected her from the entire wing at the first mention of pregnancy. Just so that she wouldn't sully his reputable name any further.

Yet, Bas stared at her, taking far too long to answer her.

'That will come, of course,' he managed eventually, and she had the oddest impression that it hadn't actually even crossed his mind.

But that couldn't be right, either.

'First, however, we're going for a scan.'

Fear rose in Naomi's chest.

'We most certainly are not. I told you, I don't want the entire hospital gossiping about me, which will be inevitable if they know I'm pregnant. Let alone if you're the one accompanying me. I've had a scan. Everything was fine. I am definitely *not* going for another with you.'

He cast her a cool look.

'Are you quite finished with your rant?'

'I'm not being *that* conversion nurse who got pregnant with Bas Jensen's baby.'

'And you won't be. Grace is utterly discreet and she will come here.'

'No.' Naomi shook her head.

'You will have that scan, Naomi. And I will be with you.' He folded his arms again, and this time she was struck by quite how authoritative the man was. How had she failed to appreciate quite what *power* looked like on a man? He didn't just bear the Jensen name, rather he epitomised everything it represented.

She glowered at him, but it seemed to bounce off his solid chest without making a dent.

'So you're…what? Taking charge now?' The idea of it should baulk more. So why didn't it? 'I told you, I don't need your help, I'm perfectly used to taking care of myself.'

'And I'm beginning to think you *tell* me a few too many things whilst you aren't as keen to listen. But I suspect that part of the reason for telling me now is because this is beginning to overwhelm you.'

'You're deluded.'

'No, I'm not, but I think you are.' His voice dropped to a sudden, quiet hum. 'I suspect that whether you want to admit it or not, deep down, you don't want to be the one taking care of everything. You want someone to take the reins for once.'

And it was odd, but it was still there, that lethal air, swirling beneath the surface like a rip tide, just waiting to drag her under. But he was controlling it with a fierceness that struck an unexpected chord in her.

As though by controlling that, he could control some dark secret of his own. As if a man like him had dark secrets at all.

Naomi laughed. Less humour, more a slightly maniacal sound.

She didn't intend to, it just bubbled up out of nowhere, taking over her until her shoulders were shaking and her arms were around her chest. And if there was a slightly maniacal edge to it, then surely she was the only one who could tell?

Because it struck her that she really was out of her depth with this pregnancy. And perhaps his assessment of her wasn't so ludicrous, after all.

So where did that leave her?

'I'm taking you home,' Bas announced abruptly. 'We'll arrange the scan for tomorrow.'

She fought to sober up.

'I'm still on duty.'

'You're done.'

'I don't think so.' She shook her head as he indicated the wall clock behind her.

'Your shift should have finished over an hour ago.'

She shouldn't feel flattered that he'd paid that much attention earlier. He clearly didn't intend it as such.

'Fine, but I don't need a lift. I'm perfectly capable of making my own way home.'

'Do you have your car back?'

His eyes held hers steadily.

'My car?' She wrinkled her nose.

He couldn't possibly have remembered.

'I seem to recall you mentioning that your sister had your car these days. For college, I believe.'

She'd told him that the night of the gala. She hadn't known why. A random conversation they'd been having on the lead up to them being intimate. The fact that he remembered all this time later was…surprising. And Naomi refused to read anything more into it than that.

'My sister still has my car,' she admitted. 'But there are buses running every half-hour from the main stop outside the hospital.'

'And you'd rather wait in the cold night, then endure a long stop-start journey home, than accept a lift from me?'

She would, as it happened. Because whether she wanted to admit it or not, she would rather he didn't see where she lived. Not that she wasn't proud of the fact that she'd bought the two-bed flat for her family, it was just that when she compared it to the luxury penthouse she imagined Bas owned, she felt a little…lacking.

'I'm perfectly…'

'Capable of looking after yourself. Yes, so you've said.' He sounded distinctly unconcerned. 'However, that was before you were carrying this baby—*my* baby.'

'I don't need clarification,' she reminded him. 'I'm not the one who has been in any doubt about its parentage.'

He chose not to answer that.

'You will not be getting the bus any more.'

A smile tugged at the corners of her mouth, despite the prickling indignation.

'You say the word "bus" as though it appals you.'

'Are you suggesting you enjoy such a journey?'

'Sure.' Naomi nodded. 'It gives me time to think. An hour where I can quietly process whatever happened in work that day. Anyway, it's called the real world. You ought to try it one day instead of all your supercars and private jets.'

'I think not.'

She stifled a giggle. If he'd been appalled before, he sounded positively horrified now. And she couldn't explain why needling him was such fun. She made herself shrug.

'Shame. You might find the real world isn't anywhere near as bad as you think.'

She might have known he wouldn't let her have the upper hand for long.

'Are you scared of me, Naomi? Do you think I'll bite?'

It took everything she had not to startle at that. Just, she suspected, as he'd intended. And now her entire body was once again prickling with awareness, and with the too-vivid recollections of their night—hours—together. As though she wanted a repeat performance.

Worse, as though she wanted more—when of course she didn't. And the disdainful man in front of her clearly didn't, either.

Yet still, she found herself following him out of his office, and down the quiet, sleek Jansen wing corridors, and to the exclusive car park reserved for the private wing's consultants only.

Without exception, the cars were all new, high-end motors. Even so, Naomi wasn't remotely surprised when Bas led her to the most muscular, uncompromisingly styled supercar of the lot.

Totally impractical for a baby, of course, she couldn't help thinking. As if that would ever be a factor for the great Bas.

'Of course not.' She forced herself to laugh, but it sounded far more brittle than she would have preferred.

'Because you know I won't,' Bas continued, far too breezily.

'I know,' she managed.

'Not even for you, *älskling*.' His grin was utterly wicked yet icily cold. 'After what you've done, not even if you ask really nicely.'

CHAPTER FIVE

BAS GRIPPED THE steering wheel tighter as he skilfully manoeuvred through the parking garage, and out onto the main road, and tried to focus on his driving. Anything that kept that tumult in his head at bay.

Now that the initial shock was beginning to recede, he could feel a fury beginning to stir. Naomi was twenty weeks pregnant, and he was only just finding out about it now.

If he hadn't walked into that resus bay, today, with her patient, if he hadn't bumped into her—would she even be telling him now?

The question threw itself angrily around his head. He needed answers, but not now. Not until he knew he could keep his cool.

'Left or right at the junction?' he demanded coldly, instead.

'Left or right?' Naomi echoed uncertainly, and a less than forgiving side of himself felt a grim satisfaction at the tremor in her voice. The one he knew she'd hoped she'd concealed from him. It betrayed how much she was struggling right now.

Good—she deserved to.

'Where do you live, Naomi?'

'Oh…' She drew in a sharp breath, before giving him her address.

He didn't know the area well—certainly not somewhere he'd visited—but he knew the direction. Slipping expertly through the gears, Bas nosed his car in the appropriate direction. It would be quicker to drop onto the motorway, maybe about a twenty-minute journey, but public transport would surely have to take at least three or four times that—and only if she didn't have to change buses.

Not that Naomi's transport arrangements were his concern, he reminded himself hastily. Or his problem.

Aside from the one, obvious fact that she was pregnant with his child. *Allegedly his child,* he reminded himself again.

He had never intended to become a father. Never intended to settle down. He knew only too well that he wasn't capable of the kind of selfless love that set a good husband, and good father apart from a bad one.

He was a potent combination of the worst traits of both his parents, and probably those violent stepfathers, too— and there was no damned way he was going to pass that on to anyone else. He would never inflict his childhood on any other poor, innocent kid.

It was why he'd planned his life's trajectory down to the finest detail. Why he'd always been so fastidious about protection. And yet, ever since that kiss with her had brought the memories of that night with Naomi crashing back—he could now remember events in all too glorious detail.

He could picture exactly how she'd looked when she'd watched him take the condom from his jacket pocket, her eyes so dark, and innocent, and greedy, her breathing catching in throat with every shallow, choppy intake, that he'd feared he might have embarrassed himself on the spot.

The way she'd taken it from him had been captivating, her hands actually shaking with the same need that had been tearing through him, right in that moment. Her obvious inexperience had been ridiculously captivating, resulting in him feeling like some unschooled adolescent rather than the notorious playboy of Thorncroft.

Little wonder, then, that the condom had failed and he now found himself in the situation he'd spent his entire adult life avoiding.

Naomi was pregnant.

The knowledge kept clattering around Bas's head, which

felt altogether too empty. Too echoing. He felt suffocated, as though the very breath were being squeezed from his lungs. Yes, Naomi was pregnant, and he was going to be a father.

Him—who should be the last person on Earth to ever subject a child to him as a parent.

Something sharp lodged within Bas's chest. He ignored it.

She was right about the fact that he ought to be demanding paternity tests. His first phone call should have been to his lawyers. They had a series of protocols in place for just such an event—his father had ensured that, being an even more infamous playboy surgeon than his son.

In fact, the protocols had been set up the very week that Magnus had discovered he had a seven-year-old son—two seven-year-old sons, in fact—and that one of them was being foisted upon him.

'Come off at the junction coming up.' Naomi's tight voice broke into his thoughts. 'Then take the second exit. It'll drop you straight onto some country lanes.'

He grunted his acknowledgement, flicking the signal to switch lanes, but didn't add anything more.

Thinking about his twin brother—and the letter still lying in his office bin—didn't help. As ridiculous a notion as it was, he'd felt as if the damned unread letter were judging him. In all the ruckus, he'd forgotten that Henrik had declared his intention to attend tonight's gala. He'd been preparing all day to do damage control, but, after Naomi's revelation, attending the ball was the furthest thing from Bas's mind.

Another thing to ask Grace to take on for him, when she finally got around to returning his damned answerphone message.

As he pulled off the motorway and onto the country lanes that Naomi had indicated, an odd feeling moved through Bas.

The road twisted and turned whilst the built-up environs of the city gave way to flatter, green areas and, as his car began to roar through the relatively traffic-free lanes, for a brief moment Bas began to feel a little less suffocated.

For five or ten minutes, as the car clung masterfully to the tight bends and accelerated through the straights, Bas felt free. But he might have known it wouldn't last. A couple more turns and the road began with ribbon housing and then, suddenly, they were in another built-up area. With an older high street and tired buildings.

The reality of the situation crashed back in.

Bas knew what his father would tell—or, more accurately, *command*—him to do once the indomitable Magnus Jansen heard the news about Naomi. Namely to agree a generous monthly sum to be paid from the lawyers directly into her account. An amount that would be more than enough to take care of this unborn child, as well as to ensure that Naomi signed a non-disclosure form to prevent her from ever telling anyone that he was father to a child. And get back to living his life exactly as before.

It was known as the Erin Contract, and it was what Magnus had put in place straight after he'd been burned by the woman who Bas barely remembered but who was, for all intents and purposes, his biological mother.

She was also the woman who had thrown him away without a second thought when Henrik had thrown him to the wolves.

And didn't that tell him everything he'd already known his entire life? Didn't that prove just how disposable he was? How, as a kid, both his mother and his twin brother had found him that easy to discard.

Magnus had been the one to catch him—though his father had never hidden the fact that it was out of a sense of obligation rather than love. Even growing up, nothing he'd done had been good enough for them. Only Mrs Jenkins, the housekeeper and cook at Redlington Castle—the country pile Magnus had purchased but rarely visited, and where Bas had grown up—had ever shown him love.

It had only been when he'd shown an aptitude for medicine that his father had finally taken notice. And more because the man had realised his son becoming a successful surgeon could reflect well on himself and the Jansen name.

Even so, whilst living with Magnus Jansen might have afforded him a luxury lifestyle, he'd still had to work bloody hard to become the surgeon he was today. Not least because Magnus hadn't so much opened doors for him as shoved his foot behind them to stop Bas from coming through.

The last thing the old man had wanted was to be eclipsed by a kid. Even his own. And even for himself, no amount of success could ever entirely erase the feeling of spending the first two and a half decades of his life hatefully unwanted. Discarded first by his mother, in part down to Henrik, and then resented by his father.

So why would he choose to inflict that kind of upbringing on any child of his own? All those hard, spiteful lessons? And he would inflict them—it wasn't as though he knew any other way to do it.

This was precisely why Magnus had contingency plans with lawyers. He could walk away from Naomi whilst ensuring that his child was more than generously compensated. It would have a better life than Naomi could ever provide herself—on the single proviso that she never publicly named him as the father.

The proverbial win-win. All he had to do was pick up the phone and call his lawyers.

So why wasn't he doing just that?

Why wasn't he kicking Naomi out of the door, and refusing to have any conversation with her until he even knew for sure that the child she claimed was his *was*, in fact, his?

He could blame it on this unexpected, wholly inappropriate, and entirely unwanted residual attraction, of course. The unwelcome fact that he still wanted her. Had wanted her ever since that night when he'd waited for her in that shower, only to discover that she'd snuck out of the hotel room.

He should have revelled in it. No pouting and no preening as she'd tried to convince him that their brief intimacy was actually the start of something new and wonderful together. No tears and no tantrums when he would have stood up, dressed, and assured her that this would never happen again.

Instead, his bed that night had simply felt cold. Empty. Without her in it. And he hadn't wanted any other woman to fill it, ever since.

Bas thought it was that truth that galled him the most. Even now, he couldn't pinpoint what it was about her that affected him so very deeply. As no one else ever had.

Presumably that was why he hadn't been acting with his head from the moment she'd dropped her bombshell on him. The reason why, despite his arguments to the contrary, a part of him had believed it was his baby the moment she'd told him it was. And the reason why he was driving out of his way into a less salubrious area of the city, just to ensure that the mother of his child was safe.

And he hated himself for such weakness.

Well, no more. As soon as he dropped her at home, he was heading back to the city, back to civilisation, and back to the lawyers who could handle the rest of this unpleasant debacle without him having to sully his hands any further. Something about this thought made Bas feel even more unsettled than he had since Naomi had appeared back in his life. But he wouldn't think about that now. He had years of practice pushing uncomfortable thoughts to hidden recesses of his brain. And what was one more to add to his already existing multitude of unpleasant memories...?

'Take a left, then the second right.'

Her quiet voice cut through his thoughts.

He peered through the top of the windscreen and grimaced. 'These are flats.'

'So they are,' she agreed, valiantly attempting to convince herself that she didn't give a rat's backside what he thought about her. 'Mine's the one on the right, next to the field.'

'Here?' He made no effort to conceal his distaste. 'This is where you live?'

'We don't all have the Jansen name. Or money.'

Could he practically feel her bristling in her seat? She probably ought to be more circumspect; he'd been remarkably patient, not levelling half the demands or accusations at her that she'd tried to anticipate he might.

But her usual patient, judicious self appeared to have deserted her. What was it about this man that left her feeling so edgy, so impatient, so unlike herself?

'Still, you're a doctor, you must have some money. This place is barely a step up from student digs.'

'Hardly.' Naomi snorted, refusing to acknowledge the heat blooming in her cheeks, and spreading down her neck even as she scrabbled for the button to raise the door. 'It's actually quite decent. Though I can imagine anything less than millionaire penthouses look like hovels to you.'

'Hardly.'

'You have no right to try to shame me.' She threw the door open before he could get around to open it for her. 'You were born with a proverbial silver spoon in your mouth. A monied plastic surgeon for a father, opening doors for you by virtue of the Jansen name alone. And that's fine, but don't judge the rest of us mere mortals.'

But just because she had got the door open didn't mean she'd managed to unfold herself out before he was there, holding his hand out to her as though she were some kind of old woman.

Or pregnant.

'What are you doing?' Naomi gritted her teeth and glared up at him from the passenger seat.

'Do I need to worry about my car around here whilst I walk you to the door?' he asked, his tone deliberately neutral as he ignored her question.

Her jaw locked tighter, if that were possible.

'We're not complete heathens around here. Not that it matters anyway. I can walk twenty metres on my own.'

'Is that so?' he pondered, almost cheerfully. 'Then I won't be walking with you for long.'

'No,' she snapped.

'Yes. Now, I don't mind if you want to stand on the street and cause a scene, but if you really don't want to be on the hospital grapevine by tomorrow, as you've declared several times already, then I suggest you tell me where we're heading. Before someone sees us.'

Naomi lurched angrily out of the car, and across the pavement to her crumbling, old building, wishing she weren't picturing it through his eyes. He'd never had to claw for every little thing the way she had. Taking care of a baby sister and grandmother whilst trying to scrape the money together to fund the years studying for the career she'd always wanted.

She'd been so proud of being able to buy this little place a few years earlier. Yes, she had the mortgage to pay but it had meant, for the first time, that they hadn't been reliant on a landlord. There was no one putting up the rent, no spending time and love trying to make it nice, only for some less than scrupulous landlord to turf them out.

Yanking open the door, she dimly realised he was taking the weight of it from her.

'Where do you think you're going?' She wished her voice didn't hold such a note of panic.

'I'm seeing exactly where you think you're going to raise my child.'

'No.'

This time it was less a note, and more a shriek, of panic.

'The fact that you don't want me to even see your apartment tells me all I need to know,' he commented pointedly.

'It isn't that.' Naomi shook her head, but whatever else she might have wanted to say didn't come. Turning around to face Bas, she deliberately blocked the doorway. 'You can't come up.'

'The hell I can't,' he rebutted, though there was no heat to his tone.

Nothing to make her feel intimidated.

Merely…uncomfortable. Her life was so far removed from his. Had it been too much to wish that the only image he'd ever had of her was as that polished woman at the gala, who had looked as though she'd fitted into his world? If only for that one night.

'You can't come up,' she repeated. 'It isn't…that is, I don't live alone.'

She wasn't ready for the thunderous expression that darkened over his too-beautiful face.

'Say again?'

'I just mean…' She stopped, and exhaled slowly. Thoroughly. There was nothing else for it but to tell the truth and trust in his discretion not to share her private business with the entire hospital. 'I live with my grandmother and my sister.'

'Your grandmother?'

He'd managed his trick of pinning her with his gaze again, Naomi realised. And even though she knew it was irrational, it left her with an inexplicable compunction to fill the dead air.

'And my sister, yes.' She licked her lips.

'You already told me about them. The sister who has your car and the grandmother who raised you. Granted, you didn't mention that you still lived together.'

'Right.' She hesitated, not sure why it was suddenly so important to explain how much they meant to her. 'It feels like it's always been the three of us, even before my mother died.'

Also, no need for Bas to know how.

'You never knew your father?'

'No. My grandmother took care of us, and now I try to take care of her.'

And still she stood in Bas's way, blocking the door. He could have pushed past her, of course. She wondered why he didn't. Why he chose instead to lean against the wall and simply…talk. As if he knew she needed a moment to get her head around the fact that he was here.

'And your sister's at the college just out of town, right? She must be about nineteen? What is she studying?'

'She's seventeen, and she's studying fashion. All she's ever wanted to be is a designer.' Despite the circumstances, Naomi couldn't help smiling. 'She's really good. She designed and made that emerald gown for me, for the gala.'

'She made that?'

The sudden heat in his eyes caught Naomi unawares. He stifled it in an instant, but it was too late. She'd seen it and it had already seared through her, leaving her struggling to even remember what they'd been saying.

'I bought the dress itself in a…*shop*.' She couldn't bring herself to tell him it had been a charity shop. 'It didn't look great, but I liked the material. Leila was the one who redesigned it and gave it a modern edge.'

'It was bloody stunning,' he announced gruffly, doing things to her.

'My point is…' Her chest was still fluttering wildly and it took all she had not to press her hand to it just to try to slow the beats. 'My point is that you can't come in. It isn't just my home, it's theirs, too. And…they don't know about you.'

'They don't know you're pregnant?' He eyed her sceptically.

'Obviously they know I'm pregnant. But they don't know

you're the father and I have no intention of telling them.' She refused to feel guilty. 'My grandmother has gone through enough between taking on me, then Leila, and then losing my mother—her daughter. She doesn't need to know that I fell pregnant to a man who is technically my boss's son, in a hotel-room fumble after the first gala ball I ever attended in my new job.'

'So what do they think?' he demanded incredulously. 'That I'm some boyfriend who left you high and dry when I heard the news?'

'Not exactly.'

'Then what? *Exactly?*'

She bit her lip, wishing he weren't pushing her so hard.

'I told them that the father is a former colleague from my army days. But that he has been deployed.'

'You told them that?'

She pressed her lips together in a thin line, wishing she didn't have to say anything more.

'I also told them that we're going to get married when he gets back home.'

Bas stared at her incredulously, and it was as though she were actually shrinking. Pressed down by the weight of his glare.

'What then? You were going to claim he'd been killed in action?'

'*No!*' she cried instinctively, then paused.

What *had* she thought she was going to say? She couldn't have pretended that he was deployed for the rest of her baby's life. Shame translated itself to anger.

'You're in no position to judge. You're the king of one-night stands at Thorncroft. I was hardly going to admit to having a brief fling with the surgeon playboy, was I? I had no husband and nowhere to go. It might not hold such shock value in today's day and age, but it would with my old-fashioned grandmother.'

Naomi drew in a deep breath, preparing herself for the next onslaught. But it didn't quite come.

She'd never been so grateful for the ring of a mobile phone, and she tried not to care that Bas had practically dropped her in order to pick it up on the first ring.

'You got my message,' Bas stated, without preamble.

So this was Grace, presumably.

'I need a favour.'

Naomi strained, trying to hear the reply on the other end without appearing to Bas as though she was eavesdropping.

'Can you make it quick? I've got a consult waiting.'

'I need you to make me an appointment.'

'Really?' Naomi heard the other woman scoff. 'You aren't pregnant, Bas.'

There was silence as the woman seemed to be waiting for Bas to laugh, but he didn't. Of course he didn't. Naomi could virtually see the proverbial penny dropping.

'No? You got someone…?'

'Not *someone*,' Bas gritted out, and Naomi hated herself for the way her heart jumped.

'How far along?' the bodiless Grace asked, her voice dropping so that Naomi found herself leaning closer before she could stop herself.

'Twenty weeks.' Bas eyed her movement towards him, narrowed his glare. But at least he didn't turn away. This conversation concerned her just as much as him. He turned his attention back to Grace. 'But she isn't showing much at all. This is all done discreetly, understand? You don't mention it to anyone.'

'She might have got away with it this far, but she won't be able to hide it for ever, Bas.' Naomi heard the woman tut softly. 'Not even much longer.'

'Thank you, I am aware. Perhaps you can tell her that yourself, however.'

'Not a chance,' Naomi heard, then tried not to bristle again when Grace added, 'This is your mess, not mine.'

'Are you going to help, or just pass judgement?' Bas snapped.

'I thought a little of both,' Grace answered airily, and Naomi found herself grudgingly liking the woman. The way she handled Bas was so simple, yet so effective. It almost made her jealous.

But, of course, that would have been nonsensical.

'How about I see you both first thing tomorrow morning? It was my day off, after the ball, but, hey, I've learned to expect the unexpected around you.'

'Dammit, the ball,' Bas gritted out, apparently belatedly remembering. 'You'll need to do something else for me. You'll have to go on my behalf and—'

He stopped abruptly, turning to look at Naomi. A shuttered expression coming down over his face. Clearly, he didn't want her to overhear whatever it was he had to say.

He turned his back.

'I just need you to look out for anything…unusual.'

Naomi couldn't hear Grace's reply, but it was clear that the other woman hadn't understood any more than she had.

'I mean, listen out for anyone who you think…shouldn't be there. I've alerted security that they need to be ready.'

Again, the woman said something, but Naomi didn't catch it.

'I trust that you'll know it if you see it,' Bas gritted out. 'As for the scan, how about now? We can use the facilities in the Jansen wing—with the gala tonight no one should really see us there.'

Naomi waited as they agreed a time, without her. As though she—the person who was actually present—was second to the plans. So what did it say that she was letting them? Allowing them to sort it all out.

It was only when Bas had moved the phone away from his face, about to ring off, that Naomi heard Grace speak again.

'Bas, one last thing. Whatever you're thinking right now—don't.'

Bas growled in warning, but it didn't stop the woman.

'I've never thought you would be the bad father you think you would.'

'I don't wish to discuss this, Grace…'

Grace, it appeared, wasn't about to be silenced so easily. He moved his finger to terminate the call, but not before Naomi heard the other woman say one more thing.

'You're not him. And you sure as hell aren't her—'

The voice went dead as Bas swiped viciously at the screen, and then eyeballed it, unmoving.

Behind her, Naomi could hear the wind in the sycamore trees as it began to pick up. She desperately wanted to ask what Grace had meant by her comments, but something stopped her.

The moments ticked by and then, with a furious glare, Bas swung around to her.

'You have five minutes to throw what you need into a bag and meet me in the car.'

CHAPTER SIX

'I DON'T UNDERSTAND.' Naomi felt as though her entire body was shaking uncontrollably. Her heart hurtling around her chest so violently that she feared it might punch its way through altogether. 'There was nothing wrong with my baby at the last scan.'

She felt her hand being enveloped in a larger one, which she dimly realised was Bas's, but she could hardly process it. She was caught in a nightmare. This had to be her punishment for even considering the option of giving her baby up.

Or perhaps for failing to tell Bas straight away.

So this was her punishment. It was too much to bear.

'This is my fault,' she whispered.

'No.' Grace shook her head emphatically. 'This is not your fault at all, Naomi. We don't know for certain how or why this occurs, but it usually happens in early pregnancy and there is nothing you could have done.'

Naomi knew better. This was where her baby was supposed to be safest, inside her. She was supposed to be nurturing it, allowing it to grow and develop. But her stupid body couldn't even do that properly.

She was usually so calm, so in control, of medical situations, even the most shocking events as an army nurse, but it was so very, terribly different being on the receiving end of them instead.

And this wasn't her area of medicine. Nor Bas's.

This was what it must be like for her patients and their families—this feeling of utter helplessness—when she was explaining things to them. The most wretched emotions washed around her.

It seemed that the excess of fluid was indicative of her baby having difficulty swallowing. Now, as she peered incredulously at the 'double bubble' of fluid in her unborn baby's ultrasound, she struggled to latch onto Grace's words.

'These dark spots here...' the doctor pointed '...and here, are what we call a double bubble. They show the baby's stomach and duodenum are fluid-filled, but as you can see there is no fluid further down the intestinal tract.'

'Which is indicative of duodenal atresia?' Bas stated, and Naomi found herself grateful for his calm, controlled presence.

He was helping her to find her way through when she knew that—without him—she might have felt even more overwhelmed than she already did now.

'So what now?' Bas continued. 'Is it surgery in utero?'

'Not necessarily. Many babies are operated on after birth.'

'So we just wait?' he demanded.

Grace was being as reassuring and positive as she would expect her to be. But even though she didn't know the woman as well as Bas did, she couldn't shake the impression that this was Grace's way of smoothing the way for more bad news.

'To correct the atresia, yes,' Grace confirmed. 'But we do need to perform a couple of other tests.'

Naomi's heart stopped hurtling and simply plummeted. She wanted to speak but she couldn't and was grateful when Bas stepped in again with quiet steadfastness.

'You're saying that duodenal atresia is associated with other birth abnormalities?'

'Not always.' Grace was trying to soften the blow but still, Naomi found she was bracing herself. She knew the language only too well. 'But we like to gather as much information as we can. Sometimes, duodenal atresia is the only complication, but it is possible that it may a heart-related birth defect or Trisomy 21 may be present.'

'What are the stats?' Bas demanded as Naomi could only stare hollowly at the screen.

'One in three babies with duodenal atresia also have

Down's,' Grace confirmed. 'One or two in ten also suffer with congenital heart defects. So I'd like to send you for an amniocentesis, and then to our paediatric cardiologist for a foetal echocardiogram.'

'So much?' she whispered, her hand reaching instinctively to cover her belly.

As though that could somehow protect the innocent unborn baby inside her.

'The more informed we are, the better care plan we can create for you, and the more the neonatologist will have to help care for your infant when they are born.' The doctor offered a bolstering smile. 'The prognosis is excellent for babies with properly diagnosed and treated isolated duodenal atresia.'

'When?' Bas demanded. 'When can these tests be carried out?'

'I'll book you slots as soon as possible,' Grace said.

'And the results?'

'The results might take a couple of days for the lab to process the amniocentesis.'

Naomi's mind lurched. Up to forty-eight hours of wondering and questions. Possibly more.

'What about the baby? Will it…? Will *she*…?' She stopped, looking to Grace for confirmation. Grace nodded. She was expecting a daughter. 'Will she be born normally?'

'With polyhydramnios, there is a high risk that the baby will be born early,' answered the doctor before turning back to Naomi. 'Hopefully, with the right care, we can get you to the thirty-seven-week mark at least. If the surgery isn't an emergency then it will most likely be carried out when your baby is two or three days old.'

'Presumably, in all cases the surgeon will open up the blocked end of the duodenum and connect it back up to the small intestine?' Bas clarified.

'Exactly. There are different subtypes of duodenal atresia,

but the basic surgery remains unchanged. During surgery a feeding tube will also be passed from your baby's mouth, through the stomach and into the small intestine, which will be used for the first few weeks after the surgery.'

'Until the small intestine has healed.' Bas nodded, and Naomi knew it was his way of maintaining some semblance of control.

She struggled to do the same.

'And afterwards...' She stalled, her tongue feeling as though it didn't even fit her own mouth. 'After the operation, will she be able to feed? What I mean is...will she be able to feed from me?'

'It will usually take a couple of weeks for your baby's bowel to be able to tolerate milk feeds.' Grace smiled gently. 'Which is why we use the trans-anastomotic tube to bypass the join in the duodenum, to enable the feeds to start earlier. Once the recovery is under way, there would usually be no reason why you couldn't begin feeding your baby by either breast or bottle.'

'And what about long-term?' Grace asked. 'Should I— we—expect anything in the future?'

'I'd like to see the results of the amniocentesis and the echocardiogram before I make that assessment,' Grace reminded them softly. 'But, in the event of isolated duodenal atresia, the prognosis is good. There aren't usually any long-term effects.'

Naomi tried to nod, but none of it was what she wanted to hear. Then again, what parent would? All she wanted was for Grace to tell her that it was all a mistake and that her baby was absolutely fine.

'Given the elevated risk of premature delivery with polyhydramnios,' Bas cut in, squeezing her hand, 'I presume we're talking additional rest, birth plans, monitoring the size of the stomach?'

Naomi felt her heart thump, and hang. There was something mounting in her that verged on the hysterical, but she wouldn't allow it to overtake her. She refused to. Her one consolation was that at every turn Bas was using pronouns like *us* and *we*.

He didn't leave her feeling as if she was alone in this. And she wondered why she wasn't more surprised.

'Easier said than done, I know—' Grace offered a rueful expression '—but try not to worry. Reduce stress as much as you can. I know you're in the middle of retraining, Naomi. But if you can take a break, or reduce the workload, try to do that.'

'I'll sort that. It won't be an issue,' growled Bas, staring at her as if daring her to defy him.

Any other time she might have. Even now a part of her felt as though she ought to argue her position and tell him that she couldn't just walk away from her career like that. But then her hand crept to her belly again.

Not every mother going through this would have the luxury of focussing solely on her baby. But if that was what Bas was offering to her, she'd be a fool not to take him up on it.

'I'll give you a moment to talk whilst I see if I can set up an echo and an amniocentesis,' Grace advised kindly as she headed for the door. 'Though I suspect Doctors Seddon and Rhodes will have left already, especially with the gala. We're probably looking at tomorrow at the earliest, if I tell them who it's for.'

She was looking directly at Bas as she spoke, and even as Naomi tried to shake her rebellious head he jerked his head up and down.

'Tell them.'

Grace bobbed her head in acknowledgement before sliding neatly out of the door.

And then it was just her and Bas.

'Thank you,' she managed stiffly, turning her neck to the

side but unable to lift her head to look at him through the swirling jumble of thoughts. 'I'd like to go home now, and—'

'I think not.'

Naomi startled at his curt tone.

'I…we just established that I need to rest. For the baby…'

'And you will,' Bas agreed tersely. 'But not there. Not a ridiculous bus-ride away. And not in those godawful flats. Not with my child.'

'Those godawful flats are my home. They're where my grandmother and sister are. My family.'

'You aren't carrying their baby,' he ground out. 'You're carrying mine. And that means you're coming home with me.'

'No…' she tried to argue, but a traitorous part of her wanted nothing more than to do exactly what he was telling her.

'My apartment is around the corner, not somewhere in the back of beyond. It's bigger, and more modern, and it's closer to the hospital for coming in for the tests.'

'What am I supposed to tell my family?'

'Tell them that you're with your baby's father,' Bas told her sharply. 'You know, the one with whom you've pretended to be in a relationship all these months? Tell them you're moving into your new home.'

'But it isn't my home,' she cried.

He eyed her coldly.

'At least, from now until this baby comes out, safely, consider my home yours.'

'You're crazy. They won't believe that. They—'

'Then convince them—I don't care how. I recommend you don't push me on this, Naomi. You won't like my reaction.'

And as much as Naomi wanted to stand her ground, and appear independent, she found herself staying silent. A Leila far more grown-up than she used to be would be on hand to look after her grandmother, after all, and they'd probably both be relieved to know she was being looked after for once in her life.

Maybe Bas was right, and she *did* need him to look out for her. For their baby. She clearly wasn't able to. The scan earlier had given her a huge shock. How could she not have known something wasn't right with her own baby? In her own way, she must be as bad a mother as her own had turned out to be.

How had she not realised that premature delivery could be a complication? She wasn't sure if that made her a worse mother-to-be, or doctor. Either way, it left her feeling somehow more lacking than ever.

Dully, she bobbed her head.

'Fine.'

Because what other choice was there? This thing was serious, and there was nothing she could do but wait.

And hope.

Naomi woke the following morning in an unfamiliar bed, the unusual sound of nothing around her, the morning sun cascading light onto the empty pillow beside her—and with it, a fresh sense of hope.

She was in Bas's guest suite—a beautifully furnished white and grey minimalist space, the footprint of which was likely bigger than that of her entire apartment back home. And strangely she felt lighter than she had in quite some months.

Her baby had every chance of being okay. The echocardiogram—taken once Bas had placed a call and brought Dr Rhodes hurrying back to the hospital—had been gloriously clear, with no signs of defects or abnormalities.

There was still the amniocentesis to go, and then the wait for the results. But all in all, she was feeling far more positive than yesterday.

No mother wanted to think of their baby needing surgery the moment it was born, but if the duodenal atresia was the only concern—and everything pointed to that being the most likely outcome—then the overall prognosis was good.

And the fact that Dr Rhodes and Grace, had been so happy to give their time for Bas—a surgeon who had apparently given up his days off and free time for them on several occasions, from what she dimly recalled—said a surprising amount about the man who was father to her baby.

But now a different question was beginning to gnaw away at Naomi. From the way Bas and Grace interacted, there was clearly something more to their relationship than simply colleagues. A sort of…unspoken closeness.

For her baby's sake, she ought to understand that better.

Throwing back the covers and swinging her legs over the side of the bed, Naomi caught sight of a small rucksack across the room. One that looked suspiciously like Leila's old college bag. Curiously, she walked over to unzip it.

A selection of her clothes, packed neatly and efficiently. And with them the dress that Leila had been diligently sewing all week, claiming it was her latest college assignment, and refusing to let Naomi see it until it was finished. Carefully extracting the garment and unrolling it, she held it up.

It had to be one of the prettiest dresses Naomi thought she'd seen. Her favourite colour, and a fabric that Naomi loved. But even better than that, the slight shaping to it told her instantly that it was a flattering maternity style. Her eyes pricked.

Trust Leila to have thought of everything.

And how had Bas got it from her sister? The faster she dressed and found him, the faster she could get her answers.

Padding through to what was clearly her own private en suite bathroom—but which was bigger than her living room back home—she stepped into an expansive shower, all gleaming glass and polished stone tiles, and luxuriated in the water jets that powered out of the walls, cleaning her body until she felt brand new.

A few minutes later, the stunning dress swirling around her legs, and her damp curls tied up in an easy pineapple on her head, she poked her head out of her room before moving slowly along the corridor.

She hadn't even been sure what she'd been expecting from his apartment—something that was part dark bachelor pad and part kinky dungeon, perhaps, but this place wasn't either.

Instead, the apartment was light and airy, with white walls, and slick, clean lines of shimmering glass and gleaming metal. Modern, yet without feeling cold, or sterile. Not somewhere she could ever imagine a sticky-fingered child, she thought with a pang. She'd rather have a house, with a playroom, and a garden—but it certainly suited Bas.

She took her time looking around. The main living areas, a study with another incredible view over the city, the guest suite, which she had slept in—and a hasty dash past the master suite where she didn't care to think of Bas sleeping—before finally returning to the vast open-plan living room and kitchen where he was, of all things, making her a cup of tea. Naturally from a minimalist boiling water tap, no mere kettle for Basilius Jansen.

'Find what you were looking for?' he asked, mildly.

She was glad he wouldn't be able to read the flush of heat that rushed to her cheeks.

'Sorry?' She feigned innocence.

'A mistress locked away? A bawdy S & M room perhaps? I suppose I should be offended that the mother of my baby thinks so little of me.'

His voice wasn't friendly, exactly. But some of the ice from the previous day seemed to have thawed, if only a little. Or perhaps that was just what she wanted to think. She frowned, a little of her earlier positivity dissipating.

'Perhaps that's because you appear to actively encourage people to think the worst of you. At least, when it comes to your personal life, you do.'

'People will think whatever they want to think,' he countered, in a tone that warned her that particular line of conversation was over.

No matter, there were always a hundred other questions all jostling for position in her head. The question was where to start?

In the end, she plumped for the first one that reached her tongue.

'What are we doing here, Bas?' She wasn't sure how she managed to keep her tone so even. So neutral.

'Doing where? In my apartment? I told you yesterday, I'm making sure the baby you're carrying—*my daughter*—is being looked after as well as she possibly can be.'

'Only less than twenty-four hours ago, you were questioning whether you were actually the father of this baby. Now you've dragged me here, to your penthouse, because I'm not doing a proper job of taking care of *your* baby. I'm not the enemy here, Bas.'

Her voice cracked on the last part, and she could have kicked herself.

'Are you not?' he asked quietly. Dangerously.

'No,' she managed as calmly as she could. 'I'm not.'

Inside, she felt like a churning mess. Not least because she was still trying to work out how things had changed so quickly from the sense of relief they'd both felt emerging from the echocardiogram. How *Bas* had changed from that uneasy truce they'd seemed to have forged.

'It is time to decide what we are going to do.'

'What we're going to do?' she echoed.

'About the baby. My daughter. We need a solution.'

'*Our* daughter,' she said, before realising she'd meant to say anything at all. 'And I have a solution, thank you very much.

Stalking wordlessly around the vast living room, Bas flung

himself into a brown leather armchair and stretched his long, muscular legs out in front of him with unexpected insouciance.

Being alone with Bas—in his penthouse—was feeling more and more taut by the minute, and it didn't matter how many times she told herself it was just the nerves of the situation, a part of her didn't quite believe it.

He, meanwhile, merely waved a hand casually in the air.

'Sit down.'

She narrowed her eyes at him. The best she could manage, all things given.

'I'm not a dog you can train to perform tricks.'

'Asking you to sit down is hardly that,' he snorted.

She arched one eyebrow in an attempt to convey the impression that she was actually irritated. With him.

'You didn't *ask*.'

He held her eyes a moment longer.

'Sit down, *please*,' he amended grudgingly, his eyes not leaving Naomi's.

For a moment, she didn't move. And then, she offered a delicate sniff as she moved to the straight-back dining chairs around the glass and resin table. No need to risk looking ungainly dropping into those sprawling plaid and leather sofas, which were so buttery soft that they looked as though they'd cost about the same as her actual apartment.

Pulling the chair out, she moved back, startled.

'There's a cat under the table.'

'Probably,' Bas replied evenly. 'There are underfloor heating pipes running under there, and he likes to lie on them. So long as he isn't on the table or chairs, I leave him be.'

'He's yours?'

Bas eyed her sharply.

'Is that so shocking?'

'Well, frankly…yes.' It suggested all manner of things about Bas that she would have preferred not to know. 'How long have you owned him? What's his name? How did you even come to own him?'

'I didn't realise having a cat was such a crime.'

Naomi wrinkled her nose.

'It isn't.'

'And yet, I feel distinctly interrogated by such a barrage of questions. Where should I even start? How about here? His name is Sonny, I'd say he owns me more than I own him, and I got him when he was a kitten some eleven years ago.'

'Eleven years?' Naomi exclaimed before she could stop herself.

That was longer than some people's relationships lasted. Even some marriages.

'Grace and I were walking down a canal towpath, back from the hospital, when I saw a plastic bag moving. When I went to investigate, I found two freezing, sodden kittens— three, actually, but one was clearly dead. Grace took one, I took the other, and he's been with me ever since.'

Naomi opened her mouth, trying to find the right words. 'Oh.'

It suddenly seemed significant that he'd had that cat for over a decade. It meant that she could no longer tell herself that Bas Jansen didn't understand the meaning of commitment. He'd committed to a damned cat. For over a decade.

Suddenly, it seemed possible that he could commit to their daughter. If that was what he wanted to do.

She wasn't sure how she felt about that. But before she could consider it in any greater detail, Bas started speaking again.

'What exactly was it that you expected from me, Naomi?' he demanded, without further preamble.

She fought away the flustered feeling that stole over her and lifted her head as high as she could.

'I already told you. I didn't expect anything. I *don't* expect anything.'

'Is that why you hadn't intended to tell me about her?'

The question walloped into Naomi, winding her. It took her a moment to catch her breath.

'I fully intended to tell you about her,' she choked out at length.

'When?' he pushed relentlessly. 'When she was born? When she became a teenager? When she turned twenty-one?'

Naomi bit her lip.

'Before she was born.'

'And I'm supposed to simply believe that? You're twenty weeks pregnant, Naomi. You've known for months, you've had scans, you even told your family. But you didn't think to tell me? The father?'

Naomi dropped her head. Of all the things she'd done in her life, that was certainly her most shameful. She watched her fingers whiten as her fists clenched and unclenched in her lap. And then—she couldn't have said where it came from— a calmness overtook her and she lifted her head back up to meet Bas's glower.

'You're right, and I'm sorry. I just…didn't know how to tell you. Or even if you'd want to know. Your reputation…' She tailed off with a shrug.

'These are your excuses?'

She shook her head vehemently.

'They aren't meant to be excuses, so much as my attempt to explain what went through my head. I was afraid you might think I'd done it deliberately for your money, or connections. I was even afraid that I would lose my bursary once your father discovered I was pregnant. And so, I kept putting it off until I could find the right way, the right time, to tell you.'

'Did you really think there could be a *right time*?' Bas demanded as she gazed at him miserably.

'No, I guess not. And the simple truth is that you had a right to know. So I'm sorry. More sorry than you can ever know.'

Was it just her imagination, or was there a thawing in the room?

'Say I choose to believe you. Say you were going to tell me…' he lifted his hand into the air '…at some point before the birth. You're claiming that you would have done it because it was "the right thing to do"?'

'Yes.' Naomi sat straight, determined not to betray any of the turmoil she felt inside. But she didn't speak.

'But you don't want anything from me? Not a thing? How very *decent* of you.'

And still, his tone lacked the bitter edge of before. A drumbeat pounded hard in her chest, and it sounded very much like the rhythm of optimism.

'I think we've just established that, so far, I've been anything but decent. But it's true. We had a one-night stand—'

'Not even,' he cut in.

'And my falling pregnant was an accident. But for me, it's turned out to be a happy one. I want this child, and I get to choose to do that. But if I hadn't wanted her, I would have got to choose that, too. As the woman, I get to make that choice. You don't. So the very least I can do is allow you to walk away without recriminations.'

'This is my child, Naomi. I can't just walk away.' He didn't need to launch himself up for her to read how tightly coiled he was. 'I'm not the monster you clearly believe me to be.'

She gawked at him in shock.

'I don't think you're a monster at all. How could I? You took me for that scan. You ensured I got the tests I needed. You even enlisted my sister's help to get me clothes when you insisted I came here.'

'Because your idea of looking after yourself would have been going back to full-time work, which you got to by sitting on a bus or two for hours every day; and living in a flat which I highly doubt is big enough for three, let alone three and a baby. I'd hazard a guess that you and your sister still have to share a room. Am I right?'

'No,' she answered, truthfully.

He wasn't convinced.

'Am I right, Naomi?'

She clamped her jaw shut, forcing herself to maintain eye contact. But, eventually, she couldn't stop her eyes from sliding away.

'I sleep on a sofa bed in the living room,' she muttered.

Something dark shifted in his eyes right then, and Naomi realised that, no matter how casual he appeared to be, he was filled with just as much pent up emotion as she was.

'And then you were going to introduce a baby into that mix? I would hardly call that a solution.'

'Plenty of people manage with less.'

She had intended to sound placating, but the words came out more defensively. Little wonder that Bas leaned forward instantly.

'Not any child of mine,' he told her. 'Just as no child of mine will grow up without a father.'

A wiser woman would have paid heed to the dangerous note in his voice. Naomi regretted that she had never thought of herself as all that wise.

'So what exactly are you proposing we should do?' she challenged. 'Enlighten me, please.'

'I am merely telling you that I will be present in her life. I will be there whenever she needs me.'

Which meant *what*, precisely? For a moment, Naomi considered that Bas might not even knew himself what he wanted.

But the next second she dismissed such a notion. Of course he would have a plan. He was Bas, he always had a plan. It didn't mean she would like it.

'Listen.' She cleared her throat, trying to get her point

in before he could voice his. 'I appreciate all you've done, and that you're trying to do the right thing now. But let me spare you by saying that you don't need to. In fact, I don't want you to.'

'Say that again. You don't want me to be a part of my child's life?'

Her stomach churned, but she fought to quell it.

'No, I don't want you dipping in and out of our daughter's life. Or mine, for that matter. It isn't an option.'

She pretended the words didn't scrape her raw inside. Because to admit that might mean she had to admit a few other home truths.

'We agree on that much,' he bit out. 'I don't intend to dip out of anything.'

She tried again.

'What I mean is, you might say that now out of some misguided notion of taking responsibility, but the reality isn't the same. You'll grow tired of it.'

'And you know me well enough to make this assessment, do you?'

Again, his words wielded a dangerous edge. And again, she chose to blandly ignore it.

'I'm not judging, but surely you can see that it's inevitable?' She forced her mouth into a semblance of an understanding smile, though it near killed her. 'You'll grow bored, or resentful. Probably both. With luck, it will be before our baby even knows who you are, so she won't notice your absence. But I think we both know that it would be better not to have that around a baby. You live your life, and I'll live mine. That can be our arrangement.'

'Enough!'

He didn't shout. He didn't even raise his voice. Yet it was clear to Naomi that something inside Bas had detonated. And so she fell instantly silent.

'That is not how things will be,' he murmured quietly. Too quietly.

'It's for the best. You're free, Bas. I release you of all responsibility.'

He glowered at her, his eyes boring into her so hard that she was sure they would leave bruises. Not that she would have been alone in her pain, she could see how tightly his jaw was locked.

'You misjudge me completely if you think that is any kind of an acceptable response,' he ground out.

She lifted one shoulder as delicately as she could.

'Perhaps, but is it any wonder? You're a closed book, Bas. I hardly think you're going to open up to me.'

This time, his eyes narrowed on her.

'If you have questions, maybe you should try simply asking them instead of going through this pantomime.'

'Maybe.' She inhaled deeply. 'But what would be the point? You'd never answer them.'

'Try me.'

Whatever she'd expected, it hadn't been that. Naomi caught her breath, trying to work out if she had the courage to ask all the questions she wanted to. Any other time, she likely wouldn't have but then, any other time, she wouldn't have even been here.

And she wasn't asking for herself; she was asking for her daughter.

Exhaling slowly, silently, Naomi lifted her gaze back to Baz. It was now or never.

'Okay,' she heard herself ask. 'Then tell me what your relationship to Grace Henley is. And explain what she meant on the phone yesterday when she said you could be a good father because *"You're not him. And you sure as hell aren't her"*.'

Bas didn't answer. He simply went still. The air in the room pulled taut, wrapping itself tightly around her and squeezing as though it would force all the air out of her lungs. Out of the room.

And she willed him to speak, to explain and open himself up to her in some way. Anything that might help her to feel as though they were more equal partners in this, instead of her and her pregnancy being an issue that he had to deal with. A problem to solve.

Because she didn't need him to *solve* anything. She'd been dealing with problems on her own for as long as she could remember. She didn't want rescuing. Wasn't this one of the reasons she'd found it so difficult to tell him she was pregnant in the first place?

Still, she silently urged him to talk. But he didn't.

And then, without warning, the mobile phone he'd spun so casually onto the coffee table blipped an alert, breaking the moment as he reached out to read the message.

In one smooth movement, Bas launched himself to his feet, tipping back his mug and finishing his drink in one mouthful. Naomi couldn't say she was surprised when he strode across the room away from her, to set the empty cup on the gleaming granite worktop.

His voice totally emotionless he said, 'For the baby's sake, I suggest you try to rest today, the amniocentesis is scheduled for midday tomorrow.'

'Midday,' she echoed, thoughts of Bas forgotten as everything felt as though it was crashing in on her at once. 'That was the message that just came through?'

'Be ready here by half-past eleven. I'll have my driver, Phillip, collect you.'

'We aren't…that is…you don't want to…'

She'd never stuttered before in her life, and she didn't like that she was starting now.

Bas eyed her coolly.

'You were quite clear that you wanted to be seen with me

as little as possible and, unlike last night, the hospital will be heaving in the middle of the day.'

'Right,' she muttered, half in a daze.

Bas continued as though she hadn't spoken.

'Also, I still have patients, and I have a packed schedule today and rounds to do in the morning. But I will be in Seddon's office at the designated time tomorrow.'

And then, just like that, he was gone. Leaving Naomi all alone in a room that was possibly the most expensive, pristine living area she'd ever seen in her life. But which didn't feel remotely like home.

CHAPTER SEVEN

THROWING HIS GOWN and gloves into the bin, and checking his hands for stains, Bas pushed through the OR doors to de-scrub.

Jimi's surgery had gone smoothly. A subcutaneous mastectomy with a direct resection of the glandular tissue.

Bas eyed his patient through the glass.

The peri-areolar approach with liposuction had been textbook, and Bas was confident that he'd achieved good contour regularity with accurate symmetry. Only time would tell whether Jimi would have numbness or loss of sensation. Or whether there would be any tissue-shedding as a result of blood loss.

It was as good an outcome as Bas could have hoped for. He ought to be happier.

But his mind—now that it no longer had the complex surgery to distract it—was already shifting back to Naomi. But not the amniocentesis from the previous day, so much as the conversation he'd walked out on the day before that.

The last time he'd been home in two days. Instead, he'd been hiding out here in the hospital, using his patients as his cover, and taking on additional on-call duties—all to avoid returning back home. Back to where Naomi was.

All because he hadn't—wouldn't, couldn't—answer the questions she had asked him.

He'd challenged her to ask whatever she wanted, with the assurance that he would answer—his opportunity to make her trust him. But then she'd asked one of the few questions he simply hadn't been expecting, and he'd cut and run, using the hospital and his patients as an excuse for not returning in some thirty-odd hours. And using the on-call room to catch some shut-eye.

The irony didn't escape him.

He scrubbed angrily at his skin, wondering what his next step ought to be. He felt wrong-footed, and it wasn't a state of being that he was accustomed to. He didn't find it suited him well.

'How are you doing?'

Whipping his head around, Bas cast his friend Grace an even stare.

'The surgery went well.'

'I didn't mean the surgery.' She moved to stand near him. 'I meant you.'

He wasn't sure he was going to answer, until he heard his own dry voice.

'You mean, aside from the fact that my unborn baby is going to need surgery mere days after she's born?'

'I'm so sorry,' Grace told him sincerely. 'I can only imagine what you and Naomi are going through.'

A strange lump lodged in Bas's throat. He told himself not to be so emotional.

'Thanks. No amniocentesis results?'

'Not yet.' She pulled a face. 'Seddon put a rush on it, but it still takes time—you know that.'

He grunted.

Knowing how things worked didn't necessarily make it any easier to wait, though.

'Do you and Naomi know what you're going to do yet?' Grace asked. 'In terms of raising the baby, I mean?'

'Do you mean how involved am I going to be?' he demanded. 'It's my child, Grace. Or do you think the same as Naomi? That I'll just *dip in and out of their lives*?'

Grace didn't take the bait. He hadn't really expected her to.

In many ways, she was like Naomi. Calm. Even-tempered. The main difference was that Grace was his friend, whilst Naomi was the woman whose face had—inconceivably— haunted his dreams at night, these past months. And whose body he'd tasted so thoroughly, so indulgently, that he thought he could have identified her blindfolded.

With an effort, he dragged his mind back to what Grace was saying.'

'Is that what Naomi thinks?' she asked. 'That you wouldn't be dependable? Then again, she doesn't know you. You hide the real you well, so I guess you can see her side of it, can't you?'

'Not really,' he replied tersely as his friend cast him a sidelong look. He might have known she wouldn't let him get away with it. 'She asked me what you meant when you talked about me not being like Magnus. Or my mother.'

Grace didn't answer immediately. Instead, she waited as though she expected him to say more.

'You didn't answer, did you?' She sighed eventually.

'I don't see that it's any of her business.'

'You can hear the absurdity of your comment, right?' Grace prodded softly. 'Naomi is the mother of your unborn child. Like it or not, she has a right to hear a little about your past, and the way it shaped you.'

'Does she?' countered Bas. 'It isn't as though we've chosen to be together. If it weren't for this pregnancy, we probably wouldn't have even spoken again.'

And yet, even as he said the words, it felt like a punch to the gut. As though something inside him fundamentally disagreed with such an assertion.

Still, he wasn't prepared for Grace's reaction.

'Wouldn't you?' she asked, carefully.

'What's that supposed to mean?'

'It means that I don't think I've ever seen you act quite the way you did around Naomi,' Grace shrugged. 'And it isn't just that she's pregnant, or that you were both dealing with the news that no parent-to-be wants to hear, because I noticed even before the scan.'

'You're imagining things,' Bas scoffed.

But it took more effort than it should have.

'I don't think so. There was just something…different, about the way you were around her. The softer side of Bas that I usually only see when you and I are alone. I think you like her, Bas. And I think you think so, too.'

He wanted to say something scornful. Or laugh at the suggestion, at the very least. But he couldn't, though he couldn't explain why.'

'How did the gala go?' he demanded instead, stepping off the foot tap and drying his hands.

Grace paused, presumably wanting to say something more. But then she seemed to dismiss it.

'The gala went very smoothly,' she assured him. 'People asked after you, naturally, but I just said you were caught up in a case here. In any case, a record amount of money was raised, and a good night was had by all.'

It wasn't the question he'd really been asking. Given the other parts of his life that were currently blowing up, he just wanted to hear that his brother, Henrik, hadn't turned up to make his presence known.

It made his voice sharper than Bas would have preferred.

'Nothing else to tell?'

Grace hesitated again, and this time there was no mistaking the wariness in her gaze.

'Are you talking about the new doctor on your exchange programme?'

It took everything in Bas not to give into a sudden urge to pound the wall. Violence had always been his stepfather's go-to, never his own, but in that moment Bas felt positively murderous.

Henrik had actually dared to go to the gala.

'He was there?' Bas choked out. 'You met him?'

'I did.' Her voice sounded odd, tight, but he couldn't focus on that now. 'Is there some reason I shouldn't have?'

Bas's mind raced.

'He was actually there? He had the bloody audacity? And you didn't think to call me?' snarled Bas. 'You didn't think to even mention it?'

'I rather thought you had enough going on,' Grace managed jerkily. 'Don't you?'

'Not more important than Henrik turning up,' Bas retorted icily.

And Grace blinked quickly. A myriad unspoken thoughts chased across her face.

'Wait. *Henrik?*' she echoed slowly. 'You mean Rik?'

'Rik?'

'Dr Rik Magnusson, the new surgeon.'

The red haze seemed to turn a darker crimson.

'That's what he's calling himself?' Bas snorted.

A few days ago, he would have single-mindedly tracked his so-called brother down to whatever rock he was hiding under, and he would have sent the traitor back to where he'd come from.

Instead, he felt torn in two. All he kept thinking of was Naomi, back at his apartment, without even the distraction of surgery to keep her mind off the impending amniocentesis results. And suddenly, Bas didn't have either the time or inclination for Henrik, right now.

Grace, it seemed, was still chasing to keep up.

'When you say Henrik, you don't mean…?' She stopped awkwardly. 'But he called himself Rik. And surely he would be a Jansen?'

'My father's name is Magnus,' Bas thrust his hands into his pockets in an effort to conceal his clenched fists. Though he couldn't be sure whether it was at Rik, or at the time this unwelcome conversation was taking up. 'Presumably, he thinks he's clever calling himself Magnusson. And shortening Henrik to Rik.'

'Perhaps he's trying to be discreet,' she managed in an anguished tone. 'Maybe he's trying not to cause a scene.'

If only that were true.

'If he doesn't want a scene, then he shouldn't have come here. He should have stayed the hell away, just as he has done these past thirty years. Just as he ought to have done when I didn't answer any of his letters.'

'Rik wrote to you?'

There was something so demanding in the question that it pulled Bas up short. He eyed his friend a little closer. Her pulse was hammering in her neck, as though she was upset.

Or guilty.

'Rik?' he demanded harshly. 'You're acquainted with him?'

The silence stretched out too long.

'I didn't know who he was,' Grace cried at last.

The implication was clear. Bas felt cold dismay bubble up inside him.

'You had sex with him?' he said coldly. 'Of all the people in this hospital, in this county, with whom you could have had sex, you chose my brother?'

'How could I have known?' Grace raked a hand through her hair.

'I asked you to go in my place and to look out for anything unusual. Anyone who was there who shouldn't be.'

For a long moment, they stood watching each other. And then Grace's panic began to die down, and she eyed him critically.

'And from that, I was supposed to know you meant your brother?'

Bas gritted his teeth. 'Anyone unusual, Grace.'

'I couldn't possibly have known that meant the brother you haven't seen in almost thirty years. I couldn't possibly have concluded that the stranger I happened to meet—the perfectly…normal man, who called himself Rik and was a surgeon like so many people at that medical ball—was someone *unusual.*'

Bas snorted his disdain.

'You think you *happened* to meet him? That it was a coincidence that he bumped into you—the person I'm closest to?'

He watched as she registered what he was saying. Then paled. She shook her head.

'You're saying he sought me out deliberately?' she whispered, her words jagged.

And even through his anger, Bas felt a pang a guilt at how the truth would hurt Grace. And he hated Henrik even more for putting him in such a position. But he knew Grace, she was strong, and fiercely independent, and he wouldn't be much of a friend if he let her believe that his brother hadn't known exactly who she was when he'd seduced her.

And then something else sneaked through him, creeping so stealthily that he almost missed it at first.

If Henrik was underhanded enough to sleep with Grace in order to glean information about him, what would his excuse for a brother do if he found about Naomi? He needed to find her. To…well, not protect her precisely, but…

Bas faltered. What did he want to do if not protect Naomi? She was the mother of his child, after all.

He shut down the voice in his head that asked if that was all she was to him.

Things were so fragile between the two of them. So delicately balanced. The last thing he needed was Henrik crashing in with whatever manipulative power game he was here to play out.

This was his baby they were talking about. He couldn't risk losing her because Naomi decided his family was so twisted and spiteful that she didn't want to have anything to do with him.

However sickeningly true that might be.

'I have to go,' he told Grace. 'But you need to meet up with Henrik again.'

She cast him a horrified glance.

'What? *No!*'

'Yes.' He nodded grimly. 'Whatever he's doing here, whatever he's up to, I need to know.'

Perhaps he should have paid more heed to Henrik's letters, but it was too late now. Now, it was all about damage limitation. Just like the most acute trauma patients who came into his OR.

'Wait, you want me to spy on Henrik?' Grace looked appalled. 'I can't. No. If you want to know why Henrik's here, Bas, you're going to have to speak to him.'

He could read the discomfort in every line of her body, and a sliver of guilt ran through him. But he couldn't give into it. He played his trump card.

'Please, Grace, I'm asking you as my friend. Whatever Henrik is doing here, it won't be good. But I have to concentrate on Naomi right now. She has to be my priority. My baby has to be my main focus.'

'Bas…' Grace bit her lip. 'What you're asking…'

'I'm not asking you to sleep with him again, for pity's sake,' Bas told her, as he realised what she thought. 'I'm just asking you to occupy him. Distract him. Maybe show him around the hospital. Take him on a tour of the city.'

'Show him around…' she echoed uncertainly.

But she wasn't saying no any more, and he took that as a good sign.

A thought struck him.

'You could even ask him to take my place in the hospital fete this year.'

'You really want Rik… Henrik, to get involved in the charitable side of the hospital?'

'Not particularly.' Bas gritted his teeth. 'But you know how long the prep work takes, between repairing the stalls and giving the tired ones a fresh lick of paint. And then there's the manning of them. It takes time. All of which I could be spending with Naomi this year.'

'I don't know, Bas.' Grace pursed her lips. Her distaste for the whole thing was evident.

And maybe he was throwing her under the bus a little, but he really needed her to do this. Because whilst Henrik was focussed on Grace, he wasn't focussed on Naomi.

He just had to apply a little more pressure—as unpalatable as that was. For Naomi and his baby's sake.

'You slept with my brother, Grace. I think you owe me.'

She opened her mouth as if she was going to argue some more and then, abruptly, she closed it again.

'Okay,' she muttered, so quietly that he could barely hear her. 'Okay, I'll do it. I'll try to keep him distracted. But there's a time limit, Bas. I'll give you a week.'

'A month,' he negotiated bleakly.

'A fortnight. So you'd better do the right thing by Naomi, Bas. And you'd better agree on your solution quickly.'

Bas offered his friend a grim nod and made his way to the door.

'Agreed. And, Grace…' He stopped briefly to turn back to her. 'Thank you.'

Naomi knew he was there without even seeing him.

It could have been the buzz in the corridor outside, or the way her colleagues suddenly, subtly changed. But really, it was the way her body came alive—the little things, from the tiny hairs on the back of her neck, to the goosebumps on her lower calves.

Or perhaps it was just the fact that she'd been half expecting him.

But she refused to turn to him, concentrating instead on the consultant standing with her in the small doctors' room along the corridor from her patient's bay.

'He presented a year ago with lower back pain, and it has been getting progressively worse. We diagnosed compressed nerves in the lumbar region and we've tried NSAIDs, corticosteroids and TENS relief. Physiotherapy has been a non-starter.'

Quickly and efficiently, she ran the consultant through the case, presenting her notes and explaining her conclusions. All the while ignoring Bas, though she could feel his eyes boring into her back.

Then, eventually, as the consultant left she finally allowed herself to turn.

'What do you think you're doing?'

Sucking in a steadying breath, Naomi plastered a neutral expression on her face and turned around.

'I'm on shift,' she told him mildly. 'Just like you.'

He took her elbow—not entirely roughly—and bundled her out of the door and into the nearest empty room which—given how hectic the hospital was already—was no mean feat.

Part of her wondered if these vacant spaces materialised just for him. He wielded that much power in the place that she wouldn't have been shocked.

But that didn't mean he had authority over her.

'You're supposed to be resting.'

His tone might seem mild enough, but she wasn't fooled. She cranked her smile up a notch.

'I rested and was monitored for an hour yesterday,' she told him. 'As you well know, since you were the one doing the monitoring, right alongside Dr Seddon. And then you walked me to the car park where your driver took me home, as per your instruction.'

'And yet here you are now. In work,' he pointed out. 'Not—as you can see—still at the penthouse.'

She could dodge, as a wiser woman might have done. Or she could bite the proverbial bullet and tell him exactly what she thought. Naomi barely thought twice.

'Because I decided that I didn't particularly want to sit around there—as magnificent as your home is—staring at four walls and driving myself slightly crazy while I think about these results. I did enough of that yesterday—which I might have told you, had you deigned to return last night.'

'I was working.'

'How convenient.' It was all she could do to sound breezy. 'So, you dragged me from my own home, where at least I would have had company—my grandmother and sister to distract me—and installed me in a place where I am basically isolated from anyone and anything.'

'I would hardly say isolated. Your family are free to visit. Provided that I am not there.'

'How generous of you.' She fought back the bitterness from her voice. 'Especially after you invited me to ask you whatever questions I needed to, but when I did you actually got up and left.'

'Because you need to rest.' At least he had the decency to look mildly guilty. 'Just as you need to rest now.'

'I need to work,' she exclaimed crossly. 'To be useful. And this place—whilst better off than most public hospitals thanks to also being home to the Jansen wing—is at capacity and always down on staff. Do you really think anyone asked twice when I turned up as an extra working doctor?'

Bas let out a low rumble of disapproval.

'And how, precisely, did you get in to work today? Did you take a bus? Don't tell me you walked.'

'If I had done, it wouldn't have been an issue. Your building is practically around the corner from this place—I can only imagine how much that must have cost, even without it being the penthouse. But no, for the record, I asked Phillip to drive me in.'

'Phillip?' Bas exclaimed irritably. 'He should have let me know the minute you called. Scratch that, he should never have agreed to drive you here in the first place.'

'Phillip is your driver, not your security guard.' Naomi actually laughed. 'And I've no doubt he would have tried to contact you, but I imagine you were already in surgery. Didn't you tell me that you had surgeries to catch up on, since you pushed them in order to be with me for the test?'

Bas looked furious.

'I never begrudged that.'

'I never suggested that you did,' she told him, deliberately sweetly. 'I'm merely pointing out likely scenarios to stop you from doing something impulsive like sacking poor Phillip. Have you checked your phone?'

'Not yet.'

'Ah. Well, there you go. Now…' ducking around him, she headed for the door '…if you don't mind, I'm sure there will already be a new patient waiting out there for me to see.'

She had no idea how Bas made it to the door before her.

'Absolutely not.'

'Bas…'

'You may be completely insensible to the seriousness of what's going on, Naomi, but I am not. And you are carrying my child.'

'I'm perfectly aware of that fact.' She dipped her head. 'And, no, I am not *insensible* to the seriousness of my baby's situation. But I do not wish to sit in a prison—albeit a luxuriously expensive one—with nothing to do all day but torture myself with everything that could go wrong.'

'This is not about—' began Bas.

But she cut him off.

'I've had the scan. I've done the tests. The echocardiogram was clear, and I rested all day yesterday after the amniocentesis, the results of which are yet to be determined. You've already ensured that I will get a battery of scans, and if I should develop polyhydramnios, and there is any suggestion of risk of early delivery, then I will go on full bed rest. Until then, I fully intend to keep working as my Jansen Bursary expects.'

His glare could have skewered her to the spot. It might have done, had she been a lesser woman. She squared her shoulders.

'Or are you the kind of person who feels that, because of their position of power, they have the right to dictate every aspect of the other person's life?'

'This isn't about me exerting power over you, Naomi. This is about me ensuring our baby is as safe as it can be.'

'And you think I'm not?' Her cool exterior began to crumble. 'You think I'm not terrified? You think the worst scenarios aren't lurking in the back of my mind? I just want a shift where I can push them aside and focus on other people's problems. Maybe try to solve a few of them, because, heaven knows, I can't solve this for myself.'

Bas eyed her wordlessly, but he refused to budge. For a moment, she thought he was going to fight her some more.

And the worst of it was that she didn't have the strength to fight back. The last few days' events had drained her, mentally and physically. More than she'd been prepared to admit.

'How about a compromise?' he said gruffly, after the silence between them had begun to fray.

She eyed him archly.

'You'll give up your work if I give up mine?'

He glared at her.

'Where are you working today?'

'Here.' She gestured to the corridor outside, and the ward they were on.

'Not Resus? Or A & E?' he demanded. 'Not Plastics?'

'No. Just here.'

He stared at her, and she wasn't quite sure how long passed.

'Fine, have it your way, Naomi.' He ultimately blew out a harsh breath. 'At least until the results of the amnio come through. But if there is any indication whatsoever of a problem, or if you get tired, or experience anything at all out of the ordinary, you get a message to me. I don't care what I'm doing, I don't care if I'm in surgery, you get a message through. Understand?'

She hadn't expected him to capitulate so readily. Blinking, Naomi offered him a brief bob of her head.

'I understand.'

'And once your shift finishes, you go to Phillip and he will take you straight home. Straight home, Naomi.'

'Straight...home,' she confirmed, as strange as that sounded to her.

'Then, all right,' Bas grunted out grudgingly. 'I shall see you back there tonight.'

And Naomi pretended that a traitorous part of her wasn't looking forward to that moment a little too much.

CHAPTER EIGHT

NAOMI HEARD THE exclusive penthouse lift ping its forewarning of someone's arrival a few moments before Bas actually appeared at the front door. Certainly long enough for her to have vacated her position on the settee, taking her book and retreating to the relative security of her guest suite.

But she didn't. She refused to run and hide. Bas was the one who had insisted she moved in with him—however long that was meant to last—and so now he was going to have to deal with her presence.

Contrary to what she'd told Bas earlier that day, she'd ended up on Paediatric A&E after all—treating a baby with an abnormally slow heart-rate, an eight-year-old who had shoved a building block in his ear, and another who had stuffed a button up her nose. None of it had fazed her.

But now, she now sat tensely, the words on the page swimming before her eyes each time she attempted to read, as Bas stepped into the penthouse.

'You had a good shift?' he asked, dropping his keys and his bag before making his way to a polished oak and resin cabinet, and retrieving two glasses.

'I did.' It was impossible not to sound formal. 'It was… what I needed.'

Truth be told, it had been an incredible relief to spend the day working. As though everything were normal.

'Good.'

He didn't sound as if he thought it was good. Then again, she couldn't tell what he sounded like. But then, how could she? When all was said and done, she barely knew the man.

The father of her unborn child.

She watched him prepare a drink—two drinks—and then cross over the room to set a sparkling water down in front of her, and a brandy down in front of himself. But he still caught her off-guard when he started to speak.

'You worried that I would want to dip in and out of your life, and that of our daughter. You asked me what Grace Henley meant to me. And you wanted to know what she meant by me being nothing like my father. So which part do you want me to answer first?'

Slowly, Naomi turned her book over on her lap, trying to stop that tremor in her hands. Working on smoothing the look of shock that was surely clouding her face.

'Start wherever you think the beginning is.' She swallowed.

Bas reached for his tumbler of brandy and took a long pull.

'My brother is here. In the UK. At Thorncroft.'

It was all she could do not to clear out her ears. She couldn't possibly have heard that correctly.

'Your…brother?'

Setting the crystalware back down, Bas offered a grim nod.

'Up until I was seven, I lived in Sweden with my brother, a sorry excuse for a wannabe singer—my mother—and the fist-flailing two-bit musician we were led to believe was our father.'

He stopped as if waiting for her to speak, but Naomi just wanted to hear what he had to say. Besides, she wouldn't have known what to answer if she tried.

'One day, after he'd sent my brother Henrik flying across the room and head first into the wall—this time for interrupting his quiet time when it was me who'd asked our mother whether I had any clean underwear for school—I told my teacher what our father was doing to us. Child Welfare came and investigated.'

'And they discovered Magnus Jansen was really your father, and sent you to him?' she asked, unable to stop herself.

'No.' He jerked his head bitterly. 'My mother told them

that I was an angry child who had a propensity for lying. When they presented her with medical records, she convinced them that I was the one who had caused the injuries to my brother because I flew into rages.'

'They believed her?' Naomi couldn't disguise her reaction.

'My mother has always been very…convincing. She told them that it had started when I'd discovered that my real father had abandoned us all, and that I resented my stepfather, even though he was a good man who had taken us all on despite the fact that Henrik and I weren't his. I can still remember my brother and I standing in that room, and the shock I felt at hearing about our real parentage for the first time.'

'What about your brother? When he told them what really happened, how could they not believe two of you?'

Bas felt his face twist into something ugly, and there was nothing he could do to stop it.

'Henrik sided with our mother. Usually, she protected him, and it was me who got hit. Their relationship was… closer. And so when my mother said that I was the one who had been lying, he backed her up.'

'Bas…'

'He betrayed me.'

Naomi hesitated. It was humbling that Bas was confiding his truth in her—*her*—and she desperately wanted to say the right thing. To help. But something niggled at her, and she couldn't swallow back her words, even though she knew she ran the risk of alienating him.

She had to be true to herself.

'I can't imagine how that must have felt for you, as a seven-year-old boy,' she began falteringly. 'But, Bas, Henrik was only seven, too. Could he have thought he was pouring oil onto troubled waters when he said what he did? Do you believe he could have known what the consequences would be?'

'By lying?' Bas snapped.

But, for a split second, there had been a hesitation. An acknowledgement of what she was saying.

'Ah,' she said quietly. 'I see it now. You blame Henrik because it's easier for you to do that and hate him, than for you to have faced all those years torn away from the brother you loved.'

Bas didn't reply, but his jaw locked tightly—the pulse flickering angrily at its base. It was the only answer she needed.

'Is it still too painful, even now, to forgive your brother?' she pressed softly. 'Or is it that it's been so long that you no longer know *how* to forgive him?'

He glowered at her—silent and imperial—and she wondered if she hadn't perhaps gone too far. And then, just as she was about to give up thinking he would confide anything more in her, he worked his jaw as if trying to loosen it.

'I have no wish to try,' he bit out. 'Once it was over, my mother screamed at me that I was an ungrateful and vindictive child—I won't bore you with the words she actually used—and she told me that I should be more respectful of the man who had taken me in as his son, especially when I was such a piece of work. And then she told me that I was going to live with my real father.'

'With Magnus,' Naomi breathed. 'It must have been a shock to find out he had a son.'

'Two sons,' Bas bit out. 'Henrik and I are twins. Fraternal—to be exact. And no, it wasn't a shock. He was aware that we were supposed to have been our mother's meal ticket to marrying an up-and-coming surgeon.'

'Magnus had known about you?'

'Yes, he'd known. But he'd paid my mother off—handsomely, apparently, though she'd blown through it all in those first few years—to never again trouble him with two babies he didn't want.'

'Oh.'

'She drove me to the airport, stuck me on a flight, and told me to take a taxi when I landed at the airport and that Magnus would pay the fare.'

'My God.'

'Magnus was livid, of course. He tried to contact her, to get me sent back, but when she threatened to go to the press and tell them that the great Magnus Jansen was an absent father unless he took me on and sent her another generous pay-off, he complied. Only this time, he had a pack of lawyers to tie her into an airtight contract.'

Bas took another pull of his drink before he continued.

'After that, he told me that having a kid around his neck was the last thing he'd ever needed, but that it was his obligation to give me a home and a decent education. He also said that it was my obligation to repay him by proving myself one day, and at least becoming a "halfway decent" surgeon, worthy of the Jansen name.'

Naomi shifted in her seat. She wanted to cross the room, and put her arms around him, make him feel the love she was beginning to think he'd never known. But she suspected that Bas wouldn't thank her for it. To the contrary, she could well imagine him pushing her away.

Was this why he was the way he was? The hospital playboy, never forming attachments, never allowing himself to get close to anyone.

'So you've been living with your father ever since? And your brother has been living with...your mother?'

'It was always going to be a better fit for him there. Henrik was always her favourite. Like I said, we aren't identical twins, so whilst we might look similar in terms of body type, he has more of our mother's features, whilst I look like Magnus—the man who she believes got her pregnant and walked away. According to her, Magnus is the devil who ruined her life. And, unbeknownst to me, I'd had his look about me since birth.'

'Ah,' she offered, uncertain what else to say.

'Henrik was also the one through whom she'd been able to live vicariously. She always said she was an undiscovered star. The singer who had never caught her big break. Since Henrik could sing and I definitely can't, she always intended for him to become the superstar she felt she'd been robbed of being.'

'So now he's here? At Thorncroft?' She wasn't sure she followed.

'He is.' Bas barked out a laugh. A hollow, scraping sound. 'But he isn't some singing sensation. He's a surgeon.'

'A surgeon?'

'A plastic surgeon.'

'Like you.' Naomi gasped before she could bite it back. Though she managed not to add, *And like Magnus.*

'Exactly like me,' Bas confirmed bitterly.

'I…see.'

Though she wasn't sure she did. Not really. Was it really a bad thing that his brother had chosen to be like him rather than like their mother, given all that Bas had said?

Was it, somehow, a compliment to Bas?

'And if that wasn't enough,' he ground out unexpectedly, 'I discovered today that he sought out Grace at the medical ball the other night and seduced her.'

Ah. Grace.

Naomi tried valiantly to swallow back the questions jumbling inside her. But it proved too much.

'What exactly is Grace, to you, Bas?'

His stare practically skewered her.

'I've heard rumours…' Naomi continued, stiffly.

The fact was that she'd only heard them that day, when she'd begun asking discreetly around the hospital. But once she'd asked, she could hardly believe she hadn't heard them before.

According to everyone she'd asked, Grace wasn't just a

brilliant doctor, but she was the suspected reason that Bas never dated the same woman twice. According to the hospital grapevine—not that she usually liked to put much stock into idle rumour—Grace was Bas's soulmate. The one who got away.

Even now, as she thought about it, a ripple ran through Naomi that couldn't possibly have been jealousy. And no matter how she thrust it aside, it still danced there, on the periphery of her mind.

And she hated herself for it because she had no right to be upset. Bas owed her nothing. They weren't a couple— she was just the woman who'd been foolish enough to fall pregnant by him.

She came back to, to realise that Bas was staring grimly at her.

'That's all they are,' he bit out. 'Rumours. Nothing more. We've been good friends since med school.'

'But that's it?' Naomi couldn't silence her tongue. 'I'm not stirring up anything by going to scans with her when I'm carrying your baby?'

She studiously ignored those odd internal undulations as he peered at her. Rather too closely. She didn't care much for that gleam in his eyes, either—the one that said he could read her uncharacteristic thoughts. And that he liked them.

The last thing Bas needed was for her to send his already stratospheric ego into the ionosphere.

He scratched his chin, as though deciding what to tell her.

'I'm aware that there are those who consider me self-indulgent, with an addiction to the finer things in life. Grace claims that it's actually my form of self-flagellation. She calls it my personally appointed hell, an adult version of the one in which she thinks I've been languishing for the better part of three decades.'

Naomi cocked her head to one side.

'And what do you think?'

'I think that I've always found her theory laughable.'

He didn't add the words *until now*. But she thought she heard them, all the same.

'And what does Grace think of…this situation?'

Bas cast her a shrewd look.

'Do you want to know what she thinks of this situation? Or what she thinks of you?'

And Naomi didn't like it that he seemed to read her so easily.

She wrinkled her nose. Clearly, he wasn't going to tell her, anyway.

'Forget I said anything.'

'Surely that isn't jealousy I can see, Dr Fox?' He frowned. 'I can't say I think it suits you.'

'Of course I'm not jealous.' She bristled, ignoring the little voice in her head branding her a liar. 'I just want to know that the woman who is going to be operating on my newborn baby isn't going to be contending with her own feelings about the fact that you're the father.'

The black look in Bas's eyes—unmistakeable anger— was hardly settling. But it was the hint of guilt that really wheedled its way under her skin. Surely guilt could mean only one thing?

'There is nothing between Grace and me,' he bit out icily instead. 'But let me make one thing absolutely clear, Grace would never, never jeopardise the life of the baby. She is an incredible surgeon, and a good friend. She would never ever be unprofessional. Do I make myself clear?'

And it was perhaps the vehement way that he defended his so-called 'just a friend' that felt, to Naomi, like the most damning indictment of all.

If Grace really was the one who got away, then there was no way Naomi intended to compete with that.

Hadn't she learned, many years ago, never to settle for

second-best? Hadn't she promised herself that she would never again be anyone's second choice?

The most terrifying part was that, for a moment there with Bas, she had let herself be lulled into believing that she wasn't his second choice.

That she and the baby genuinely mattered to him.

She wouldn't be so foolish as to make that mistake again.

Bas checked his phone for the tenth time in as many minutes.

The results of the amniocentesis were due today, and it had taken him these past couple of days to realise that the wait was practically driving him insane.

He could only imagine how hard Naomi was finding it.

He'd lost count of the number of times he'd had to wait for tests to come back on patients; he'd schooled them on the importance of the tests being done right, and he'd always believed he'd had good empathy for the people under his care, as well as their fraught families.

It turned out he hadn't understood anywhere near as well as he'd thought he had. It felt very, very different when *he* was the one feeling powerless. Useless.

All those pat little phrases he had as a surgeon—the ones that enabled him to express sympathy without actually having to experience the same loss as a family, because how could he have done his job if he'd allowed himself to feel *exactly* what they felt?—now seemed so hollow and empty.

The row—if his eruption could be called that—with Naomi the previous evening had to be testament to that. A result of the shock he'd felt to realise that he'd opened up to her more than he had anyone in the past.

Ever.

And that included Grace.

There was something about Naomi that made him want to tell her things he'd spent the past few decades trying to bury. And he couldn't explain it.

Or didn't want to.

So here he was throwing himself into work—the one thing that was meant to be his solace. The one thing that he could do to make a difference. It was the thing that he understood best.

Yet all he could think about was Naomi, and if she was okay. How she was coping with this interminable wait. Up until that last part of the previous evening, it had felt as though they had grown a little closer.

As though maybe they actually could find a resolution for the situation in which they now found themselves. Because, clearly, living together long term wasn't remotely a viable option. But when he tried to imagine when it would be best for Naomi to leave—he found it impossible.

The idea of being apart from his daughter felt…wrong. And yet he didn't doubt that the more contact he would have in her life, the more he would eventually mess her up.

Just as his own parents had done to him.

How could it be that Naomi, who hadn't had either parent in her life, seemed so much more together and in control than he thought he would ever feel?

Being a surgeon was one thing. But being a father…? It held a terror he would never before have believed.

The worst of it was that, for the first time in his career, it was as though he was going through the motions. He was doing all the right things, saying all the right things, but all he could think about was Naomi.

Automatically, his hand reached for his mobile, punching in the keys to speed-dial her to ensure that she was okay, and that she was resting the way she needed to be. As if they really were some kind of couple. As if she would want him to be that solicitous.

Bas stopped, his finger hovering over the button to make the call, and it took him all his self-control to cancel it and drop the mobile back in his pocket.

The original agreement for Naomi to move in with him had been one born out of practicality—out of a desire to have Naomi close to the hospital after discovering that their unborn baby had a serious medical condition.

It hadn't been something they'd discussed—it had just happened. But now the initial shock had worn off, he felt it was time to start making plans. To discuss what would happen once their daughter was actually here.

In his head, the logical move would be for Naomi and their baby to remain here, so that their daughter could have the family and emotional security that had been so lacking in his own upbringing. It was a chance to offer his child more than he'd had.

But was he fooling himself to think that he was capable of that?

More than that, would it open the door to Naomi imagining that something more was going on? He was fairly sure she hadn't thought that a few days ago, but since then the lines had begun to get blurred. And he wasn't sure he could pinpoint why.

Bas was still pondering the matter when his pager went off, calling him downstairs.

'Talk to me,' Bas stated as he hurried into A & E.

'Fifty-five-year-old male with subtotal hand amputation following accident with a circular saw. He's in bay five.'

'Another DIY accident,' Bas noted grimly, cutting a path across the room.

Accidents involving home owners and electric saws were all too common, and they were rarely straightforward. He could only hope that this one wasn't too serious.

Especially when he'd heard that Henrik was on call somewhere in the hospital.

The last thing he wanted was some run-in with his long-lost twin brother.

'Someone paged me,' he announced himself as he reached

the bay, his attention immediately drawn to the man—ashen and blood-soaked—lying on the trolley.

One glance at the hand told him that this was more than a little accident. The message he'd been given had stated it was a subtotal hand amputation, but that didn't begin to convey the fact that the man's extremity had been almost severed in two places and was only still attached thanks to the faintest sliver of skin and bone.

He cursed inwardly whilst maintaining his usual poker face. It was going to take some skilled work if he was going to stand a chance of saving this man's hand. Many surgeons might have considered it unsalvageable, but Bas had sewn hands and feet to groins before now in an attempt to save a dying extremity.

The most crucial initial step was going to be to get him into a surgery to repair as much as possible and establish a good blood and nerve supply to the fingers. Or what fingers remained.

'Book an OR,' he murmured to the ward sister as he watched the patient being wheeled away to be prepped for surgery.

'It's booked.'

Bas stopped, an iciness stealing over him at the sound of the voice, the faintest Swedish lilt. If the hospital had crashed down around him, Bas couldn't have felt any more razed.

He certainly wasn't sure how he managed to turn around.

'Henrik,' he bit out. 'What the hell are you doing here?'

Staring at his brother was like staring at a ghost. Bas had thought he'd imagined this moment in enough detail to know what he was going to do. And say. But he hadn't foreseen the gamut of emotions that would run through him the moment he looked into those familiar blue eyes again.

It was a body-blow. A reminder of a time when he and his brother had been so close that he'd thought nothing could ever come between them. A time when he'd never dreamed

Henrik would ever betray him. A time of innocence—no, of gullibility.

How dearly he'd paid for such naivety.

'It is the Jansen exchange programme.' The faint Swedish lilt and a set of painfully familiar eyes cast Bas to stone on the spot. He couldn't have jerked away if he'd tried. 'I have been writing to you three times.'

Slowly, slowly, Bas's breath seeped back into his lungs. He worked his jaw a few times.

'I am aware. It landed me with the task of having to throw them in the trash where they belong.' If he hadn't known it was himself speaking, Bas didn't think he would have known his own voice. 'My mistake—what I really meant to say was, get away from my case.'

'The way I am to keep away from Grace?'

Bas eyeballed him.

'Grace is a grown woman. She makes her own decisions. And I never told her to stay away from you.'

'No. You merely told her that I have targeted her because I knew you two were friends.'

'I can't imagine Grace told you that,' Bas said levelly.

Though when put like that, it sounded even worse than he remembered.

'Of course not. She is loyal to you. But she asked me, and I knew it had come from you.'

'Perhaps so.' Bas wasn't about to apologise. 'But it wasn't a lie, was it?'

'I went to that medical ball to talk to you, Basilius. I did not know who Grace was when I first spoke to her that night.'

Bas eyed his brother shrewdly.

'But you knew who she was when you slept with her. Didn't you?'

And it was odd, wasn't it, that even after all this time he didn't need Henrik to respond in order for him to know the answer to that question?

'As I thought,' Bas spat out, disgusted.

He wasn't prepared for the look that shadowed his brother's face.

'What is Grace to you, Basilius? Do you love her?'

Bas stopped, taken aback.

'Grace is a friend,' he rasped. 'Nothing more. Has she not told you that?'

Henrik eyed him in frank assessment.

'That's exactly what she told me. But I'm not a fool, brother. I know you sent her to watch me. What is your saying? *Keep your enemies close?*'

'Something like that,' Bas murmured.

'So, I shall ask you again, do you care for her, Basilius? Because I think I might, and I am willing to fight for her.'

And he looked so sincere that if Bas hadn't known his brother's tricks first hand, even he might have believed Henrik.

'You're not capable of fighting for her. Or anyone.' Bas snorted, making no attempt to conceal his disdain. 'You don't know what love is, Henrik. Neither of us do. The only thing we know is that sick, twisted version of love that we learned from *them.*'

He didn't need to say their names for his brother to know he was talking about their mother and the man she'd passed off as their father for years.

But then something flashed across his brother's face. Something that looked incomprehensibly like…sadness.

'Is that what you really believe?'

'It's what I know.' Bas glowered. 'She might have favoured you, but it didn't make her idea of love any less dangerous. There were always strings attached to her affection.'

'And what about Mrs P? And Bertie?' Henrik asked quietly. 'Were there always strings attached to their love? Or have you forgotten them, Basilius?'

But Bas couldn't answer. He thought his brain might have shut down.

Mrs P. Even the mere name was enough to send emotions cascading through him, throwing open memories as if they were coffins, uncovered in a dark crypt where he'd forgotten he'd even buried them.

Mrs P, the kind, lovely cook, and her husband, Bertie, who had worked in the mechanics garage down the road from their home. How could he ever, ever have forgotten them, and the way the pair had treated him and Henrik like the children they'd never had?

With kindness. And care. And *love*.

They'd been the stable family that he and Henrik had never had. And then, one day, they'd simply left.

'They deserted us,' he bit out.

Because they too had seen something fundamentally unlikeable in him. And they'd rejected him like everyone else.

'They didn't leave,' Henrik told him softly. 'We left. We went from that suburban house to that flat in the city. Don't you remember?'

Bas shook his head tersely. He didn't. Or, at least, he hadn't. Now, all of a sudden, something was beginning to unfurl in the back of his mind. Hazy and dark, but there nonetheless.

'Mother was always so jealous of them,' Henrik said jerkily. 'The way we always used to go to them first for things. Don't you recall running into their kitchen on the way home from school and they'd be waiting to hear about our day, with milk and home-baked fairy cakes? Sometimes, we got to decorate them.'

Bas blinked. He couldn't say he remembered exactly, but things were beginning to take shape. As though his past was slowly, *slowly* pulling into focus.

How had he forgotten all of this?

Something pricked at the backs of Bas's eyes and he blinked it back viciously. *No.* It couldn't possibly be tears.

No weakness. Wasn't that what Magnus had always taught him?

Impulsively, he shoved the alarming tangle of memories back into their boxes. But they were too messy, and they wouldn't go back properly. They kept spilling out.

Bas folded his arms over his chest and forced his head up.

'Is that why you called me for a consultation on this patient?' Cold, precise, his voice did a remarkable job of disguising the storm of emotions that raged inside him.

And Henrik paused. Faltered. Then offered an almost imperceptible shake of his head.

Whatever conversation the two of them hadn't quite been having, it was not over. And they both knew it.

'I did not call for a consultation.'

'I was paged,' Bas gritted out.

'I called for another surgeon.' His brother shrugged. 'I could not have known that would be you. It is an urgent case.'

And even though he didn't believe Henrik, Bas realised he couldn't dwell on it. There wasn't time. There was a patient who needed urgent care and, like it or not, he now had no choice but to work with his brother to save the patient's hand.

'Fine,' he growled at length. 'Run me through it.'

Henrik dipped his head in assent and swiped his screen to his notes before passing the tablet over.

'Preliminary tests have been run, and a CT. The sooner I operate, the better, but it's likely to run late into the night. Two surgeons working together will make it a faster surgery for the patient. Less time under anaesthetic means less stress on the patient.'

It made sense. He'd worked on relatively similar injuries before, and the operation could run to ten, twelve, even fifteen hours. Two surgeons would mean that one surgeon could be harvesting grafts from lower limbs whilst the other worked on the hand. And Henrik had a point: the less time the patient was under anaesthesia, the better for them.

The choices ran through Bas's head.

The thought of spending hours effectively locked in an operating room with no way to avoid his brother certainly didn't appeal. And yet…the surgeon side of him was drawn to the case. How could he pass up this operation to someone else?

How could he choose not to be part of the case when he knew he could well be this patient's best hope?

'I've seen cases like this before, but this is probably one of the worst cases I've seen,' Bas stated in a clipped tone, which was nonetheless too quiet to be heard by the patient, or his family. 'I suggest you pass this case to me to take lead. I can bring in a surgeon on my team to assist.'

Henrik fixed him with a steady gaze that was all too familiar. He had seen it in himself any time he looked in the mirror.

'If you don't feel able to assist me…' his brother's voice was equally low, but firm '…then by all means send another member of your team. However, I have completed several of these procedures in the past. The last case I worked on involved cutting a flap of skin from the groin to embed my patient's hand, to allow the skin to grow and provide new covering.'

Bas schooled his features. His brother's words virtually mirrored everything he'd been thinking when he'd first seen the patient and it was simultaneously galling and…something he didn't care to examine further.

'You've harvested veins and nerve grafts from the foot and forearm, to reconstruct the hand?'

'And joined tendons and arteries, yes,' Henrik confirmed. 'As I know you have. So it is up to you to choose whether to work with me on this patient, or not. But right now, I really need to get him into surgery. The sooner I can re-establish blood supply, the better his recovery is likely to be. Are you joining me, or sending someone else?'

It galled him that Henrik was right. And apparently more skilled than he'd wanted to believe. Bas couldn't remember the last time he'd had to be second surgeon to another plastic guy. But this was Henrik's patient and, personal feelings aside, there was no way the surgeon in him could walk away.

'I've worked on these microsurgical repairs many times before,' Bas stated. 'It's quite draining. You'll need to be good.'

'As will you.'

Bas met Henrik's level gaze. He refused to be the first one to blink.

'You have to be realistic about his prognosis. This will never be a normal hand, but, with time and effort, physio can help him regain strength.'

'I made his family clear that even holding a pen will be good progress,' Henrik agreed. 'He'll need multiple surgeries over the next few months, even years.'

'In time perhaps we can go for a power grip.'

'In time,' Henrik agreed. 'Either way, I must take him in and begin now. I need a decision, Basilius. Can you work with me? Or no?'

Bas paused for one fraction of a moment longer before dipping his head in tacit acquiescence. Then, with a signal from Henrik to the rest of the team, the bay once again became a flurry of activity as they prepped to bring the patient up to Theatre.

They had hours of surgery ahead of them, and Bas couldn't stop himself from wondering how he would ever get through it with the brother he had vowed never to have any contact with, for the rest of his life.

Slowly, methodically, they began, until at last, fourteen hours later, they found themselves peeling off their gowns and gloves, after a successful operation. And Bas thought he should probably say something.

'Good surgery,' he muttered, rolling up his gown and

gloves and hurling them into the medical waste bin, before marching through the doors of the surgical suite to scrub out, leaving his brother to finish up his debriefing.

'Very good,' Henrik agreed, joining him at last. 'Would you care to join me in telling the family?'

It was on the tip of Bas's tongue to agree, but seeing a message on his phone stopped him. Finishing his sterilisation routine, he reached for it.

The results of the amniocentesis.

Without a backward glance, Bas hurried out of the room. It was Henrik's patient. Let his brother deal with the family himself.

He had to find Naomi and tell her. Not to mention trying to rationalise those memories that Henrik had so unexpectedly raked up.

CHAPTER NINE

BAS TRIED TELLING himself that he wasn't panicking, that he never panicked. But as he moved slickly through the gears, his car speeding down the dark deserted city streets, he began to feel something rising inside him which felt a lot like he imagined panic to feel.

Naomi was supposed to have been in the cafeteria, waiting for him. But when he'd got there only to learn that that she'd already left for home, it had been terrifying.

Was she tired? Ill? Was something wrong?

It was all he could do not to smash the speed limit as he hurtled around corners. But he was a surgeon. He'd seen too many accidents, put too many broken bodies back together, and faced too many devastated, grieving family members.

But at last, he was home. Stepping into his penthouse lift and willing it to hoist him up to his floor faster.

He saw her the moment he crashed through the door, standing on the decked balcony, her hands on the cool metal balustrade as she looked down to the city below. Hauling the doors open, he stepped through, and just about restrained himself from hurrying over.

'Naomi, is something wrong?'

'I'm fine. I just thought the fresh air might help to clear my head.'

She didn't turn her head to look at him but her voice carried through the air assuredly as though she'd sensed his approach. Yet the sensation that shot through him only bemused him all the more.

'Is that your apology for not being in the hospital cafeteria where I instructed you to wait for me?'

It wasn't what he'd intended to say. He wasn't even sure where it had come from.

This time, she did turn her head.

'Were you expecting me to sit obediently like a trained animal, waiting for you? If so, I suggest you get yourself a dog. Preferably a working one, like a border collie, or a German shepherd.'

Her dry tone licked at him in ways he didn't care to analyse further. He told himself it was resentment, but he wasn't sure he was convinced.

'The results of the amniocentesis are back,' he told her gravely.

She gripped the railing tighter.

'What do they say?'

'See for yourself.' He held out his phone and, stiffly, she turned to take it.

A few seconds later, she stumbled and fell against him. Half choking, half sobbing.

'Oh, thank God.'

'We should discuss how we proceed from here.' At least his voice sounded cool. Controlled. Even if he felt anything but.

For several seconds, she didn't speak. She merely continued her laugh-crying. And then, slowly, she regained control and turned back to the balustrade.

'*We* don't need to discuss anything,' Naomi managed quietly. 'I told you about the baby because it was the right thing to do—and, again, I'm grateful for yesterday—but I don't need you. *We* don't need you. You're free, Bas. Why must we discuss this any more than that?'

'Because we're not discussing some inanimate object here,' he exploded. 'That's my *child* you're carrying. Which makes her my responsibility.'

She flattened her hands on the metal balustrade.

'But it doesn't *have* to,' she murmured. 'That's what I'm trying to tell you. I understand this isn't what you bargained for. I get to choose whether I want this baby or not, and for the record I do want it. You don't get to make that decision for me. So I'm saying that I won't blame you if you walk away.'

'How very magnanimous of you.'

He wasn't sure how he was keeping his temper in check. It was hammering through every inch of his body, threatening to punch its way out.

Did she really think he'd thank her for pushing him out of his baby's life?

'You think I'm being high-handed here.' She met his eyes and, this time, she didn't let her gaze slide away. 'But I believe you'll thank me for it later. You might be prepared to do what you think is the honourable thing, and step up as a father, but deep down you don't want the responsibility of a kid weighing you down.'

'And you do?'

'It might not have been what I planned, but I intend to be there every step of the way. I *want* this baby, Bas. I'm ready for her. But you can't say the same.'

'I'm as ready as you are,' he managed evenly as Naomi snorted delicately.

'That certainly isn't true. You expect me—us—to return here. To a less than baby-friendly pristine penthouse of metal and glass.'

'As opposed to that cramped place that wasn't big enough for three of you, let alone one of you having a baby.'

'At least it was a home. It was cosy, and it was real. This is a bachelor pad with white walls, and marble tiling, and shiny metal. A place which boasts unparalleled views of the city through sparklingly clean, floor-to-ceiling glass. How long is a child going to last in a place like this?'

'You're objecting because of where I live? One of the most prestigious postcodes in the city?'

'You're an intelligent man, Bas,' she countered softly. 'You understand what I'm saying. You didn't even think about that side of it, did you?'

He hadn't. And it galled him to admit it, even to himself.

'So where, precisely, would you live, Naomi? If you could live anywhere in this city?'

And he couldn't have said what rattled through him as he watched a faraway look enter her eyes—the corners of her mouth pulling up a fraction.

'It's a cliché, I know, but I always wanted a place in the country, with rambling roses, and a pretty fence. It wouldn't have to be fancy, just homely. A house for a family. A home. With a garden, and a room where my child could play. A place where there might be a few sticky fingers, or pencil marks, but, more than that, there would be lots of laughter.'

'A place like that would be totally incompatible with working at Thorncroft,' he dismissed. 'That's an impractical fantasy, whilst I'm talking about realities.'

'I know the reality, Bas.' Her eyes sparked, and he thought he preferred that fire to the wistfulness of before. 'I'm the one who was telling you about reality. I'm the one who wants this child and will be there for her.'

'And I intend to be there every step of the way, too.'

'How? By dropping in and out of her life when the demands of your career and/or your love life allow?' She shook her head. 'I want my baby to grow up knowing it's loved, wholly and unconditionally. By me. I want it to feel like the most important thing in my life. I don't want it growing up thinking that it is, at best, a mild inconvenience. Or, at worst, unloved. Believe me, I know how that feels.'

She stopped sharply, biting her lip as though she hadn't intended to say anything. But Bas was already caught up with his own fury.

'Do you imagine that you have the monopoly on unwanted feelings?' he demanded furiously. 'That you have been the only child in the world not to be wanted by their parents?'

'You're the son of Magnus Jansen.' Her brow pulled tightly

together, as though she was irritated by him. 'Your father taught you everything about becoming a surgeon.'

'It didn't mean he wanted me. You think I have a reputation as a playboy, but my father was King Lothario. If he wasn't at the hospital, he was with a woman. Practically a different one every night.'

'Yet he still taught you all he could. Imagine a kid like me, with a mother who dumped my sister and me for the next man who took an interest. Social services visited us so many times that my grandmother had no choice in the end but to take us in.'

'I thought you said she loved you. That she was a good woman.'

'She did love us. But that didn't stop me from feeling second choice. It's all relative, isn't it?' Naomi shrugged. 'My mother never wanted me so my grandmother *had* to take me on. And then take Leila on, when the same thing happened to her.'

'I understand,' he murmured.

But Naomi seemed caught up in her own thoughts.

'My grandmother kept a safe roof over our heads, but I was the one who cooked, and cleaned. She didn't have much choice, of course. She'd been a cleaner all her life and had no savings. The meagre pension she received didn't stretch far when it came to feeding and clothing two growing kids.'

He didn't answer. What was there to say?

As private a person as he'd always prided himself on being, it was nothing to the way Naomi pulled her secrets around her like a warm cloak on a cold winter's night.

Or a shield.

They stood in silence for so long, and he was beginning to think she wasn't going to tell him anything more, when she began talking again.

'She bought what she could from second-hand shops, and some of it wasn't bad. But the other kids always knew, anyway. Always last season's stuff, or older. And every time I got laughed at, or my schoolbooks knocked to the ground, it made me feel second rate. Not good enough.'

'Which is why I don't want that for our baby.' He didn't intend to sound so abrasive, but he didn't apologise when it did, either. 'I felt that, too, Naomi. But our daughter never has to.'

She watched him, her breathing shallow. And he got the sense she was trying to compose herself.

That made two of them, then. Although he didn't intend to let her know it.

'I know that,' she managed at length. 'I don't want my child to go through what I went through, either. And that's why I let myself get drawn in by your suggestion that I move in with you. That we try to raise this baby together. But it won't work.'

'It will work,' he told her firmly.

'No.' She shook her head fiercely, and he wondered if she knew how attractive a quality he found it. 'It doesn't. It doesn't make the slightest bit of sense. And neither does the fact that I was so desperate to have a family that I leapt at what you offered. But it isn't real, is it? It's just an illusion. And what happens when that illusion shatters?'

Bas pulled his jaw tight.

He let his gaze wander over her. He wondered if she knew how often her hands cradled that baby bump, as though she could protect it from the worst this world had to throw at it. He considered all the things he might say to sway her back to his original plan. But he didn't let himself think about what she was saying.

Because he didn't think he could answer her questions.

Or *would*.

'It won't shatter,' he bit out. 'You and I will ensure it doesn't. Regardless of the circumstances, we both want what's best for this baby. She will have every opportunity she needs. I'll make sure of that.'

And finally, Naomi met his gaze. Eye to eye.

'Financially, I don't doubt you,' she told him earnestly. 'But in terms of being in her life, day in and day out…? I don't think you can do that.'

'Then you don't know me,' he cut her off coldly.

'Bas…'

'I've been understanding up until now, Naomi,' he growled. 'But let's be crystal clear here, I will not be shut out of this child's life because *you* had a poor childhood and you've suddenly realised that you don't want to trust anyone but yourself.'

'It is *not* because I had a poor childhood. But that does give me some true perspective.'

'You don't even know what kind of perspective I have,' interrupted Bas. 'But this child will have two parents who love and cherish them. No matter the personal cost.'

Naomi threw her hands into the air.

'But that's exactly my point. There won't be a personal cost for me. I *want* this child.'

It was crazy. He understood the logic of what she was saying, but, no matter how earnest she was, he couldn't reconcile it. The words made sense in his head, but then they mixed with this *thing* swirling around his chest, and everything became confused.

'I will be recognised as this baby's father. I will be present in its life. I won't relinquish that just because you're afraid I'll walk away. And I won't keep having this conversation with you. We already settled this, a week ago, when you accepted moving here with me.'

She blinked rapidly.

'I know…but I was wrong. I accepted for all the wrong reasons. I accepted because I was scared of doing this alone. But I shouldn't be. I can do this. I know I can. So I'm offering you the *out* now.'

'Have you ever considered that you're making these decisions based on your own fear of letting go of control?' he demanded.

'What?' She snapped her head around. 'No. This isn't about control. This is about wanting the best for my baby.'

'Which you seem to think doesn't include a father who actively wants to be there for his child.'

He recognised that defiant tilt of her chin.

'I've told you—this isn't about being there some of the time. This is about the day-in-day-out banality of being a parent. You live your life at full throttle, Bas. The two don't mix. At least, not well.'

'For all intents and purposes, you've been the one running your family all these years,' he continued, as though she hadn't spoken at all. 'I'm just suggesting that maybe the idea of relinquishing control, or even just sharing it, terrifies you.'

'No…' She shook her head.

'Let's be absolutely clear, Naomi. I am this baby's father, and I will not let you sideline me.'

She opened her mouth to argue. He could read it in every line of her lush body which still—against all appropriateness—called to him as if she were some siren and he were a sailor enthralled in her song.

'I'd think very carefully about what you say, or do, next,' he cautioned, though a part of him wondered who he was really warning. Naomi, or himself?

He watched, unduly fascinated as she drew in several steadying breaths.

'I think we're going around in circles here,' she offered at last.

'I couldn't agree more, which is why I have a solution,' he replied, and though he knew he had said the words, he had no idea where they'd come from.

She eyed him uncertainly.

'What kind of solution?'

'You're worried about coming to rely on me only for me

to abandon you, so you're trying to draw a line between us from the start.'

She inclined her head but didn't answer.

'So we make it so you don't fear me walking away.'

'And how do we do that?' She laughed scornfully. 'Some legal contract drawn up by any of your highly experienced team of lawyers?'

He didn't laugh.

'Of a sort.' He shrugged. And then heard himself say, 'I'm talking about a marriage contract.'

'A marriage contract?'

She gaped at him as though he was half mad. Possibly he was.

He certainly had no idea where *that* suggestion had come from.

'What does that even mean?' she choked out, when he didn't answer.

'It means marriage, Naomi.' The words were still coming out of his mouth despite the fact they appeared to have completely bypassed his brain.

He had no idea what he was saying. Yet, at the same time, it all seemed so logical. So practical.

'No…you don't mean it?'

And Bas felt it spoke volumes that her words came out a little more like a breathy question than the incredulous refusal that he believed she'd intended.

'You're proposing marriage?' she added when he didn't respond.

'I thought I was quite clear,' he answered, his voice calm. No mean feat given that he didn't even understand what he was doing.

Naomi sucked in another sharp breath, though it did little to settle the manic fluttering in her chest. He struggled to drag his gaze away.

'You can't be serious. It's an insane suggestion.'

If he wasn't very much mistaken, she looked altogether too tempted to say *yes*. A sense of victory rolled through him.

'I disagree.' He sounded far too calm. 'Your main concern is coming to rely on me, only for me to walk out. You don't want to feel second-rate. Not enough.'

'I don't want my child—our daughter—to feel that way,' she corrected.

He wondered if she knew that slight tremor in her voice gave her away.

'That's why you want to take it on all on your own from the start, right?' he demanded. 'You believed that, at least that way, you would already be geared up to do this alone.'

She stared at him mutely, and he knew then that he had her.

'You will marry me, Naomi. You will marry me because you are carrying my child and because I will not have my child growing up as I did. Or, indeed, as you did. She deserves better.'

'Bas...'

'It's our responsibility, as the people who have brought her into this world, to do everything we can to give her the childhood we never had. I know that's how you feel, too.'

Marriage would be his punishment for breaking all his rules, and for wanting Naomi too much.

And if a part of him wondered why his punishment didn't feel more...punitive, then no one else needed to know it but him.

CHAPTER TEN

THIS WAS ABSOLUTELY CRAZY.

A hundred objections tore through Naomi's head, but the one thing she couldn't shake was quite how Bas seemed to be able to read her so easily.

As if he really *got* her when no one else ever had done in the past.

She thrust the notion aside, and tried valiantly to remind herself who the man standing in front of her really was. Because if she didn't do that then she was terribly afraid she would agree to this crazy suggestion there and then. But Thorncroft's resident Lothario wasn't really the marrying kind.

'And what of your playboy ways?'

'That part of my life is over.'

'You can simply give that up?' She frowned, as if a part of her didn't feel so joyous at the idea. 'Not just like that.'

'I'm sure I've already told you that those stories were exaggerated anyway.'

'But not complete lies,' she pointed out. 'And even if there's only a fraction of truth in them, how could I expect you to stop completely just because you're married? Especially when ours won't even be a true marriage.'

A sickening thought struck Naomi. So hard that it actually winded her.

'Or are you expecting me to turn a blind eye? Because I can tell you now, that won't happen.'

'I think I rather like the fierce side of you, *älskling*.'

He actually sounded amused, and she had to bite the inside of her mouth to refrain from saying something uncouth.

'But you can sheath your claws, there will be no other women.'

'So you intend to become a monk?' She laughed, though it sounded vaguely maniacal. 'Forgive me if I can't picture it.'

'Who said anything about becoming a monk?' he demanded, his voice low and rich and deep.

And then he was inches from her and suddenly she wasn't laughing any more. Though she was still gasping for air.

Before she knew what she was doing, she found that she'd lifted her hands and splayed them against his chest. It wasn't at all what she'd intended—she had meant to brace against him. But now everything was ten times worse.

A hundred times worse.

Because she was touching him. And the heat of his body was permeating through her hands, and it was all she could do not to give into the crushing urge to let her palms roam the solid chest that felt so deliciously familiar to her.

'I'm not sleeping with you again,' she managed, but her voice was breathy, and unsubstantial.

Was it any wonder? It had been hard enough to get enough air before but now she couldn't breathe at all, which left her feeling light-headed. The *only* reason she was feeling light-headed, she tried telling herself firmly. Because, of course, it couldn't be anything else.

She couldn't possibly be so foolish as to actually believe this ludicrous marriage idea had any legs at all, could she? Worse, she—the girl who had grown up knowing romance and real life bore no relation to each other—couldn't possibly *want* to believe it had any merit.

'Sex,' he corrected thickly. 'Not *sleep*.'

His low, rich tone snaked inside her, winding its way around her chest. Lower and gloriously lower.

Naomi swallowed.

'You can't think I'll have…sex with you again.'

'Oh, I know it,' he rasped. 'Lots of sex. Raw, urgent, desperate sex. As a married couple, we'll have a lifetime of sex together.'

'I don't want that,' she lied, barely recognising her own voice.

His mouth twisted into a smile. He could read the truth in every line of her traitorous body, and there was nothing she could do about it.

'I don't believe that,' he muttered. 'And you don't either.'

And, God, what was wrong with her that he made her ache for him all the more?

It was just the physical, Naomi decided desperately, a physiological reaction. Because that was easier to deal with right now. She had a ready-made excuse for that. And she was dreadfully afraid that if she hadn't had the excuse, she would have willingly given herself to him already.

'Bas… I…'

'Not now,' he assured her. 'Nothing will risk our baby. The next few months will be about doing everything in our power to ensure our unborn daughter gets to term. And we will give our child the stable, family home that neither of us ever got to enjoy.'

It was insane, how badly she wanted to believe him. Standing here with him, like this, she almost did. Naomi had no idea how she found the strength to pull her hands back and step away.

'Real life doesn't work that way,' she managed. 'Couples staying together for the sake of a baby are doomed to fail, never mind one-night stands like us.'

'Personal experience?' He quirked his eyebrow at the emphasis in her tone.

She hadn't meant to say anything. She hadn't even been aware she was going to, until the words came tumbling out of their own volition.

'My mother begged my father to stay, and for a while, he did. I don't have many memories of the time before I lived with my grandmother, but I do remember that it wasn't pleasant living with the constant rowing. Or the screaming and crying. One often resents the other, or they end up resenting each other. Or they cheat.'

'We will not be *most* couples,' he growled, though he didn't move to close the gap between them again.

'You can't promise that,' she countered softly.

But Bas wasn't so easily deterred.

'I can tell you that I didn't get to be a surgeon by being *most* men, and I didn't get to become a top surgeon by being *most* surgeons.'

From anyone else, it might have sounded arrogant, yet from this man it just sounded factual. Still, it was all she could do not to step back into the circle of his arms, where it had felt safe, yet dangerously thrilling, all at the same time.

'And you didn't get to join the army to look after your family by being *most* women.'

She jerked her head up, the unexpected compliment piercing what little armour she'd been trying to gather about herself.

'Most people are stronger and more resilient than they would give themselves credit for.'

'They are,' he agreed. 'I see it every day, with the way some families rally themselves when a loved one is suddenly desperately ill. Therefore, I see no reason why we can't equally rally together. For this baby.'

'Not if it means me being embarrassed when you finally realise that you can't give up your playboy lifestyle. And I can't quite see you settling down, wife, children, pipe, slippers.'

'No.' He let out an unexpected laugh at that, free and wild, the way she'd only ever seen him be with Grace before that moment. But *she* was the one who had elicited it from him.

It was a heady realisation, as if something were reaching inside her chest, filling it with something she couldn't identify.

Or didn't want to.

How was it that a simple laugh had shifted things between them in an instant?

She didn't realise he'd closed the gap between them until he was there again. And he was dragging a thumb pad across her lower lip.

'But who says our marriage has to be like that?' he demanded. 'We've already demonstrated that we can enjoy a far more...*carnal* connection.'

There was no stopping the delicious shiver that rippled through her at that. Tangling inside her and threatening to turn her inside out. Just from his thumb on her lip.

How quickly would her already weak defence crumble if he replaced his thumb with his mouth?

'I can still taste you,' Bas growled, and she wondered if her thoughts were imprinted, shamefully, on her face somehow. 'In my dreams at night. Some couples make it work on far less.'

Never mind a kiss, how fast would she come apart if he placed his mouth somewhere else altogether? Naomi gasped quietly as the memories came back to her in a rush, charging her right through.

Now, all she could picture was his dark head as it had been nestled between her legs, all those months ago. That expression of wanton greed that had darkened his expression as he'd looked up at her, moments before she'd lost herself completely.

When had any other man affected her quite that way?

It had only ever been Bas.

And then, as if to prove who was in control, he slid his hand around the nape of heck, lowered his head, and claimed her mouth with his own—his skill as devastating as ever.

With any other man, it might have been just a kiss. But with Bas, there was no *just* anything.

It was a magnificent assault on her senses. His touch, his smell, his taste, even the way he sounded when he made that low growl of possession that rumbled straight through her. To where she was hottest for him.

Molten.

And even though her brain screamed at her to resist him, to stand firm and demand more from him, to show him that she wouldn't simply capitulate every time, to her shame Naomi felt helpless to stop herself from opening up to his kiss, her body already on fire.

He claimed her again, and again, with the same wild intensity that she remembered from that first night. Skilful, and bold. Making her his.

And there was nothing she could do about it. She was lost, and she didn't care.

Without warning, Bas stopped. Pulling his head away as he set her body aside from him. Leaving her blinking, and desperately struggling to right herself.

'I rather think that proves the point,' he rasped, his eyes big and black, mirroring her own desire. 'Does it not?'

Naomi didn't answer. She wasn't even sure how she was breathing. Or standing. But one of them needed to walk away from this, otherwise who knew where this night could end up?

Still, she didn't move. In the end, it was Bas who moved across the room. Bas who controlled the shots—as ever.

Because, when it came down to it, she was his—whether she liked it or not. But Bas Jansen wasn't hers in return.

He never would be.

'Talk to me,' Bas instructed as he joined the rest of the multidisciplinary team that had been gathered for the latest case on the resus floor. He'd been finishing a protracted surgery, which had been yet another much-needed distraction from thoughts of Naomi.

He'd been working at the hospital for the last few days, ever since the night he'd asked her to marry him. Or, more accurately, ever since the kiss when he'd almost forgotten himself completely—the way that only Naomi seemed to make him do.

And though he knew he couldn't avoid her for ever, throwing himself into work seemed like a good temporary option.

'What's the case?' he prompted, biting back his irritation when the doctor didn't answer.

'I'm not running this shout.' The young man edged away, flustered.

Bas blew out a breath.

'Then who is?'

'I am.'

Naomi's unmistakeable voice came over his shoulder, steady and controlled. But even so, it had the ability to reach inside his chest and squeeze. Not that she even gave him a second glance.

'Thirty-two-year-old female came in with significant thermal injuries a short while ago after being caught in a caravan explosion while on holiday with her family,' Naomi advised the team smoothly. Professionally.

Had he expected anything less?

'The patient came to us alert,' Naomi continued, 'though we understand she was unconscious for about a minute on scene. She was intubated for airway protection, and she presented with bilateral breath sounds, and readily apparent fullthickness burns to her face, neck, anterior torso, and bilateral arms, and right leg.'

'Wait.' Stepping forward, Bas made a quick visual check of the patient. This might be Naomi running the shout, but he wasn't about to go easy on her just because working with her was the last thing he needed right now.

So much for his distraction.

Nonetheless, he diverted all his attention to the patient. The extent of her burns was clear enough to see, covering around sixty per cent of her body. 'Secondary imaging?'

'Carried out,' Naomi confirmed. 'No further injuries were revealed. No internal haemorrhaging. I'm bringing her up to the Jansen suite now for excisional debridement of her wounds.'

'Good.' Bas nodded. 'We need to get her into operating room two—the sooner we start, the better for her. Okay, are we ready to move her?'

'Ready.'

'You've taken into account burn shock?'

Naomi nodded.

'Yes, given that it's a major burn covering more than twenty per cent of total body surface injury.'

'Good,' Bas agreed.

The burn shock was a unique combination of distributive and hypovolaemic shock, similar to an ischemia-reperfusion injury manifesting at both cellular, then systemic levels. Early resuscitation of the burns injuries had been proven vital to the survival of a burns victim suffering with burn shock.

'What's your full course of action?'

'I want to get her to the OR for debridement and antimicrobial dressings. She can then resuscitate for the next thirty-six to forty-eight hours with various fluid replacement, bearing in mind the released cytokines with this heat injury, given that the burns are greater than twenty per cent of her total body surface area.'

'Good.' Bas nodded his approval.

Regardless of anything, given the extent of the woman's burns, she would require multiple excisional debridement and wound prep procedures over the course of several weeks, and significant treatment, most likely including cultured epidermal grafts over the coming months, along with local grafts.

'One more thing.' Naomi held Bas back as the porters took over manoeuvring the trolley into the lifts. 'She keeps asking about her son and her husband, but they died in the fire. I don't know whether I'm supposed to tell her or not.'

The twist inside Bas was sharp, and deep.

Just looking at Naomi and thinking about her and their unborn baby suddenly choked him. He didn't even care to imagine how horrific it would be if anything happened to them.

'Do not tell the patient yet,' Bas gritted out under his breath, though he hated having to keep news like that from somebody.

And the sharp intake of breath from Naomi told him that she felt the same.

'Nothing?'

'Nothing,' he insisted. 'We'll need to keep it from our patient for as long as it takes to get her stable because I can't say what effect that will have on her recovery. And she has enough of a mountain to climb without the added mental anguish.'

As long as the woman was fighting for her life right alongside his medical team, then maybe he could save her life. Though whether she would actually thank him for it was a different thing altogether.

And it struck Bas that if he didn't handle things properly, there was a possibility—in years to come—that neither Naomi nor his unborn baby would thank him for his intervention in their lives, either.

It was late into the night when Naomi and Bas finally finished and were headed back to the penthouse together. In silence. Neither apparently having anything to say.

But that didn't mean her mind wasn't racing. Still trying to process that last, dreadful case.

If working with that young woman had taught Naomi

anything, then she thought it had reminded her how short life was.

One moment, her patient had been loving her life with her husband and child. Now, she in the ICU, fighting for her life, and to get back to her family. Not even aware that she didn't have a family to get back to.

Naomi swallowed down the lump that currently clogged up her throat. What if that were her? With Bas, and their daughter?

It didn't bear thinking about.

Shoving the thoughts out of her mind, Naomi hurried to her suite and stripped off her clothes, as though that could somehow help her to also divest herself of the horror of the day. Then, padding through to her en-suite bathroom, she spun the jets for a long, hot shower, and stood under them until her skin was red, and scoured clean.

She couldn't have said how long she stayed like that, but by the time she wandered back through the apartment to find Bas, he was knocking seven shades out of a punchbag in his home gym.

For a short time, she simply stood silently by the door and watched him.

He moved so gracefully that it was almost like a dance. Moving in and out, to one side then the other, as he jabbed and lunged at the heavy bag hanging from the ceiling. It was almost mesmerising.

By the look of the sweat dripping from him, and the pumped muscles, he'd been here a while—probably ever since she'd stepped into the shower—but he showed no sign of stopping.

Was this his way of trying to clear his mind of that dreadful case?

After the other night, she didn't want to step in and invade his space. But neither could she manage to tear herself away. And then, without warning, he turned as though he could sense her there, and Naomi found herself pinned to the spot where she stood.

She thought she ought to speak, but she didn't know what to say. And Bas turned back to the punchbag. *Left-right-left. Right-left-right.*

'That was a bad day,' she blurted out, when she couldn't take it any longer.

Left-right-left.

'We didn't lose our patient.' The exertion made his breath choppy. But she knew that wasn't why it sounded so harsh. 'In fact, we saved her.'

'For what, though?' she whispered. 'When she finds out the truth, she's going to wish we'd let her die right alongside her husband and child.'

Right-left-right.

'For a while.' He shrugged. 'But then…she won't. She'll stop wishing she was dead though she may not like being alive. And then, in time, she'll start living again. It's human nature. Either that, or…'

He stopped talking, but Naomi could hear the words as surely as if he'd spoken them.

And then, the only sound was back to the beating of the punchbag.

'I'm sorry,' she offered eventually. 'I shouldn't have intruded on you.'

Turning, she headed for the door and was halfway through it when Bas stopped and caught the bag.

'Why are you here, Naomi?'

He didn't want to hear what she'd come here to say. But that was too bad, because she needed to tell him. There was nothing else for it.

'What happened today…it made me think.'

'Is that so?' he growled, his voice low.

'Yes.' She forced herself to continue. 'It made me realise that life is too short. You don't know what's around the corner.'

Bas didn't look impressed.

'I've no doubt that working as an army nurse gave you plenty of those days.'

'Not like this.' Naomi took a step forward before she realised what she was doing. 'Today was different.'

And maybe it was because of the baby. Maybe she realised her own mortality. Either way, it didn't change how she now felt. Or how she now *knew* she felt.

'What is it you've come to say, Naomi?' Bas gritted out, his tone far from encouraging.

But she didn't care about that either. She sucked in a steadying breath.

'Today, I realised what I want. What matters to me,' she told him boldly. 'Today, I realised that a marriage in name only isn't what I want.'

Bas dropped the punchbag and took a step towards her. She wondered what made her notice the slight hesitation in his step, as though he wasn't as brimming with confidence as he liked to make out. Or why the bandages on one of his fists were hanging low, as if a part of him was somehow defeated.

As if she was finally seeing the truth behind that suit of armour that he'd always drawn around himself.

'I warned you not to try to take my daughter from me, Naomi,' he bit out.

But she wasn't fooled.

'I'm not trying to take anyone away from you.' She lifted her hands in placation. 'I'm saying that I agree. I'm in.'

'You're in?' He eyed her sceptically.

She told herself there was nothing to feel nervous about.

'Our baby will be better off with both of us in her life. So… I accept.'

'You accept.'

'I do.' Naomi dipped her head, albeit a little jerkily—though she told herself that was nerves, nothing more. 'I will marry you.'

CHAPTER ELEVEN

'PLEASE, YOU HAVE to help me!'

The desperate voice had Naomi jerking her head up from the nurses' station. A young woman gripped the desk white-knuckle tight, her words tumbling urgently out of her mouth.

'I'm looking for my husband. I had a call to say he'd been in an accident this morning. He was hit by a car on his way to work. Oh…he was cycling.'

Quietly, soothingly, Naomi moved to the computer, almost forgetting to reach over her bump—still small for over thirty weeks, but evident nonetheless—as she placed her fingers on the keyboard.

How was she already this far along? It seemed as though the past few weeks…no, wait…*months,* had passed by so quickly with Bas.

Shaking the thought from her head, Naomi focussed on the young woman.

'What is your husband's name?'

'Dave. Dave Kiffleson.'

Naomi paused, not needing to type. She'd been working on that case with Bas a couple of hours ago, when the patient had arrived in Resus—cyclist versus car. A young newly-wed who was little more than a kid.

And now his life was in Bas's hands on the operating table—not that she was about to tell their patient's young, terrified, new wife.

Naomi offered another comforting smile.

'Let me see if I can find someone who can talk to you.'

'Oh, no!' A loud sob escaped the girl's throat as her hands flew up to her mouth. 'It's bad, isn't it? Oh, please don't say he's… I can't be without him. I can't.'

'It's Becky, isn't it?'

Another gasp, as the young woman nodded.

'You spoke to him?'

'A little. Dave was quite badly injured, but he kept wanting us to wait for you to arrive. He said you'd be here any minute.'

'He did?'

The relief was evident.

'He did.' Naomi smiled kindly. There was no need, at this point, to frighten her by telling her that her husband had been slipping in and out of consciousness. Or quite how bad a state his body had been in. 'You're newly-weds, aren't you?'

'Two weeks.' Becky pulled a face that was both awkward and defiant. 'We eloped. Our families said we were too young, but we love each other.'

Naomi didn't react. She had no intention of judging. A part of her even half admired the passion in the girl's voice. The same passion that had been in the young lad's reaction, despite his obvious pain.

What must it be like to love a person that much? To feel as though you couldn't go on if they were no longer in your life? To feel such pure love?

Like the love you're starting to feel for Bas?

The question slammed into her brain from apparently nowhere, and Naomi fought to shove it aside.

The girl peered at her through her tears.

'Oh, you understand exactly what I mean, don't you?' Becky managed to sob out.

'No... I—' Naomi began to speak, but the girl clearly wasn't listening.

'I can see it in your face. You know what I'm saying.'

And as hard as she tried to deny it—if only to herself—Naomi found she couldn't say a word.

She loved Bas.

How had that even happened?

It had snuck up on her so sneakily she hadn't even realised it—ever since that night in his gym when she'd agreed to marry him.

It had been like flicking a switch. As though the assurance that she wasn't trying to tear his daughter away from him had revealed a whole different Bas, who Naomi had never anticipated.

A kind Bas. An attentive Bas. A caring Bas. All revealed in every tiny little thing that he did to make her pregnancy—her life—easier. Each one of them seemingly unimportant in and of themselves yet which, when put together, meant that her life had changed without her even realising it. And for the better.

When had she started to feel as though she mattered—really mattered—to someone? To *Bas*? When had this...*thing* inside her suddenly flickered into life? When had it breathed out its first body-warming breath, heating up her frozen heart with each passing day?

How had Bas made her feel alive again?

And one day had bled into another, and then into a week, and suddenly she was here, unable to imagine how she would feel if she were Becky, and Bas were Dave. It would be...unbearable. And not simply because he was her unborn daughter's father.

He *mattered* to her. How had that happened?

Thrusting the unwelcome, unhelpful thought from her brain, Naomi turned her full concentration to Becky.

'But we wanted to help him as quickly as we could so your husband is in Theatre right now,' Naomi said firmly but with as much comfort as she could. 'He's with the best people to help him. Let me get someone who can explain what's happening more fully.'

Beckoning a colleague to make the call, Naomi moved around the desk and led the woman to a relatives' waiting area.

'As soon as one of my colleagues comes down, I'll take you through to them.'

'You can't tell me?' Becky pushed anxiously, and Naomi shook her head.

'I'm sorry, but it's better that you speak to one of my colleagues who has been in the OR with your husband. He'll have far more up-to-date information for you. Can I get you tea? Coffee?'

The girl offered her a momentarily blank look, then managed a small smile.

'Tea, please.'

'Tea it is.' Naomi dipped her head as she headed over to the machines.

It felt like the least she could do. Because even if Bas could save his patient from being wheelchair-bound for the remainder of his life, the young lad's spinal injuries meant that it was going to be a long, long road back to recovery. It would take months to learn to walk again. Perhaps even years to run or cycle.

'In sickness and in health,' Becky blurted out as she returned with the tea.

Naomi caught herself abruptly. Had she uncharacteristically betrayed herself in her expressions?

'Sorry?'

'I was in and out of hospitals as a kid.' The girl shrugged, suddenly more composed. 'Childhood leukaemia. I learned to read micro expressions, though you hide yours pretty well. But I can tell it's bad.'

'My colleague is the best surgeon I know,' Naomi offered sincerely as the girl flashed another half-smile.

'We vowed to love each other in sickness and in health, and I intend to honour it, whatever happens,' Becky said firmly. 'I guess I never expected the sickness to come so soon, and we always thought it would be the cancer coming back for me rather than something happening to him, but it doesn't change anything.'

Naomi choked back an unexpected sob. Put like that, it

cast a whole different perspective on how young these two
newly-weds were.

'People say *life's too short* all the time,' Becky continued quietly, taking a small sup of her tea. 'But I don't think
many of them understand it the way that Dave and I do. And
I guess, in this job, you must see that too, right?'

And for a moment, Naomi could only stare at Becky. A
wise old woman in the body of a teenager.

'Right,' Naomi managed abruptly. 'Life's too short.'
So what was she going to do about it?

Bas eyed Naomi sceptically. It wasn't so much that he didn't
understand the words she was saying, it was more that he
didn't understand his body's reaction to them.

Or perhaps he did understand, all too well, and it was
more that he feared it.

These last few months with her living in his penthouse had
been…a revelation. It had made him see things, feel things,
want things that he'd never wanted before. And he found the
prospect terrifying.

He'd decided over a month ago that it was better to pretend
it didn't exist than have to deal with it. But now, he couldn't
ignore it any more. Not when Naomi was standing right in
front of him saying all the things he'd never imagined wanting to ever hear anyone say.

He still didn't want to hear, Bas reminded himself
brusquely.

'I'm saying that I want more,' she continued defiantly
when it became clear he hadn't been intending to answer her.

'More?'

One simple syllable that was a sentence—a warning—all
on its own. But Naomi clearly had no intention of heeding it.

'More,' she confirmed. 'More than just a paper marriage.
More than just a marriage of convenience. More than just
marrying for the sake of our daughter.'

It took him an eternity to answer. And when he did, he wasn't even sure what he was saying.

'More, how?' he managed.

Naomi flicked her tongue out over her suddenly parched lips, but he couldn't help his gaze from being snagged by the motion. His body reacted predictably, even as he tried to shut it down. Having her live with him the past few months, getting closer, had been difficult enough without this added fire in the mix.

'I want something real, Bas. I want love.'

He laughed. An unpleasant sound that scraped, painful and deep, inside his own body.

'*Love?* Love doesn't exist, Naomi. It isn't real. It's an illusory construct dreamt up by those too desperate, too lonely, too pathetic to know better.'

She shook her head.

'It's real, Bas. You want to know how I know?'

'Not really,' he snapped.

She chose to ignore him.

'I know it's real because I feel it. For you.'

'No.'

'I love you, Bas.'

The silence between them was oppressive. Menacing even. Though he didn't know if it was only him who felt it.

Something boiled through Bas and even though that terrified part of him feared it wasn't temper—not at all—a dull part of his brain channelled it into such. Because it was easier to be angry than to face whatever that dark, viscous...*thing* was that swirled within him.

'You do not love me.'

Still, he didn't realise he'd roared the denial until it began bouncing back to him, off the cold, stark walls.

He wanted to punch it away again. Keep it from touching him. But at the same time, there was a deep ache in his chest.

A yearning, that began to cleave him in two right there, where he stood. And there was no punching *that* away.

'People do not love me, Naomi,' he tried again, even though he barely recognised his own voice.

'And yet I do.' She offered a smile so soft that he thought it might suffocate him. 'There is nothing fundamentally unlovable about you, at all. I love you. Grace does, in a different way. That much is evident. Even Henrik, I think. Since he came all this way.'

'That's impossible,' he made himself insist. Though he couldn't explain why it was getting harder and harder to remember a truth he'd known all these years. 'Henrik isn't capable of it, any more than I am.'

'You're wrong.' She flashed that damned soft smile again. 'I think you're capable of a lot more than you like to pretend.'

'No.'

'You didn't take me—us—in because it was your duty, or at least you didn't take us in *simply* because you felt it was your duty. You took us in because I am carrying your daughter.'

'Why do you seem so intent on thinking of me as a much better man than I actually am?'

'Why do you seem so intent on seeing yourself as less than you are?'

And Bas thought it was that gentleness that might prove his undoing. He wanted to refute what she was saying. He found he couldn't. He wasn't sure what that said about the situation.

'I'm taking responsibility for my child. That is a matter of doing what is right. That isn't about love.'

'Except that we don't need to get married in order for you to meet your responsibilities.'

'This baby will have two parents who care for her. To…'

'To love her?' Naomi supplied when he stopped. 'When I told you I was pregnant, I did so because I knew it was morally the right thing to do. But I told you, even then, that I didn't want or expect anything from you.'

'So because I chose to take my responsibility seriously, you think that means I love you?' he demanded. 'I have no wish to hurt you, Naomi, but that wasn't love. I told you, I'm not capable of such an emotion. I wish I were.'

'You *are* capable, Bas.' Naomi shook her head. 'I think you only wish you *weren't*. Which makes me wonder if talking to Henrik is the solution. Not so long ago I asked you if you couldn't forgive Henrik because what happened when you were kids is still too painful for you, or if it was more that it has been so long that you no longer know *how* to forgive him.'

'I didn't answer you,' he bit out.

'You did not,' she agreed. 'And now I know why. Because it's both of those things. And it's something else as well.'

'No.'

'Yes,' she continued gently. 'The reason you won't forgive Henrik—the reason you still hate him—is because you're scared of yourself, Bas. You're scared to love again. Him. Me. Our baby. And that's why you keep everyone at arm's length.'

'You're wrong,' he rasped, wishing that there weren't that unwelcome sliver of him that thought it might agree with her.

'Are you sure about that?' She pressed her lips against each other sadly. 'Because I wonder what your brother has come all this way to tell you. Why he turned his back on you for all those years?'

'I don't care.'

If only that were true. It ought to be true.

'I think we both know that isn't true,' she told him, as if reading his mind. 'Why you refuse to meet him. What you've buried in the recesses of your memory that you don't want dredged up. Are you hiding from him? Or yourself?'

Bas stood paralysed. Frozen right through. He had no

idea how he managed to work his jaw enough to reply, but he barely recognised his own tight, seething voice.

'He betrayed me, Naomi,' he managed. 'He lied almost thirty years ago to social services, choosing our excuse for a mother, and the man who had no right being any child's stepfather, over me—when I was the only one standing up for him.

'And it has eaten you up inside ever since,' she exclaimed. 'Yet right now you have the chance to find out the truth about why Henrik did that. Maybe he had a good reason to? At the very least, maybe he wants to apologise.'

'It's too late for apologies.' Bas snorted, not surprised at the earnest expression that crossed Naomi's lovely features.

It might have been endearing, had he not felt so livid. And so…knocked sideways.

'I don't think it's ever too late for that,' she told him softly. 'And I'm not saying that if he did apologise you would have to forgive and forget. I'm just saying, for your own sake, let it give you some peace.

Another wave of silence washed over them as he couldn't help wondering if she had a point.

What was the use of all this bitterness and hatred he felt towards his brother? What good did it do him? But even as the thoughts entered Bas's head, another thought chased them along.

'If he came to Thorncroft to apologise, then he shouldn't have tracked down my closest friend and seduced her. He made her betray you, too.'

'Grace never betrayed you,' Naomi countered. 'She was devastated when she found out who he was, you said it yourself. And what if Henrik really didn't know who she was? What if he simply fell for her that night? No ulterior motives.'

'That's ludicrous,' Bas barked. 'No one—'

'Like the way I fell for you,' she continued, refusing to let him take over. 'Like the way I think you feel for me, too. If only you'd let go long enough to see it for yourself.'

'This is not a conversation we will be having.'

He moved back to the punchbag then, dismissing her. Every fibre of her ached on his behalf. His demons were right there, on the periphery, and she couldn't just let him hide away from them for another thirty years. She wouldn't.

Lurching forward, she grabbed the heavy PVC bag as it hung there, stopping Bas from continuing.

'You need to let go,' Naomi whispered. 'You've been clinging to the edge for so long without knowing it.'

'This isn't going to happen. It's in the past. I'm not going to speak to Henrik. He may be a good surgeon but he is my brother in name only. I have no intention of meeting with him.'

'I can't help feeling that would be your loss, Bas,' she pleaded.

His face twisted into a mask of ferocious hurt, though she doubted he realised it.

'So be it.'

'Let go. And if you fall, I'll be here to catch you.'

'I will not fall,' he growled. 'And, if I did, I would never need you to catch *anything*.'

He hadn't wanted to hurt her, but he'd needed to stop her from talking. He'd needed to do something—anything—to stop the sharpness of her words from stabbing into him like a thousand tiny needle points.

Even so, he wasn't ready for the look of anguish that twisted up her lovely face.

'Then if you can't let go of those awful parts of your past,' she choked out, 'you need to let go of me.'

'Say again?'

'I love you, Bas. But that means that I can't watch you devouring yourself from the inside out. I don't want to see you putting yourself through that suffering over and over, like it's on some kind of crazy loop in your head.'

'What exactly are you saying?' Bas bit out coldly, as Naomi threw her arms around herself as if to ward off anything bad.

'I'm saying that you should let me go, Bas. Forget marriage. Or living together to raise this child. You're Basilius Jansen, of course. Thorncroft's resident playboy surgeon. I knew you would remember that eventually, however much we both tried to pretend otherwise.'

'You tried to pretend otherwise,' he ground out, hating himself. 'I seem to recall warning you who I was all along.'

'Someone who is incapable of love. Or forgiveness. Or even basic human decency. Yes, you're making that as clear as you can, aren't you, Bas? Well, then, fine. Have it your way. But you need to let me go back to my grandmother and my sister.'

'I think not.'

'I think yes,' she countered. 'I need to go home. More than that, my baby needs to come with me. She deserves better than you, Bas. She deserves a family. People who won't be afraid to tell her that they love her. Who will teach her how to be a better person.'

And if Naomi had taken a scalpel to his chest, and sliced it wide open, it surely couldn't have pained him any more than this.

For several moments, he couldn't answer. He was sure he stopped breathing.

'Fine,' he heard himself answer, at long last. 'That might indeed be for the best.'

And if she looked destroyed, then there was very little he could do about that. He felt decimated.

It was sickening to realise that this baby—his unborn daughter—would be better off without him.

That he wasn't the kind of role model she should ever have to deal with in her life.

'No marriage. No contact between you and I,' he continued. 'But that is still my daughter, and I won't let her be taken from my life so easily.'

'I'll move back home, until I…we…come to some kind of arrangement.'

'As you wish,' he agreed coldly, ignoring the tumbling and twisting inside him at that moment. 'I'll sort out a more appropriate apartment for you—one that is closer to the hospital, but where you can live with your family without being on top of each other.'

'I don't need you to take care of me. I need you to—'

He cut her off again.

'It's done, Naomi.'

If only his mind were as clear as his voice sounded. What else did he need to sort out? His thoughts were a confusion of emotions.

She had just had her last weekly foetal nonstress test; it would be another week before there was another.

Bas vacillated. The tests checked for movements because she couldn't feel much any more, beyond the usual pain from sheer fluid. But the baby had been fine the past few weeks, and he didn't care to deal with Grace at the moment. Most importantly, he didn't want any confrontation between the two of them to upset Naomi.

For her sake, it would be better for him not to be there this time.

If he could have wrapped her, and his baby, in cotton wool and tucked them away in his apartment, not to emerge for the remainder of the pregnancy, then he was sure he would have done so. And the notion bewildered him.

He, who had never wanted children. Or a family. Or even a wife. He, who had never felt so protective of any woman who he'd dated. Although, admittedly, *dated* probably wasn't the most appropriate term.

Which brought him to the other reason behind hauling the mother of his unborn baby to his private apartment.

Had a part of him hoped that bringing her here, to his 'sanctuary' where he'd never brought a lover in all his life, might help him to get a grip on whatever this *thing* was between them?

As unchivalrous as it was, Bas considered that such a motive had indeed formed part of his plan. But then, how chivalrous could a self-proclaimed playboy really be?

He suspected that he'd imagined seeing her here would feel wrong. Ill-fitting. And might thus help to dull this inconvenient attraction he felt for her.

But it hadn't helped at all.

It was still there, squatting on his chest. A little too bright, and too encompassing.

CHAPTER TWELVE

BAS POUNDED THE STREETS, running faster, harder, better than he'd ever done in his life.

But he didn't feel better.

He felt as if he were a mere shadow of himself. The last month without Naomi had been torture. His own private hell, which more and more he was beginning to think he'd brought upon himself.

He was free. Back to his pre-Naomi, pre-baby life. His apartment was his own. His lawyers were drawing up the contracts for Naomi to sign.

Finally, he could begin to breathe again.

Only, he couldn't seem to.

Instead, every last second of their row began to run through his head. Replaying in all too vivid detail. To his shame.

The way she'd looked. And that devastated expression on her lovely features when he'd sliced her with his words. As if she truly believed what she'd been telling him. As if she truly couldn't see the darkness that lurked within that made him so impossible to love. Or, that he'd always believed made him impossible to love.

And if he was, in fact, deserving of the love of a woman like Naomi, then could she also be right that he was capable of love, too?

He picked up his speed to a brutal pace, but it didn't help.

Everything swelled and crashed through Bas's brain, shifting and tilting the way his whole life seemed to have been doing recently. Starting with the night he'd met Naomi and peaking the night he'd severed her from his life.

He could still picture the way she'd looked. The way she'd felt in his arms as they'd swept across that floor together.

She hadn't known how to dance, and still, the way she had followed his lead as though they were one and same. Hand-crafted for each other.

And nothing dulled the pain.

Once upon a time, whiskey had numbed his feelings. Peaty and rich, it had seemed to help him to fool himself that life was good. But now he found he could barely touch it. Naomi had changed everything. Taking him higher than he'd ever felt before. More intoxicated than ever, without ever having had a drop.

He just hadn't wanted to admit it.

Suddenly, he realised that he didn't want to argue any more. At least, not with her. Not with the woman who had brought him back to life when he hadn't even realised that he'd been dead inside.

As much as he loathed the idea of speaking with Henrik— good surgeon or not—he could concede that Naomi had made a good point when she'd reminded him that they were all different people than they had been ten, twenty, thirty years ago.

So, even if he knew his brother could have nothing to say that Bas wanted to hear, he could at least hear Henrik out. If only for Naomi. And if only for the baby that was growing in her belly.

He was soon to be a father, with all that entailed. The least he could do was be one worthy of their daughter.

Turning back to the house, Bas began running faster, despite the fact that his legs no longer felt as if they were his.

Home.

Or at least, he would be, once he brought Naomi back. And soon—their daughter.

'What the hell happened?'

Bas burst into the hospital, his lungs on fire. He wasn't sure he'd breathed ever since he'd returned to his penthouse only to see a missed message.

Naomi turned her head to him and his stomach twisted at the expression of pure anguish in her eyes.

'What are you doing here, Bas?'

'Your sister left me a message.'

The words felt strange in his mouth, and he realised it was the fact that Leila shouldn't have had to call him in the first place. He should have been there. He should have never let Naomi go through this alone.

But this wasn't the time or the place.

'What happened, Naomi?'

'I don't need you here,' she bit out. The pained expression belying her words.

But it was only what he deserved.

'We can talk about how much of a lie that is later,' he managed. 'Just as we can talk about what a jerk I've been.'

Naomi gritted her teeth.

'You don't want to be here. You said it from the start. It's fine.'

'I was wrong,' he said, shocking her. 'I was coming to tell you that when I got the message.'

'You were?'

She lifted her hands up and stopped. As if she'd been going to reach for him but had thought better of it.

Bas took her hands in his.

'I was,' he assured her. 'But now isn't the time. What happened?'

She looked at him, then exhaled on a shaky breath.

'Grace found an issue during this week's foetal nonstress test. They brought me straight into hospital.'

Bas didn't dare speak. He bit back a curse. This wasn't a scenario with which he was familiar, and still all he could do was try to keep from swaying on precarious legs as he stared at her.

'What was the issue?'

Naomi swallowed once, twice, as she fought not to cry,

and Bas found himself hurrying across the room to take her hands.

Her grip was white-knuckle tight.

'The baby's heart-rate dipped a couple of times so they carried out an ultrasound. I'm having contractions.'

'Contractions?'

His gut twisted further. She was thirty-six weeks; if the baby was born now it would be preterm. Late pre-term, but pre-term all the same.

'I'm in labour, Bas.' There was no mistaking the agony in her voice. It echoed that dark thing that was currently skulking around his chest. 'And I couldn't even feel it.'

'That's not uncommon,' Grace said quietly, returning to the room. 'With all the fluid, and the discomfort you've been feeling up to this point.'

'So bed rest?' Bas cut in, unable to help himself. 'You can give her something to stop the contractions, Grace. Betamimetics? Try to keep the baby in just a little longer. Preferably to at least thirty-seven weeks.'

'Her cervix is already beginning to change and your little one isn't tolerating the contractions too well.' Grace shook her head, before turning back to Naomi. 'We'll prep you for a C-section now, Naomi.'

'I'm coming in.' Bas lifted the side of the bed and prepared to move it.

'You'll wait here,' Grace told him firmly. 'I'll take good care of her, Bas. But you're the father right now, not the surgeon. I'll make sure we call you as soon as she's prepped.'

There was an unspoken test in there, and Bas knew they were both waiting to see whether he trusted his friend enough to look after Naomi. And he didn't care. All that mattered was her. And their baby.

'Go,' he grunted, dipping his head to kiss Naomi's forehead.

Words hovered on his lips, but he couldn't say them. Not yet. Not until he'd done what she'd asked him to do.

He sat in the room for what felt like a lifetime. Maybe two. And even Bas—accustomed to the speed of treatment during a medical emergency—found he wasn't processing it as he might have expected.

It was one thing being the surgeon in control of the event, but quite another being this side of a scenario, at risk of being consumed by his concern for both the baby, and the mother of his unborn child.

And then, finally, a midwife came for him. He wasn't sure how he managed not to run down the corridors to the operating room, barely noticing as they gowned him up and led him through.

The sight of her on the operating table wasn't one he was prepared for. He'd performed countless procedures over the years, but this was surreal.

Unconscionable.

'The local anaesthetic means you won't feel any pain as we pull the baby out, Naomi, but you'll be aware of the movement.' Grace smiled kindly. 'I've had some patients describe it as being a little like a washing machine churning around.'

'Understood.' Naomi forced a tight smile of her own, even as she reached for his hand again, gripping it just as tightly as before.

Bas didn't dare to look around the curtain. He just kept his eyes locked with Naomi's, talking to her as quietly and soothingly as possible, though he wasn't sure he had any idea what he was talking to her about.

And then, at last, their baby was out and he stopped breathing, his stomach twisted into the tightest knot as they manually cleared her airways and the room was silent, waiting for that first cry.

'Is she okay?' Naomi choked out as the silence seemed to stretch on for an eternity. 'Is she...alive?'

He moved his hand to stroke the hair from her face, not trusting himself to answer. Then, without warning, a loud cry rent the air and Bas thought it was possibly the most beautiful sound that he'd ever heard.

'She's strong.' Grace appeared, the tiny bundle in her arms. 'Do you want to hold her before we take her through to NICU?'

Naomi lifted her arms and took her daughter, staring in awe at the tiny, puckered face. If he could have frozen this moment for ever, he thought he might have. And then Naomi glanced up at him and carefully offered their daughter for him to take.

'I've carried her for eight months,' she whispered. 'I think it's your chance now.'

He didn't wait to be told again. Taking his new baby in his arms, Bas looked down in undiluted rapture.

She was more perfect than he could have imagined. And he couldn't even speak to tell Naomi. He didn't need to. Once glance at her face told him she knew it too.

Holding their baby out for Naomi to kiss, he touched his own lips to her head.

'Aneka,' Naomi whispered reverently. Like a prayer.

'Aneka,' Bas echoed quietly. Then, long before he was ready, Grace appeared to reluctantly take her away again.

'Sorry,' she murmured, extending her arms.

Bas couldn't answer. His whole world had upended in an instant, and it hadn't even taken him a full glance to realise there was nothing he wouldn't do for this baby.

This was love—*real* love. And he was capable of it.

More than capable. It felt as though he had been waiting for this moment—for these two incredible human beings to enter his life. This wasn't about being a husband and father because it was the right thing to do, this was about being a husband and father because he knew his life would be all wrong if he didn't.

He loved them. And that meant he wanted to be the best version of himself that he could possibly be.

There was one thing left to do.

'Thank you,' he murmured sincerely as Grace turned to look at him.

Her smile broadened.

'Any time.'

Beside him, Naomi squeezed his hand once again, though she didn't say anything.

She didn't need to.

Bas watched as they took the baby to the NICU, then he waited for them to take Naomi to post-op recovery. And then he peeled off his gown and left the OR.

His new life with Naomi, and their daughter, could start the moment he spoke to Henrik. It might be the closure that Naomi had once suggested he needed.

Or maybe, just maybe, it could end up being so much more than that.

'I was surprised to receive your call.'

A few weeks ago it would have taken every ounce of Bas's self-control to look at his brother without reacting. As though his presence didn't both Bas at all.

Now, here in the hospital coffee shop, he couldn't help but notice that he didn't feel the same antagonism. Naomi—and now their beautiful little Aneka—were having more of an effect on him than he could ever have imagined possible. Healing him; making him feel whole for the first time in his life.

'Let's get on with this, shall we?' he suggested instead.

'How is fatherhood?' Henrik asked without warning.

'Fine,' began Bas. But it was impossible not to say more when his chest felt as if it might swell enough to burst. 'I never thought I would ever be a parent, yet I've learned how to be a father. A proper father. I've begun to understand what it is to love, and to accept love.'

'And you didn't know that before?'

The tone of the questions was like a grate rubbing the wrong way over Bas's soul.

'How could I know?' he demanded. 'I had no idea what love felt like. It's taken me until now to understand it.'

'Then I envy you.' Henrik bowed his head slightly, leaving Bas confused.

'You envy me? Are you completely deluded?'

'I always envied you. You got away.'

'I got away? I was the one who envied you.'

Henrik looked genuinely confused.

'I can't imagine why.'

'You had it all,' Bas blasted out. 'You were the one she wanted—the one she heaped love onto—whilst I was the one she cast aside.'

'Say that again,' Henrik demanded slowly, his tone unexpectedly dangerous.

Not that Bas was remotely cowed. Not when his stomach was churning so violently.

'You were the one she wanted to keep, whilst I was the one she couldn't wait to get rid of.'

'Have you seriously forgotten what it was like in that house when things didn't go our stepfather's way? Did you consider that, with you gone, I was the only punchbag left? Did you think she'd suddenly stop turning a blind eye to his tempers?'

'That was your decision. You're the one who told authorities I was lying when I'd had enough. At least she wanted to keep you. I got sent to be with a father who never wanted me around.'

'You can't really mean that?' The chill in Henrik's tone could have frosted the entire hospital.

But Bas didn't care. He gritted his teeth at his brother.

'How do you think it feels to be the son so awful that even his mother couldn't love him? I spent years wondering what was so wrong...so flawed about me, that wasn't you. You were always the perfect son.'

'That's...preposterous.' Henrik shook his head in disbelief, and Bas felt his own temper rise.

Bas took a step back, folding his arms over his chest—whether to protect himself or to create a barrier from his brother, he couldn't be sure.

'That's the truth. The last words she told me were that you and I might be twins, but that I lacked your compassionate side. That I was a horrid little bastard who no one could ever love.'

'Is that what you truly think?' Henrik laughed, but it was a hollow, cold sound.

Bas stopped, taken aback.

'Is that the way you remember things in your head, Basilius? That she somehow favoured me?'

'Didn't she?'

'No.' Henrik didn't hesitate. 'Our mother was a master of manipulation. She used to tell me that I lacked the kind of personality that you had. She told me that I was a pathetic excuse for a boy, and that no one could ever love me.'

Bas didn't answer. How could he when he had no idea what to say?

'Have you really forgotten what our mother was truly like?' Henrik demanded, after a moment. 'Have you forgotten how she used to play one of us against the other? Always trying to drive that wedge between us? All for attention?'

'I haven't forgotten anything,' Bas ground out. 'I remember how she more than loved attention, she *craved* it. She couldn't live without it. Attention to her was like air is to every other normal human being. Without it, she might as well be suffocating, dying. And you gave it to her.'

'I was trying to keep her sweet.' His brother shook his head. 'In a good mood. Especially when *he* came along, and it went from her manipulation to his fists.'

There was no need to discuss him further, they both knew who they were talking about.

'You never really bore the brunt of that, did you?' Bas couldn't help saying.

He wasn't prepared for his brother's response.

'Not as much as you did, I know that. You made sure of it.'

He paused, as if waiting for Bas to acknowledge, but the memories were hazy, and Bas couldn't work out what he was supposed to be remembering.

'Don't you remember how you would take the blame for me?' Henrik demanded. 'Taking responsibility for things I was supposed to have done wrong, even though you'd had nothing to do with it? If we were out of milk. If a light had been left on. Even simply if we walked down the stairs the wrong way.'

'I remember all that,' Bas began, 'but I don't remember taking the blame for you.'

'Well, you did.' His brother jerked his head. 'Almost all the time. You were always a protector, Basilius. Even for me. The only reason you didn't try to protect me that day was because you were concussed. Not that either of us understood that at the time.'

'Say that again?'

'You got walloped the day before. Only, it was so rough that you'd actually been sick. You told me that everything had gone black. If it hadn't been for that, you would have leaped in for me again. The way you always did.'

Bas stared down his six-foot-three brother. It was anybody's guess which of them might have a millimetre's edge on the other. And the images were fuzzy, but, now that Henrik had reminded him of them, something was beginning to pull into focus.

Henrik had been born half an hour after him, and hadn't he himself always felt like the *big* brother, needing to protect his younger brother?

'So why did you betray me?' Bas demanded abruptly; the one question that had niggled at him most, all these years, finally spilling out. 'Why did you back her up, that final time, instead of me?'

Henrik peered at him, incredulously.

'Because we agreed that was what I was going to do.'

Bas could only gawk at him.

'What are you talking about?' he ground out. 'Why would we ever, *ever* agree that?'

Disbelief was etched into his brother's face.

'You really don't remember?'

He felt as though he were going to explode.

'Remember what?'

'We agreed that if Child Welfare took us, then they'd probably end up splitting us up. We didn't want that.'

'That conversation never happened,' Bas scorned. His memories might be hazy, but they weren't non-existent. 'Besides, we got split up anyway.'

'How could we have foreseen that?' his brother bit out. 'We didn't know Magnus existed. We didn't even know that deadbeat wasn't our father.'

That much was true enough. But as for the rest of it...

'So that's what you're claiming? That was our plan?' He was getting angry now. And he couldn't seem to swallow it down. 'That we agreed I would tell the truth, only for you to back up our mother's lie? I don't think much of that so-called plan.'

'Our plan was that we would get rid of Child Welfare, and then we were going to run away and find Mrs P and Bertie,' Henrik fired back. 'You really don't remember?'

'I don't remember because it didn't happen.'

It was a strong denial. And yet, still, it cleaved into two that hard ball of resentment and anger inside him.

'It must have been the concussion,' Henrik realised abruptly.

And Bas hated that it made sense.

Hated it, and at the same time wished with every fibre of his being that it could be true.

That maybe his brother never had betrayed him the way he'd thought, all those years ago.

'You're saying you told them that I was lying so that they would go away?'

Surely it was sickening how desperate he sounded. Not that Henrik seemed to have noticed. He was wearing his own fervent expression.

'And we wouldn't be torn apart before we'd had chance to escape and find Mrs P,' Henrik added.

The two men stood in contemplative silence.

Could it really be that simple? He wished his memory weren't so hazy. But then what Henrik had said about a concussion would make sense.

The strangest part about it all was that Bas thought he might actually believe his brother. Because he *wanted* to believe Henrik? Or because his subconscious knew something he didn't? He couldn't be sure.

'I tried to find you,' his brother offered, after another pause. 'But I had no idea where to start looking or how. I asked, but she never told me anything, of course.'

'I find that harder to believe. Even back then, Magnus Jansen had made a name for himself as a surgeon.'

Henrik cast him a long look.

'Up until our mother's death, before Christmas last year, I thought my name was Henrik Magnusson. I've spent a decade looking up every Magnusson in Sweden. I had no idea you were even in the UK, let alone that I should really be looking for the name Jansen. The only thing I ever gleaned from her, growing up, was that he was a surgeon. It was the one nugget I held onto. So damned tightly. My one connection to you.'

'So much so that you became a surgeon?' Bas rasped.

It sounded so plausible, but he hated the idea that he might be being gullible.

'Yes.'

So simple. So frank. It rattled Bas—the idea that he might have got it all wrong, all these years.

'You expect me to believe that you only found out the truth when our mother told you…what, on her deathbed?'

'I can't tell you what to believe, Basilius. I can only tell you the facts as I know them to be. And she didn't tell me anything, whether on her deathbed or otherwise. Finally telling the truth would have been too kind an ending for her, Basilius. She was bitter and vengeful until the end.'

'Then how?' Bas bit out.

'When she died, Mrs P saw the obituary in the paper and made contact. When I told her what had happened all those years ago, she was able to fill in some of the gaps. Once I pieced it together with what I knew, I was able to find you.'

Bas felt as though he'd been walloped in the gut. It took him a moment to regroup.

'Mrs P is still out there?'

'She is.'

'And Bertie?'

Henrik's expression changed. 'He died. About a decade ago. Apparently, they'd both been waiting. Hoping we would one day seek them out.'

'They didn't seek us out,' Bas gritted out, as though he didn't care.

When this swirling mess inside him betrayed just how much he really did.

'They didn't know where we'd gone, Basilius. And they didn't want to risk causing problems for us when we were younger. They'd hoped that with them out of the picture, our mother's jealousy would have dissipated. And when we never got in touch, they let themselves believe it.'

He grunted, unable to speak.

'She would love to know about you and Naomi. I can only imagine how much joy it would bring her to hear about your new baby girl.'

Bas jerked his hand up for Henrik to stop.

It was too much to take in at once—his head was swimming. He needed time to process. Even just a moment to breathe.

Henrik, it seemed, had other ideas.

'You seem to think you have the monopoly on being rejected, *bror*. On being mistreated, and wronged. But, from my perspective, you got the better deal. You got away from her. And maybe Magnus wasn't any more welcoming, or loving, I can't speak to that,' Henrik rasped, 'but at least his fists were never the answer.'

Bas glowered at Henrik as though it was all somehow his brother's fault. The man—the surgeon—standing opposite him wasn't quite the stranger he'd always told himself.

Naomi had told him that, at the very least, he might get some closure. But this felt as far from closure as was possible.

'How long did you stay?'

Henrik's expression was closed off, but he forced himself to speak all the same.

'I got away when I was fifteen. Then, as soon as I could, I joined the army and I got my education that way.'

Clearly, his brother wasn't even telling Bas the half of it. He didn't need to. What little he was saying was enough.

It meant that Henrik was more like Naomi than he himself. Only she'd had her grandmother, and her sister. And he'd had Magnus.

Henrik was right—any of those choices would have been better than their mother. Or, worse, their stepfather.

'What about him?' Bas forced himself to ask. 'Where is he now?'

Henrik scoffed indelicately.

'Who knows? Without you or me there as a punchbag, he

turned his attention onto her. She saw her chance to take him to court for compensation and she divorced him.'

Bas stopped breathing.

So she'd been willing to stay with him when he'd hurt Henrik or himself—innocent babies, just like his own precious Aneka, who needed his protection more than anyone— but when it came to him hitting her, everything changed?

It felt as if his life had been smashed wide open, exposing some great, cavernous black hole that he'd spent his entire life trying to fill. Work, whiskey, women. He hadn't cared. He'd tossed it all in there and when it had been swallowed up, he'd slung in some more.

And then Naomi had come along. Her brilliance, and warmth, and…love…were all counter to that void within him.

She'd brought colour into his life for the first time in so, so long. She'd given him Aneka.

Family.

And now, she might even have delivered his brother—and Mrs P—back to him. It was more than he'd ever thought possible. More than he'd dared to dream.

More than he deserved. It was going to take him a life-time—more—to repay her.

And suddenly, he couldn't wait to start.

CHAPTER THIRTEEN

'WHERE EXACTLY IS it that we're going?' Naomi asked the driver as the car glided silently through the quiet streets. Not quite the direction for Bas's penthouse.

She'd been in the NICU, reading to Aneka, for the past few hours. Her baby was growing stronger and stronger with each passing day, and it seemed that tomorrow was going to be the moment she'd been waiting for. The moment when Grace was going to finally operate on her tiny baby girl.

It made Naomi feel elated, and terrified, all at once.

She was only grateful that she'd been able to lean on Bas. He was the only reason she was ever able to tear herself away from the incubator. Because even though he was never there when she was, she knew he had nurses monitoring her coming and going, and the moment she left through one door, she saw him step through the doors at the other end.

'I'm under instructions just to drive you, ma'am,' Phillip apologised.

Of course he was, Naomi thought irascibly. It was another way for Bas to keep his distance. For him to close himself off. For a moment, in that delivery room, she'd felt as though everything had shifted.

As though she'd finally pierced through that armour of ice, after so many weeks of chipping away where she hadn't even managed to make a dent. Or every time she'd thought she had, something had happened and it had iced over once again. And each time, harder than the last.

But none of that was Phillips's fault, so she simply offered him a soft smile.

'I understand.'

It was alarming quite how quickly she'd come to rely on Bas, Naomi thought as she stared out of the window, but instead found herself staring at her own reflection. She who had always been the one other people relied on.

At least, it *ought* to have been alarming. Instead, she'd found it somewhat thrilling. But from the moment they'd called it quits that night, she'd felt lost. Alone. The past month had been like some kind of hell, though she'd gritted her teeth and smiled through it.

What good could come of worrying Leila and her grandmother by sharing the fears that kept her up night after night?

Such as if her baby was going to be okay. And if she could really do this alone.

But this is what you wanted, she reminded herself sternly.

Far better to be alone and know it, than to be with someone who she loved—but who would never let himself love her in return. A man who left her feeling lonelier than ever. And if he couldn't love her—or their precious daughter—the way they would love him, then it would only be all the more hurtful to them both.

Didn't she know that from experience?

There was nothing worse than loving a parent who could never really love in return.

For a brief, reckless moment, she had considered asking Grace to contact Henrik for her, thinking that perhaps if she better understood what had happened when Bas had been a kid, she might be able to help him—and their daughter.

Now she was grateful that she'd dismissed the crazy idea almost as quickly.

No matter the circumstances, this was still Bas's secret. She couldn't violate it. Not even for Aneka.

But if he loved her the way she suspected he did—even if he hadn't admitted it to himself—then he would work it out for himself.

In the meantime, she could focus all her attention on her beautiful daughter. And trust that whatever was going to be, would be.

It was only as the car turned onto the main drag that Naomi felt a prickle of…anticipation. She wasn't sure why, but she realised she'd been holding her breath. Every one of her limbs felt leaden and when the driver rounded the car to open the door for her, Naomi wasn't convinced that she'd be able to slide out.

She wanted *too much*. And she was terrified of how desperate and hopeful that made her.

And then, without warning, he was there. *Bas.* Opening the door and reaching in to offer his hand.

Wordlessly, she took it, allowing him to draw her out of the limousine, and into his arms. She waited, her entire body yearning for him to simply lower his mouth and kiss her.

But he didn't.

'What's this about, Bas?' Her tongue felt too outsized for her mouth.

Tucking her hand through his elbow by way of an answer, Bas turned her around to look at the house.

'It isn't the country home with the rambling roses, or the pretty fence. But it is a family house, with a playroom, and a garden. Even a kitchen where you could make jam, if only you didn't burn the water trying to boil an egg.'

She craned her neck to look at him and he offered a soft laugh.

'Oh, you thought I didn't notice? You were with me long enough to reveal a few flaws in your otherwise perfect character.'

'Hardly,' she breathed, but the emotion in his voice was what slid inside her the most.

The warmth.

Turning back, she gazed up at the Georgian town house with the stone steps leading up to the big door. A warm light spilling out of the semicircular window above it.

'It's perfect.'

'It's ours. If you want it,' he told her. 'A family house, but together we can make it a home.'

For Naomi, in that moment, time might as well have stopped. Or perhaps sped up, whirling around on some unseen lever before hurtling off into nothingness.

And it was hard to remember all the reasons why she'd walked away from him, when Bas was gazing at her with such unadulterated love in his eyes.

But she *had* to remember them. Because they hadn't changed.

Had they?

'I should have realised eight months ago that you were the thing I didn't know I'd been looking for, my entire life,' he told her. 'I knew you were different from the first moment we met. When I saw you moving around that room, I thought you'd reached inside and stolen my breath, but now I know you stole something far, far more valuable.'

'I want to believe you,' she whispered. 'I do. But you're talking about half measures. You won't even talk to your brother because you don't believe in love. Or forgiveness.'

'I believe in them now,' he confirmed, with a certain steadiness to his tone that convinced her every bit as much as the words themselves. 'I don't want half measures, either, *älskling*. I thought I was better alone. I thought I was incapable of love. But I was wrong. You unlocked something inside me that I could never have believed existed.'

Naomi wanted to speak; her throat, her chest, ached with the need to say something. But she couldn't. She could only listen, transfixed, as Bas stood in front of her, his hand brushing a stray strand of hair from her face in a movement that was so simple, yet so intimate, that it stole the breath from her lungs.

'I'm a different man with you in my life, a *better* man. And I want our daughter to know that man. I don't want to be my father. I thought I did, but now I realise how much he lost out on. He was the kind of man who held onto things tightly, with his fists. Grasping them so tightly that he ended up suffocating them. All the way, never acknowledging that he needed or wanted them at all.'

Without warning, he dropped to one knee.

'Over the better part of the past three decades, I've learned to silence all my rage, and frustration. But along with that, I learnt to stuff down everything that could make me a better man. That isn't the kind of father, or husband, I want to be. I want to be the best version of myself, and you are the only person who has helped me to find that.'

'Bas…'

Pulling an elegant box out of his pocket, he lifted it up until it was between then, but didn't open it.

'You told me you wanted more, that you *deserved* more. And you were right.

'You made me face up to my demons. More than that, Naomi, you gave me the weapons I needed to defeat them.'

'Henrik was never your demon,' she choked out.

'No, he wasn't,' Bas agreed thickly. 'But my bitter hatred for him was. You taught me to love instead. You showed me how to listen. And how to forgive.'

'You have forgiven your brother?' She could scarcely believe it.

It felt too good to be real.

'We have a way to go,' he admitted. 'But we're getting there. Though it turns out he didn't really need forgiveness.'

'No?'

'No,' Bas confirmed. 'Rather he sacrificed more than I knew. *For* me. And if it hadn't been for you, I would never have known that. I would have carried around that weighty, debilitating burden for the rest of my life. You've given me chance to become a different man. A *better* man. You've given me back my relationship with my brother.'

That warmth in her chest had swelled so much that she thought it might spill out everywhere.

This was the Basilius she had always thought lurked beneath that suave exterior and naughty reputation. She wasn't sure she had really believed she would ever see it, though.

She certainly hadn't imagined that she would have anything to do with it.

'You did that yourself.' She couldn't keep the smile from her lips, even as the prickling in her eyes finally spilled over.

He didn't answer. He merely reached out his arms and pulled her to him, his lips pressed to the top of her head.

'You're the only one for me, Naomi,' he muttered. 'How could I ever have thought different? My life is nothing without you in it. You, and our baby.'

'I feel the same,' she murmured, her hand moving to cup his face. His jaw sitting squarely in the softness of her palm.

'I already strong-armed you into moving in with me,' he told her. 'And then agreeing to marry me. But, now, I think it's time I asked you. Properly.'

She opened her mouth ready to agree, but then he opened the box and she could only stare at the ring in front of her. Five stones winked back at her, three diamonds and two stunning emeralds, which she could have testified were the exact colour of the gown she had worn for the gala.

It was as though Bas had taken the very essence of that first night and poured it into such an exquisite piece of jewellery. Along with his heart and soul.

'Will you accept all that I have, Naomi Fox?' he asked solemnly. 'And I promise you that I will spend each and every day making sure you never live to regret that decision.'

It was everything she could have imagined. And more. The romantic notion she'd told him she didn't need, but it turned out that she thoroughly wanted.

As though he understood her better than she understood herself.

She offered a wry smile. It turned out he had a few lessons of his own that he wanted to teach *her*.

And she found she liked that. Very much.

'You've tattooed my name on your heart. I was half a man before I met you. I'd still be half a man now, if it hadn't been for you. I love you, Naomi. I think I fell in love with you that first night—I just couldn't have believed love existed for me. But we're a family. We were always meant to be. Come home with me, and promise me you'll never leave again.'

He was so earnest. Almost as though a part of him actually doubted she would agree. Did he really not know that she couldn't have denied him even if she'd wanted?

'I promise,' she choked out. 'You've given me everything I could ever have wanted. I love you, too, Bas. I always will.'

She watched as he slid the ring out of the box and onto her finger. Finally claiming her as his. The way she hadn't even allowed herself to dream it could be. Moments later, he stood back up and swept her into his embrace, before dipping his mouth to hers, to seal their promise.

The three of them already a little family.

For ever.

Finally.

* * * * *

FORBIDDEN NIGHTS
WITH THE SURGEON

CHARLOTTE HAWKES

MILLS & BOON

Derek.
I love you enough to let you talk over songs
on my playlist…
(But not every time—let's not push it.)
xxx

CHAPTER ONE

HENRIK 'RIK' MAGNUSSON—or Henrik Jansen, as he supposed he should call himself, now that he knew that to be his real name—cast his eye around the ballroom of the opulent venue that was hosting tonight's exclusive medical gala, and his eye caught her straight away.

The arresting stranger was standing within a small group, smiling politely, a part of it and yet somehow not. She wore a long blue-grey ball gown with a plunging neckline that nonetheless only offered brief, tantalising glimpses of what lay beyond. No more than any other woman in the room—decidedly less, in fact—and yet he couldn't seem to stop staring.

And when she lifted her eyes and looked right at him—as though some sixth sense had compelled her to do—Rik couldn't find a way to drag his gaze away.

But he had to.

Because he wasn't here to be distracted. And because he hadn't earned his hated reputation as *den iskalla Munk*—the stone-cold monk—for nothing.

A split second later, though he couldn't have said how, his focus was back where it belonged—namely, in the architecturally stunning room.

The place was unequivocally magnificent, from its stone columns to the vaulted, ornately crafted stone ceiling, some twenty-five feet above their heads. Clearly no expense had been spared with the opulent décor, with flower garlands wound lovingly around the pillars, the ornate iron fretwork and over the expansive arched doorways.

Even the big band playing flawlessly on the dais couldn't have been more perfectly selected for the occasion. The architecture of the room enhanced the acoustics spectacularly.

But it was the guest list that was even more striking.

The ballroom heaved and swelled with the monied and influential, all of whom were here because it was the place to be seen, rather than because of any deeply held charitable values. These people were only eager to part with their money if it meant they were the subject of a sharp, media-bound photograph with the gala's keynote speaker—the eminent plastic surgeon to the stars, Magnus Jansen. Or perhaps with his rising star surgeon son, Basilius Jansen.

Whilst Rik himself remained, well...if not invisible—it was impossible to stay unnoticed given his six-foot-three, blond-haired Viking appearance attracting admiring glances wherever he went—then at least *anonymous*. Certainly no one here had any idea that he, too, was a Jansen.

And how would they? Indeed, for thirty-six years—up until six months ago, in fact—neither had he.

As far as the world was concerned, there were only two Jansen miracle men. The renowned Magnus Jansen, who headlined for his skill both as a surgeon and as a playboy, and his son Bas, who the media feverishly declared had come for his father's crown on both counts.

Either way, there was no second son. No third Jansen. Bas—it was universally agreed—had broken the mould.

Rik knew that even if he got up on that stage and declared who he was to the entire ballroom, no one would believe that he was the young Lothario surgeon's brother.

People certainly wouldn't believe that he was Bas's long-lost twin—and not just because they weren't identical.

Besides, he would never do something as wild as declaring it to everyone. That kind of impulsive, spirited daring had never been him. There had only ever been room for one wild, crazy Magnusson brother—as they'd both once believed they were—with a flair for the dramatic, Rik thought with a pang of nostalgia. And that person had always been Bas.

A low punch walloped into Rik's gut, as he weaved an efficient path around the room. It seemed that even the mere name of his beloved, long-lost brother echoed through the neural pathways of his mind much as an ethereal spirit might haunt the corridors of some medieval castle. It conjured up dusty memories of a childhood that Rik could never really have described as 'happy', but which—thanks to Mrs P, and Bertie, and the irrepressible Bas himself—had nonetheless offered some happier moments. Some love.

The past almost thirty years had been notably lacking in either. He'd had friends, of course, and girlfriends at uni, but that visceral loss he'd felt as a seven-year-old meant that he'd never felt truly able to let anyone in completely. He'd been trapped in some dark dungeon of his mother's creation. Because, as far as Erin Sundberg was concerned, why should she be the only one to suffer if she could cause pain to those around her, too?

Had it not been for Bas, Rik knew he would have cut Erin out of his life. The same day that his fifteen-year-old self had finally had enough of being his stepfather's punchbag, and had walked out of the so-called family home once and for all. The only reason he hadn't turned his back on Erin completely had been because he'd been desperately hoping for just one scrap of information from her that might help him to finally track down the brother he'd always idolised as a kid.

And still, she had deliberately said nothing. Raising him as a *Magnusson*—wilfully letting him search for Bas *Magnusson* for the better part of three decades—had just been the tip of her deception, not that he'd realised it at the time. And then a year ago, she'd finally died, taking her secrets to her grave—snuffing out his hopes in the cruellest act of all.

Another circuit of the ballroom completed, Rik moved up the luxuriously carpeted stairs to survey the floor beyond, shocked when his eyes instinctively sought out that tall vision in blue-grey from before.

Since when had he believed in self-sabotage? That wasn't his style. He was more renowned for his dogged determination. Even if Bas wasn't here—and Rik was beginning to suspect that he wasn't—was that any reason to let himself be distracted?

This time, however, instead of snatching his focus back to the room, Rik found his eyes lingering on the figure. Allowing his gaze to track down as he took in the narrow blue velvet ribbon belt that circled a waist that his hands suddenly itched to span, before falling away to a full flowing skirt that skimmed the polished wooden floor as she moved.

More than that, those movements made her sparkle captivatingly—and Rik feared it had nothing to do with the subtle, glittery patterns, almost like fireworks, that shimmered as she moved.

Den iskalla Munk, he reproved himself tacitly—coldly—dragging his eyes away once more, ignoring the fact that this time it was even harder to do so than last time.

How could he be distracted tonight, of all nights? Being here was supposed to be about finally reconnecting with the brother he'd thought he'd never see again.

As if that could somehow kick-start the life Rik felt had been on hold, all these years.

With Bas gone, it was as if the light had been snuffed out in his little seven-year-old's world. He had frozen over. And that thing in his chest that most people called a heart had initially petrified. Then, as the decades had marched inexorably by, it had ultimately crumbled, leaving a nothingness in its wake.

Stone-cold, indeed. Rik knew it, and in a twisted way he welcomed it.

Far better to have shut himself off, than to have the people he loved snatched from him, one by one. Mrs P. Bertie. Bas.

He had never dreamed that there could be a chance to resurrect anything from that petrified dust.

Shaking off the odd, unfamiliar feelings, Rik tried to keep his focus on the ball.

Indeed, if it hadn't been for a chance encounter six months back, he would still have no idea of the Jansen connection, even now. No idea that Magnus Jansen was his father—not *somebody* Magnusson—and no idea that he should be looking for Bas *Jansen*.

That one nugget of information had been enough to allow Rik to finally track them down. And even though his letters to Bas hadn't been returned, it hadn't stopped Rik from making his way here—both to the UK, and to this monied medical ball—where the hospital grapevine had led him to believe that his now playboy brother would be guaranteed to attend.

Yet there was no sign of Bas anywhere. It seemed another circuit of the room was in order.

Dropping back down the steps, Rik moved skilfully through the crowd as it swelled and heaved, deftly avoiding the flirtatious women stepping into his path. He didn't need the distraction, and one-night stands had never been his style.

He'd seen from the cradle just what they could do. His mother flaunting her indiscretions to get a rise out of his stepfather, which had invariably resulted in the angry drunk taking it out on him and Bas and then, once Bas had gone— just him.

It was why he'd decided long ago that he would never, *never* permit anyone, or anything, to get under his skin. Even as a kid, Rik had known he'd begun to turn into himself, just as Bas had begun to act out.

Now, thirty years on, Rik was beginning to learn that not a lot seemed to have changed. His brother was apparently still daring—a fun, coveted playboy—whilst he himself had his own decidedly less scandalous reputations.

Aside from the Stone Monk, he was known as *den ishand kirurg*—the ice-hand surgeon. Because his hand never shook, and he never made a mistake.

So why did tonight feel like a bomb inside him, waiting to explode?

Dragging himself back to the moment, Rik decided to make one more sweep of the ballroom, and if there was still no sign of Bas, then he would return to his hotel suite upstairs, and he would try to find his brother again, in the morning.

However much the idea frustrated him.

Executing a sharp about-turn, Rik ploughed a fresh path through the parting throng. From the snippets of conversation he was catching, it appeared that he wasn't the only one to be speculating on the party-loving Bas Jansen's unexpected absence.

So much for tonight's reconciliation. It was time to cut his losses and leave.

'Excuse me,' he muttered automatically as someone stepped into his path.

Another woman wearing the familiar expression that inevitably meant she was keen to introduce herself to him. Rik smiled and returned the greeting, before expertly disengaging himself, but as he moved her aside and continued his striding to the exit, he might have known that flash of blue-grey would, once again, seize his attention.

Before he could stop himself, he had turned. Looked. And this time, there was no fighting the attraction that had been arcing between them from that first shared glance.

It shot through him like a thousand volts. Only somehow thrilling, rather than deadly.

A plethora of thoughts crowded his usually logical brain, but the one that pounded in his mind loudest of all was that he'd been right. That shimmering, dazzling, breathtaking light wasn't coming from her sparkling dress—it was a brilliance that was all hers. A lustre. *She* was the real draw. The reason he couldn't seem to drag his gaze away. The reason he didn't want to.

Without even knowing what he was doing, Rik plunged back into the crowd, and it didn't matter that he lost sight of her for a moment because his body suddenly seemed to have an inbuilt compass, and it was heading directly to her.

It was almost a relief when the stranger disappeared into the swell of guests, Grace Henley told herself, as she fought to remember how to breathe again.

It was an unsettling experience. Hadn't she made herself immune to any man years ago? Near enough a decade and a half ago, to be a little more precise.

And yet the impact of this particular man's gaze had landed on her like a net around a butterfly, trapping her without even having to touch her. Just as it had that first time. And the second. Not that she was much of a butterfly, more like a wallflower.

Even so, each time he'd emerged from the crowd—each time his eyes had seemed to find hers—she hadn't been able to move, or breathe, or even blink.

And then he'd disappeared, and the net cage around her had simply…evaporated.

Grace glanced surreptitiously at her watch for the hundredth time already that night and gave herself a half-grin, half-grimace.

It was finally time that she could make her excuses and leave—not that anyone was likely to be bothered. She wouldn't have even been at the ball had Bas—the closest thing she'd ever had to a best friend—not demanded it of her. Some cryptic request to look out for 'anything unusual'.

But there was nothing unusual about this gala. It was as predictably magnificent and depressing as ever. She would far rather be in the operating room saving mums and babies than networking with a bunch of people who thought money and the latest designer accessories were matters of life and death.

It was only Bas who had made these things fun for her. Even if it was just her amusement at watching him fend off the advances of a multitude of women throwing themselves—sometimes quite literally—at one half of the eminent Jansen duo.

Look up playboy surgeon on any Internet search, and a picture of Bas or Magnus, or even both of them, would surely appear.

But there was another side to Bas, her friend. A side that was raw, and sad, but fiercely loyal. And she'd thought it was perhaps that friendship that she'd miss the most when she finally left Thorncroft Royal Infirmary.

She'd planned to share her plan tonight. To explain that she'd recently begun to feel restless. Unsettled. That her reason for coming here—coming *back* here, if she was going to be strictly accurate—had begun to fade, and that there was a part of her—a guilty, secretive slither inside her—that had begun to think it was time to move somewhere other than Thorncroft.

Though she couldn't tell Bas why. She'd never been able to share that long-buried secret with anyone. Perhaps it was the sheer, crushing pressure of it that had finally convinced her that it was time to go.

So, tonight was supposed to have been the night she'd been going to broach it with him. She'd rehearsed her speech so many times. And then he'd called with the most startling news she thought she'd ever heard. That he was about to become a father.

The irony of it hadn't been lost on Grace.

But there'd been no time to dwell. Worse than that—far worse—had been the fact that she'd been the one to have to tell the accidental couple that there was something wrong with their baby. No parent wanted to hear that their baby was going to need complex surgery within days of its birth.

God, it had just been a horrific night, all around. The sooner she got home, to a hot shower, a light movie, and her cat, the better. And she didn't care what that made her sound like.

Taking her leave from the cluster of guests around her—who had only really stopped to talk to her because they'd wanted to know where the 'incredible Bas' was—Grace turned with relief, ducked her head and hurried away.

Straight into some unyielding, muscled wall of a man.

'Oof.' Her breath was knocked out of her, even as a pair of strong hands reached out to steady her.

'*Ursåkta mig.* Excuse me.'

By the way her blood pressure was affected, she didn't need to lift her head to guess who the man was.

'Sorry...that was... I wasn't looking where I was going,' she blurted out awkwardly.

'Don't be sorry.'

But his voice was muffled somehow. Distant. It took her a moment to process that it might have something to do with the fact that she was still held against a solid, hot, unmistakeably male chest.

Sinfully defined.

Grace felt her palms begin to actually itch with the effort of not reaching out to touch it. She lifted her head slowly, so slowly, and half wished she hadn't. And it was impossible to say what affected her most. The electricity that arced through her at his touch, the exquisitely low rumble of his sensual male voice, or the breath-stealing masculine beauty of what had to be one of the most stunning men she'd ever seen in her life.

Seeing him from a distance had been one thing, but up close was a whole different experience. And she didn't feel like a wallflower any longer—not with this stunning man staring down at her.

The man who had been causing a series of rumblings through much of the female contingency of tonight's illustrious guest list. No wonder a dozen or so pairs of baleful, heavily fake-lashed eyes were launching sharp, invisible daggers into her from all sides.

And still, Grace couldn't seem to move her body. To escape. So, instead, she allowed herself to indulge for a moment.

The man was six-foot-three, at a guess, and incredibly well-built, with broad shoulders and a strong neck, not too thick. He looked like some kind of model and, in a way, she hoped he was.

The last thing Thorncroft Royal Infirmary needed, she decided, with some inexplicable degree of maniacal amusement, was another wild Lothario like Bas. The man might be the closest thing she'd ever had to a best friend, but she wasn't oblivious to the trail of broken hearts in his wake.

Two heartbreakers would be more than the hospital—than the entire county—could possibly cope with.

And still, she couldn't seem to drag her eyes from his. She felt pinned to the spot, barely able to breathe let alone move—though the rest of the ballroom seemed to have faded into nothingness.

Her pulse hammered hectically in her neck, at her wrists, and somewhere else—somewhere lower, however much she tried to deny it—and whatever she might try, Grace knew there was no calming it. As long as this man's gaze was on her, its chaotic pace was beyond her control.

Like something she might have read about in one of those thrilling magazine stories she'd sneakily read as a kid—before her academic of a mother had thrown them out, loftily reminding her that she had a whole library of far more intellectually stimulating journals and classical masterpieces to choose from. As if it had been the Great Library of Alexandria, rather than the book collection right there in the front room of their bland, suburban, three-bedroom family house.

But, right in this instant, Grace couldn't think of a single one of those dusty tomes that could possibly have been more stimulating than whatever it was that she was pretending she wasn't feeling just now.

This scraping, shimmering thrill that made her body feel as though it was more awake than it had ever been in her life before. And then, he spoke.

'Can I buy you a drink?'

Inexplicably, the corners of her mouth tugged upwards despite her suddenly jangling nerves.

'It's an open bar.'

Why had she said that?

Grace frowned—though whether at her own gaucheness or at her uncharacteristic reaction to the stranger, she couldn't quite be sure. She should have just accepted. Now she looked as though she wasn't interested.

Which, of course, she wasn't.

So why was she still standing in front of him? Waiting?

Everything about the man screamed wealth and power, which meant that he was most likely a wealthy guest. A man accustomed to getting exactly what he wanted, when he wanted it. The kind of man with whom she definitely didn't want to share her future.

Grace blinked abruptly.

Since when had she started to think of sharing her life with someone again?

That was a dream that she'd let go of when she was sixteen—in that one year that had changed everything. The year she never talked about. The year she was never allowed to talk about.

Was this all part of the way everything had been shifting inside her recently? Could it be that her decision to leave Thorncroft meant that she was finally ready to let go of the past, and move on with her life?

Obviously not with this stranger. But, after years of being the wallflower and watching other people have fun, maybe this was her place to start. A flirt and drink, at a party, with a handsome man, didn't seem a bad place to begin.

It certainly accounted for why she was still standing in

the same spot, still staring at the beautiful stranger as she waited for the world to stop spinning and willing herself to say something. Anything. Though preferably something at least slightly witty.

'Do you work at Thorncroft Royal Infirmary?'

So, not witty at all, then. *Embarrassing.*

CHAPTER TWO

'I DO,' THE stranger answered seriously, as though her inquiry was perfectly acceptable.

It took Grace a moment to remember that she'd asked if he worked at the hospital with her. And try as she might, she couldn't stop herself from frowning again.

'I don't recognise you.'

His mouth curved up into a small smile of his own.

'Should I be flattered? Or do you know everyone who works at the hospital?'

'I wasn't trying to flatter you.'

'Yet there you go again.' He grinned.

And it was the strangest sensation, being teased by this man. Thrilling and terrifying all at once. But she hadn't fought her way to where she was now by being easily intimidated.

Lifting her head up, Grace met the full intensity of those mesmerising eyes—not quite green, but not entirely blue—head-on.

'What can I say?' She offered a delicate shrug. 'It seems I haven't been housebroken yet.'

It was the quirky, funny side of herself that few people ever saw. She usually repressed it around anyone except for her friend, Bas—certainly around strangers. It was impossible to say what it was about this man that made her feel so comfortable—and yet so damned *aware*—from this initial encounter.

For a split second, he simply looked at her, then the stranger threw back his head and let out a low, magnificent laugh.

And something warm and liquid-like slid smoothly through Grace.

'Clearly you haven't been working here long, though,' she noted evenly, trying not to feel so ridiculously victorious as his head cocked to one side when he studied her a little more carefully.

'What makes you say that?'

'Because the hospital grapevine at this place is alive and flourishing. If you'd here for more than a minute, it would definitely have been buzzing with gossip about you.'

He grinned at her, and it burst inside her like fireworks. Sparkling around her and raining down excitement.

'Ah, but you don't even know that I'm a good enough surgeon to warrant discussion. Or a bad enough one, for that matter.'

She narrowed her gaze.

'I didn't even know that you were a surgeon,' she pointed out. 'I'm simply stating that new faces equal new discussion. But I think you already knew that.'

She certainly wasn't going to highlight the fact that having a new surgeon who could easily moonlight as a London billboard model would make the interest in him even more feverish.

'Faktiskt?' He arched his brow. 'Indeed? And am I to take *that* to be a compliment?'

She shrugged elegantly.

'Take it however you want,' she quipped. 'I'm Grace Henley, by the way.'

She thrust her hand out, as though hoping the banality of it could somehow stifle the heat that had been building higher and higher between them, even during the course of the conversation. Though deep down, she suspected it wouldn't muffle anything at all. Least of all her inexplicably excited libido.

It was all so unlike her. So strange. So thrilling.

She cranked her polite smile up another notch.

Still, her heart seemed to hang for a fraction of a second

when he paused before ultimately reaching out his own hand. And then, as electricity arced between them once again, so fast and so shocking, Grace was almost surprised when the gargantuan, grandiose chandeliers in the ballroom didn't flicker, and hum, and then explode.

'Rik Magnusson,' he introduced himself, his voice little more than a low rumble like a lick against the softest part of her body. 'So, Grace Henley, if I can't buy you a drink then the least I can do is inject a little fun into your evening. Do you dance?'

'I…do,' she heard herself answer before her mind had time to engage.

Some atypical, spontaneous devil sneaking out of her without warning.

The only other person to ever make her see her fun, wild streak had been Bas. But this—Rik—was a whole different level of sinful. She could feel it in her bones.

Lower, actually. If she was going to be entirely truthful with herself.

'Good.' His voice rumbled through her as he spun her around and guided her to the dance floor simply by the lightest of touches from his hand at the small of her back. 'Then enough talking. Let's dance.'

And though she meant to say no, she found herself being guided across the ballroom, the palm of his head searing into the small of her back, and then swept into his arms as they danced into the beat of the big band.

It was like some kind of dream, or perhaps a fairy tale, Grace thought, rather breathlessly, a lifetime later. Or perhaps it had only been minutes, who could tell? Though if glowers were scalpels she would have had a hundred of them embedded between her shoulder blades right now.

But when he held her body against his, his heat seeming to seep right through every layer of dermis to permeate her very bones, she couldn't seem to care the way she knew she ought to. It was all still something of a blur and she thought perhaps she was still waiting for the whole world to tilt completely and go spinning off its axis.

There was something so inescapably beautiful, mesmerising even, about him.

A study in masculinity that even Rodin would have ached to capture in bronze. And it made her feel unsteady inside, as if she'd been scooped out and left hollow. Grace couldn't explain it, but the longer he spun her around the ballroom floor, the edgier, the more thrilling the sensation that wound through her.

Surely she ought to do something—anything—to mute it.

'So, how long have you been at Thorncroft?'

Amusement danced within those green-blue eyes and… something else. Something she couldn't quite identify. She might have thought…*wariness*? But that didn't seem to fit.

'Is this to be our discussion this evening?'

'We have to talk about something,' she retorted, though there was an uncharacteristic shake to her voice.

Fortunately, he didn't know her well enough to notice. Or perhaps it was that, whilst he spoke English fluently, the hint of an accent indicated that it wasn't his native language. It reminded her of the accent Bas put on when he knew it would make women puddle at his feet.

'Do you know Bas Jansen?'

'Pardon?'

Was it her imagination, or was his voice sharper than before?

'Or Magnus?' she guessed, instead.

'Magnus?'

Did his step falter for a split second as they danced?

'Magnus Jansen,' she clarified, watching him a little more carefully this time. More prepared.

'What makes you think that?'

But this time there was nothing. He seemed quite relaxed.

Too relaxed? a voice in her head asked, before she dismissed the foolish notion.

'I don't know.' She shook her head, a rueful smile creeping over her. 'I just thought…the faint accent, the name, the somewhat Viking appearance.'

'By Viking, do you mean slightly dishevelled, with battle scars, and kohl-framed eyes?'

And there it was again. He was teasing her, yet there was an almost imperceptible edge to his voice that she couldn't quite explain.

'I meant more your…what six-foot-three, six-foot-four height?' Dammit, she hadn't intended to sound so fan-girlish. 'Your blond hair, and your green-blue eyes.'

Not to mention the fact that he was so well-built that it was only too embarrassingly easy to imagine him hauling her over his shoulder and carrying her off into the night. He had such thrillingly broad shoulders, it could happily take a woman a lifetime to explore them properly.

'Know many Vikings, do you?'

What was it about him that made her wish she'd never started this line of conversation?

'Well, like I said, there's Magnus Jansen. And there's his son, Bas.'

'And they look like me, do they?' His voice whispered down her spine, but she still couldn't explain it.

'Not exactly,' she answered carefully. 'They're both tall, too, but they have almost white-blond hair. Yours is more a dirty blond.'

'Is that right? Dirty blond…' he echoed, somehow making it sound ridiculously sexy.

Grace plunged on desperately.

'Plus, they don't have any accent, of course. Unless Bas is seducing a woman who's making him work for it.'

'I've only been here a day and already I've heard a lot

about Bas Jansen. He has quite the reputation for burning the candle at both ends.'

'Bas has a…"work hard, play hard" ethos,' she conceded with a smile. 'He's certainly a brilliant surgeon.'

'With a legion of female suitors, I believe.' Rik's expression darkened.

Was he jealous? One alpha male studying another alpha male? Grace fought back a wave of disappointment. He hadn't seemed the type, but there was no doubt that he was interested in learning about Bas.

'I'm sure you'll agree that what a person does in their own time is their business, just as long as they are professional in their working life. Whatever rumours you've heard about Bas Jansen are just that, rumours.'

Which she thought was a fairly decent speech, given that her head was still scrambled from the feel of Rik's arms around her, still swirling her around the dance floor,

'You're very defensive of Bas,' he noted. 'Are you one of his admirers?'

'I'm his friend,' Grace retorted, telling herself to stop there. Reminding herself that anything more was none of this man's business. '*Just* his friend.'

And she wondered why she felt the need to put quite so much emphasis into it.

'Is that so?'

There was a lift to his tone that thrilled her even as she tried to pretend it didn't. Even as she forced herself to concentrate on her dancing, and her footwork, rather than the solid feel of the man—the heat from his thighs—as their bodies moved so slickly together.

This was…ridiculous.

'It is so,' she muttered firmly. 'There has never been anything more between us.'

Namely because she'd been nineteen when she'd met him

at her first year of her medical degree at university—and still numbed from what had happened only a few years earlier.

The fact that it had been Bas who had made her laugh for the first time in almost four years—a sound that had shocked her the first time she'd heard it after so long—was surely how he had become important to her, so quickly.

And the fact that she was possibly the first woman who hadn't toppled into lust with him was no doubt what had appealed to Bas, too. It didn't mean she hadn't noticed quite how beautiful a man he was, of course. It just meant that she'd been too shell-shocked to feel anything. Certainly to act on it.

And Grace was eternally glad that she hadn't, because if she had, then they would never have become the close friends they were today.

Nevertheless, it didn't stop people gossiping, or speculating that there was more to her relationship with Bas the playboy. And, as much as she might tell herself otherwise, she didn't want this particular man thinking the same.

'And there never will be anything more than friendship between Bas and me,' she added, before she could check herself.

Which had been the case before she'd decided it was time to leave Thorncroft for pastures new, and before Bas had found out that he was set to become a father.

Not that this man—*Rik*—needed to know any of that.

The music was coming to an end now, the band seamlessly moving from a waltz to a foxtrot, and Grace prepared for Rik to let her go. And of course it meant nothing that she couldn't decide whether she was relieved at that, or frustrated.

'Then it seems you're in the minority,' Rik commented, which she couldn't help thinking was neither accepting her word, nor refuting it.

She also noted that he wasn't letting her go, instead transitioning them both into a smooth foxtrot. And it didn't matter that she told herself the fluttering of her stomach was just nerves that she'd get the steps wrong, deep down she knew that wasn't the real reason.

It likely explained why her voice suddenly sounded so prim.

'That's as maybe. But it doesn't make it any less true. What's more interesting is your apparent interest in him.'

'You're right,' Rik noted abruptly, his expression rueful and his tone light again. 'It's my fault, not yours. It's simply that I'm here at Thorncroft Royal Infirmary because I've secured a place on the Jansen Surgical Exchange programme.'

'Ah, I see.' She nodded, understanding suddenly. 'You're trying to get to know the surgeons you think will be your bosses.'

'Mmm, something like that.'

It wasn't exactly a full-hearted agreement, but Grace was too preoccupied with her own thoughts. She couldn't help wondering what kind of surgeon Rik might be. Typically, anyone who won a place on the Jansen Surgical Exchange programme had to be good. More than good. They had to have the potential to alter the course of surgery in whatever their specialist field happened to be. Just as Magnus, and now Bas, were pioneers in the field of plastic surgery.

And with a face and body like Rik's, it wouldn't surprise her if he was one, too. It was certainly majestic enough to be a walking advert for flawless looks.

'What is your specialist field?' she asked abruptly.

He offered another rueful smile, as if he could read her thoughts.

'Plastic surgery.'

She laughed out loud.

'Of course it is.'

But at least that meant that he hadn't been acting like some weird, jealous alpha male before, checking out the competition for dating. He'd simply been acting as a competitive alpha surgeon—and that was something she could easily cope with. A man who was clearly dedicated to his career.

Looks aside, a healthy competitive streak when it came to work was something she found particularly attractive. The question was whether Rik had what it took to keep up with the Jansen pair.

Many didn't, yet there was something about Rik that made her think that he might even be able to give Magnus and Bas a run for their money. Or perhaps it was just that she wanted that to be the case. For his sake, of course. Nothing to do with her.

'Can I offer you a little advice?' She hesitated. Had Rik been anybody else, she was fairly sure that she wouldn't have said anything.

'I would welcome it,' he replied easily, allowing her to feel a little less tense.

'Don't listen to everything you hear from the hospital rumour mill. Yes, Bas has a reputation as a playboy, but that doesn't stop him from being a brilliant surgeon. There's a reason the Jansen name is so esteemed.'

'Because Magnus Jansen has been pioneering new surgical techniques, pushing the boundaries of what plastic surgeons can do, for the past three decades.'

No, she certainly wouldn't be telling anyone else what she was about to tell Rik.

'Magnus Jansen is a good surgeon. A *great* surgeon,' she corrected. 'There is no doubt that he pushed the boundaries of his field. But the advances attributed to the Jansen name from the last ten years have been Bas's. Any patient would be lucky to have Magnus as a surgeon, but Bas is the one you want to watch. He is the one you should spend the next few months learning from. If it hadn't been for him, I wouldn't be a doctor.'

For a long moment Rik was silent. But then, Grace didn't need his words in order to read every taut line in his body.

'You seem very defensive of him, for just a friend.'

Grace opened her mouth to explain herself, then changed her mind. The foxtrot was coming to an end and Rik was deliberately moving her out of his arms. Clearly, their dancing was over.

'Thank you for the dances, anyway.' She dredged up a bright smile.

It shouldn't feel like such a wrench. Especially since it somehow managed to irk her new acquaintance. She shouldn't want him to wrap his arms around her or pull her back in for another dance.

Yet, it was almost terrifying how badly she wanted precisely that.

'Enjoy the rest of your evening.' Rik dipped his head politely, but his smile—like hers, she feared—didn't quite match his eyes.

Whatever that tiny, exquisite seed had been between them—it was gone now.

'I'll be leaving anyway.'

'No need to leave on my account.'

His gaze trapped her in place, making her blurt out an explanation.

'I'm not. Of course I'm not. I was leaving anyway. I mean, I was just on my way to the exit when I bumped into you.'

Grace fought off another deep, giveaway blush. He didn't think she'd engineered their encounter deliberately, did he? She'd watched plenty of women crash into Bas accidentally on purpose in the past.

'Don't tell me you're Cinderella, and you have to leave the ball before midnight?' He was teasing her, but there was still an edge to it.

Still, she tried to smile again.

'I'm not Cinderella. But yes, I have to leave the ball. Or this gala fundraiser, anyway.'

He seemed to hesitate for a moment.

'Then I'll walk you out.'

She wanted, so badly, to accept. Instead, she offered a light shake of her head. Truth be told, she wanted far more than for him to just walk her out. Which was crazy, since she never did anything like that usually. It was one of the reasons she had such a reputation for being a little bit too much of a nerd.

Sometimes, it seemed that her reputation as a nerd grew in equal proportion to Bas's reputation as a playboy. As though it was her role, as his best friend, to balance him out.

But then if that were the case, given his current serious situation with Naomi, this was the time for her to cut loose and have a little fun, for once.

It was harder than it should have been to dismiss the notion as preposterous.

'Don't be silly, you should stay and enjoy yourself. The gala will go on for a few hours yet.'

'Not for me,' Rik told her, his hand pressed too distractingly against the small of her back as he guided her away from the dance floor. 'Believe it or not, I was leaving, too.'

She eyed him sceptically.

'You didn't look like you were leaving. You look like you are searching for someone.'

To her surprise, Rik's eyes darkened. Only a fraction, but it was there nonetheless. She certainly didn't expect him to answer.

'I was just looking out for Magnus. I thought I might introduce myself before formally meeting him on Monday. Only now, after what you've told me, perhaps I should also look out for Bas.'

It sounded perfectly logical, so why did she feel as though she was missing something? Grace dismissed the niggling thought. Surely it wasn't any of her business, anyway.

'Bas isn't here tonight.' She thought about her friend, and Naomi—the woman he'd just discovered was the mother of his child—and hoped they were doing okay. 'As for Magnus, he wouldn't thank you for introducing yourself. Especially not at a gala like this.'

She clamped her mouth shut, shocked at herself. No need to tell Rik that his new boss would be far more interested in any of the beautiful, eager women here tonight than in his newest surgeon.

She didn't customarily go around criticising colleagues, especially senior surgeons. Unless it was to Bas, of course. He had always been her sounding board for when hospital life frustrated her. Just as she'd been his sounding board for his all too exacting father.

Magnus might be a great surgeon, but he'd been sorely lacking as a parent.

What was it about Rik that had her almost sharing such personal information? Something she had never, *never* done before.

'I spoke out of turn.' She shut down the conversation. 'Forget about it. Anyway, goodnight, Rik. Thank you again for the dances.'

But as she turned to leave, she was acutely aware of Rik moving alongside her. His long, casual stride easily keeping pace with her. Apparently, she was going to have to wait a little longer to shake him.

If only her unexpectedly traitorous body weren't trying to tell her that shaking this man off was the last thing it wanted to do.

CHAPTER THREE

'ARE YOU A DOCTOR?' They were barely out of the ballroom before they were accosted by a concierge who was bustling their way. 'There's a woman giving birth in the lift.'

Grace knew the ideal response. It was drilled into them from almost the start of their medical careers—outside the hospital it was never advised to admit you were a doctor unless there was absolutely no choice. Too many well-intentioned doctors had been sued after attempting to help in an emergency.

But it went against everything she believed in.

She gritted her teeth.

'Where's the patient?'

This was about doing the right thing. And it absolutely wasn't influenced by wanting to put some space between herself and the too tempting man who had walked out of that ballroom beside her.

In an instant, her mind switched from the awkwardness of the evening, into clear, professional mode.

'This way.' The concierge looked past her, straight to Rik. 'We've phoned for an ambulance, but it isn't here yet. Follow me.'

'I'm not an obstetrician.' Rik shook his head, and Grace liked that he wasn't arrogant enough to take charge.

'But I am,' she murmured.

Hurrying from the ballroom, down a plushly carpeted hall and then onto the polished granite floor of the main lobby, the concierge led them to the lifts, where a young waiter looked shell-shocked as he stood in the lift doorway, stopping the doors from closing.

Inside, a young woman was almost doubled over, each hand tightly gripping friends on either side of her.

'We didn't even know she was pregnant,' one of the women cried.

'We're supposed to be on a hen weekend,' the other added. 'She's getting married next week.'

'She's never even had the slightest bump,' the first woman chimed back in. 'I mean, a wedding dress was a bit tight at the last fitting and she was upset because she didn't know how she gained a few pounds. But that was about it.'

'Not a problem.' Grace shot them all a carefully crafted, soothing smile. 'I'm a doctor, I deal with babies every day and I'm here to help. Can I just get in there?'

The two friends looked at each other over the pregnant girl's head, apparently trying to decide which of them should go. It was evident that they both wanted to stay with their friend.

'Okay, you have two very good buddies here,' Grace told the pregnant girl as she took control. Then she stepped into the side of the lift that had more room and gently disengaged one of the girls' hands, chivvying her out. 'Is there anyone you need to call?'

The friend shook her head, still resisting leaving the lift.

'Perhaps the groom?' Rik stepped up gently, steering the girl away as he shot Grace a meaningful look.

One that told her, without him even having to say a word, that she was free to concentrate on the case in hand, whilst he would deal with sorting everyone else out.

Whatever awkwardness had sprung up between her and Rik in that ballroom, it was dissipating quickly now. And for that, she was grateful.

'Oh, God, we never thought,' Grace heard the girl cry, flustered, as Rik led her away. 'He's my brother. I'll call him right now and tell him what's going on.'

'Good, great. We can sit in these chairs, where you can still see your friend. Shall I come with you?'

'Thanks.'

Briefly, Grace watched them leave, grateful for the way Rik stepped in so easily to handle that side of things. Then she turned her attention back to her patient.

'Okay, sweetheart, let's see what this baby is up to, shall we? You're doing really well, and we're here with you now. I'm Grace, what's your name?'

'Her name's Emma,' the other friend answered for her.

'I didn't know.' The woman—Emma—gasped, a slick sheen of sweat covering her forehead and neck. 'I thought it was the stress of the wedding…that made me miss a few periods…'

She tailed off with a low moan as a contraction hit her. Grace waited until Emma was done.

'Well done, sweetheart. How far apart are the contractions?'

'I thought…they were period pains,' Emma began, puffing slightly. 'I thought it had come at last. I thought they would…ease off if we went shopping. I wasn't trying to hide it. I just…didn't know.'

'I understand,' Grace soothed. 'I'm not judging you, sweetheart. I just need to know how far apart your contractions are, and if you can walk.'

She looked out of the lift doors and across the shiny, dense granite of the lobby floor just as Emma shook her head emphatically.

'No. I…can't move.' She emitted a low cry.

Evidently, the contractions were very close. At least the inside of the lift had a somewhat more forgiving rubber floor.

'Not a problem, don't worry,' soothed Grace. 'I'm just going to take a look and see exactly where baby is up to, okay?'

'Okay.'

'Are you on any medication?'

'No.'

'The pill?'

'No, I came off it about a year ago.' Emma puffed, her breathing erratic and her words choppy as she fought past the waves of pain. 'We were supposed to get married six months ago but the wedding got postponed because of restrictions at the time. We…'

She let out a sharp sound, and Grace rubbed her hand over Emma's back.

'Take your time. You're doing brilliantly.

The mum-to-be offered a grateful, if exhausted smile.

'We were going to…try for a baby as soon as we were married.'

'That's good,' encouraged Grace. At least that meant they'd both wanted a baby. That would hopefully lessen the shock of the birth a little. 'Any history of disease or illness in the family?'

'Nothing,' Emma managed, after a moment.

After a few more questions and an examination, Grace was as confident as she could be that her patient was presenting without any additional, obvious complications. Emma was fully dilated and the baby was head-down and definitely coming. She craned her neck up to Rik, who was watching her even as he encouraged the rather flustered friend as she talked animatedly on her mobile phone.

'Rik, can you see where the ambulance crew is, and tell them we have a twenty-five-year-old female, prima-gravida, and that it's a precipitous birth,' she instructed him before turning swiftly back to her patient. 'It's okay, sweetheart. Everything is going to be okay.'

'Can we get her into a private room?' asked the hotel concierge.

Grace shook her head.

'I don't think we can risk it. She feels like pushing now so I think the best thing we can do is stay where we are. You could get some towels, clean water, and paper towels though.'

'I really don't think…'

'And maybe some gloves, too,' George told him firmly. 'That would be most helpful.'

Whatever objections he had to a woman giving birth in his hotel lift, he was going to have to set them aside. There was no way she was going to risk trying to move the mother-to-be when the birth was this imminent.

'Good girl, that's it. Keep trusting your body, you're doing really well.'

Then, as the concierge scurried off, muttering under his breath, and the young waiter was still holding the doors open, Grace crouched down ready to catch the baby if it fell.

In what felt like a few seconds later, Rik was over with all the supplies she'd asked for, plus a large parasol from the garden restaurant.

'To afford our mum-to-be a little privacy,' he said simply. 'Now, what do you want me to do?'

'Thanks.' Grace couldn't help but like his consideration for her patient. 'What happened to the friend?'

'She's still talking to the groom—her brother—but I told the concierge to stay with her.' He dropped his voice a little lower so that only she could hear. 'I felt he was a little more interested in getting Emma out of his hotel lobby than in the fact that she was in labour.'

'Agreed,' Grace murmured in reply.

But whatever else she'd been going to say was cut off as Emma gave a deep grunt, which sounded to Grace as though she was bearing down. Another brief check, and Grace nodded.

'Okay, Emma, sweetheart, you're doing really well. On the next contraction, you give a push and we'll let gravity do the rest.'

'But my baby...'

'I'll catch baby, don't you worry.'

'Should she be lying down?' the remaining friend asked, worriedly.

'No, Emma's fine.' Grace offered a smile of assurance.

'In fact, standing up will help to facilitate the birth since it helps to widen the baby's pathway through the pelvis. That's it, Emma, you're doing well.'

Emma let out another primal grunt.

'Keep going, sweetheart, that's great. Your movement is an instinctive, age-old way to help humans manage the discomfort of labour. It's only in recent times that women have begun to give birth lying down.'

A few minutes later, it was all over. A flash of purple, and the baby came out like a rocket, straight into Grace's arms. Gratefully, she took the towel that Rik promptly offered her, and cleaned the baby.

'You're not cutting the cord?' he asked sharply.

'Not yet.' She continued attending to the baby. 'It gives time for some of the baby's blood to come back from their side of the placenta. Can be up to one hundred ccs.'

'That will make the blood quite a bit thicker,' he murmured.

'Yep, and it works as additional iron cells for the baby to help make red blood cells.'

'So how long do you wait?'

'I like to wait a few minutes, at least until the umbilical cord stops pulsing.' She smiled, as a loud cry rent the air.

'Good set of lungs.' Rik smiled at the half-smiling, half-sobbing new mum.

'It's a girl,' added Grace, finally cutting the cord and wrapping the baby up to hand to a still shocked Emma as she finished off. 'Ten perfect fingers and toes.'

She kept her voice upbeat, but Emma was still staring at the tiny, pink, shrivelled creature, as though she couldn't quite believe what had happened. Grace couldn't blame her, but before she could talk to the new mum, the concierge came bustling back over.

'The paramedics have just arrived,' he announced, with two cleaners in tow, and obvious relief.

Grace gritted her teeth.

'Great.' As she glanced over his shoulder to the crew hurrying in, her smile become more genuine. 'Over here, guys.'

They were colleagues she knew fairly well, and both of them shot her a brief greeting as they all crouched down around the new mum, and Grace began her handover.

'This is Emma, twenty-five. She has just given birth—less than ten minutes ago—to a baby daughter following a cryptic pregnancy. She had pseudo-bleeding, which she took to be light periods due to the stress of her upcoming marriage. The patient had no form of pain relief and there were no apparent complications during labour and delivery. There was no hormone injection to help the placenta to come out but, again, it hasn't even been ten minutes since delivery. She isn't on any medication and has no prenatal history. Mum and baby will need full assessment upon admission, and I recommend providing her, and her husband-to-be, with someone to talk to before they are discharged.'

'Thanks, Grace, we'll take it from here.' The paramedic shot her a rueful smile. 'You go back and enjoy what's left of your gala.'

'Thanks,' Grace replied, not bothering to tell them that she'd been leaving anyway.

They were more concerned with getting Emma and her newborn baby back to Thorncroft as quickly as possible. Still, Grace waited until the pair was safely loaded onto the ambulance, and it was on its way.

The concierge, having been blocked by Rik from rushing his cleaners in to clean up even around the poor ambulance crew's ankles, fired off a few snarky comments as he finally got his team to work.

'Thanks for your patience, guys,' Grace told the cleaners sincerely. She didn't miss their discreet eye-rolls of apology when the concierge's back was turned.

And as she made her way to the ladies' washroom to clean

up, she heard Rik also offer a word of thanks. She couldn't stop herself from liking him all the more—not that it meant anything because by the time she'd finished tidying herself up, he would already be gone.

As he should be.

So why, when she emerged from the washroom some time later, did her face feel as though it were going to crack with smiling when she saw Rik heading across the lobby towards her?

'Well.' He smiled that heart-stopping smile of his at her. 'That was a bit of unexpected drama.'

'It was,' she agreed as he cast her an amused look.

'One which I rather think you preferred to the gala.'

She wrinkled her nose.

'I did a bit, yes. And about the umbilical cord...'

'I wasn't criticising,' he assured her. 'Clearly you knew what you were doing back there. I was just curious. It's a long time since I did a training stint with Obstetrics.'

And what did it say that she liked his compliment as much as the fact that he was still so keen to learn new developments in other fields?

There was nothing worse than an arrogant surgeon, but Rik clearly wasn't one of them.

'Anyway—' she forced herself to speak '—I ought to leave.'

'How are you planning on getting home?'

Grace glanced around the lobby.

'I'll ask Reception to call a taxi for me.'

And then it was back—that strange undercurrent that ran between them. Only this time, there was something more substantial to it. As though their moment of working together with the birth had lent weight to their attraction.

Or perhaps she was reading into it because that was what she *wanted* to see.

Thrusting it aside, she headed to the desk.

'I'm so sorry, madam,' the receptionist apologised. 'There has been some kind of incident on the Metro, so all the taxis have been booked out for at least the next couple of hours. As a result, the hotel is keeping its restaurant open later, if you would like to dine with us.'

'No, that's okay.' Grace smiled, despite her suddenly pounding heart.

As if her body wasn't as unhappy as it ought to be at the idea of not being able to leave, after all.

'It's time I bought you that drink,' Rik announced abruptly.

And even though she knew she ought to decline, there wasn't a bit of her that seemed capable of doing so.

'That would be nice.' It was definitely her voice, but she hadn't intended to speak the words.

And as he led her across to the bar, she found her legs moving of their own free will. Apparently, both her body *and* mind were acting entirely independently of each other, God help her.

'Ahh, excuse me? Madam? If you please?'

Grace and Rik swung around as the concierge scuttled across the expanse of floor towards them.

'It seems our friend has found something else to irk him,' Rik muttered quietly under his breath, making her stifle a laugh.

Almost as if she were some recalcitrant schoolgirl.

'You can't go in there.' The concierge slid himself between the two of them and the bar area.

'I believe we can.' Rik's tone might have been steady, and even, but disapproval seeped through nonetheless. 'And if you're going to address my companion here, I think I'd prefer you addressed her as *Doctor*, not *madam*.'

And Grace found it mirrored her own objections perfectly, even as the concierge twisted his face into a genteelly offended expression.

'You, sir, may of course go in, but I'm afraid your companion here may not.'

'I rather think we've earned it, no?' she added carefully.

'That's as may be.' He narrowed his eyes at them. 'But your dress is covered in blood, madam. I can't let you upset our other guests simply because you feel you deserve a drink.'

Grace halted abruptly, shame and humiliation slicing through her—emotions that she'd struggled to work out of her psyche for years. With Bas's help, she'd actually thought she'd overcome it. Which only made it all the more embarrassing now, that this man could make her feel so small.

'I...didn't realise,' she began apologetically. 'I just—'

'I believe what you're trying to say,' Rik cut in, his gaze firmly on the concierge, 'is that you're incredibly grateful for Dr Henley's intervention back there. Without her expert medical help, the situation with that young mother could have turned tragic.'

'However—' the concierge began, but Rik didn't allow him to continue.

'And, of course, *Dr* Henley wouldn't want to upset any of your other guests. Which is why, I imagine, you have another suggestion in mind. Especially as it appears we are being filmed.'

He jerked his head to the couple of mobile phones that were clearly pointed in their direction.

Grace edged self-consciously behind Rik, only too aware of the state of her attire.

The concierge, however, plastered a tight smile to his face.

'Of course, sir,' he noted with a polished air. 'The hotel would be only too happy to offer you the complimentary use of the Thistle Suite, complete with its own private entertaining area, where you and Dr Henley can enjoy your drink in peace.'

Grace nearly choked on swallowed air. The Thistle Suite in this place was famously one of the most coveted, and expensive, in the city. It was usually reserved for only the most exclusive VIP guests.

'*Underbart.*' Rik nodded his approval without a trace of sarcasm, and Grace could only admire his style.

'Perhaps Dr Henley would also prefer a change of clothes, complimentary of course, from our hotel boutique?'

'That would be very kind,' Grace managed, hoping she could sound even a fraction as relaxed as Rik.

The concierge looked considerably happier.

'Very good. I'll take you up there now, and have the clothes sent along shortly. You can also send your dress for dry-cleaning, if you wish. I'm sure we can do something for those bloodstains. It is a designer dress, after all.'

'Thank you,' Grace managed again as they followed the man when he scurried across the floor to the reception desk.

'For the record,' she whispered to Rik, without knowing why it mattered to her, 'this dress might be designer, but I didn't buy it. I rented it.'

'I've heard about that.' He actually looked impressed and, despite her best efforts, Grace felt a sense of triumph. 'It's becoming something of a movement, is it not?'

'It is, and that's a good thing,' she agreed. 'But I've been doing it for years—ever since I was a med student with not a lot of money.'

'I don't think I attended many of these things when I was a student.'

'No.' She laughed. 'I wouldn't have normally. But I have a friend who used to invite me to several galas, and other functions, each year, so that I could network—and so that I could throw his father off the scent when he inevitably snuck out of the party with some new female.'

'Nice of him,' Rik noted, though she couldn't help but think there was an odd tightness to his voice.

It was probably just her imagination.

'It was, actually. He had any number of contacts he could

draw on, whilst I had none. He knew that and so he opened up his world to me. Without him I wouldn't be where I am now.'

Rik frowned.

'I'm sure that was your own talent, and hard work.'

'I'm not saying I didn't have to work hard.' She lifted her shoulders lightly, and then dropped them. 'Nor am I saying that I might not have got here eventually. But having those contacts made things easier. That's all.'

'This way, please.'

Obediently, Grace followed the man to the lifts, with Rik sauntering along in easy fashion, as though this happened to him every day.

Perhaps it did. He was certainly the sort of man for whom she imagined people jumping to attention.

By the time they reached the suite, Grace had just about managed to settle her jangling nerves. And then the concierge opened the door, and the jangling reached a deafening level.

Nothing that she'd heard about the Thistle Suite could have prepared her for its sheer size. The footprint had to be about as big as the flat she'd worked so hard to buy and was so very proud of.

There were probably about as many rooms, too.

'It's just a series of spaces,' Rik whispered quietly.

She cast him a grateful smile. Clearly, he was somewhat accustomed to this kind of thing, which made her wonder quite how successful a plastic surgeon he had to be. Perhaps on the Jansens' level, after all.

Whilst here she was, struggling to pretend there wasn't some ridiculous thrill that ran though her at the idea of being in his hotel room.

'Go and get your shower,' Rik suggested. 'It's about three rooms away, but if you prefer, I can wait downstairs.'

She told herself that wasn't her heart kicking up another beat.

'Right. Lovely. Thank you.' She started through one door,

before realising the bathroom was in the other direction. 'I'll be as quick as I can, and out of your hair as soon as possible.'

And she had to remind herself that it was just a turn of phrase when, in his low, rumbling voice, Rik told her to take her time.

CHAPTER FOUR

RIK WATCHED THE doorway for several minutes after Grace had left, trying to puzzle out what was going on.

He stared until some complimentary wine arrived, along with the fresh clothes for Grace. And then he glowered some more.

He'd spent his entire life keeping people at arm's distance—it was the safest way to handle them. And yet, from the moment he'd seen Grace Henley, that magnetic attraction had caught him off guard.

One dance with her and he'd felt greedy, and feverish, and a whole lot more when her firm, perfectly curved body had melded itself to his.

He felt strangely unbalanced, unable to remember when was the last time that any woman had managed to get under his skin quite like this. Had they ever? Either way, Rik only knew he wanted more. He wanted *her*. The hottest, hardest part of him did, anyway.

He sipped his wine, and wished it were something stronger. Richer. Something that would stop this inexplicable feeling of…jealousy…that seemed to be swirling around inside him.

He snorted to himself. He sounded drunk, yet he'd barely touched a drop. Perhaps it really was time to call it a night. He'd always been so tough. So unreachable. And yet…recently Rik thought he'd felt his famously ice-cool façade slipping. Ever since he'd found out who he really was and tracked down what remained of his so-called family.

As if finally achieving his goal of finding his brother had caused something to shift inside him. To…change.

Either way, there was no other way he would have let a

woman, even one as captivating as Grace Henley, distract him from his main goal. Yet here he was.

Rik tried to shrug it off, but it was impossible.

For the better part of three decades, he'd stuffed down memories because they'd hurt too much to remember. It was odd, wasn't it, the things a person remembered? How the tiniest things could dislodge memories so deeply buried that one might have been forgiven for never knowing they existed.

Like playing schoolboy pranks, stealing pocketfuls of apples from Old Man's Nilsson's orchard, and sneaking out of their bedroom window at night to go and watch for the hedgehog family that had lived under the hawthorn hedge on the edge of the farmland.

How that wild, fun, free part of himself had died the moment he'd lost his beloved brother. How, the minute Bas had gone, it had felt to Rik as though the light had gone out in the entire universe.

He'd spent the better part of three decades mourning his bold, brave, full-of-life brother. He'd spent over twenty years actively searching for him. And he'd spent the past five months waiting for this very moment, when they would finally be reunited.

And now he was here—so close that he could practically taste it, like the finest, peatiest bourbon—he could feel the floodgates in his head being pushed and strained as he fought to hold back the slew of memories and emotions that were threatening to crash down on him at any moment.

It made Rik wonder if choosing the gala to approach Bas had been the best choice, after all. His intention had been neutral ground, outside the hospital where his brother—and he, as of Monday—worked.

But the closer the moment seemed to get, the more he was starting to wonder about why his brother hadn't replied to either of his previous letters. The thought that maybe Bas was deliberately ignoring him was finally began to gnaw into his brain. And the idea of it was almost too much to bear.

Three decades of missing his brother. Of imagining that glorious moment when they reunited. He'd never once stopped to consider that Bas might not feel the same way.

That Bas…might not even have thought of his twin at all.

Something slithered through Rik. Something that felt like cold, hard rejection, all over again. But he didn't care to analyse it further. Bas *had* to want to see him. No other option was possible. And tonight was meant to have been their reunion.

Only his brother wasn't here.

But the mouth-watering Grace was.

The knock on the door came just as Grace was sliding her feet into the pretty flat pumps that had come with the clothing. She smoothed down the gorgeous steel-grey soft jersey trousers, and adjusted the short, floaty sleeves of the delicate cream top. As complimentary outfits went, it was surely the most expensive one the concierge could have chosen.

At last, she opened the door to the suite.

The time away had done little to diminish the impact of being face to face with Rik Magnusson.

'I didn't want to disturb you, but—' he apologised before stopping abruptly.

He stepped closer, and Grace realised she'd stopped breathing. And she couldn't seem to start again, no matter how hard she tried.

For what felt like an eternity—though logically she knew was probably only a few seconds—she didn't dare to move as Rik's rich, disreputable eyes seemed to roam over her.

She felt ridiculously hot, and flustered. And molten.

Right *there*.

'You look stunning,' he told her, at length. But his eyes told her so much more. They whispered all the wicked thoughts that were already dancing around her head. Things she hadn't done before—not even in her dreams.

Disgracefully molten.

Grace smoothed down the jersey material again and tried to laugh it off—as though to prove she wasn't another of his adoring suitors.

'I don't think our concierge friend chose the clothes, do you?'

And if her voice was a little shaky, well, that could be her little secret.

'No?' Rik still seemed gratifyingly distracted.

'I rather suspect the boutique assistant did that,' she continued, if only to fill the silence. 'The outfit is too put-together, and he barely even wanted to help. Or maybe I'm being unfair on the man.'

'Han var en pompös röv,' Rik began hotly before correcting himself. 'He was a pompous ass.'

'Thank you.' She grinned.

'Reception have just called up to offer us a complimentary dinner on the house, and I wondered if you might like to get something to eat with me.'

'You don't need to do that. It's...' she checked her watch '...just after midnight. You could go to bed.'

Too late, she realised the folly of her suggestion. The last thing she needed was images of a semi-naked Rik in her head. Grace felt the familiar heat flushing through her and tried to beat it back.

She was more than a little grateful when Rik didn't appear to notice.

'And leave you sitting alone in the hotel lobby?' He quirked his eyebrows up. 'That wouldn't be particularly chivalrous, would it? So, will you dine with me?'

She hesitated, shoving all the uncharacteristically naughty thoughts out of her head. It *had* been several hours since she'd only picked nervously at a couple of elements of the sumptuous five-course gala meal. Even now, her stomach grumbled—its way of reminding her that the last time she'd eaten properly had probably been the day before.

Plus, she found that the offer of dining with this particular man was simply too good to pass up.

'If you're sure…' an odd grin tugged at the corners of her mouth, and it was all she could do to suppress it '…your company would be…very nice.'

Which didn't get anywhere close to articulating exactly what she thought spending a night in this man's company might be like.

Rather, she focussed on retrieving his key card for the suite before they left together, letting the door close behind them with what felt altogether too much like a click of finality.

As if her body wanted things that her brain would never allow itself to even contemplate.

'So,' Rik began as they made their way down the sumptuous hallway together. 'Tell me about Thorncroft.'

'Thorncroft,' she echoed, her brain struggling for a moment to right itself before reality plonked itself squarely on her chest.

So this was why he'd invited her to dinner. So that he could pump her for more information about the famous Jansen team—as outsiders tended to call it. She should have known.

'Which one do you want to hear about first?' Somehow she dredged up a smile.

'Which one?' he echoed neutrally.

He played it well, but she wasn't a fool.

'Magnus? Or Bas?'

'Neither,' Rik replied.

And, as daft as it seemed, for a moment she was almost convinced that he'd surprised even himself.

'Don't be silly, I'm not offended.' She pasted on another bright expression. 'Everyone wants to know about Magnus and Bas Jansen. Even new colleagues who aren't on the surgical exchange programme.'

'And yet, what I want to know most is what brought you to Thorncroft.'

'Me?'

'You,' he confirmed. 'Dr Grace Henley. Tell me your story, *älskling*. I find I want to hear it all.'

And even though a part of her desperately wanted to believe he was interested, her more sceptical side tried to remind herself to be on her guard for him using her to get inside information on Magnus and Bas.

This wasn't at all the way he'd intended his evening to go when he'd first decided to fly to the UK early, in order to attend the Jansen medical ball.

But he couldn't seem to regret a moment of it—not when he was spending it in the company of this woman. Yet, none of this made sense.

He wasn't like the playboy brother he'd travelled all this way to meet again. He didn't pick women up in bars—or at galas, if he was going to be technical—and take them home for one night of wild abandon. He wasn't a monk, of course, but he picked his companions carefully.

Always professional women who were as career-minded as he was, so who wouldn't want more from him than he was prepared to give. Attractive, too, admittedly. There had to be some chemistry.

Though never like this. Never so strong that he'd had to physically remove himself from the suite upstairs, lest he draw her into the bedroom and tear off all those new clothes that she kept subconsciously skimming down over a body he could already tell was nothing less than luscious.

Because she wanted him, just as badly. He knew women well enough to read her dilated pupils, her erratic pulse, and the way she responded to him. Just as he'd read the way her body had moulded itself so exquisitely to his when they'd been dancing earlier.

They might well have passed one perfect lifetime just spinning around that floor together. And Rik could easily imagine passing several more lifetimes doing the same.

He could pretend that he'd only brought her here to try to find out a little more about his brother, and his father, but Rik knew it would have been a lie. Despite his questions about Thorncroft, she'd seemed wary, almost cagey in her replies, and in a way he hadn't cared.

Given the choice between plugging her for information about his long-lost family, and spending more time just enjoying her company, he'd known exactly what he preferred.

'Another coffee?' he asked as she replaced the delicate cup back on the saucer.

Anything to prolong the meal, and their time together. *What had got into him?*

She tipped her head from one side to the other, ruefully, and the soft blonde bun—a 'messy' bun, he had once heard it called—tilted with her.

He wanted to know what that would look like down, cascading over her bare, elegant shoulders.

'I shouldn't have had that one really,' she answered with mock sorrow. 'I'll never sleep tonight.'

He bit back the suggestions in his head, and he knew it wasn't just his imagination when she plastered on an overbright smile.

'I guess I really ought to see if there are any taxis available by now.'

'Of course.' It shouldn't have been a struggle for him to sound gentlemanly. 'We'll go and speak to the front desk.'

He stood, letting her step out in front of him; her blue eyes were just as bright when they met his. Then he placed his hand at the small of her back to guide her and, without a word, she seemed to melt into him, and Rik knew there was no fighting it any longer. Not for either of them.

Without a word, they left the still-busy restaurant together, heading across the lobby and towards the bank of lifts rather than the reception post.

It was only when they were inside, the metal doors sliding closed in front of them, that Rik turned her to face him, pulling her in, as she looped her arms around his neck.

'You're quite sure, *älskling*?' Rik's voice was gruff, and needy. And he watched with satisfaction—and not a small degree of triumph—when it raked over her, leaving her skin goosebumping with desire.

'Do I look unsure?' she challenged, inching that fraction closer to him.

He wondered if Grace had any idea of *how* she looked. Breathless, dizzy, and charged with adrenalin. She was every last schoolboy fantasy he'd ever had, and more. So much more.

But she still didn't really answer his question until she reached up onto her toes, pushed her face closer to his, and pressed her lips to his.

And he felt astoundingly reckless.

It was not a feeling he was accustomed to, having spent his entire adult life—and much of his childhood one—being the voice of reason. Grounding his alternatively self-aggrandising then self-sabotaging mother. Caring for her when she pushed everyone else away with her temper and her cruelty.

As if it had been his penance.

But now, he felt as though this—Grace—was somehow his reward for all of those years.

She made him feel…free. Alive. As though life was finally meant for living.

At least, that was what Rik told himself as he pressed her back against the wall of the lift. His mouth plundering hers, over and over, as if he couldn't get enough of her taste. As if he'd been waiting for her his entire life.

That alone should have been enough to make him stop—this *thing* wasn't why he'd worked so hard, and sacrificed so much, to get where he was—but instead, the only thing it did was spur him on.

It felt too *right*.

Rik had no idea how they managed to draw apart, moments before the lift doors slid smoothly open at his floor. Nor how they made it down the infernally long, deserted corridor to his room. But as soon as the key card was activated, he found himself hauling her back to him as they tumbled through the door.

It wasn't enough.

He wanted more. To touch her, to taste her, to make her his—especially when she opened her mouth to his tongue and rolled her hips against the hardest part of him. As if she wanted all that, too.

Rik wasn't sure how long they stayed there, against the hotel-room door, kissing like a couple of passionate teenagers. It could have been a lifetime. Longer. But when he hoisted her up into his arms, with Grace wrapping her legs around his hips as though she'd been specially crafted just for him, he found he didn't want to wait any longer.

Carrying her across the room and depositing her on the luxurious bed, he made short work of divesting her of those clothes that had been a symphony to every last, glorious curve.

'*Härlig...*' he breathed. 'You are stunning, *älskling*. I want to taste every inch of you.'

'Show me,' his vision whispered huskily.

Rik needed no further invitation.

An instant later, his own clothes had followed hers onto the floor of the suite, and his body was moving deliciously slickly over hers, as if they'd been waiting for this moment all night.

'Rik...' she breathed, shifting beneath him, the softest, hottest, wettest part of her skimming his as though she was ready for him.

If he didn't move now and slow it down, he wasn't sure that he wouldn't embarrass himself. He wanted her so badly that his body actually physically hurt. It would have been so easy to take what she was offering to him.

But he wanted so much more than that. For both of them.

So instead, he silenced her by dipping his head to the sensitive hollow at the base of her neck, and kissing her whilst she sighed and let her hands explore their way up his biceps and to his shoulder muscles. As if learning his body, the way he intended to learn hers.

All night, if he had to.

Slowly, with a leisureliness that almost killed him, Rik acquainted himself with every curve, every line, every ridge of this magnificent creature. He explored one side of her collarbone, then the other, delighting in the shivers that ran through her body as she arched this way, then that, in response.

Then, he trailed his kisses across the tempting swell of her chest, drawling whorls with his tongue before reaching one perfect, pink-nippled breast, and lavishing it with attention that had Grace writhing sweetly beneath him.

He used his fingers, his tongue, even the faintest hint of his teeth, as he licked, and played, and teased. And when she cried out his name again, her hands raking over his back, he simply turned his attention to the other side, and played some more.

Rik lost all sense of time. There was only Grace, and him, and the long night stretching complicitly out before them.

He made his way from one side of her incredible body to the other, using scorching-hot kisses and teasing patterns with his tongue. He blazed a trail downwards to her lower abdomen, then dropped to halfway up the inside of her thighs where he took his time working his way back upwards. Until finally, *finally* he was *there*. Where he most ached to taste her.

And then, he made himself slow down even further.

It was like some kind of exquisite torture, lifting his head to instead let his hand wander over the sensitive skin at the top of her legs. Revelling in the way her hips rolled for him as he moved from one side to the other, doing nothing more than deliberately skimming her wet heat with his knuckles. The sound of his name on her lips possibly the sexiest thing he thought he'd ever heard.

As if her sweet scent weren't driving him almost crazy with need.

Finally, when he didn't think either of them could take it any more, he dropped his head between her legs and licked straight into her core.

And, Lord, her luscious, honeyed taste was even better than he'd been dreaming of. He couldn't get enough. Again and again he tasted her, teased her, feeling that heavenly pressure build up in her as her hips moved and her body danced that dance of old.

'Rik…' she murmured, half a question.

But he could tell everything that he needed to from her taste, and he simply slid his hands under her perfect backside, growling into her until she shivered with need. Until she slid her fingers into his hair and began to writhe against his mouth.

And then he licked her some more. The sound of her moans—thicker and faster now—and his name on her breath making his body tighter than he thought it had ever, ever been. As if no woman had ever counted before her.

He could feel the tension building in her, banking hotter, and higher, until suddenly he knew she was close to the edge, bucking against him as she half gasped, and half cried. And then Rik slid his finger inside her as he sucked on the very centre of her need. Hard, and long, as she screamed out his name and shattered around him.

The most perfect sound he thought he'd ever heard.

By the time Grace came back to herself, feeling more torn apart, yet more whole than she thought she'd ever felt, Rik was already moving his body over her. The feel of his solid, muscled body making her ache to touch him more.

To offer him the same flawless high that he'd just given her.

Dimly, in the furthest reaches of her brain, it occurred to her that—from this moment—she was ruined for any other man. No other encounter she'd ever had—not that there had been many—had even come close to this. She suspected no man in the future ever would.

But she didn't care. Because if this was the best she would ever have the fortune to experience, then she was damned well going to revel in every single, last moment of it.

'That was…' she began, hoping he couldn't hear the slight shake in her laugh.

The one that revealed how come-apart she still felt.

'Only the beginning,' Rik cut in, dipping his head to kiss her throat, her neck, and that sensitive hollow below her ear.

She sighed with pleasure, even as she shifted beneath him. And then, suddenly, he was between her legs. His hard, dizzying maleness nestled right against where she was still molten and soft. Making her want, *need*, all over again.

And it was only then that an alarm started to sound in her head. Dim. Muffled. But there, all the same.

She paused, her mind floundering as she tried to work out what the ringing was. And then it struck her.

How could she possibly have forgotten? *She*, of all people.

'Wait,' she muttered, pushing herself upright from beneath

him, though she had no idea how she had the strength to do so. 'Do you have…protection?'

'Protection?' He looked at her for a moment—stunned.

It occurred to Grace that it was more than a little flattering to realise that Rik had been as caught up in the moment as she'd been. That, like her, he'd almost forgotten himself.

'I think they have something in the minibar,' he managed grimly, after a moment.

Yes, now that he mentioned it, she thought she'd heard that, too. She nodded jerkily.

'Intimacy kits.' Her tongue felt thick in her mouth, and she hated that the moment had become so awkward.

'Shall I?' Rik asked, moving across the room with no hint of embarrassment as her eyes traced his magnificent naked form.

He was asking her if she wanted to continue. Making sure her hesitation was simply a matter of practicality, and that she hadn't changed her mind.

What did it say about her that his consideration felt like the most romantic thing anyone had ever done for her?

'Yes,' she managed thickly. But with certainty.

And she watched as Rik obliged, retrieving the kit and removing a condom with an efficiency of movement that helped to erase any awkwardness between them. And then he was heading across the room, taking a moment to roll it on in a way that made her breath catch in her throat, before slipping back between her legs as though nothing had happened at all.

Making her feel at ease, all over again.

Bending her knees up, Grace let her hands glide down his hewn, muscled back, and arched up to him.

'There's no rush,' he murmured.

But it was the tight edge to his voice that thrilled her the most. As if he was barely restraining himself. As if he wanted her too badly.

'You call this rushing?' she complained on uneven breaths

even as the corners of her mouth turned upwards. 'Glaciers move quicker.'

'You're taunting me.' His eyes darkened. Rich and delicious.

'I am,' she agreed, her voice still choppy.

'Is that so, *älskling*?' His intent eyes darkened to almost black. His tone deceptively even. 'Because, trust me, that cuts both ways.'

It could have been a threat or a promise—most likely it was both. A thrill rippled through Grace. She might have tried to start this little game of dares, but she had a feeling he planned on winning it.

'Suit yourself,' she retorted deliberately. Her pulse speeding up as he trailed a finger down her body.

If he wanted to win, that was fine by her. In fact, anything was fine by her so long as…

She gasped with pleasure as Rik thrust into her. Slick, and slow, and deep.

He was big, stretching her everywhere. Making parts of her *feel* things where she didn't think they ever had before. Not that she'd ever thought her previous boyfriends had been *bad* at sex. They just hadn't been as good as *this*.

As intense, and incredible, and breath-stealing as being with Rik felt like.

And then he began to move, and every other thought fled her brain. There was only this. Only now.

He slid out, then in, Out. In. All the while his gaze was holding hers, his mesmerising eyes reflecting back that same raw hunger that coursed through her very veins. The entire world fell away as Grace gave herself up to this captivating man.

Again.

Stroke after stroke, he built the fire inside her. And all she could do was cling on. Wrapping her arms, her legs, right around him, and letting him take them wherever he pleased—their breath intermingling, drawing them closer together.

Rik began to move faster now. Harder. Each slick thrust propelling her on to a new high. She didn't know how she broke the eye contact. She only knew that she needed to lift her head so that she could press her lips against his neck. She had to taste the faint, glorious tang of salt with her tongue. To graze his skin with her teeth.

He groaned—a low sound that seemed to rumble right through her, and to her very core—and plunged in harder. Grace gasped, lifting her hips to meet him, revelling in the faster rhythm. Matching him, thrust for thrust.

And then she felt that wave building above her, ready to crash over and tear her apart. She was ready for it. She needed it. Raking her hands down his back, she arched her body, and he did something magical, and she was lost. Completely and perfectly.

Crying out his name as she soared into blissful nothingness.

And the last thing she remembered was Rik calling out her name, too, as he soared right along with her.

CHAPTER FIVE

'GOOD MORNING.' RIK glanced around the teaching hospital's Jansen Auditorium—yet another reminder of his father and brother's power. 'My name is Rik Magnusson and I'm here as part of the Jansen Exchange Programme,'

Why invite unwanted gossip by introducing himself by any other name?

He glanced around the audience again, not particularly surprised that neither of them was present. He didn't even feel disappointed. It was only what he'd expected.

What had caught him off-guard, however, was that he also found himself looking for Grace in the audience.

Grace, the woman who had shared his bed for the weekend. The woman who was supposed to have been nothing more than an unanticipated yet pleasant diversion from the disappointment of not seeing his brother at the Jansen Gala.

Yet now he was searching for her. Eager to see her. Rik didn't care to examine what that said about him. All he knew was that being here, in the UK, a stone's throw from his long-lost brother, was playing with his head.

It was making him feel…odd things. He couldn't explain it exactly, but it was making him want to share his reasons for being at Thorncroft with this woman. He—who had never told a single soul about his childhood, or his twin brother.

So instead, he yanked his wayward thoughts back into line, opting to engage with the group of doctors and surgeons who would be his colleagues for the next three months.

'But you guys aren't interested in why I'm here, are you?' He smiled, moving away from the podium and walking across the floor. 'You want to know about the case I've brought with me. So, let's get started.'

A low rumble of laughter ran around the room, and Rik

started the programme on his laptop, perched on the side table, and watched the images flash onto the main screen on the stage.

This was what he did best—the medical side. Not the emotional.

'This is Kenny, a nine-year-old boy who presented with occult craniosynostosis.'

Another rumble went around the room. This time of interest, rather than laughter.

'Craniosynostosis, as I'm sure most of you know, is the premature fusion of cranial sutures—otherwise known as the fibrous joints—between the skull bones,' Rik continued, conversationally. 'Would any of the junior house officers care to tell me what makes this case particularly interesting? Yes, you. Go ahead.'

'Craniosynostosis occurs in approximately one in every two thousand live births,' the young doctor Rik had selected sat up in his seat confidently. 'It's usually diagnosed and treated within the first year of life, though.'

'Good.' Rik nodded. 'Delayed diagnosis craniosynostosis beyond those first twelve months is uncommon. However, as you can see from this photo, our patient presents as a relatively normocephalic nine-year-old. He displays none of the normal head-shape anomalies or syndromic diagnosis which would usually have alerted a paediatrician to potential craniosynostosis, earlier in infancy.'

Rik stopped, his attention broken as the door at the top of the room opened unexpectedly. It wasn't loud enough to distract the audience, not least since it was behind them and they were all still assessing the images on the large screen. But despite every part of his brain roaring at him to ignore it, instinct made Rik look.

Grace. Somehow, he'd known it was her even before she'd stepped into view.

His eyes tracked her movements as she walked down a

couple of steps, then a couple more, before stopping abruptly and sliding elegantly into an end seat.

Suddenly, it was as though her presence—her interest—made him feel taller. Lighter.

Ridiculous.

And yet, as she settled in one of the seats near the top, it cost him far more than it ought to have done to drag his attention back to his presentation.

'The patient presented with increasingly debilitating migraines, optic nerve oedema, and issues consistent with ICP—increased intercranial pressure, which was confirmed by invasive monitoring. Additionally, CT scan showed pan-suture craniosynostosis. Initial questions?'

'Is there any family history of craniosynostosis?' called out one voice.

'There is not,' Rik confirmed.

'What about a family history of migraines?' another voice added after a moment.

'Good. Yes.' Rik nodded. 'The patient's biological father has always suffered with debilitating migraines, but, again, had never been diagnosed with any craniofacial abnormalities.'

'So, then, you're recommending cranial vault remodelling?' asked one doctor.

'Obviously he is, or we wouldn't be here,' another joked.

Still, Rik liked the way the original speaker didn't back down.

'My point is, given that the father may have dealt with occult craniosynostosis all his life, and also given the debate surrounding the functional benefits of cranial remodelling, I was simply wondering how you came to the conclusion that surgery was the right option in this case, Dr Magnusson?'

'It's a good question,' Rik agreed, 'and one which I find important. Any thoughts?'

A lively debate sprang up between those cautioning

against surgery when there was no clear need, and those who thought it was worth trying to see if it could alleviate the issue.

And then Grace spoke out.

'I would want to know what the impact has been on the patient's life. Most notably, the migraines and his ability to lead a normal life.'

Rik dipped his head in agreement. It might not be her field, but it didn't surprise him how quickly she got to the crux of the issue.

'According to the family, the migraines began as head-aches that have become increasingly debilitating over the past couple of years.'

'He's nine,' Grace mused, her eyes locked with his. 'So what about his schooling? Has it been affected?'

There might as well have been no one else in the room. He could see only her.

'The patient's migraines have resulted in a significant number of days absent from school,' confirmed Rik. 'His family have noted increasing difficulty in learning, and there are issues concerning the patient's temper along with an in-creasing number of violent outbursts—most likely as a re-sult of the pain—which have led to our nine-year-old being expelled from school.'

'In that case,' she noted, those green-blue depths still fixed with his, 'I would agree that surgical intervention looks to be the most beneficial treatment. Whilst the patient may not need cranial vault remodelling to rectify any craniofacial ab-normalities, the procedure would nonetheless create a space into which the brain could expand.'

'That could help to alleviate the migraines, and the optic oedema as mentioned before,' another voice noted thought-fully.

'Which was the conclusion I came to,' Rik confirmed.

But it took more effort than it should have done for him

to drag his eyes from Grace and remember to address the rest of the group.

Every second of their weekend together was burned, so insanely brightly, into his brain. If he closed his eyes, he was certain he could still see her, smell her, *taste* her. He still wanted her with a feverishness that he couldn't explain. It made him physically ache. Worse, it made something ache deep inside his chest.

Incredibly, no one else appeared to have noticed anything amiss.

So much for his 'stone-cold' reputation. All he had seemed to feel, since that moment at the gala, was fire.

And molten heat.

Rik had no idea how he concluded his lecture but finally, finally, they were wrapping up and he was accepting words of thanks, and offers to assist in Theatre, as the group filed out of the lecture room.

And then it was just him and Grace alone in the vast space, and common sense tapping valiantly against his brain.

This couldn't happen.

'Good lecture,' she complimented as he busied himself disconnecting the laptop from the system and shutting it down. 'You had them eating out of the palm of your hand.'

'It's an interesting case.'

He was deflecting, but it was either that or haul her back into his arms to take up where they'd left off.

Back where she belongs, a strange, uninvited voice whispered.

He silenced it.

Maybe there was still an unspent attraction between them, and maybe they could explore it during the course of the next couple of months. But not yet. Not until he'd found his brother and had the conversation that was decades overdue.

He could tell himself it was because he always put the priority tasks ahead of pleasure, and that he'd come here to find his brother long before he'd laid eyes on this woman. And perhaps there would even be a degree of truth in it.

But it wasn't the entire reason.

The truth was more along the lines of the fact that he hated lying to her. Or, more accurately, avoiding telling her the truth.

How many times, this past weekend, had she asked him about himself only for him to have to divert the conversation simply because he hadn't been able to answer her the way a part of him had wanted to do?

He was renowned for playing his cards close to his chest, yet even from that first night he'd wanted to tell this woman the secrets that he'd never told anyone else.

He hadn't, of course. Because that would have been illogical. And he was all about sense, and rationale.

And rationally, Rik knew acting out of character had to be down to finally being in contact with his brother, after decades of searching. It was understandable that being so close after all this time had stirred emotions within him whether he'd intended it to, or not.

That didn't mean he had to share his innermost thoughts with some stranger. Besides, it wasn't just his secret to share.

The sooner he tracked his elusive brother down and finally spoke with him, the better.

Grace had always thought of herself as a normal woman. Perhaps a little quiet at times, and something of a wallflower at parties, and she'd never had a one-night stand before. She was committed to her career far more than she was committed to a relationship, though she couldn't call herself a nun, or even a virgin.

That one night when she'd been sixteen had seen to that.

But then she'd gone to that ball before the weekend where she'd met Rik, and all those hitherto ridiculous books and films about *wanting* and *lusting* meant nothing when held up against this tumultuous, febrile *yearning* that seemed to tumble and roll underneath every inch of her very skin.

This *aching* that was almost too much to bear.

It was the reason she'd been unable to keep away from his lecture. Not simply because she'd been interested in the case he was bringing to Thorncroft, but because she'd actually itched to see him again.

So much for her immunity to men. She'd found herself in the corridor outside the lecture theatre before she had even realised she'd been drawn there.

The next thing she'd known, she'd been opening the door and creeping inside. When he'd looked up to see her walking down the steps, she'd almost forgotten anyone else had been in there, and so very nearly kept moving all the way down to the bottom, and onto that stage in front of him.

And now, she was here, having waited for everyone else to leave. As though he would have wanted her to stay behind. As though he saw her as anything other than the extended one-night stand that she knew she'd been.

If she didn't want to look desperate, then she needed to pull things back to a more professional footing.

'You didn't mention that you were one of the foremost authorities on craniosynostosis,' she countered.

'I seem to recall that we didn't do a lot of talking,' he drawled, and she felt herself flush—the stain creeping down her neck and beneath the neckline of her top.

And it only made it all the hotter when his eyes watched every inch of its journey. She tried to speak but couldn't.

'Do you have a particular interest in this area of medicine?' Rik asked at length, rescuing her.

She bobbed her head a little over-eagerly.

'I have a case of a two-month-old, which I think may be craniosynostosis.'

That much, at least, was true.

'My speciality is delayed diagnosis of craniosynostosis,'

Rik pointed out. 'Usually in pre-adolescence, and adolescence. Not in babies.'

'I understand that,' she acknowledged lightly. 'But you must have carried out multiple surgeries on babies diagnosed within the first year of life, before you specialised in delayed diagnosis craniosynostoses?'

'I have,' he admitted, though she got the sense he hadn't meant to.

It gave her a certain kind of hope, and she wasn't sure how she refrained from reaching up and pressing her lips to his. Just to see if he tasted as good as she remembered.

'Is the family in the hospital now?'

Grace shook her head.

'I have the case notes, though. Although you'll have to brace yourself—the main part of Thorncroft Royal Infirmary is nowhere near as luxurious as the Jansen wing.'

'That's hardly surprising,' Rik remarked dryly. 'I have to say that, although I had heard the Jansen clinic was a top-spec facility, I wasn't prepared for quite how luxurious it is. Even the damned coffee machines in this wing are espresso machines that wouldn't look out of place in a high-class coffee house in town. Complete with barista.'

Grace grinned.

'Everything in this place is top of the range,' she confirmed. 'From the marble floors to the latest light fittings in the bathrooms. There are even two helipads on the roof, one for emergencies and the other for VIP clients.'

'Of course it is.' Rik exhaled. 'And what about the building annexed to the hospital? The low-rise vertical garden apartment building?'

Grace was surprised.

'That's the one I was telling you about the night of the gala.' She flushed suddenly, but pressed on. 'It belongs exclusively to the Jansen wing. The lower floors are dedicated rehab areas, luxury pools, and spas, and gyms, and the upper levels are given over to VIP patients and/or their entourages.'

'So it's basically a luxury hotel for patients and their stylists, PR, make-up?'

'Not just them.' Grace refused to take the bait. 'The mid-levels are for visiting consultants. That's where you would have been put up had you not opted for The Marham.'

'I asked to be put up in a hotel,' he corrected swiftly. 'I never said it needed to be as luxurious as The Marham.'

'You wanted a bolt-hole away from the hospital?' she guessed.

It was something she probably would have wanted, too. She loved working at Thorncroft, but it was also nice just to be able to go home.

Which brought her right back to her recent hankering for a complete change of scene.

'I knew the Jansen clinics catered to celebrity clients,' Rik noted. 'But I didn't realise quite the scale.'

No, she didn't suppose he did. That was the art of what Magnus and Bas achieved—however much they differed on the means—in medical arenas, the Jansen name was more synonymous with pushing the boundaries of their field.

'Magnus makes the Jansen facilities their money by carrying out some of the best elective procedures in the country, and to do that he needs to attract the elite. Bas used that income to push the boundaries of reconstructive surgery from some of the neediest patients worldwide.'

'So effectively, Bas gives the Jansen name its medical kudos, whilst Magnus makes enough money that it would make your eyes water?'

'I suppose you could put it like that,' though it sounded a little harsh. 'Also, as far as those vertical gardens go, Magnus wanted one of the most acclaimed British architects to design the apartment complex, whilst Bas insisted it should be environmentally friendly. Eventually, they agreed that a leading botanist of Bas's choosing would work with the architect Magnus wanted.'

Rik arched his eyebrows tellingly.

'I can't deny that the result is incredible. It looks as if a lush, green, leafy park has met the most cutting-edge building.'

That was exactly what it was; Grace nodded.

'All part of the Jansen brand,' he remarked dryly. 'I see that you're setting the bar extremely high for me.'

And she liked quite how self-effacing he was. In fact, it turned out, she liked an awful lot about Rik Magnusson.

'By all accounts, you've already set the bar high for yourself.' She flushed. 'Obvious, I guess, since you wouldn't have been selected for the exchange programme if you hadn't, but you have to know that the craniosynostosis you just presented is going to be the talk of the hospital.'

He eyed her for a moment.

'If it interests you, put your name forward to work on the surgery with me.'

She started, surprised.

'I'm Obstetrics. I'm not Plastics.'

'Nor are half the doctors who were just in that room, and you had plenty of good suggestions—you weren't exactly a lurker. Besides, isn't this hospital supposed to be about teaching?'

She chewed her lip thoughtfully. The idea was tempting, but she couldn't decide if he was suggesting it because he truly felt she would benefit from it, or simply because they'd had sex—and he wanted more.

And you don't? A wry voice crept into her head.

She shut it down—just as Rik started speaking again.

'Okay, so I have another meeting to get to now, but perhaps we could meet tonight for dinner? Say half-past seven?'

She was sure she forgot how to breathe—if only for a moment.

Crazy.

'Dinner sounds lovely.' She wasn't sure how she succeeded in sounding so composed. 'But it won't let you see my case files on my patient.'

'I see.' His lips twitched. And she had the insane urge to kiss them into submission. 'Then how about we meet around lunchtime in the coffee shop I saw downstairs?'

'Julian's?' Grace clarified. 'All right. Shall we say around half-twelve?'

Rik took out his mobile.

'Give me your number in case either of us get held up.'

'At lunchtime?' she verified, before she could stop herself.

'At lunchtime for the case. And also tonight, at dinner.'

Lord, he was too perfect.

'Right, fine. Good.' She blinked at him as he eyed her steadily, his fingers on the buttons of his phone as he waited for her details. But she couldn't think. Her mind had gone completely blank. 'Wait…may I?'

Taking his phone, she drew in a steadying breath as she took a moment to fire her brain back into action. Then, punching in her digits quickly, she handed it back to him.

Within moments, he'd texted her a silly face, which made her grin inanely.

'I should get back to the ward, but I'll see you then.' She spun around and hurried out of the room, leaving him in her wake.

Before she did anything foolish, as much as because her morning of scans was about to begin.

She really shouldn't feel so giddy. Grace lifted her fingers tentatively to her still-grinning face as she hurried along the corridor.

But surely she could bask in it for a few more moments—when did this kind of thing ever usually happen to her?

When had she ever let it? That one mistake as a sixteen-year-old had been enough to frighten her off acting on impulse for good. Not least when it came to men.

But then, she'd never met any man quite like Rik before.

CHAPTER SIX

'How are you doing?'

Grace stepped into the scrub room, where Bas was cleaning up after one of his surgeries.

'The surgery went well,' he acknowledged, his tone neutral.

Grace tried not to grimace. This was so like Bas, to shut people out. Though not usually her.

Still she pressed on.

'I didn't mean the surgery. I meant you.'

For a moment, she wasn't sure he was going to answer. He sluiced his arms side to side under the water.

Left.

Right.

Left.

Right.

Grace waited, unsure what to say. Something had…shifted between them recently. It had started a few months before.

He'd received a letter: he'd thought she hadn't seen it, but she had. One morning, it had been sitting on the desk in his opulent office in the Jansen wing. By the time she'd visited in the afternoon, the letter had been in the bin. Unopened.

And he'd started to shut down from there. Little by little.

It was one of the reasons that she'd held off from telling him that she was thinking about leaving Thorncroft. That, and the fact that a part of her was scared to make such a big move.

But it hadn't stopped the niggling voice inside her from growing louder. Telling her that this wasn't the place for her any more.

Had it not been for Naomi's scan the night of the gala, she would have told Bas then. It had been her plan. But then there had been Naomi. And then she'd met Rik. And everything seemed to have drifted between her and Bas.

Would he shut Naomi out the same way? She couldn't help but wonder. Bas's deep voice pulled her back to the present.

'You mean, aside from the fact that my unborn baby is going to need surgery mere days after she's born?'

'I'm so sorry,' Grace told him sincerely. 'I can only imagine what you and Naomi are going through.'

'Thanks.' His voice sounded almost unfamiliar to her. It took her a moment to realise that it was emotion. 'No amniocentesis results?'

'Not yet.' She frowned. 'Seddon put a rush on it, but it still takes time—you know that.'

His only response was one of his trademark grunts. She dreaded to think what was running through his head.

'Do you and Naomi know what you're going to do yet?' she asked. 'In terms of raising the baby, I mean?'

He cast her a dark look.

'Do you mean how involved am I going to be? It's my child, Grace. Or do you think the same as Naomi? Namely that I'll just *dip in and out of their lives*?'

Ah, was that what was bothering him?

'Is that what Naomi thinks? That you wouldn't be dependable?' Grace asked gently. She could see how that would get under Bas's skin. But she could see Naomi's point of view, too. 'Then again, she doesn't know you. You hide the real you well, so I guess you can see her side of it, can't you?'

'Not really,' he bit out. 'She asked me what you meant when you talked about me not being like Magnus. Or my mother.'

Grace didn't answer straight away. If she'd known Naomi could overhear the telephone conversation then she might have been a little more guarded. Yet perhaps it was no bad thing for Bas to be forced to open up to this woman a little more. After all, Naomi was carrying Bas's baby. For better or worse, the two of them were going to be part of each other's lives for ever, surely the poor woman deserved to know a little more about the father of her unborn child.

She doubted Naomi had deliberately set about getting pregnant by Bas—though many a woman had certainly tried. But there was something about the other woman that Grace had instantly liked. She got the impression that random hook-ups were about as common an occurrence in Naomi's life as they were in her own.

Or had been, until the other night, Grace thought abruptly as a sinful image of Rik filled her mind.

She shoved it away hastily and blew out a breath.

'You didn't answer, did you?'

'I don't see that it's any of her business.'

She almost felt sorry for her friend. *Almost.*

'You can hear the absurdity of your comment, right?' Grace prodded softly. 'Naomi is the mother of your unborn child. Like it or not, she has a right to hear a little about your past, and the way it shaped you.'

'Does she?' countered Bas. 'It isn't as though we've chosen to be together. If it weren't for this pregnancy, we probably wouldn't have even spoken again.'

If it hadn't been for that odd shadow that skittered across his features, she might have believed him.

'Wouldn't you?' she asked, carefully.

'What's that supposed to mean?'

Grace wrinkled her nose, trying to choose her words carefully.

'It means that I don't think I've ever seen you act quite the way you did around Naomi. And it isn't just that she's pregnant, or that you were both dealing with the news that no parent-to-be wants to hear, because I noticed even before the scan.'

'You're imagining things,' Bas countered scornfully.

But Grace couldn't help feeling it lacked any real emphasis. As if he was just playing a part.

But to fool other people—or himself?

'I don't think so. There was just something…different, about the way you were around her. The softer side of Bas that I usually only see when you and I are alone. I think you like her, Bas. And I think you think so, too.'

He glowered at her for a moment then, tellingly, abruptly changed the topic.

'How did the gala go?' he demanded, stepping off the foot tap and drying his hands.

Grace paused. She'd wanted to say more about him and Naomi, but it didn't seem like the right moment.

Not least when thoughts of Rik were now suddenly tearing around her head.

'The gala went very smoothly,' she assured him. 'People asked after you, naturally, but I just said you were caught up in a case here. In any case, a record amount of money was raised, and a good night was had by all.'

Guilt chased through her and, as if he could tell, Bas's voice sounded slightly sharper than usual.

'Nothing else to tell?'

Or perhaps it was simply her imagination. She eyed him warily.

'Are you talking about the new doctor on your exchange programme?'

Something flitted across her friend's expression just then. Something so dark and bleak that it caught her unprepared.

'He was there?' Bas choked. 'You met him?'

Did Bas know? Was that what this was about? But even if he did, why would he care?

'I did,' she admitted tightly, not understanding where the sudden animosity had come from. 'Is there some reason I shouldn't have?'

'He was actually there?' Bas was practically snarling at

her now. 'He had the bloody audacity? And you didn't think to call me? You didn't think to even mention it?'

What on earth was she missing? It made no sense.

'I rather thought you had enough going on,' she managed jerkily. 'Don't you?'

'Not more important than Henrik turning up,' her friend roared.

Grace froze. Her mind wasn't so much racing, as it was hurtling around her skull, wholly out of control. He couldn't possibly mean...

'Wait. *Henrik?*' she echoed slowly. 'You mean Rik?'

She knew about Henrik. She was possibly one of the only people with whom Bas had shared stories about his past— just as she had shared hers with him—but Henrik Jansen certainly wasn't an individual Grace had ever cared to meet.

The way he'd betrayed his brother—even as kids—had been horrific.

'Rik?'

'Dr Rik Magnusson,' she managed, though her tongue felt far too unwieldy for her mouth. 'The new surgeon.'

Oh, Lord...but she hadn't just met him. She'd slept with him.

No, it still didn't make sense. It couldn't.

A wave of nausea swelled in Grace's belly, and there was no missing the fury in her friend's glower.

He snorted.

'That's what he's calling himself?'

This couldn't be happening. She couldn't quite process it.

'When you say Henrik, you don't mean...?' She stopped awkwardly, afraid that she sounded dumb. 'But he called himself Rik. And surely he would be a Jansen?'

'My father's name is Magnus.' Bas bit out every word as though it pained him. It certainly hurt her, to think that she'd contributed to her friend's anguish. 'Presumably, he thinks he's clever calling himself Magnusson. And shortening Henrik to Rik.'

Grade didn't want to believe it, however much it fitted. But then, the expression on her friend's face—that flicker of hesitation—made her wonder if he'd remembered something else.

'Perhaps he's trying to be discreet,' she managed hopefully. 'Maybe he's trying not to cause a scene.'

'If he doesn't want a scene, then he shouldn't have come here. He should have stayed the hell away, just as he has done these past thirty years. Just as he ought to have done when I didn't answer any of his letters.'

Except that her friend's tone lacked the absolute anger of a moment ago. As though he was a little less sure.

Grace swallowed down a cry of exasperation. If only Bas had said something, if only he'd *told* her, then she could have been on her guard for Rik... Henrik.

She'd known Bas for too long, her loyalty to him was absolute. However strong the attraction to Rik, that night of the gala, had she known his true identity she would never have risked her friendship for a one-night stand.

Not even one as glorious as the other night had been.

But, dammit, Bas hadn't told her a thing. The guilt she'd felt before was being chased now by anger. If her friend hadn't been so closed off—if he'd trusted her enough to confide in her—then this would never have happened.

'Rik wrote to you?' she demanded fiercely before she could check herself.

But how she wished she could bite the words back when the infamous black gaze bored into her, skewering her in place.

A different colour from Rik's green-blue eyes, admittedly, but how could she have failed to see the similarities between the two men? Notably, that characteristic, all-commanding expression.

But then, Bas had never made her feel as sensual, as all-woman, as Rik had. Her friend had come into her life at a time when she'd needed precisely that—a friend. Ultimately, he'd made her feel as if he were a protective big brother.

Rik had made her feel something quite, quite sublimely different.

'Rik?' Bas demanded harshly, yanking her attention back into the room. 'You're acquainted with him?'

The silence stretched out so very long between them.

Part of her wanted to confess the truth, perhaps even explain herself. But another part of her—a stronger part—wanted to hold onto the sweet perfection of her weekend with Rik. Even if only for a little bit longer.

But even now, she feared that memory was tarnished for good. Because however glorious it had been with Rik, however much she'd hoped something more might have come of it, the ugly truth was that he'd lied to her.

He wasn't Rik Magnusson—he was Henrik Jansen. Brother to the person she thought of as her closest friend.

The one man who was utterly off-limits to her. Her heart hammered harder against her ribs—enough to bruise. And yet she drew in a deep breath and mentally squared herself. She might not know what was going on here, but she knew she didn't deserve to be attacked.

'I didn't know who he was,' she cried out at last.

But the implication was clear and her friend's face turned to disgust.

'You had sex with him?' he said coldly. 'Of all the people in this hospital, in this county, with whom you could have had sex, you chose my brother?'

'How could I have known?' Grace thrust her hands in her hair.

The worst of it was that she wasn't sure what she was most angry about. That she'd hurt her friend? That Bas hadn't trusted her? Or was it that something inside her died at the thought of not being able to see Rik again?

She thought it was that possibility that shamed her above all others.

'I asked you to go in my place and to look out for anything unusual. Anyone who was there who shouldn't be.'

For a long moment, they stood watching each other. And then Grace's panic began to die down, and she eyed him critically.

'And from that, I was supposed to know you meant your brother?'

He gritted his teeth at her.

'Anyone unusual, Grace.'

'I couldn't possibly have known that meant the brother you haven't seen in almost thirty years. I couldn't possibly have concluded that the stranger I happened to meet—the perfectly…normal man, who called himself Rik and was a surgeon like so many people at that medical ball—was the someone *unusual*.'

Another disdainful snort was directed her way. But she didn't care.

'You think you *happened* to meet him? That it was a coincidence that he bumped into you—the person I'm closest to?'

It took her a moment to work out what he was saying. And when she did, she felt that nausea from before beginning to rise. She shook her head as vigorously as she could.

As if that could stop his words from being true.

'You're saying he sought me out deliberately?' she whispered, her words jagged.

For a long time, he didn't speak. Grace could practically see the wheels in his head spinning around.

But she couldn't say anything. Or do anything. She was still feverishly trying to process the last thing Bas had said. Trying to make sense of it.

Had Rik… *Henrik*…really used her? Had he known exactly who she was when he'd approached her at that gala?

Had he slept with her because he'd thought she was a way to get to his brother?

Her gut screamed that it wasn't true. That it wasn't the man she'd met. She opened her mouth to tell her friend, but then she stopped. And she swallowed her denial.

Because she wasn't exactly renowned for her ability to read people, was she?

Grace opened her mouth again, this time to apologise. But Bas started speaking before she could.

'I have to go. But you need to meet up with Henrik again.'

She cast him a horrified glance.

'What? *No!*'

'Yes.' He nodded grimly. 'Whatever he's doing here, whatever he's up to, I need to know.'

Grace gaped at him, appalled.

'Wait, you want me to spy on Henrik? I can't. No. If you want to know why Henrik's here, Bas, you're going to have to speak to him.'

He glanced at her, but seemed entirely unmoved.

'Please, Grace, I'm asking you as my friend. Whatever Henrik is doing here, it won't be good. But I have to concentrate on Naomi right now. She has to be my priority. My baby has to be my main focus.'

'Bas…' Grace bit her lip. 'What you're asking…'

What made it all the more abhorrent was that there was a sliver of her that welcomed the excuse to see Rik again. Despite everything.

What awful things must that say about her?

'I'm not asking you to sleep with him again, for pity's sake,' Bas snapped, as if reading her thoughts. 'I'm just asking you to occupy him. Distract him. Maybe show him around the hospital. Take him on a tour of the city.'

'Show him around…' she echoed uncertainly.

'You could even ask him to take my place in the hospital fete this year.'

'You really want Rik… Henrik, to get involved in the charitable side of the hospital?'

'Not particularly.' Bas gritted his teeth. 'But you know how long the prep work takes, between repairing the stalls and giving the tired ones a fresh lick of paint. And then there's the manning of them. It takes time. All of which I could be spending with Naomi this year.'

Her head was such a jumble that she couldn't think straight.

If she agreed, would she be agreeing on her friend's terms? Or merely because it meant she didn't have to stop seeing the first man who'd made her feel alive in a long, long time.

The only man.

'I don't know, Bas.' Grace pursed her lips.

'You slept with my brother, Grace. I think you owe me.'

That was below the belt. Especially for the man who had been her only true friend for the better part of a decade. But though she wanted to, she didn't dare argue for fear that she might betray more than she wanted to. Even to herself.

Perhaps she could do it. As much to get answers to her own questions as to get answer to Bas's. Like, had Rik known who she was that night? Had he used her?

The very thought of it made her feel sick. No, there was no choice—she couldn't possibly agree.

It would be the second time she'd been used by someone in such an intimate way. But at least the fact that Rik had used protection meant that she wouldn't pay the ultimate price this time.

She wouldn't end up spending a lifetime wondering, and searching, and hoping for someone else.

One was enough.

Without warning, grief slammed into her. And with it, guilt.

She owed Bas so much. If it hadn't been for him, she wasn't sure she'd be where she was now. Certainly not here—

a sought-after obstetrics doctor at a hospital with ties to one of the country's most prestigious private medical centres.

Before that propitious day when she'd first met Bas, the nineteen-year-old, first-year medical student that she'd been had been just about ready to throw in the towel. If not on life, then certainly on any idea of a fulfilling career.

She hadn't thought she'd deserved it.

But Bas had rescued her. He'd pulled her out of the dark, sinking pit that had been claiming her, inch by inch, for years—even if he'd never known it. Even if she'd never been able to share her terrible secret with him.

She owed him. And if spying on his brother—the one man who had made her feel physically alive, for the first time since she'd been sixteen—was the dues she had to pay, then she would do it.

'Okay,' she heard herself mutter quietly, at length. 'Okay, I'll do it. I'll try to keep him distracted. But there's a time limit, Bas. I'll give you a week.'

'A month,' he countered, though he sounded as grim as she felt.

A shiver ran through her. Though, Grace suspected, not for any of the reasons it really ought to. Because she could tell herself it was her penance, but that didn't stop some perfidious part of her from thinking that she might actually enjoy *having* to spend time with Rik.

'A fortnight,' she managed. 'So you'd better do the right thing by Naomi, Bas. And you'd better agree on your solution quickly.'

Because she was terribly afraid that the longer she spent with Rik, the easier it would be to forget why she had agreed to it in the first place.

She needed answers. Not to fall for the last man on Earth that she should find attractive.

'Agreed.' Bas offered a terse nod and made his way to the door. 'And, Grace, thank you.'

A moment later, he was gone, leaving Grace all alone. And as if it couldn't get much worse, her phone started to vibrate in her pocket.

She didn't know how she sensed it would be Rik, even as she slid her shaking hands into the fabric to retrieve it. Still, she stared at the ringing screen for a moment before shutting it off.

How had she gone from looking forward to spending time with the magnificent Rik, to spying on the hated Henrik, in the space of a few minutes?

It was too much.

Agreement or not, she needed to cancel their dates—the surgical date as well as the dinner date—until she got her head straight again and figured out precisely how she was supposed to spend time with Rik without him realising that something was now very wrong.

CHAPTER SEVEN

LEANING ON THE DOORFRAME, wondering when he'd last done something so out of character, Rik lifted his knuckles to the wooden door and knocked. Loudly.

Moments later it swung open and Grace stood in front of him, barefoot and ponytail swinging.

It should ring alarm bells how possessive that made him feel.

'I do have neighbours, you know...' she began, then tailed off when she saw it was him. 'Oh, I thought you were someone else.'

Something knotted in Rik's gut as he took in the worry lines that were suddenly etched into Grace's lovely face. Something was wrong. She hadn't cancelled their dates because of a patient-related emergency—his instinct had been spot-on.

To be fair, it usually was, but this time he'd really hoped he'd misread the situation.

'Who were you expecting?' he asked, before he could stop himself.

Lightly, non-aggressively, so she couldn't see how desperate he was to know—as uncharacteristic of himself as it felt to even care.

She hesitated, as though she wasn't going to answer. The knot pulled tighter.

Finally, she relented.

'I thought you were my grocery delivery,' she confessed after a moment.

And it shouldn't have made him anything like as relieved.

'Good. Then I can come in?'

It didn't escape him the way her eyes kept sliding from

his, as though she found it too hard to look straight at him. As though she was…fighting with herself.

Or perhaps that was just what he wanted to think.

'I'd rather you didn't.' She stood in the doorway as if to block him.

In effect, however, the action brought her—and her body—all too mouth-wateringly close. And by the way her pulse beat erratically at the base of her smooth, elegant neck, he wasn't the only one feeling that familiar rush of heat.

It practically sizzled through the air between them.

Was he to take heart from the knowledge that whatever had caused her to cancel their dates—both medical and personal—it wasn't because she'd decided she was no longer attracted to him?

'Do you want to tell me what's going on?'

At least his voice was even, back to his usual control. Even if inside felt like a jumble of unfamiliar emotions.

Her eyes flickered to his—just for a split second—and then dropped away again.

'I'm career-focussed at the moment,' she bit out, as though it was a speech she'd been rehearsing but couldn't quite commit to. 'I don't have time for…flirtations.'

'Rubbish.'

He didn't intend to move but suddenly his fingers were under her chin, tilting it up so that he could look right into those expressive eyes of hers. And this heat between them was so intense that it glowed blinding white.

The force of it walloped into him, practically knocking him off his feet.

'Fine…' Her breath was a whisper that he might have felt, more than heard. 'Perhaps we should start with the fact that your name is actually Henrik Jansen.'

'Ahh.'

Guilt moved through him.

'*Ahh*, indeed,' Grace echoed, but her voice shook a little

beneath the surface. 'Bas is my friend and you're his brother. A fact about which you clearly lied to me.'

'Not lied,' he qualified, hating his own words in that moment. 'Omitted.'

'That's your apology?'

Her expression grew disdainful, and the sense of guilt that had been rumbling quietly through him now grew.

'You're right.' He held his hands up, palms outstretched, in front of her. 'And I do want to apologise.'

As if that could magic it all away.

There was a beat of silence, as though she thought the same thing.

'Then why did you do it?' she asked, when he didn't offer anything further. 'Did you target me because you already knew he and I were friends? Was I your way to get closer to him?'

'No,' he ground out, abhorring the suspicion in her expression.

As well as the fact that he was the one who had put it there.

It made him wonder how many people had used Grace in the past, in order to get closer to the infamous Bas. Women—undoubtedly, given his brother's womanising reputation, but men? Possibly—especially if they were surgeons wanting to learn from someone with his brother's reputation and skill.

And Grace was glowering at him.

'Then was sleeping with me your way of getting under your brother's skin?'

'That's absurd,' he bit out, riled despite his attempts to stay calm.

Another chink in his usually irreproachable control. What was it about this woman?

'Is it?' she cried. 'Bas believes—'

'*Bas* believes?' he echoed incredulously, though a lot quieter than Grace. '*My brother* is the one who put such a damned insulting idea in your head?'

'He's looking out for me.'

'He is looking out for himself,' Rik ground out, even as he hated himself for letting those old fears sneak out.

He tried valiantly to stuff them back. He hadn't come all this way to resurrect an old argument with his long-lost brother. On the contrary, this trip—all this effort—was supposed to be about healing. Funny how one woman could put all that at risk. He ought to walk away right now.

But he couldn't.

Instead, he stood motionless, waiting for her to speak. To answer his question.

But Grace didn't say a word. Instead, the lift of her shoulders was almost delicate. And a part of him longed to answer her—to explain himself—but then there was something else moving through him, too. Something strange.

Something that—had he not known better—he might have mistaken for a sliver of jealousy.

But of course that couldn't be the case. She was a one-night—weekend—stand. There was no reason for jealousy to figure into it. He opened his mouth to say something practical. Logical.

'What's really going on here?' his voice cracked out instead, the low tone doing nothing to soften that almost lethal edge. 'Are you worried I will tell him about your little indiscretion?'

'My...indiscretion?'

That unwelcome, misplaced sensation slithered around the pit of Rik's belly. He'd never known anything like it before. He certainly didn't like it.

And still, he was powerless to stop it.

'Come now, I think we can dispense with the games. It's clear you're preoccupied with what will happen when Bas hears about your night with me.'

'No,' she denied quickly. 'That isn't true.'

'Then you would take no issue with him knowing that happened between us?'

'None…' She bit her lip uncertainly.

'As I thought,' Rik cut in with an expression of disgust. Though less at her, and more at himself.

'Wait…no,' she cried out quietly as he swung abruptly away from her. 'It isn't like…that.'

'More lies, *älskling*?'

Grace blinked, momentarily stunned, and the slithering and churning sensations intensified.

'Let me guess, my brother uses that same phrase—*älskling*—and you thought it was unique to you?'

What was the matter with him? Why couldn't he stop talking? It was so out-of-character for him, but then his usual iron will had deserted him from that first night he'd met Grace.

'I've heard Bas use it,' she admitted. 'Though rarely. And certainly not to me.'

'Is that right?' he added.

And finally, finally, Grace jerked her head up to meet his eye.

'I told you once before that he and I have only ever been friends.'

'Given his reputation, I find that hard to believe.'

Although he wanted to believe her. Perhaps more than he'd ever wanted to believe anything—though that made no sense.

'Then, regrettably, that's something for you to reconcile,' Grace said quietly. 'Not me.'

The weight of her soulful gaze was almost too much for him to stand. He still wanted her. Even now. Even though he couldn't explain this dark, covetous thing that moved inside him.

'We are both adults here.' He had no idea how he kept his tone so mild. 'We had sex—incredible sex, I might add, in which you screamed out my name many times—but now that you know who I am, it seems you're desperate for my brother not to find out what happened. If you and he are not together, explain that to me, if you will.'

He waited as she chewed on the inside of her cheek, and shifted her weight first from one side, and then the next. And then, when she still didn't answer, he decided he needed to intervene...just as a movement dragged his attention away and he snapped his head around. A blur of grey-green was hurtling down the corridor to the lift doors at the end, just as they pinged and began to close.

'*Cooper!*'

As Grace cried out, Rik didn't even pause to think. He spun around and chased down the corridor after the flying missile, throwing himself into the lift just as the doors closed. He scooped the grey-green blob into his arms and realised it was a young cat. And for all its athletic display a few moments earlier, it was quite a friendly one at that—purring contentedly the moment he tickled its chin.

By the time he got back to Grace's floor, it—Cooper, if he remembered correctly—was virtually his best friend.

He strode up the corridor, half expecting Grace to yell at him for frightening her pet. Half looking forward to it, if he was going to be honest, because at least it meant she would no longer be trying to ignore him.

Instead, she laughed ruefully as he strode up the corridor and, just like that, the ice was broken again between them.

'Yours, I presume?' He held out the wriggling feline.

'Thank you.' She reached out to take it. 'Though you didn't have to break your neck to catch him. He would have been okay.'

Rik might have frowned, but at least the unexpected interlude had broken the ice between him and Grace again. For that, he was grateful.

'From the way you called his name when he escaped, I thought you were afraid he would get himself lost.'

'He startled me, that's all.' She shook her head. 'He goes

out a fair bit. Sometimes to my neighbour across the hall because she has a cat, too. And lots of cat treats. And sometimes out of the window. It's one of the perks of having a ground-floor apartment that backs onto hectares of woodland. Thank you, though. It was very sweet of you to chase after him.'

'I ought to object to being called *sweet*…' He arched his eyebrows. 'But if it's enough for you to now invite me in…?'

Grace bit her lip, then stepped back in tacit agreement as she placed the cat—who now seemed content to stay inside the apartment—onto the floor. Rik stepped through as she closed the door behind them.

'You haven't had him long, I take it? Cooper, I mean.'

'He's eleven years old.'

'Really?' Surprised, Rik eyed the cat a little closer. 'I thought he was much younger.'

'He's small,' Grace acknowledged. 'But he's still very active.'

Her soft smile was almost proud. Clearly Cooper was a good way to her heart.

'How did you come to have him?'

'I've had him since a kitten.' She seemed to pause before plunging on. 'Bas has his brother.'

Rik stopped, not sure he'd heard properly. Not certain of the implications. But he didn't need to ask more, since Grace was already speaking again.

'It was a summer night, just as it was starting to go dark, when we were on our way back from the hospital one night. As we passed the canal, Bas saw a plastic bag under the bridge and… I don't know what he saw, or whether it was instinct, but the next thing I knew, he was scrambling over thorny undergrowth. When he opened the rubbish bag, there were three kittens inside. One had clearly died, but the other two were alive. Though barely.'

'My brother rescued abandoned kittens?'

It was so unlike the man he'd been hearing about these

past few years, yet so like the brother he remembered. Especially that impetuous boy who had always thrown himself into whatever he'd perceived as the right thing to do, without ever thinking twice.

Sometimes, without even thinking it through.

'We took the kittens to the local vets,' Grace continued, 'who said that the remaining two kittens were really too small, and too weak, to survive. That they would need round-the-clock care and that, sadly, they simply didn't have the staff or resources to do it right then.'

'So my brother took them on, did he not?'

Rik knew the answer without her even needing to tell him. He could well imagine the brother he had known staying up, night and day, to care for them. To tend to them.

'He did.' Grace nodded. 'They needed feeding every two to three hours initially, and Bas took that on. He risked his place on the course to care for them—not that it mattered academically since he was way ahead of the rest of us anyway, partly due to having Magnus as a father, and partly due to Bas's own innate ability. I tried to help whenever I could, but I couldn't afford to risk my education the way Bas did.'

'So Magnus was a good father to Bas?'

It was odd, the way that knowledge made him feel relieved, and yet twisted and scraped at him, all at once.

Relieved, because Bas had got the parent he deserved, after what their mother had put him—an innocent kid—through, but bitter because, at the end of the day, he himself had never been able to escape her. Or her cruelty.

But Grace's expression changed and became closed off.

'You would need to speak to Bas about his relationship with Magnus.'

'It must have been relatively good,' Rik pressed. 'You don't take time out of a medical degree to care for a couple of kittens, without risking your education.'

Grace bristled, and, even though he could see she didn't

want to rise to his comment, he needed to know more. To understand.

'I imagine having Magnus guiding him has been a bonus,' Rik noted evenly.

Grace glowered at him.

'The Jansen father-son team is certainly world-renowned,' he continued. 'I think everyone has heard the stories about how the great Magnus Jansen would bring his ten-year-old son to the OR to watch operations.'

'You shouldn't believe everything you read,' she managed, her voice stilted.

And it only made him all the keener to learn more. To know that Bas had landed on his feet with the father who hadn't had anything to do with either of them during the first seven years of their lives. Which was, at the end of the day, why he'd left Stockholm to come here—if only for a few months.

And to understand exactly what the nature of this woman's relationship with his brother was—which *wasn't* why he'd come here.

'So you're saying the stories aren't true?' he pressed her, mercilessly. 'That Magnus didn't help Bas?'

'Yes, they're true,' she gritted out, at last. 'And of course that exposure has helped to make Bas the surgeon he is today. But that has always been about your father's ego.'

'I believe Bas is the one with an ego.'

'No. Maybe. But Bas is all about the patient. And taking him to surgeries was all fine when Bas was a kid, idolising his hero surgeon father.' She swallowed, but forced herself to continue. 'But what I'm saying is that Magnus didn't do him any favours once Bas turned eighteen and went to uni to study medicine. And your father certainly didn't do Bas any favours when it came to starting plastics as a speciality.'

'Bas is here, isn't he? Running the private Jansen wing at

this hospital. His name above the door. His reputation intact as one of the country's fastest rising surgeons in his field?'

'You really ought to talk with your brother about this,' she told him desperately.

'I'm talking to you,' Rik pointed out. 'Since you seem to have a vested interest.

She bared her teeth at him. Actually bared them. And it might have had an impact, had he not immediately imagined them pressed against his naked flesh.

As if he were a man possessed.

'No vested interest,' she bit out, bending down to stroke the cat.

It took him a moment to realise this was her attempt at regrouping.

'You seem pretty clued up on my brother,' he countered. But this time, some of the heat had gone out of his tone.

Enough to let Grace relax a little.

'All I can tell you is that Bas had to be twice as good as any other surgeon for his father to even allow him into the Jansen wing. Your father only really allowed him any say when he realised that Bas being there brought in more money than ever. And money is what motivates your father.'

'And it doesn't motivate Bas?' Rik scoffed.

'Not particularly.' She stood firm. 'Bas is all about the patients, every time.'

'And the women, of course. Don't forget his playboy reputation.'

He saw the temper swirl beneath her skin moments before it burst out.

'Listen, *Henrik*, you might think you know Bas from all the rumours, and stories, but you don't. You haven't been in his life for almost thirty years, but I can tell you that Bas never really had a childhood. He didn't go to parties, or have friends over, he grew up with nannies, or in observation galleries to operating rooms as Magnus performed his surgeries. The only things that interested Magnus were his career, and women.'

'Like father, like son, then.'

'Not really. But if it makes you feel better to think that, then go ahead. Bas is twice the man you are, by all accounts.'

'Why? Because he risked it all in order to raise two kittens, like some kind of rebellion?' Rik threw back scornfully.

He couldn't have said why. Though he suspected it was because he didn't want to accept the fact that he'd spent the past thirty years believing that it didn't matter that he'd lost his brother—his best friend, and the best anchor he'd had in his life—because Bas had a better life with his father.

'No,' Grace denied, dragging him back to the present. 'I think it was his attempt to capture the youth he'd never had.'

'Why?'

But Grace was already clamming up, clearly regretting having said anything at all.

'All I can tell you is that Bas was already years ahead of anyone else on the course and had perfect scores in almost everything he did, so any attempts to get him kicked out of uni ultimately failed. The kittens—who were never supposed to have survived—began to thrive. We named them Sonny, and Cooper, and Bas has one whilst I have the other.'

Something clicked suddenly in Rik's head. Something else, pushing its way through the fog that had suddenly dropped in his brain.

'So when you say you're friends with Bas, you don't mean as colleagues.'

'No, I mean as friends.' She wiped her hand over her forehead. 'Good friends. The kind you trust with your life.'

He hesitated. His thoughts might as well have been trying to race through treacle.

'I didn't appreciate that.'

'I know. But I meant it, the other night, when I told you

that if it hadn't been for Bas, I wouldn't be a doctor today. You didn't believe me, but it isn't exaggeration, it's a fact.'

'Then I apologise for that, too,' he told her sincerely. 'Perhaps we could start over. I'm Henrik Magnusson.'

He held his hand out, waiting for her to take it.

'You're lying, even now,' she cried instead, heading for the door and yanking it back open again. 'You're not Magnusson at all, are you? You're Jansen. Henrik *Jansen*.'

And what did it say that he wanted, so badly, to defend himself on that score, at least?

'As far as my name goes, I didn't lie to you,' he heard himself saying. 'The reason I didn't introduce myself as Henrik Jansen was because, up until a few months ago, I didn't even know that was my father's real name. I was brought up as Henrik Magnusson.'

'But, what about Bas?'

'He was called Bas Magnusson, whether he remembers it now, or not,' Rik told her firmly. 'At first, I didn't mention Bas being my brother because I wanted to speak with him before I told anyone else who I was. It was the only reason I was at the gala that night.'

'Even when I told you that he and I were friends?'

'I'd heard enough about his playboy reputation already. How could I have known that you were genuinely so close?'

'Yet you pursued me. Why? Because you thought I was your way to your brother? How selfish do you have to be to do that, Rik?'

'It wasn't like that.'

He kept his hand out. But although Grace stared at it for an inordinately long time, she didn't take it.

Instead, at last, she shook her head.

'I can't. I won't. Bas and I will always be there for each other, because I owe him that much. And because he is my friend.'

'Just as he's my brother.'

'No. No, he isn't,' she gritted out, feeding that dark, icy thing that had squatted inside him for as long as he could remember. 'Because you…don't exist to him. Not after what you did.'

The words slammed into Rik.

Everything he'd been beginning to fear was being all wrapped up in one.

Did his brother genuinely believe that he had been the victim, even though he'd been the one to escape? How could Bas hate him so much that he pretended not to even have a brother?

It made no sense, but, more than that, it made Rik feel a hurt and a vulnerability that he'd refused to feel for decades. A weakness that he'd learned to stuff down the day that his brother had been taken from him.

He'd thought he'd ripped down his heart a long time ago. Thought he'd buried it in the deepest, darkest black hole where it could never be found. Because that way no one could ever hurt him again.

But hearing what his brother—his beloved, morally upright brother, who he'd idolised his entire life—had said about him, Rik felt an overwhelming urge to lean on the wall behind him, and just let his legs go until he slid down it to the floor.

The way he'd done as a kid—just once—before his brother had hauled him to his feet and made him swear that he'd never, *never* let their mother, or anyone, make him feel as if he was nothing, ever again.

Instead, Rik stood his ground. Because weakness wasn't even in his vocabulary any more.

'You don't exist to Bas,' Grace was saying, and he didn't know if it was her gritted teeth, or the tumult in his own head, that was muffling her words. 'So, you don't exist to me. Now please, leave.'

And even though a thousand things cluttered up his brain,

and his chest, they were woven so tightly that he couldn't unpick them. He didn't even know where to begin.

So Rik did the only thing he could do—he left.

CHAPTER EIGHT

'LET'S PREP THE patient for CT, and get a good set of images for me,' Rik instructed, as he left the resus bay to contact another senior plastic surgeon who he knew was on call. 'I'm going to need them to work out whether there are any bones left in there, and what I can work with. And book an OR, please.'

'Do you really think you can save anything of the patient's hand?' A resident caught him as he left the area, making sure they were both out of earshot of the patient or his screaming family. 'There's nothing there. I've seen patients with injuries not even as severe as this that surgeons have deemed unsalvageable.'

'And for them, that may be true,' Rik answered without pomp. 'It certainly looks bad, but I believe I can give him something of a hand.'

Though it would be no mean feat. One look at the man's extremity had shown that it had been almost severed in two places and was only still attached thanks to the faintest sliver of skin and bone. If he were to stand any chance of saving his patient's hand, he was going to have to start as quickly as possible, before everything turned necrotic.

Establishing good blood and nerve supply to the fingers would be vital. And he'd sewn hands and feet, even ears and nose, to groins before now, in an attempt to save dying body parts.

He tried his colleague a few times, but there was no answer. He would have to put in a call to the Jansen wing and see if anyone from Plastics was on call up there.

Hopefully not his father or brother.

Shoving the phone into his pocket, Rik strode quickly

back to the resus bay, in time to hear his brother speaking to the ward sister, just his side of the curtain.

'Book an OR.'

It seemed that someone had already contacted the Jansen wing, and that fate had decided to play a prank on him. But there was no time to take it personally. His patient was depending on him to do everything in his power to save the remnants of his hand.

With a steadying breath, Rik stepped forward, his voice calm. Controlled.

'It's booked.'

His brother froze, then turned slowly.

And Rik felt as though everything had stopped.

He'd spent years—decades—imagining this moment. But now that it was here, it felt surreal.

The eyes were the same colour that he remembered, but the expression in them was nothing like the love and care his brother used to have for him.

'Henrik,' his brother bit out icily. 'What the hell are you doing here?'

Rik opened his mouth to speak, but realised that all the questions charging around his head were in Swedish. He couldn't seem to remember a word of English.

'It is the Jansen exchange programme,' he began. 'I have been writing to you three times.'

His brother worked his jaw a few times. The look of hostility in his regard every bit as harsh as before.

'I am aware. It landed me with the task of having to throw them in the trash where they belong,' he clipped out, making Rik wince. Though not through any weakness, but more because it was heartbreaking to hear the bitterness in his brother's voice. 'My mistake—what I really meant to say was, get away from my case.'

'The way I am to keep away from Grace?' Rik asked

softly, though his brother would have to be an idiot to miss the steely core of his tone.

Bas eyeballed him.

'Grace is a grown woman. She makes her own decisions. And I never told her to stay away from you.'

'No,' Rik agreed easily enough. 'You merely told her that I have targeted her because I knew you two were friends.'

'I can't imagine Grace told you that.' Bas narrowed his eyes, though he didn't deny it.

Rik hadn't expected that he would. His brother had never been a liar.

'Of course not,' Rik replied. 'She is loyal to you. But she asked me, and I knew it had come from you.'

'Perhaps so. But it wasn't a lie, was it?'

There were so many things that Rik wanted to say to that. But instead, he had to content himself with sticking to the basic facts. And not only because they didn't have much time to talk whilst their patient was on his way to CT.

'I went to that medical ball to talk to you, Basilius. I did not know who Grace was when I first spoke to her that night.'

Bas eyed him shrewdly, but Rik had no intention of backing down.

'But you knew who she was when you slept with her. Didn't you?'

Rik didn't answer—he didn't believe his brother's question dignified one. But he certainly didn't expect Bas to take that as confirmation.

'As I thought,' Bas spat out, disgusted, and a sudden anger shot through Rik.

'What is Grace to you, Basilius? Do you love her?'

Bas stopped, taken aback.

'Grace is a friend,' he rasped. 'Nothing more. Has she not told you that?'

Rik eyed him in frank assessment.

'That's exactly what she told me. But I'm not a fool,

brother. I know you sent her to watch me. What is your saying? *Keep your enemies close?*'

'Something like that,' Bas murmured.

'So, I shall ask you again, do you care for her, Basilius? Because I think I might, and I am willing to fight for her.'

He wasn't sure which of them was more shocked at the unexpected declaration, and when his brother didn't respond, for a moment, Rik thought Bas had actually listened to what he was saying.

But then a sneer curled his brother's upper lip, like a scalpel to Rik's chest.

'You're not capable of fighting for her. Or anyone.' Bas snorted, making no attempt to conceal his disdain. 'You don't know what love is, Henrik. Neither of us do. The only thing we know is that sick, twisted version of love that we learned from *them.*'

And Rik didn't care what his brother said about their mother, or the man she'd passed off as their father for years. Instead, what scraped at Rik the most was that his brother— the one person in the world who had always had his back as a kid—no longer believed in him. Not at all.

A kind of sadness settled down on Rik, like a heavy, wet, woollen cloak worn in a lightning storm. It offered no solace. Only a depressing weight.

'Is that what you really believe?' he demanded quietly.

'It's what I know.' Bas glowered. 'She might have favoured you, but it didn't make her idea of love any less dangerous. There were always strings attached to her affection.'

'And what about Mrs P? And Bertie?' Rik shook his head, unable to accept that his brother was dismissing them so easily. So heartlessly. 'Were there always strings attached to their love? Or have you forgotten them, Basilius?'

Surely his brother couldn't have buried all the memories of the sweet, kindly Mrs P. The cook who had lived down the road from them, up until they were about seven. Could

Bas really have forgotten how Mrs P, and her husband, Bertie, who had worked in the mechanics garage nearby, had treated the two young boys like the children they'd never had?

With kindness. And care. And *love*.

They'd been the stable family that he and Bas had never had. Until their own mother had grown jealous and reacted with her predictable volatility.

'They deserted us,' Bas bit out, and it took Rik a moment to realise that his brother was talking about Mrs P. About Bertie.

And from the bleak expression in his eyes, Bas genuinely thought he knew what he was saying was the truth.

'They didn't leave,' Rik told him softly. 'We left. We went from that suburban house to that flat in the city. Don't you remember?'

His brother shook his head tersely. But there was something in the turn of his face that made Rik think his memory might be beginning to kick back into action.

'Mother was always so jealous of them,' he prompted his brother. 'The way we always used to go to them first for things. Don't you recall running into their kitchen on the way home from school and they'd be waiting to hear about our day, with milk and home-baked fairy cakes? Sometimes, we got to decorate them.'

Bas blinked and, to Rik's shock, he thought he saw tears in his brother's eyes. But then Bas blinked again and they were gone. An unyielding expression taking over his features as he folded his arms over his chest and forced his head up.

It almost made Rik despair. *Almost.*

'Is that why you called me for a consultation on this patient?'

Bas's voice was cold again. Deliberate. But it didn't quite disguise the emotions that Rik suspected lurked beneath the surface.

'I did not call for a consultation,' he denied.

'I was paged.'

'I called for another surgeon.' Rik shrugged. 'I could not have known that would be you. It is an urgent case.' Which was certainly the truth.

It was clear that Bas didn't believe him, but they both knew they couldn't afford to dwell any longer. There wasn't time. There was a patient who needed urgent care and, like it or not, he now had no choice but to work with his brother to save the patient's hand.

'Fine,' Bas growled at length. 'Run me through it.'

It wasn't exactly the breakthrough that Rik had hoped for, but at least it was a start. Swiping his screen to his case notes, Rik passed the tablet over.

'Preliminary tests have been run, and a CT. The sooner I operate the better, but it's likely to run late into the night. Two surgeons working together will make it a faster surgery for the patient. Less time under anaesthetic means less stress on the patient.'

It was the most rational, efficient solution. An operation as this would be likely to be could run to ten, twelve, even fifteen hours. Two surgeons would mean that one surgeon could be harvesting grafts from lower limbs whilst the other worked on the hand. Plus, the less time the patient was under anaesthesia, the better for them.

But he could still see his brother trying to weigh up the pros and cons. Trying to avoid doing the surgery with him, and no doubt trying to find a way that might allow him to take control of it for himself.

There was one thing working at Thorncroft, and the Jansen wing, had revealed about both Magnus and Bas, and that was their inability to share cases.

'I've seen cases like this before, but this is probably one of the worst cases I've seen,' Bas stated in a clipped tone, which was nonetheless too quiet to be heard by the patient, or his family. 'I suggest you pass this case to me to take lead. I can bring in a surgeon on my team to assist.'

Rik watched him, but opted not to speak. Not until he knew exactly what plan his brother was hatching. As sad as that was.

So much for them having worked together. It wasn't supposed to have been this way.

'If you don't feel able to assist me...' Rik lowered his voice without losing any of his own self-control '...then by all means send another member of your team. However, I have completed several of these procedures in the past. The last case I worked on involved cutting a flap of skin from the groin to embed my patient's hand, to allow the skin to grow and provide new covering.'

Bas stiffened and, with a jolt, Rik realised that his brother agreed with him. He just didn't want to admit it out loud.

'You've harvested veins and nerve grafts from the foot and forearm, to reconstruct the hand?'

'And joined tendons and arteries, yes,' Rik confirmed neutrally. 'As I know you have. So it is up to you to choose whether to work with me on this patient, or not. But right now, I really need to get him into surgery. The sooner I can re-establish blood supply, the better his recovery is likely to be. Are you joining me, or sending someone else?'

It galled Bas that he was right—that much was obvious. Evidently, Bas wasn't accustomed to playing second surgeon to another plastics guy. But then, neither was he. And this was his patient, not Bas's. Personal feelings aside, there was no way the surgeon in him could give that up.

'I've worked on these microsurgical repairs many times before,' Bas stated. 'It's quite draining. You'll need to be good.'

'As will you.'

They met each other's gazes and Rik wondered how pathetic it was that neither of them wanted to be the first one to blink. He wasn't much surprised when his brother took another high-handed tone.

'You have to be realistic about his prognosis. This will never be a normal hand, but, with time and effort, physio can help him regain strength.'

'I made his family clear that even holding a pen will be good progress,' Rik agreed, refusing to rise to the bait. 'He'll need multiple surgeries over the next few months, even years.'

'In time perhaps we can go for a power grip.'

It took Rik a supreme effort not to grin. Despite everything, Bas was echoing exactly the same thought that he himself had entertained.

And if they were in agreement, then it would make working together on the case that much easier.

'In time,' Rik agreed carefully. 'Either way, I must take him in and begin now. I need a decision, Basilius. Can you work with me? Or no?'

Bas paused for one fraction of a moment longer before dipping his head in tacit acquiescence. Then, with a signal from himself to the rest of the team, the bay once again became a flurry of activity as they prepped to bring the patient up to Theatre.

They had hours of surgery ahead of them, and, for the first time in a while, Rik found himself actively looking forward to it.

Slowly, methodically, they began, until at last, fourteen hours later, they found themselves peeling off their gowns and gloves, after a successful operation.

'Good surgery,' his brother muttered grudgingly to him, rolling up his gown and gloves and hurling them into the medical waste bin.

Before Rik—still finishing up his debriefing—could reply, he'd marched through the doors of the surgical suite to scrub out.

By the time Rik joined him in the scrubbing out, Bas was already nearly done.

'Very good,' Rik agreed, nonetheless. 'Would you care to join me in telling the family?'

Bas hesitated, and Rik couldn't be sure what he'd been about to say before his mobile interrupted him. And then he was taking the call and hurrying out of the room without even looking twice.

But it didn't matter. Not really. Because Rik's mind was back to Grace.

Shoving thoughts of Rik from her mind during the daytime was one thing, Grace decided as she hurried through the doors into the resus department and ducked past yet another pair of colleagues who were gossiping about the 'hot new Swedish exchange surgeon'. But trying not think about him at night time was another thing entirely.

Especially after their confrontation at her apartment the other night meant that she'd abjectly failed in her promise to stay close to him and find out what he was really doing at Thorncroft.

No matter how vigilant she had been during the day, he always invaded her dreams at night, inviting her to relive every perfect moment of their forty-eight hours together. And every morning she woke up disconcerted and hot, and feeling as though she'd done anything but enjoy a restful night in her own bed—*alone*.

She was grateful for her work and the welcome distraction it provided for her errant thoughts—if only temporarily. And she felt guilty that she was even grateful for emergencies like this, which engaged her brain more fully.

Searching for the doctor running the shout—the one who had paged her five minutes earlier—Grace made her way quickly across the room.

'You paged Obstetrics?'

The resus doctor turned to her—Alison, a woman Grace knew quite well.

'Hey, Grace. Janine is a twenty-four-year-old in her third trimester, primigravida, brought in with absent foetal sounds, meconium-stained liquor, and non-progressive labour.'

'Okay, but she should have been brought straight to the women and children's wing.'

'Agreed, but she was brought in by ambulance, having already been brought in last night following a low-impact RTA. Patient was in a stationary vehicle in a car park when another vehicle reversed slowly into them. No apparent injuries sustained, however the patient became distressed that it was her father's car. Foetal scans show the baby was in no distress, and she was discharged without need for further treatment.'

'Right.' Grace nodded. 'If there's nothing else, I'll take her through to the labour ward now.'

Most likely the woman would need a caesarean section.

'One thing.' Alison beckoned her over, lowering her voice. 'The patient has significant childhood post-burn contracture of abdomen, which I suspect would complicate any C-section.'

'Ah.' Grace absorbed the new information. 'Is she comfortable with me taking a look here?'

'So-so.'

'Understood.'

Stepping forward, Grace smiled at her patient.

'Hello, Janine, I'm Grace. I'm an obstetrician. You're in good hands with my colleagues here, but, if they step out, do you mind if I just take a look at your abdomen?'

The patient glanced at the other medical staff and offered a terse nod, and Grace waited until it was only her and Alison before lifting the gown to inspect the area. For additional discretion, she positioned herself between the curtain and her patient, which seemed to help to gain the young woman's trust.

Alison was right, the childhood burns had clearly been quite severe.

'The contracture of the abdomen is visibly tight,' Grace murmured as casually as she could. 'Can I have a little feel for baby?'

Again, her patient nodded, and Grace began a quick examination.

'Does any of this hurt?'

'No.' The young woman shook her head. 'Is my son going to be okay?'

'You know the sex?' Grace checked, her smile in place.

It was the ideal way to keep the mother distracted and as relaxed as possible whilst she carried out an ultrasound and checked for the heartbeat.

'Yeah, I wanted to know as soon as possible.' The young woman half laughed, half sobbed. 'I picked out names and everything. Please look after my baby.'

'You and baby are in the best place for us to help you,' Grace replied, as upbeat as possible, without making promises she might not be able to keep.

Her examination completed, she carefully lowered the gown and stepped back to Alison, her bright smile in place until they'd let the rest of the team back in and they'd rounded the curtain.

'There is a foetal heartbeat, but he's clearly in distress. I need to deliver the baby now. I'm guessing you contacted Plastics?'

'I did,' Alison confirmed. 'In fact, he's just coming over now.'

But Grace didn't need to turn around to know it was Rik. Of course it was, because who else would it be?

Every fibre of her body screamed it to her, from the fine hairs on the back of her neck to the way her stomach dipped and soared.

But no matter how they'd left things, and no matter what

they'd last said to each other, Grace knew that here, in this scenario, Rik would be nothing but professional.

They both would be.

'Dr Henley. Grace,' he greeted her on cue, before turning to introduce himself to Alison. 'Rik Magnusson.'

'Yes, I've seen you around this week, it's nice to finally meet you. I'm Alison.'

There was nothing remotely unprofessional about her colleague's reaction, but Grace knew her well enough to notice that her smile was a little more...dazzling than usual.

A little flirty.

Grace's chest tightened, though it had no right to do so. Not since the last thing she'd said to Rik had been that he didn't exist to her.

Words that she'd wished a hundred times that she could take back.

But that wasn't possible—because it wasn't just about her. It was about her loyalty to her friend—to Rik's brother. Something that should be perfectly easy to remember.

So why wasn't it?

So instead, she forced herself to be patient whilst Alison caught Rik up with the case, and he then performed his own examination. Several minutes later, they were all back outside the cubicle.

'You saw that the post-burn scarring extends over the abdomen and down to the mons region, with some deformity of the lower area?' Grace asked him quietly, grateful for his unerring professionalism as he turned to look at her.

'I did.'

'Given the foetal heart sounds and the fact that he's in distress, I'd like to perform an emergency caesarean—ideally right now—but I realise any incision might not be easy to close.'

'I agree.' Rik drew in a thoughtful breath. 'Contracture is severe and so reconstruction may be necessary, but if you need to do a C-section now, I can make that happen.'

'You're confident?' Grace asked.

'Yes.' He didn't hesitate. 'I'll run you through the ideal incisions, most likely an inverted T-shape which can extend horizontally as far as the contracture vertically to the mons area. Depending on what we encounter, the rest of the C-section might be able to be completed in the usual way.'

'And if it can?'

'Then the uterus will be repaired and the anterior abdominal wall closed as usual, and then I can re-contour and re-shape depending on the extent of the displacement.'

'It's that easy?' Grace was impressed, despite herself.

Though she pretended that she didn't feel a thrill of anticipation at the idea of having to work alongside him.

As if even that little contact could help to quench this interminable thirst she'd felt, ever since the night he'd left her apartment.

As if a part of her wished she'd complied with Bas's request for her to keep Rik close. But Rik wasn't her enemy—he was Bas's. And she couldn't help but wonder if he was even that.

'It is possible I need to harvest some skin grafts from her thighs.' Rik's voice tugged her back to reality. 'I could also resurface some other areas of her abdomen to reduce the scarring for her.'

'Okay.' She nodded. 'Let's get our patient to Theatre and see if we can't deliver this baby successfully.'

And she wished that traitorous part of her weren't actually looking forward to going into the surgery side by side with this particular man.

CHAPTER NINE

'NICE JOB,' RIK complimented her as he and Grace removed their gloves and gowns and deposited them into the bin, before moving to scrub out.

The baby had been delivered a while ago—remarkably strong and healthy, all things given, and Grace had handed the newborn boy to one of her colleagues to take to the PICU and stayed to assist him with the closure.

Logically, he knew it was because any surgeon would be a fool to pass up such a learning opportunity—the observation room above them was full of residents all eager to fill the vacancy if Grace had vacated it—but there was still a part of him that wanted to believe she'd also stayed because it was him.

Since when had he ever let his ego rule him like this? And yet something sloshed inside him.

'That was…stunning,' Grace qualified.

He wondered what she'd been about to say before she'd caught herself. Surely her words shouldn't heat him in this way? Like the sun permeating his skin and warming up his bones?

'About the other night—'

'I think we should forget it happened,' Rik interrupted quickly. 'Move on, as you say in England.'

'Move on?' She hesitated.

'Or perhaps, start over.'

Grace cast him an indecipherable look.

'I think I'd like that,' she agreed, after a moment.

They both fell silent, and for a moment Rik wondered what to say.

'I can see now why you were selected for the Jansen programme,' Grace burst out awkwardly. 'You're honestly…a great surgeon.'

He grimaced, reading between the lines.

'After everything you told me about Magnus refusing to help Bas become a surgeon, did you believe that he'd given me a place on the programme merely because I'm his other long-lost son?'

She wrinkled her nose, and he wondered if she had any idea how much that quirk made him ache to reach out and smooth the puckered skin.

'I guess not,' she conceded. 'But I couldn't help but wonder.'

With anyone else, he probably wouldn't have cared. But with her, he felt the oddest need to defend himself.

'He did not,' stated Rik simply. 'In truth, I don't even know if he's aware that I'm here. Presumably, he doesn't even read the applicants' files. He must have a team who do all of that for him, as well as make the decision.'

And, if he did know, the man had certainly made no attempt to make contact.

'He knows,' Grace told him. 'No one gets onto any of the three nationwide Jansen Suites without his knowledge. It's his magnum opus, he watches everything that happens.'

'So, then, he has chosen not to bother with me,' Rik noted as Grace bit her lip wryly.

'I'm sorry, I shouldn't—'

'Don't be sorry,' he cut in easily. Truthfully. 'It makes no difference to me. It was Bas I came here to speak with. Not a man I never met.'

'Still…'

'Bas and I were close, and he was the brother that I lost. Magnus was the father I never had to begin with. When my brother was first sent to him, I think I might have harboured some childish hope that he might seek me out. But he didn't.

I came to terms, a long time ago, with the fact that he never wanted to know me.'

'His loss,' Grace whispered. Though Rik didn't think she'd intended to.

And suddenly, despite everything he'd said, he felt her empathy slide inside him like a comforting blanket for his bruised soul.

He shut it down quickly. Hating the fact she'd found another chink of weakness in him.

'If it's all the same to you, I'd prefer to reserve this conversation for my brother.'

If Bas ever stopped avoiding him.

'Rik...the things you said, about not even knowing what your real name is...?'

'It is not a conversation we will continue, *älskling*,' he told her firmly. 'That is a conversation between my brother and me.'

'I understand, but Bas believes—'

'You will not be caught in the middle of us,' he cut her off.

If he couldn't do anything else for her, he could do that much. Though he didn't care to examine why it was so important to him.

Neither of them spoke for several minutes. And then, at last, Grace straightened up from the sink.

'There's a fete...a festival. The hospital runs it every year and Bas and I usually help out. This year, he can't.'

'Can't? Or won't?'

'*Can't*,' she emphasised.

'Why not?'

'It's a long story, and not mine to tell.' She bit her lip, and he couldn't explain why he actually believed her. 'Suffice to say that there's an empty slot if you want to help.'

Despite their improved conversation, the offer wasn't what he'd expected.

He folded his arms over his chest, liking the way her

eyes were dragged to the movement, and her nostrils flared slightly. Maybe he liked it too much.

It told him the things that she wasn't saying.

'Is this your idea of an apology?'

'Something like that,' she muttered, as if she was making the admission with difficulty. And he liked that, too. 'Forget it, I shouldn't have asked.'

And that *need* still sloshed around inside him. It was rather too telling that his brother's absence didn't deter him from agreeing to help—just so long as Grace was there.

'If you hadn't asked, I couldn't have agreed.'

She blinked and peered closer at him.

'You'll do it?'

'Maybe.' Rik shot her a rueful grin.

'You understand Bas won't be there? It isn't an opportunity to meet your brother and talk to him.'

'You made that perfectly clear.' He dipped his head. 'But there's more than one way to get to know a person. The friends he chooses to keep can sometimes reveal a lot more about someone than anything anyone says about them.'

Grace's breath caught, and the impact was like a hot lick along his very sex.

'You mean me.'

'I do,' he murmured. 'People claim he's a rampant playboy, bouncing from one woman to the next and never ready to settle. But the fact that he has chosen you as his friend—the person I think he confides in—tells me a whole other story.'

'Is that right?' Her voice was deliciously husky. As if she was fighting back sinful thoughts.

Or was it more what he was doing?

'It is indeed.'

He was teetering so close to the edge of the rabbit hole here, where he wanted to simply sweep her up and throw her over his shoulder—caveman style—and carry her back to his private cave. Or, in his case, luxury hotel suite.

He might have had his fair share of partners in his life, but none of them had ever got under his skin the way that Grace had.

He needed to try to get the conversation back to a more level footing.

'So...' He paused. 'What exactly does this festival helping out entail?'

She blinked at him, her dark pupils taking a moment to adjust. He understood what she was feeling all too well.

She coughed briefly, to clear her throat. To regroup.

'Okay, so you'd be repairing some old booths, reviving others, and then manning a couple of stalls on festival week.'

'Bas repairs booths? Himself? He doesn't pay someone?'

'It's for charity, so everything we can do for free puts more money into the hands of those who need it.' Grace smiled at some memory that didn't include him, and he hated that his gut clenched so tightly.

'You've been doing this for a few years, then?' He forced himself to sound casual.

'Yeah, near enough ten years.' She sounded proud. 'Bas is quite the handyman when he wants to be, but don't worry if you're not so good. I can repair whilst you paint.'

She was teasing him, Rik realised. Tentatively, but teasing nonetheless. He found he rather liked it.

'I built my own house back in Sweden—I think I can help repair a few booths.'

'You built your own house?' Grace exclaimed.

He thought about the simple house, set in such a gloriously quiet location.

'It's more of a log cabin really, right in the Tyresta National Forest. It's a place to go if I want to escape modern life. No internet, no TV, limited mod cons.'

'It sounds isolating.' She didn't sound keen.

He didn't realise he'd moved until his hand reached out to brush a stray hair off her cheek.

'You make it sound like a bad thing,' he pointed out quietly. 'Are you that much of a city girl?'

'Through and through.' She nodded, though it didn't escape him how her breath caught. 'I make no apologies.'

'Where did you live before Thorncroft?' he asked abruptly. Not sure why.

Still, he wasn't surprised when that shuttered look slammed down over her features.

'Here and there.'

It shouldn't needle him so much that Grace was so guarded with him. Yet it did. Somehow, he fought his way to easing the tone again.

'So—' he made himself sound cheerful '—you build and repair stalls for a charity fete?'

She raised one shoulder.

'I like the idea of giving back a little. And it's always for good causes.'

'And it's a tradition you do with my brother?'

'It is,' she affirmed. 'Does that surprise you?'

Rik didn't know why he thought about the question. He didn't need to.

'No. It doesn't,' he conceded after a few seconds.

How many times had he and his brother stopped to help someone after school? Whether it was collecting their prescriptions or running to the local shop for a bottle of milk, Bas had always been keen on helping people.

Why would he have grown up any different?

'I have a free day at the weekend,' she told him. 'How about then?'

He thought of his schedule, and his determination that this would be the weekend he finally made his brother talk to him.

Then he thought about spending the day with Grace.

And he told himself that it wasn't about spending time with Grace, so much as getting to know the person who seemed to know his brother best.

He wasn't sure he believed it.

'Okay.' He dipped his head in agreement. 'A day at the weekend seems fine.'

'You don't need to flannel me, Doc, I can take it.' The old man was clearly choking back tears as he stared through the glass of the isolation room to where his son lay.

Rik looked through the glass, too. He didn't need to see the clock on the wall to know that he was late for his painting date with Grace; he already knew that. But his patients came first—they always did.

But he figured she would understand. The more he worked with her, or people who had known her a while, the clearer picture he got of her.

She was quiet—not the kind to normally go having one-night stands—which shouldn't have made him feel as punch-drunk as it did. She was loyal to a fault, though, according to everyone, that loyalty was primary reserved for his brother. And she was committed to her job.

It just made him like her more. And though that should set alarms bells off in his head, Rik didn't hear a single warning sound.

'It isn't flannel,' Rik replied gently.

The old man made an odd *tsk*ing sound.

'I was a firefighter myself, and I've seen plenty of my guys with third-degree burns as extensive as this. I know the odds are against my kid.'

'Then you'll also know that medicine is improving year on year,' Rik continued. 'I deal with burns every day, and the study that I'm working on at the moment is showing a reduced mortality in full thickness or third-degree burns, from around forty-five per cent down to eight per cent when excise and grafting are carried out within the first three days of the initial injury.'

Slowly, the man twisted to look at Rik.

'You're talking about improving his survival odds from fifty-fifty to over ninety per cent?'

'If they're good surgical candidates, yes,' Rik confirmed. 'Your son is a good surgical candidate.'

For a long while, the man just stared through the window.

'He's all I've got,' he whispered, more to himself than to Rik.

Another moment of silence ticked by and then the man turned to him again.

'So what are the options?'

'There are two types of graft used to cover the wound bed,' Rik told him carefully. 'Skin replacement and skin substitute. The first is when we harvest healthy skin from the patient themselves, while the second—skin substitute—is a mixture of cells or tissues and includes biomaterial and engineered tissue.'

'You're talking about skin substitute for my son, then?' the older man said slowly. 'Looking at the extent of his burns, he doesn't have enough healthy skin for you to harvest for a graft.'

'Which is why I am recommending a split-thickness skin-graft approach. It only takes the epidermis and upper layer of dermis, and it means the same donor sites can be harvested after one or two weeks.'

'That still won't give you enough, though,' the old fire-fighter noted grimly. 'Will it?'

'Not as it is,' Rik agreed.

'Then…what?'

It was always a fine line, deciding how much of the finite detail of the procedure that his patients and their families needed to know. With a parent like this, who had no doubt seen more than his fair share of horrific injuries, and deaths, it was clear that the more information he could give, the better.

'Then we have a further option known as meshing graft.

This is where we cut slits into the skin graft to enable it to stretch over more surface area. Sometimes as much as four times greater. A further benefit to this is that meshing can prevent seroma and haematoma formation beneath the graft. However, this method can result in significant scarring, tissue-tightening at the site, and an increased risk of infection.'

'But my boy could survive,' the man whispered.

'There is a greater chance, yes.'

There was another long silence as both men observed the young lad lying in the bed beyond the glass. Until the older man shook his head as though trying to free his thoughts.

'And what about the skin substitute? The engineered tissue?'

'The substitutes I'm looking at are biosynthetic products—skin regeneration templates that we can use to build a sort of scaffolding for the new skin. It will give a temporary wound coverage, which we would then have to remove before skin grafting.'

He was also considering an amniotic membrane graft as a short-term dressing. In any main hospitals, the cost of virus testing made it a prohibitive option. But wasn't that the beauty of being backed by someone like the Jansen Centre, with its almost unlimited resources.

The biggest potential hurdle he faced as a temporary member of the Jansen surgical team, however, was having to go to either Magnus or Bas for ultimate approval.

'And this will work?' the old man demanded suddenly. 'Really work?'

He was looking for assurance. A guarantee. Rik couldn't blame him—after all, it was his only son. But he had to be honest.

'As with anything, there is no one hundred per cent guarantee,' he said gently. 'And even if the skin grafts work, there will be a trade-off with cosmetic and functional outcomes.

Burn scars can cause depression, pain, decreased range of motion, among others.'

'But he'll be alive, which is more than many of the guys I've worked with are.'

'Then I'll leave you to think,' Rik confirmed. 'In the meantime, my team will continue debriding the wound. He *is* in good hands.'

'And if I have more questions?'

'Then you can speak to anyone here, day or night,' Rik assured him. And that was the beauty of the Jansen Centre—there was always a liaison staff available, any time, to talk to the patient's family, and allay their fears, or to find someone who could. 'And either I or another member of my team will talk you through everything you need to know.'

With the final, discreet nod to the nurse at the station behind them, Rik headed out of the unit.

He was late.

He wasn't supposed to be working, he'd only called in to check on his patients before heading out to meet Grace for this stall-painting business. But seeing the man standing there like that, the old firefighter side of him warring with the grieving father side, he'd known he couldn't walk away. Not without talking to the man.

But he suspected that, of all people, Grace would fully understand that.

'You're late,' Grace observed casually as he walked through the door where they'd agreed to meet. 'I was beginning to think you'd changed your mind.'

He wondered if the idea had dismayed her at all. From her upbeat demeanour, one might have thought not. But there had been a moment there, when he'd first walked in, when he thought her eyes might have lit up. Just a little bit.

'I wanted to check on a couple of my patients and I ran into their family member, who needed answers,' he explained, pulling off his jacket and grabbing a paintbrush.

'Ah,' Grace acknowledged simply. As if it didn't matter either way. 'Anyway, take your pick. You said you were good with a saw.'

'Right.'

Rik suppressed a wry grin and glanced around the room obligingly. Huge pieces of wood and plastic, in various states of repair, were propped against the warehouse walls, whilst several eight-foot panels glistened already with fresh coats of paint.

Grace had clearly been busy.

'So, what's the plan?'

She cast him a long look, clearly expecting more comment. He merely waited patiently.

'See that panel over to your right? The next one. Yes, that one. Can you start repairing it? Materials are on the other side of that wall.'

Away from her. He couldn't help but wonder if that was deliberate. Was she trying to keep some distance between them?

'Wouldn't it be easier if they were on hand around here? There's plenty of room.'

'There is now, yes.' The sober, serious look she assumed almost made him grin. 'But in a few weeks there'll be more of us here, things get cramped and the sawdust gets into the paint if we don't separate it all.'

He wasn't sure he liked the idea of more people in this space. He preferred the idea of being alone with Grace.

So much for telling himself that he was doing all this to get to better know the friend of his long-lost sibling, and not because he harboured any secret desire to actually get to know her better.

'Understood,' he replied impassively.

And she found she hated this closed-off side of Rik. The one where he kept her at arm's length. It made her think that he was more like his brother than either of them would care to admit.

'So, tell me about this cabin that you built,' she asked at last, hoping to draw him out.

To get back to the Rik who had made her feel...so feminine.

'What would you like to know?' he asked. His tone still deliberately even.

'Whatever you want to tell me.'

But he locked his jaw and looked distinctly underwhelmed.

'I can tell you that it isn't like this bright city. Though the hospital where I work is. Clearly not your scene.'

And she found herself bristling before she could stop herself.

'Maybe not so much my scene,' she bit out without meaning to. 'I was thinking about leaving this place anyway.'

She could pretend that she knew what she was doing, and that she'd dropped a crumb in order to get him to open up, too. But Grace didn't think that was what had happened.

She rather feared that she'd told him because she'd wanted him to know her better. Because she'd hoped he would understand.

'Leaving to go where?' he demanded, and some small victory shot through her that he looked so intent.

'Anywhere,' she answered truthfully. 'Everywhere.'

Because, before she'd felt compelled to return to Thorncroft, her childhood dream had been to travel. She'd spent half her formative years studying the books her parents had pushed her way, and half her time scouring geography books and planet guides, dreaming of the places she would visit when she was older.

And she didn't think she'd visited a single one of them.

'What about ties?' Rik asked curiously. 'Family, I mean.'

The question shouldn't scrape at her as it did. Grace forced another smile.

'Not really.'

He eyed her with interest.

'Sorry for your loss.'

But the way his regard caught hers made her feel more exposed than ever.

'They aren't dead,' she told him quietly. 'They're just… distant.'

He didn't answer, and she found herself talking some more. If only to fill the silence. Or that was what she told herself.

'They must be proud of you.'

'Of course,' she answered automatically.

Though the truth was that they weren't. That nothing had quite made them proud enough to forgive her the way she'd let them down as a teenager.

'So my brother has been the family you never had.'

That was one way of putting it.

'Does that surprise you?' Grace asked.

'Not really. It's more like the brother I remember. Kind. Empathetic. If there was a kid on their own, or getting bullied, Bas was always in there, pulling them into his gang. He would always stand up to the bullies.'

'And what about you?' she asked. 'I'm guessing you were the same.'

Rik laughed suddenly, making her jump.

'We might look similar now, but at six or seven, I weighed three stone wet through. Bas was more like a tank. Where he led, I followed. I might have stood beside him, if half a step back, but I never instigated.'

She frowned.

'I just can't see that. You're so…you. I can't see you standing on the sidelines, too scared to step forward.'

'I never said I was scared.' He flashed a devilish smile. 'But Bas was always the bold one, throwing himself into the fray. Looking before he leapt.'

Yes, she could see that. Rik, the cautious one. Quietly confident to his reactionary brother.

'Anyway, I should do some work.' He effectively shut the conversation down, that easily. And Grace let him.

Because chasing the hurricane that was Rik might be exhilarating, but it was also draining.

CHAPTER TEN

IT DIDN'T TAKE him long to decide the best course of action to effect a repair, and for half an hour he worked on the panel. The radio playing in the background eased the need for conversation, and Rik couldn't help smiling to himself when, after a while, Grace began humming to herself. Then singing.

A few old tracks that made him think of Mrs P, and the way she'd taught him and his brother to jive a little, when they'd been kids. Not that he remembered it now, of course.

But it was the sheer happiness, the freedom in her voice, that conjured up those unexpected memories and made him smile.

He was pretty sure she'd even forgotten he was there.

'You do this every year?'

Grace stopped singing, looking up at him in surprise.

'I do. I mean, I don't do it alone, there's a whole team of us, from the hospital and the wider community. Some of them work the booths on the day, and some paint or repair, and others might do both.'

'There's no one else here now, though,' Rik pointed out.

'You don't say?' Grace laughed. 'Give it an hour or so. It's still early but someone is bound to turn up. They would have had a group working last night when we were on shift.'

'And do you?' he asked curiously. 'Help out on the booths?'

'If I'm not working.' Grace nodded. 'For the last two years, I've worked the water-dunking stand with your brother. I just gather the sponges whilst he sits on the trap door above a glass water tank and people throw the sponges at a target.'

'Bas does?'

'Yep.' She nodded with a grin. 'He wears jeans, no top, and the queue is always incredibly long. It always raises an insane amount of money.'

'I thought he was Thorncroft's playboy surgeon.'

It didn't seem very playboy-like to him. And, from what little he'd heard about their father, he couldn't see Magnus liking it, either.

'It is for charity, after all.' She narrowed her eyes at him. 'You don't have to believe me, but you wanted to know more about your brother, and this is what he likes to do—help people. He also helps set up before the fete, man a booth during, and helps clear up after.'

'I wasn't mocking,' Rik told her.

If anything, it was more like the man he'd spent decades imagining his brother would have turned into. Before the ignored communications, and the Lothario reputation.

But Grace didn't know any of that, and Rik wasn't sure why he chose not to tell her.

'And what about you, *älskling*? What other things do you like to do?'

It was as if he'd asked her the theory of quantum mechanics, rather than make a simple enquiry into her personal life. After one beat seeped into the next, he told her as much.

Slowly, she lowered her paintbrush.

'Work doesn't leave a lot of time for hobbies.'

'You must have some?'

'Of course,' she agreed, but didn't elaborate until the silence between them seemed to demand it. 'I like...going for runs. And reading. Sometimes, I like ice skating when they bring a small rink into the city centre at Christmas time.'

'Is that it?' he challenged, and he didn't know why he was pressing the matter.

Perhaps because a part of him sensed she was keeping something back from him, and it bothered him. Far more than he thought it had a right to.

'As I said, I don't really have time for hobbies.' She winced.

'Not even dancing?' he demanded, deliberately lightening his tone as he strode across the room and cranked the music up.

'What are you doing?' She clutched her paintbrush tighter.

'The night of the gala you clearly knew how to dance. Just ballroom, or do you know a little jive?'

'Why?'

'Such suspicion.' He grinned. 'Though I note you aren't denying it.'

'Because I don't see what dancing has to do with painting these booths.'

'It doesn't,' agreed Rik. 'But when my brother and I were kids, we had a cook for a while. And she taught us how to jive, and lindy hop.'

'How…nice.' Grace wrinkled her nose. But that quirk of her lips gave her away.

'I rather think I'd like to try again now,' he told her.

'You're asking me to dance?'

'No. I've forgotten how to do any of it,' Rik confessed. 'I'm asking you to teach me.'

'I don't think—'

'Not a lot,' he cut her off. 'Just a little. Just for a bit of fun.'

She was clearly tempted—though he wondered how he could read her so easily.

'Here?' she asked, eventually.

'Why not? There's plenty of room.' He extended his arms and turned. 'Where better than a vast warehouse?'

'A dance hall?' she asked wryly.

'I don't know any dance halls around here.' He laughed. 'Do you?'

'Only Miss Beverley's. It's where I learned ballet and tap as a kid, before my parents decided that was too frivolous.'

Grace clamped her mouth shut instantly, her cheeks colouring as she realised her mistake. He could have let it go—it was clear she wished she hadn't forgotten herself.

But he couldn't. Some inexplicable desire to understand her better coursed through him.

'When you were a kid?'

'Forget I said anything,' she clipped out, trying to back away but hitting the wall behind them.

Swiftly, he followed, placing his hands on the wall either side of her. Effectively caging her without ever laying a finger on her. Though she could have ducked away, had she really wanted to.

Rik thought it spoke volumes that she didn't.

'You told me you met my brother at university? That you only moved here to Thorncroft to complete you career training?'

'I did…sort of.' Grace sucked in a breath, her eyes glittering with emotions he couldn't read as she stared up at him. 'The truth is, I was born here.'

'In this county?'

'In this city. In Thorncroft Royal Infirmary, to be exact.'

'Then why the big secret? Why pretend you only moved here in your twenties?'

'Because no one knows.' She lifted her shoulders lightly, as if it were no big deal. Her tense body language told a different story. 'We left when I was sixteen. My parents got offered jobs at a university in a different city, so we moved. I always wanted to return.'

'Do you have family here?'

Grace blinked at him for a moment.

'My grandparents are dead, and I was an only child, like my father. My aunt lives in Australia, though she and mother were never really close anyway.'

Which sounded like a denial but, Rik couldn't help but notice, wasn't quite one.

'So when my brother suggested moving to Thorncroft to complete your residencies…?'

'I joined him because it felt like more than just a coincidence that the world-renowned Jansen Suite should be based here. That it was *fate* somehow telling me it was time to return.'

'Why?'

This time, she jerked her chin up and glowered at him.

'It doesn't really matter.'

They both knew that she was lying, but clearly she'd said all she was going to say.

He had to think that it would have to be enough. For now.

'You don't have to talk about it.' Rik pushed off the wall without warning and took a step away.

He didn't think it was his imagination that her hand twitched—as though she'd been going to reach for him.

As though she felt too exposed to be left there alone.

'It's been pleasant so far. I don't want to ruin it by prying into your personal life.'

Except, inexplicably, that was exactly what he wanted to do.

He wanted to know this woman. To understand her. Yet she was supposed to be simply a pleasant diversion from the main business of being here, so it didn't make any sense at all.

'I promise I won't ask anything more. Wait, this is a good track.'

Moving quickly over to increase the volume on the radio, Rik strode back and held his hand back out to her, gratified when she took it with only the briefest hesitation. But the mood had started to lift in the room. Just as he'd intended.

'Okay.' He grinned. 'Let's see how good a teacher you are. Then, if I can hold my own, I might let you take me to a dance.'

'How lovely for me,' Grace remarked dryly. Then laughed, as though in spite of herself.

The sweet sound glided over him like a silken hand—just as it had that first night together. He'd missed that laugh, though he hadn't realised how much until now.

They danced through several good songs, with Rik quite surprised at how quickly Mrs P's lessons came back to him. He lacked the surprisingly easy fluidity of Grace's movements, but he felt pleased that he'd held his own.

Especially because it seemed to have restored some of the effortless banter between the two of them.

But, in many ways, the revelation had raised more questions than it had answered. And he could pretend that getting to know Grace was about getting to know his brother all he liked. The truth was that, with Grace around, it was getting harder and harder to remember why he'd come here in the first place.

'This was more fun than I remembered,' he told her, after the last song finished. 'I think we ought to discuss other potential hobbies that may interest you.'

'Is that so?' Grace asked, grabbing her bottle of water before collapsing onto a stool.

She drank deeply, then offered the bottle to him.

'Thanks.' He took a couple of quick swigs. 'Over dinner tomorrow, I think. Somewhere nice and exclusive. I'll pick you up at seven-thirty.'

And he liked it rather too much that Grace didn't even attempt to object.

Grace stared up at the restaurant frontage and tried not to gawk.

The Cherry Icing was one of the city's finest restaurants. Its waiting list was famously months long.

'We aren't eating here, surely?'

Rik had only invited her out the day before. She was fairly certain that even the Jansen name couldn't have gained entrance that quickly.

'Bad choice?' Rik grinned wryly. 'I was told it's a dining experience not to be missed.'

'Definitely not to be missed. But how did you even manage it?'

'Turns out I operated on the patron's son when I first arrived here. The kid is sous chef here, and he'd had an accident—cycling accident, not kitchen related, I might add. Still, the fear was that he would have to have his hand amputated.'

'How awful.'

'Not to brag—' he grinned '—I managed to not only save it, but restore almost full use.'

'So modest,' she couldn't help but tease him.

Surely it should worry her more, how easy things always seemed to be between them?

'Indeed.' Rik's grin broadened. 'Anyway, my patient's father was so grateful that he made me promise to visit the restaurant while I was in the city, and assured me I could count on a table whenever I wanted it. I called him last night, and he was as good as his word.'

And he'd used his invitation for her. Grace felt ridiculously special.

Taking her arm to escort her in, Rik leaned down to murmur in her ear, his hot breath tickling her neck and sending her pulse spinning off erratically.

'Just promise me one thing.'

Grace flicked her tongue out over her suddenly dry lips. 'What's that?'

'That you'll enjoy the meal, and not just order salad only to push it around the plate.'

She twisted her neck around so fast that it almost stung.

'If I hadn't spent the past five years dreaming of eating here, I think I should take offence at that.'

'Then I apologise.' Rik laughed.

That low, rich sound that always rumbled through her so deliciously, and made her wish that things between them were different.

Wish that they were *more*.

His laugh always made her forget she was supposed to be keeping a close eye on Rik, and then reporting back, when all she really wanted to do was enjoy whatever time she could snatch with this intelligent, caring, sexy-as-hell Viking.

And then, as he removed her coat for her and handed it off, the look of frank appreciation in his gaze made her forget everything all over again.

He leaned into her, his lips brushing the side of her head tantalisingly.

'I also should apologise for not telling you how incredible you look tonight.'

She valiantly tried to supress the delicious shiver that tripped its way over her, but by the curl of lips against her skin, Grace didn't think she'd succeeded.

'Thank you,' she murmured. 'You don't look so bad yourself.'

And then his palm settled on the small of her back as they followed the maître d' through the tables and to their own, and she felt all the more cherished, and sensual. Like the kind of effortlessly sexy woman that no man had ever made her feel like before.

It almost made her feel bereft when they reached their table and sat down—the contact lost. *Almost.* The exquisiteness of the restaurant just about made up for it.

Grace took a few discreet looks around and exhaled softly to herself.

'I've never been here before,' she confessed, running her hand along the impossibly smooth burr oak surface of their table.

'I'm pleasantly surprised,' Rik confessed. 'I thought you might have been here before. Look up.'

Dutifully, she did, gasping at the sight.

'It's one of the earlier examples of Italianate Renaissance architecture.' Rik leaned in once again, his head close to hers so that he could point out the tiny features that she might otherwise have missed. 'Possibly based on some of the work of the architect, Inigo Jones, in London.'

'I never even knew.' She shook her head. 'The reviews I've heard always seem to focus on the food, not the atmosphere.'

'Here, you have both. Jones, like many of the educated men of the sixteenth century, travelled quite extensively, including to places like Rome. It is said he particularly admired the work of the architect Andrea Palladio.'

'How do you know all this?' Grace turned to look at him.

It seemed the more she learned about the man, the more there was to learn. A whole lifetime, perhaps?

The thought startled her.

'It interests me.' He waved a hand almost dismissively. 'Call it a bit of a hobby. But at one time, I did consider becoming an architect.'

'What made you change your mind?' she asked, genuinely curious.

He didn't answer immediately, but peered at her intently. As if trying to decide how much to share. But before he could decide, they were interrupted by their waiter, and the moment was lost.

'So...' Rik reclined in his seat in that casual way of his that seemed to highlight every bit of his masculinity. 'Other than your work, and volunteering to repaint old booths for charity fetes, what do you like to do, Grace Henley?'

'Other than the two things that seem to take up fourteen or fifteen hours of most days?' She laughed. 'Not a lot.'

'What did you used to do, then?' He wasn't deterred. 'Before your life got so full?'

'Is it full?'

Grace stopped abruptly as she heard the words that she hadn't intended to say. Hadn't even thought. No wonder Rik was watching her curiously.

And even though the voice in her head was commanding her to retrace her steps, when she opened her mouth, she heard herself continuing.

'I don't think my life has ever been what I thought it might be,' she confessed. 'Which isn't to say that I don't like being a doctor, because I do. If I'm honest, it's the only part of my life that I'm sure about. But when I was a kid, I used to dream of so much more.'

'Such as,' he prompted softly when she fell silent.

And she lifted her shoulders to shrug the question off but, once again, she heard her own voice speaking the words she hadn't even allowed herself to think.

'I used to dream of going places, of seeing things. Not just through books, but with my own eyes. I don't know.' She glanced up at the ceiling. 'I wanted to visit Florence. I imagined going to the pyramids in Egypt. I wanted to stand in front of the Taj Mahal.'

She stopped abruptly, feeling foolish.

'That sounds silly. I'm sorry.'

'It doesn't sound remotely silly.' Rik frowned. 'So, why didn't you?'

And it was on the tip of Grace's tongue to tell him the truth. To confess the story that she had never told another living soul.

The reason why she'd felt so compelled to return to this place. The connection that was probably imagined but meant that she couldn't leave. The uncertainty that meant she hadn't really been able to move on with her life, in more than a decade.

She caught herself just in time.

'My job is here in Thorncroft.' She tried to sound casual but failed, even to her own ears.

'You can be an obstetrician anywhere,' Rik pointed out.

And Grace knew there was no answer to that. None that would make any sense to this man, anyway. But then, as the silence began to bulge and press between them, he rescued her.

Just as he'd done in the warehouse yesterday afternoon.

'Well, I've travelled to those places, and done those things, so I can tell you that if it's what you want to do, then do it. We each only have one life, and it's worth going, and seeing, and experiencing, as much as you possibly can.'

'I thought you preferred simpler things. The simple life?' she asked, fighting to get her hand back into the conversation. 'Didn't you say you'd built a log cabin?'

Rik looked surprised by her question.

'I did. But you don't want to know about that.'

'I do.' She lifted one shoulder elegantly. 'You made it sound like a nice place to get away.'

'It's quiet. Not like the cities. You said you were a city girl.'

'I realise that.' She hesitated. 'And it's true, I used to love the city, with its bright lights and nightlife. There's always something to do, somewhere that's open.'

'But…?' he prompted, when she stopped.

'I don't know.' She gave a half-laugh. 'It doesn't feel like… *me*. It hasn't for almost a year now.'

'So, change it.'

'I am changing it.' She snapped her eyes up to his. 'Or, at least, I was changing it. I was getting ready to make a move a few months ago, but then…'

She tailed off and Rik didn't speak, but she felt the weight of his gaze on her as she toyed with the stem of her wine glass.

'Anyway, where did you say it was? In a national forest?'

Rik almost didn't answer. She got the impression that the cabin was his private bolt-hole and he never shared it with anyone. Apparently, not really even in conversation.

But then, just as she was about to take a sip of wine and try to change the topic, he started speaking.

'It's on the edge of the Tyresta National Park. About a twenty-mile drive from Stockholm.'

Did she dare ask more? She certainly wanted to know what it was about it that had so captivated him.

'How did you end up with it?'

He peered at her, as though assessing her motives. But she didn't know what she should say, so she stayed silent.

'I'd run into another obstacle in my search for my brother,' he confessed, unexpectedly. 'I started lurching from one surgery to another, probably just to try to regain some kind of control, I suppose. Anyway, I was treating one patient who told me that he and his wife had always wanted to go on a round-the-world trip, but they'd always put it off because of time, or money, or family.'

'Sounds like me.' She laughed, but it was a shaky sound.

She wondered if he could read how much she was beginning to find this place—even the hospital—was suffocating her.

'My patient told me that if he recovered, he intended to sell a rare plot of land that his family had owned for almost one hundred years, and they would go. So, I made him a deal. If I healed him, I'd buy the land.'

'It was that simple?' She sounded incredulous, and Rik smiled.

'It was that simple. I bought the land on the Thursday, I headed down there on the Friday and camped overnight in the forest, and by the time I was back on shift on the Sunday I'd already started drawing up plans for a home.'

'So what's it like in this forest of yours?'

He looked at her, met her eye.

'It's incomparable,' he told her quietly. 'A stunning landscape, sculpted by the hand of the Ice Age itself, with a coniferous forest boasting ancient, giant trees as old as four hundred years.'

She was enthralled. The look in his expression drawing

her in as much as his words. Painting a picture so vivid that she thought she might truly be standing there, right now. It was so utterly enticing.

'Also, unlike the ice rink you love that gets transported into the city at Christmas time,' he reminded her of their previous conversation, 'there are lakes in the park on which you can skate all winter long.'

And Grace couldn't decide whether it was the idea of the cabin or the man that bewitched her the most.

CHAPTER ELEVEN

'I HAD NO idea the fete was going to be quite like this,' Rik marvelled, even before the pair of them stepped onto the field.

There was a variety of rides, from mini roller coasters to spinning teacups, a huge inflatable slide that had to be about thirty feet high, with a vertiginous set of covered steps leading to the top, and a plethora of different booths and stalls. Many of which she assumed he recognised from their many painting sessions over the past month.

At least he'd finally got to meet the rest of the charity board team, even if the ever-more-crowded warehouse *had* put a stop to their impromptu jive dancing.

'Infectious, isn't it?' Grace grinned as she soaked up the buzz of the carnival atmosphere.

She didn't think it was her imagination that everything was injected with that much more joy whenever Rik was around.

'I have to admit that, even having seen all those panels in that warehouse, I thought it would be a few stalls in the car park. I had no idea it would be such an extravaganza.'

Rik glanced over the multitude of booths, carnival rides, and bandstands filling up the local fields behind Thorncroft Royal, and she chuckled merrily.

'It was a bit like that when I was a kid,' Grace confessed. 'But now it's a big event, and it seems to get bigger every year. This year we've got a new bungee-trampoline thing that I think I'll be too terrified to try.'

'I can't imagine you being terrified of anything.'

His voice was even, yet he watched her for one long moment. As if there was something about her that he was trying to work out. As if she...mattered, to him.

She shook the foolish notion from her head and injected a deliberately cheery tone to her voice.

'Well, I can only say that I think I'll be sticking to hooking a duck or throwing a dart at a balloon wall.'

'Will that be before the dunking stall, or after?'

'After.' Grace danced gleefully. She couldn't seem to help herself. 'We don't open that until it's warmer, say around lunchtime?'

'Is that so?' Rik grinned, making her stomach flip-flop. 'Then, is there anything I can do?'

'Face painting.'

'Sorry?'

She didn't even try to conceal her amusement.

'We're going to do some face painting.' She led him to the stall and took over from the two colleagues who looked more than ready for a break.

The line of kids snaked around quite a way.

'Okay, first take your sponge and get some of the white face paint, like this. Good. Right.'

Rik's altogether serious expression made Grace grin.

'Now, you're going to paint the face white down the nose, see? And around the mouth, here? Great, and finally sponge in two tiger ears above his eyebrows, like so.'

She leaned back critically to inspect her work, and Rik's. She had to admit, his looked pretty good. Too good for a beginner.

She eyed him suspiciously, not trusting his innocent look for a second.

'Have you done this before?'

'I have not.' He grinned. 'But it's face painting, *älskling*. Not surgery.'

'Tell that to the kid whose tiger face you mess up,' she warned good-naturedly.

'Point taken. Now what?'

If it hadn't been for the little ears around them, she might have said something different.

'Now, load up your sponge with some yellow. Okay, here we go.'

They worked together for about fifteen minutes, with Grace working slowly to give him time to copy.

By the end, it actually looked like the tiger it was meant to be, and Rik leaned back to admire his handiwork just as Grace sent the kid off with a lollipop as a reward for his patience.

'Okay, I know I said you needed to be accurate, but it isn't a gallery opening at the V&A, you know.' She laughed. 'Turn around and look at the line.'

Obediently, Rik turned. The queue was already beginning to snake around the corner.

'Speed up, slow coach,' she told him, winking at the child seated at her table and making them giggle. 'We have a lot to get through before you have to get ready for your dunking.'

And she laughed at Rik's muttered response as they both concentrated on their new roles for the next few hours.

'Are you hungry?' she asked as a couple more colleagues came over to relieve them of their face-painting duties.

With a final flourish, Rik dropped his brush into the cleaning tub.

'Famished. What time is it?'

'Nearly lunch time. We get an hour free, and then it's time for you to delight the crowd with your shirtless dunking.'

'I can't wait.' He grimaced as his stomach gave a loud grumble of concurrence. 'Where do you suggest eating, then?'

'There are a couple of good food trucks.'

Rik glanced around sceptically.

'I think not.'

'Snob.' She laughed before she could help herself. 'There's nothing wrong with eating here.'

'I beg to differ.'

'Come on.' She elbowed him playfully in the ribs before she realised what she was doing. 'Live dangerously.'

She felt the weight of his gaze on her, but she refused to turn around. Had she just ruined the easy repartee between them?

She certainly hoped not.

After a long moment, to her relief, Rik let out a dramatic groan.

'All right, then, you've convinced me. Which one do you suggest?'

She was pretty sure she already knew, but she turned a complete three-sixty all the same, taking in all the trucks.

'Xavier's Home-Cooked Chilli,' she declared.

'Xavier's it is,' Rik agreed as they headed over to the mobile kitchen together. The place was pristine, but then it had to be, catering to a hospital of medical professionals and their families.

Still, it didn't take long for their food to come to them, complete with little wedges of lime and a swirl of soured cream.

They strolled across to where a collection of tables had been set out, and sat down, with her on a chair whilst Rik straddled the bench.

'This,' Rik exclaimed, after the first mouthful, 'is truly incredible.'

Grace closed her eyes and savoured the taste.

'It is,' she agreed after a moment. 'And just think, if I'd left you to be a snob, you would have missed out completely.'

And there she was, teasing him again. As if it was the most natural thing in the world.

'Lesson learned.'

For a few minutes, all they did was eat, the rush and hassle of the day ebbing away as peace fell, and their growling bellies began to feel a little fuller.

'You know, I think I'm going to have to get this recipe and try it for myself some time.'

Grace eyed him for a moment, unaware of the words gathering on her tongue until she heard them spill out.

'Do you cook?'

Rik's head turned slowly, so slowly, to look at her again. For a moment, she wasn't even sure that he was going to answer.

'I do.'

Without warning, the weight of it struck her.

'So does your brother,' she said. 'Incredibly well, in fact. I'm guessing it's the cook you mentioned. The one who taught you to dance?'

She watched his jaw lock tight. And the harsh tic of his pulse. Then, somehow, he loosened it off again.

'Yes.'

'She taught you as seven-year-olds?'

It had to be before those awful events Bas had told her about had happened.

Another long silence.

'Sort of. We moved away from her just before our seventh birthday. But, yes, she'd been there all our lives up until then.'

'And she taught you both how to cook?'

'She taught us how to bake at first. Fun fairy cakes. Then, when she realised what home life was like, and how sometimes we wouldn't get anything to eat at night, she taught us how to make basic meals. I guess that must have given both of us a love of cooking. My brother really enjoys it, too?'

'He's always conjuring up mouth-watering stuff,' she managed, but she still caught up on the other thing he'd said.

'What do you mean, you didn't get to eat?'

But Rik ignored that part. It clearly wasn't a memory he wanted to revisit, but she thought she understood well enough.

'Mrs P taught us more than just how to cook. She taught

us how to be good men. She taught us what was right. What is it that Aristotle said? Give me the boy until he is seven, and I will show you the man. Mrs P made us into the men we are today. At least, the better part of the men we are today.'

'I… I didn't know,' Grace admitted quietly.

'My brother never mentioned her?'

'Maybe he forgot about her?' she suggested tentatively. 'After all, he was only seven.'

'No.' There was no heat in the denial, more a quiet, grim certainty. And…something else. Something Grace thought looked a lot like a kind of anguish. 'He couldn't have forgotten about Mrs P. He couldn't have forgotten exactly what happened with her. With us. With our mother. It would make everything we went through…meaningless.'

She couldn't stop herself. Reaching forward, she touched her fingers to Rik's.

'If you're suggesting that Mrs P was part of the reason Bas ended up getting sent away, perhaps it's better that he's forgotten. Or, at least, buried it.'

'That's precisely why he needs to remember.' Rik eyed her again, his penetrating gaze locking with hers. 'I don't understand why he blames me for what happened. Or why he has chosen to forget Mrs P or her husband. But you need to help him.'

'I can't.'

'You have to. But you need to help him find the real truth.'

'He won't really listen to me any more.' She shook her head.

If he ever really had.

They'd been friends, but she'd listened to him more than he'd listened to her. Besides, Grace wasn't sure why, but she got the impression that Naomi stood more of a chance than anyone of making Bas listen.

They stopped talking, just giving themselves some time to sit and eat in peace.

But, surprisingly, it was more of a companionable still-ness than an awkward silence. It was odd, but this…*thing* she had with Rik was closer than she'd ever been with her friend.

But in a matter of weeks, Rik would be gone. His stint on the exchange programme would be over and he would fly back to Sweden.

The prospect made Grace's stomach actually churn, and it took all she had to drag her mind back to nicer things.

Back to the idea of a water-drenched Rik, barefoot and shirtless, and his dark denim jeans soaked through and cling-ing lovingly to the legs she knew first hand to be sculptured masterpieces. Never mind her stomach, the mere thought of it was enough to set other body parts racing.

This was so *not* what she was supposed to be doing. But the truth was that she'd abandoned her original task of keep-ing an eye on him a while ago.

Probably from that first moment in the warehouse when they'd started dancing instead of painting.

Laughing, and having fun, as though they were a real couple. Or, if not that, then at least two people who were genuinely attracted to each other without any other agenda.

She'd stopped thinking about it because she hadn't wanted whatever they might have to be tainted any more. Now all she had to do was find a way to explain everything to Rik with-out telling him exactly what was going on with his brother and the baby.

Because, however else she might feel, that part of the story wasn't hers to tell.

Giving herself a mental shake, Grace dropped her fork into a near-empty bowl and cast Rik a wicked grin.

His dark gaze was her reward.

'Hurry up, I want to try my hand at the skittle wall and win a squeaky toy for Cooper. And then, we've got an afternoon on the water-dunking booth to look forward to.'

'Don't remind me.' He laughed, though she sensed that it was a little forced.

As if he was trying as hard as she was to get back to the breeziness of earlier. As if, like her, he didn't want to waste the rest of the short time they had left on things that didn't make them laugh.

And, abruptly, Grace wondered what she was holding back for. If there were only a few weeks before Rik left, how could she get hurt if she indulged just a little bit more?

What would happen if she threw caution to the wind with Rik, and indulged in the less uptight side of herself? Just this once.

Grace sank into the soft leather seat of the back of the limousine taxi—one of a number reserved exclusively for the VIPs of the Jansen Suite—and closed her eyes in bliss as Rik slid in beside her. His hair was still wet from the dunking, but his change of clothes mercifully dry.

'Better?' he asked as he pulled the door closed on them, cocooning them in the darkness.

'Everything hurts,' she complained with a laugh. 'My feet, from racing around retrieving wet sponges, my hands from punching tickets, and my head, from all the screaming and laughter.'

'I seem to recall you were doing plenty of laughing,' he accused, with raised eyebrows. 'Every time that sponge hit the target and that trapdoor opened beneath me.'

Grace pulled her mouth into a tight line to keep from laughing again, as her deep blue eyes held his—so long that he could feel himself falling back under her spell.

But he shouldn't. He *mustn't*.

'Don't you know that actions have consequences, *älskling*?' Rik murmured, laughing when her eyes widened. Darkened.

'What consequences?'

'Allow me to show you.'

Before he could stop himself, or even think, he pulled her across the seats until she was sprawled across his knee, and his mouth was crushing hers.

Claiming her.

The way he'd been dreaming of doing all day.

All month.

A part of him might have expected Grace to fight him. If only for a moment, and if only for show. But she didn't even pretend that much. She simply collapsed against him, her chest pressed to his, and her arms looping around his head as if being with him was the only place she wanted to be.

'That's good,' she murmured. 'Because I think I have a few consequences of my own, given the way you kept deliberately splashing me every time.'

'Is that so, *älskling*?' he demanded.

And when she nodded, she kept her forehead pressed to his. Her mouth curved up in happiness.

'Oh, yes,' she told him. 'That's definitely so. A few lessons to be taught, I think. And they may take quite some time.'

And Rik forgot his promise to himself. He forgot who she was. He even forgot that they were in the back of a damned car. The need for her pounded through him, like a secret that he'd tried to lock away for too long now.

He was happy to tell himself that what he was doing now was nothing more than indulging in a last bit of fun before he returned home in a few weeks. He would happily stomp on any voice in his head snidely suggesting otherwise. But deep down, a different truth began to snake, and move.

But he could deal with that another day. For now, he just wanted to lose himself in the woman currently shifting on his lap. Meeting his kiss head-on, twisting herself around so that she was suddenly straddling him and he was no longer sure which one of them was teaching consequences to the other.

Worse, he didn't even care. So long as it never stopped.

She slid her fingers into his hair, pressing her body so tightly against his, as if she couldn't bear for there to be even a millimetre of space between them, making Rik groan. No matter that his mouth was still fused to hers. And no matter that he could feel the replying shiver work its way through her body as she rocked against the hardest part of him.

He had never willed a car-ride away so badly.

By the time they arrived at the hospital site—neither seeming to care that the limousine deposited them right outside the main entrance of the Garden Complex—it was all either of them could do to tumble out, thank the driver, and make their way up to Rik's rooms.

And then they were stumbling inside—a perfect echo of that first night together in the hotel suite. Only here, he had a suite of rooms, all bigger, and higher, and furnished even more luxuriously than the hotel.

Not that he cared about any of that, especially at this moment, save for the fact that he didn't think they would even make it to the bedroom. Already, their clothes were off in a shocking economy of movement, and they had barely made it into the elegant sitting room. If he didn't manage to take control they were going to be doing it down there, on the cold, hard solid wood floor.

Without warning, Rik scooped her up into his arms, and carried her directly to the bedroom. Taking matters, quite literally, into his own hands.

'You'd better hold on, *älskling*,' he muttered, depositing her onto the large bed.

But as he joined her he wondered which of them needed to hold on the most. Especially when he lay on his back, hauling her back to him to straddle him once again—the position that allowed him to see every inch of her delectable body. And every slick, perfect slide in and out of her.

She was never going to get enough of Rik, Grace thought some time later as he carried her exhausted, tingling body into the shower room and the to-die-for walk-in shower.

If she'd thought what had happened between them that first night—the night of the gala—had been spectacular, then she had no words to describe what had just happened now. Because somehow, impossibly, it had been even better.

She could still taste him on her tongue. That generous gift of satin-wrapped steel. And she could still picture the look on his face when she'd first pushed him backwards to drop kisses down that solid wall of his chest, used her fingers to toy with the smattering of hair on his chest, and taken her tongue to the mouth-wateringly defined V-lines where his obliques met his lower abdominals.

And then, that moment of power that had jolted through her as she'd lowered her head to take him in her mouth—her eyes not once leaving his—whilst his breathing had changed in an instant. A ragged, rapid sound that had guided her, and thrilled her, all at once.

God, how she'd enjoyed that. Thrilling him and celebrating him at the same time. Taking him deep into the heat of her mouth, sucking on him, then sliding him out to let the cool air dance over his tip before flicking her tongue over him.

She knew she would remember those deep, guttural noises for ever. So utterly carnal, making her feel as though she held every inch of control in the situation. It was a heady experience.

Still, she hadn't been entirely surprised when he hadn't let her finish. Not the way she'd wanted to, anyway. Not in any way that would have meant him giving up control completely.

Because he hadn't wanted to with her? Or because he couldn't bring himself to do that with anyone?

Grace found she couldn't bear the idea that he still didn't quite trust her.

'Are you joining me?'

She turned abruptly as Rik's voice floated to her in the air. The sound of the shower cascading down like some glorious waterfall, the steam filling up the room. And when he reached for her, she didn't hesitate for a moment, allowing him to pull her gently under the blissful flow and revelling in the way his soaped-up hands sought out her body again.

As if they didn't have a care in the world.

'Do you need me to?' she teased hoarsely.

With a smile, Rik slid his arms around her, their naked bodies moving slickly against each other. It caused a delicious kind of friction.

'I just might.' He sounded raw. Half undone already.

Just the way that she felt, too. She leant back on the glass—already warmed by the water—and pulled him with her.

'Show me,' she commanded.

And loved that he dutifully obeyed.

CHAPTER TWELVE

GRACE STOOD ON the balcony of Rik's hotel suite, gazing down at the twinkling lights of Thorncroft spread out before her. The air was damp, and it had been raining all evening, but even that hadn't been able to dampen her soaring spirits.

It had been creeping up on her ever since that night at the gala when she'd first met Rik—slowly at first, so that she hadn't noticed it, but now the feeling was so intense that she couldn't deny it.

She was happy. Not just happy—blissfully happy. So happy that she could actually feel it, like a warmth heating her from the inside out.

And it was Rik who had done that. The last two months had been like nothing she'd ever imagined. He'd helped her to shake off the fusty idea of love that she'd learned from her parents, and he'd shown her something so intense, and incredible.

Even better, she was beginning to realise that she might have done the same thing for him. The only proverbial fly in the ointment was that dark, niggling secret she desperately, terrifyingly, wanted to tell him.

Because how could this thing between them be real if she couldn't even tell him about the one event in her life that had shaped her the most?

'Come back to bed.'

Grace heard Rik stir behind her, and even as her heart leapt into her mouth a delicious trail of goosebumps raced over her skin.

'Join me,' she murmured softly, almost hoarsely. 'You have quite the view from up here.'

There was a brief pause, and then she heard him slide

out of bed and into a pair of trousers that she knew without needing to see would be low-slung over his sculpted hips.

As he padded across the room towards her, she steadfastly kept her head to the city lights below, lest she lose her nerve.

'Beautiful, isn't it?'

'Stunning,' Rik agreed, and she knew he was looking at her rather than the view.

It would have been so easy to swallow her words. And her courage.

Grace wasn't sure how she managed not to. But she needed to tell him the truth. Some deep need was driving within her, willing her to finally tell someone. No, not just *someone*. Rather, to tell *Rik*.

Though she had no idea how to even begin. Grace opened her mouth, hoping to find the words to ease into it.

'My daughter is down there,' she blurted out instead. 'Somewhere.'

The words she'd never spoken aloud in her life, except for that one night. They rolled oddly around her tongue.

'Pardon?'

'I mean. Maybe.' She was losing her nerve now. 'I'd like to think so, anyway.'

The silence was almost unbearable. Grace had no idea how long she waited for Rik to reply. A lifetime, perhaps? Maybe two?

And then, at last…

'You have a daughter?'

It sounded so…*real* coming from him.

'I do,' Grace managed, suddenly feeling awestruck.

'You have a baby? You? The most level-headed, career-orientated person I've met since I've been here?'

Her eyes pricked and heated unexpectedly.

'You have to stop putting me on this damned pedestal,' she burst out, not even aware she'd been so close to the brink until she heard her own voice bouncing back at her, off the balcony walls, and the cool, inky night sky beyond. 'I'm not this perfect person.'

He advanced on her, putting his hands on her shoulders in a gesture that she knew he intended as soothing.

'You're the most perfect person I've ever met,' he told her solemnly.

It should have been romantic.

Inspiring.

Instead, she clutched at her chest as though she could somehow rip off the tight, invisible cloak that felt as though it were suffocating her.

'No.' She jerked her head from side to side. 'I'm not. And it's too much. The pressure of it is too much.'

'There's no pressure.'

'There feels like pressure,' she countered.

'Why?'

'I don't know,' she cried, though quieter, this time. 'I'm not perfect, and shiny, and all the things you seem to think I am.'

'When have I told you that?' Rik demanded softly.

But her agitation was too far gone to rein in so easily.

'I can't be the person you look to as the epitome of all that is right and good, because that's not me. I'm every bit as flawed, and damaged, and broken as you. Just for different reasons.'

And she knew these were all her own fears, finally escaping after years of her stuffing them down, but that didn't seem to make it any easier to bear.

'You don't have to tell me this,' he assured her. 'If you don't want to.'

'I do.' She nodded vigorously, even as she still couldn't find the courage to turn and look at him. 'I've never told anyone this before. *Ever*. But I need to tell you now.'

Another tenuous moment pulled taut in her chest.

'Say as much or as little as you need,' Rik reassured her.

And, somehow, it was the nudge she needed.

'I *had* a baby,' Grace managed, slowly at first. 'A long time ago. But she'll be fourteen now.'

And then she stopped, as if uncertain how to continue.

'And she's somewhere down there?' Rik prompted just as she thought she might flounder.

Grace grasped the lifeline gratefully.

'Yes,' then, 'no. Well…maybe.'

'Maybe?'

For another impossibly long moment, Grace felt Rik's stare bolting her down. She saw her own knuckles turn white on the railing. And she wondered if her legs were going to start swaying and collapsing beneath her.

But whatever she might have expected, it hadn't been for Rik to begin piecing it together so quickly. Faster than she could even begin to explain.

'This was the event that happened when you were sixteen,' he said. A statement, not a question, though his tone was carefully neutral. Non-judgemental. 'The reason that your family left Thorncroft.'

'It was.' Her throat felt suddenly parched.

'And this is the reason you came back here a decade ago.' It was impressive, just how easily he was working things through. 'This was what you meant by feeling it was *fate* when my brother suggested both of you should continue your training here. You came back for your daughter.'

'I did.'

It felt unimaginably good to finally be able to admit that aloud, after all this time. Grace felt a sob make its way through her chest, but she fought it back.

'Yet you haven't met her?'

The elation dulled in an instant. It took her a few attempts to work her mouth again.

'I haven't.' The words felt like glass paper, abrading her throat, her mouth, her ears. 'The truth is, when I say she's down there somewhere, I don't actually know if she is. I might have passed her on the street out there. Or she might live halfway around the world by now.'

'You didn't want to know?' Rik asked, and a kind of stillness settled over her.

'I was never allowed to.'

'You were never allowed to know about your own baby?'

And finally, finally, Grace permitted herself a sad laugh that, even to her own ears, she could hear was tinged with bitterness.

'I once told you that my parents were academics. They weren't unkind, or harsh, but they believed in rules, in studies, in application to my schoolwork. They didn't believe in frivolous toys, or days out that weren't also educational, or parties.'

She gripped the bar tighter, but Rik didn't speak. As though he was giving her time. And space.

'When I was sixteen, I went to a party. My first ever one. Two of the kids in my school threw it when their parents had gone out of town for a weekend, and their older brother was supposed to have been babysitting them.'

'You parents couldn't have agreed to that,' Rik prompted carefully, when she hesitated again. 'You didn't do parties, and that stuff. You told me you were a boring kid.'

'They didn't,' she confirmed, and even now she could almost feel the emotion of that time washing through her, all over again. 'They forbade it, of course. But I was desperate to go so I slipped out of the house. I didn't want to be the geek. The nerd. Just for one night, I wanted to be like every other normal kid. But…'

'But you met a boy, had sex, and fell pregnant,' Rik said for her, when she couldn't find the words herself.

'I was foolish, and over-excited, and I'm not really sure I knew what I was really doing. I think I even believed I couldn't possibly get pregnant the first time.'

'That was your first time?'

Her cheeks grew hot with shame.

'That was my only time,' she bit out. 'Until you.'

And she had no idea what that low, guttural sound that Rik made was, but even to Grace's untrained ear it sounded deliciously like possessiveness.

'It took me seven months to admit it even to myself,' she made herself continue. 'Hiding my growing figure with baggier and baggier clothes. But, in the end, I couldn't hide it from my parents any longer. They were horrified, of course.'

'What happened?' Rik growled, and somehow Grace felt as if it was a protective sound.

For her, rather than against her.

'My parents told me that I would have the baby adopted, they would move universities, and we would start again. So that's what happened. I had the baby—it was a girl, I know that—but I never got to hold her,' Grace admitted, though the words seared in her chest. 'My parents had her taken away and I never saw her. We never spoke of it again. We moved house. That was that.'

Rik didn't answer immediately. She got the feeling he was taking it all in. Absorbing it.

'So, why come back here if you don't even know this is where she is?' he asked eventually.

Wordlessly, Grace stared out over the blanket of lights that was Thorncroft.

'I don't know,' she admitted, after what felt like an eternity. 'Probably because this was where she was born. Being here is the closest I can ever feel to her. It's the only comfort I have.'

'What about tracking her down?' he asked. 'Putting your name on one of those databases?'

Grace gripped the railing tighter than ever.

'I've wanted to,' she confessed. 'A thousand times. But...'

She tailed off. How could she explain that terror that lodged so intently in her chest every time she came close to contacting the Adoption Contact Register. Her daughter might not be able to register herself until she was eighteen, so right now Grace could tell herself that age was the reason they had no contact.

But what if her daughter turned eighteen and still never registered? What if she never wanted to know her. It was her greatest fear- that her daughter would reject her.

'That isn't my point,' Grace bit out, abruptly changing the subject. 'My point is that I wanted you to know the truth. I wish other people knew. I've hated her being kept like some dirty secret. I just didn't know how to tell anyone…until now.'

He didn't ask why, and for that Grace was grateful. She didn't think she had an answer for that.

'I'm honoured that you did,' he said quietly.

Then, at long last, she allowed him to peel her hands from the balcony and turn her around, that dark look of his snagging hers instantly, as though there were no one else in the place. Hot, and intent, sending liquid heat pouring through her, the way that it always did when Rik was around.

And Grace had no idea how long they stood there, with his arms around her, but it was long enough to finally gather herself again.

'You know, just a few months ago—before I'd even met you—I'd decided it was time for me to stop living in the past. Time for me to let go, and finally move away from Thorncroft on my own.'

She wasn't sure he'd heard her—her voice muffled as it was against his chest—until he moved her back, his eyes searching her face.

'You want to leave Thorncroft.'

'I do.' She nodded. 'I just don't know if I was fooling myself that I could have done it. Not when it really came down to it. But, now that you're here, I don't think I need to. Maybe it could just be…a fresh start.'

His gaze changed in an instant. Almost imperceptibly,

but Grace knew this man too well already not to notice it. It was a look that she didn't recognise. A look that sent a trickle of premonition down her very spine. She faltered, sure that whatever was going on in his head, she didn't want to know.

'A fresh start?'

His sympathetic tone was humiliating, and still, Grace forced herself to continue. To hear the words she didn't want him to say.

'I thought you and I...here in Thorncroft...'

'Grace.' He spared her from finishing, and though his eyes locked with hers, steely and unyielding, she thought it was the unguarded softness in his tone that wounded the deepest. 'Once my stint here with the exchange programme is done, I return to Sweden. Staying here, with you, has never been an option for me. I didn't think it was for you, either.'

Rik hated himself.

He could see the pain, and misery etched into every line on her face, and he knew that he had caused it.

What kind of a man was he to do that? Especially after she'd just shared what had to be her most private secret with him.

But what else was he to have done? He couldn't have lied to her and pretended that staying in Thorncroft was an option for him—especially not with his relationship with his brother so fractured and irreparable.

'I'm sorry,' he apologised, and he felt the weight of every syllable. 'Our time together has been good, *älskling*. And we have both shared things that we've never shared with anyone else, have we not?'

She eyed him warily, suspecting she was stepping into some kind of trap but couldn't quite see where it was.

'We have,' she muttered huskily.

'But I do not belong in Thorncroft. It isn't the place for

me. It wouldn't be, even if not for the fact that my brother does not want me here.'

'And what if I want you here?' She lifted her chin defiantly. 'Does that count for nothing? Because there is something between us, Rik, you can't deny it.'

'I'm not trying to,' he heard himself agree. 'But we both know that whatever either of us might think we feel, this... *thing* between us is based on a lie.

'What are you talking about?' she whispered, as if he was punishing her for something she didn't even deserve.

As if there were a noose around her neck exactly like the one that he felt encircled his own.

'I asked you once before if you were spending time with me because you wanted to, or because my brother had asked you to keep a watch on me. I told you that it didn't matter to me either way, but that I wanted to know. I asked you to do me the decency of telling me the truth or, if you couldn't do that, at least not lying to me.'

And she wanted to deny it, he could see it in Grace's elegant face. She wanted to explain, but even though she worked her jaw, no sound actually came out.

'You told me that it had nothing to do with my brother. But that wasn't true, was it? You were running down a clock, playing me and keeping me away from him until my time at Thorncroft ran out.'

'You're wrong.' She gasped, but Rik shook his head.

'I'm not wrong. But I didn't think it mattered because I told myself that you were just a distraction. I convinced myself that it didn't matter if you were manipulating me, because I was using you, too. In the absence of my brother talking to me, you were my way towards understanding him a little better.'

She blanched, and Rik hated himself a little more.

'So...you used me,' she rasped out. Painfully.

'I told myself that I was, just as I think you told yourself that you were only with me to help my brother.'

'The difference is—' she jerked her back straighter, as if that might lend her more strength '—that the person I was fooling most of all was myself. I pretended getting close to you was a plan because it was the excuse I think I needed.'

'Maybe so, but—'

'Because, deep down, I knew I was attracted to you. I had been since that first night at the ball, before I even knew who you were. What's more…' She leaned forward and, inconceivably, poked him in the chest. Hard. 'I know you felt that same attraction.'

'Whether I did or not, it makes little difference,' he told her bleakly.

'It makes every difference,' Grace cried.

He shook his head.

'No,' he told her firmly. 'It doesn't. It doesn't matter whether this thing between us is real now, because it was all based on a lie. And my entire life has been based on lies, Grace. Lies, and deceit, and betrayal. I can't have another thing like that.'

'But this isn't. Not any more.'

'Not any more,' he echoed sadly. 'And that's exactly the point. *Any more.* Which means you know it once was, just as I do. Whatever we think we have, or could have, it's too late. It has already been tainted by the lies from the start.'

'It doesn't have to be,' Grace breathed. 'For my part in it all, I'm sorry.'

Her gaze was holding his so sincerely that he almost believed her.

Almost.

Something shifted and fractured inside him. Something he wasn't yet prepared to acknowledge.

'You have nothing to apologise for,' he bit out. 'Your loyalty to my brother is admirable. There's no need to qualify it.'

'My loyalty to your brother isn't why I slept with you.'

He opened his mouth to answer, but then Grace edged closer to him and the familiar red-berry scent of her hair conditioner conjured up a dozen memories that stopped him in his tracks.

Desperately he tried to mentally scramble backwards, searching for some kind of purchase for his thoughts. Because as much as he hated to admit it, Grace deserved better than a man like him.

'I told you, aside from the one single time I slept with a man—boy, really—and fell pregnant, every other time was with you.' Her voice cracked. 'And do I need to remind you how many times that has been? I wouldn't have done that for anyone, not even someone I called my closest friend.'

Without warning, the truth of that statement hit Rik. And it felt like some precious, fragile gift that she'd given him. Her trust after what had to be years of feeling betrayed.

And suddenly, he felt unworthy.

Whether they'd started out using each other, or not, when it really came down to it, Grace had had a lot more to lose from it than him. Being intimate with him, when the last time she'd been intimate with anyone had been when she'd been sixteen, meant more than just words.

More than he had to offer.

He'd caused her enough harm. If he was the kind of decent man that he'd always believed himself to be, then he had to let her go.

'You were right when you once accused me of being selfish,' he ground out. 'I didn't care about your friendship with my brother, as much as I may have told myself that I did. You told me time and again that he was your friend and that you didn't want to hurt him, but I still pursued you. Because I wanted you.'

Rik had thought it would be hard to admit those truths. The fact was, once he'd started speaking they'd come out naturally.

'Is that so?'

He inhaled deeply.

'It is. I think perhaps a part of me wanted to get back at him, after all. It seems I'm not the man I wanted you to think I was.'

Without warning, Grace closed the gap between them and the heat that emanated off her body seemed to bounce straight to his. And straight to that frozen block that he thought had once been his heart.

'So you've just contradicted your own argument, Rik,' she observed. 'You were with me because you wanted to be. Anything to do with your brother was just an excuse. A sideshow.'

'No.' Had he contradicted himself?

He thought he might have.

'Yes,' Grace confirmed. 'And it's precisely that acknowledgement which makes you exactly the man you wanted me to think you are,' she murmured. 'You weren't selfish, Rik. You never were. I was wrong to say it. What your mother did left you as damaged and closed-off as it left Bas. And why wouldn't it?'

'I stood by and let her send Bas away. My own brother.'

'Neither of you could have predicted what happened that night.'

'Perhaps not, but I should have done more.' Rik heard the self-loathing in his voice. But there was nothing he could do to stop it. 'He was my *brother*.'

'You were seven,' countered Grace, lifting her hands to his cheeks and cupping his face as though *she* wanted to provide *him* solace.

When they both knew it should have been the other way round.

'I was supposed to be the calm one. The measured brother. I should have waited for her to calm down, and then found a way to talk her around. I should never have let it happen.'

'You're asking a lot of a child,' Grace pointed out. 'Even when that child was yourself.'

'Maybe, but it informs the man I am today. And it seems I'm not as without fault as I had thought I was.'

'None of us are, Rik. But you should stay and give your brother a little longer to come to terms with it. More importantly, you should give yourself a break. How long have you been squashing this down inside? Punishing yourself to the point where you can't even give us a chance?'

'That isn't what's happening here,' Rik denied.

Only he felt twisted up in knots suddenly, unsure of exactly how he felt. The only thing he knew was that, if it hadn't been for Grace, then he would never have opened up this pit of emotions.

He just couldn't tell if that was a good or a bad thing. Either way, it didn't change one thing. The issue that had started the conversation in the first place.

'The point is that I can't stay here in Thorncroft, Grace. I have to leave. My life is in Sweden.'

'It doesn't have to be,' she countered.

'But I want it to be,' he assured her quietly. Then, before he realised what he was saying, he added, 'Come with me.'

He wasn't sure which of them was more shocked.

'To Sweden?'

'Why not?' He hunched his shoulder suddenly. It didn't sound like such a bad idea. 'You said it yourself, you were looking to leave anyway. To travel.'

'I was,' she agreed slowly. Uncertainly. 'But I can't. I can't quite let go.'

'Of the daughter who might not even be in this city? Even in this country.'

Grace hesitated before dropping her head.

'Yet she might be.'

Rik breathed slowly.

'So we're at an impasse.'

'It seems so.' She cast him a look of misery.

And even though something in his brain was telling him to fight for her—to say something—he found that he couldn't.

He'd been fighting for his brother for so long that he had nothing left. Which meant that there was nothing else for him to do but to make the right decision for both of them.

Wordlessly, Rik slipped on the rest of his clothes, gathering his wallet before heading to his suite door. The fact that she didn't say a word told him all he needed to know.

'You can leave in your own time. I'll stay at the hospital tonight.'

And before either of them could say anything more, he pulled open the door, and left.

CHAPTER THIRTEEN

'Hi, Kate. I'm Grace.' Smiling encouragement, Grace crossed the private room to where her patient was lying on the bed in labour. 'I'm here to have a look at your baby.'

She smiled again, but the truth was that it was hard to smile these days. She wasn't sure she had that first week after her break-up—for want of a better term—from Rik. The second week, she'd had to find a way to smile for her patients. And this week, it was easier to pretend.

But she certainly didn't feel it on the inside.

Who knew that having this kind of feelings for a person could leave you feeling so bare, so hollowed-out inside, once they were gone?

The only other time she'd felt like this, she'd been a young girl in a bed like this one, screaming as some nameless doctor walked out with the baby daughter she hadn't even had chance to see, let alone hold.

'The midwife said the umbilical cord is around the baby's neck,' Kate said shakily, reaching for her husband's hand for support.

'That's right,' Grace confirmed, making sure she included both worried parents. 'It's what we call a nuchal cord but, although it might sound terrifying, it's actually a very common occurrence, happening in around one in three births.'

'Won't it… I don't know…' Darren dropped his voice as he feared the word itself might harm their baby '…strangle the baby?'

Grace shook her head.

'Your baby is still getting all the oxygen and nutrients he needs through the cord, and he won't need to take a real breath until he's actually out in the world.'

'What if it gets a kink in it, like a hose?' Darren asked,

as though he were speaking a foreign language, and he were having difficulty remembering how to speak it. 'How will the oxygen get through then?'

She watched as he and Kate gripped each other's hands even tighter, her heart going out to both of them.

'The umbilical cord has its own little set of tricks and skills,' she assured them. 'It's filled with a soft, gelatinous fluid—like a jelly—which protects all the vessels inside, and helps to protect against being compressed, or *kinked*.'

'Oh. So, we just…leave it?'

'Often intervention can cause more problems than if we just give the delivery chance to progress on its own. But to make sure the baby stays okay, I have this machine called a pulse oximeter device, and I'm going to insert the sensor into you, Kate, to your baby. That way I can monitor his oxygen saturation levels and ensure that he isn't in any undue distress.'

'Okay.' They both nodded quickly, exchanging a sweet, private look with each other.

For some inexplicable reason, it made Grace think of Rik. She shoved the errant thought from her head.

But their relationship hadn't been real, had it? Not like the couple in front of her.

She and Rik had only been together in the first place because they had a mutual connection in Bas. Rik wouldn't have bothered with her if not for his brother, and she would never have asked him to help at the charity fete if Bas hadn't demanded it.

Except that the attraction between her and Rik had been there from that first night at the gala—before they'd known they had Bas in common.

She concentrated on the task in hand.

'These are good oxygen saturation levels, Kate,' Grace encouraged her patient as she checked the results. 'Your baby is doing well.'

Still, the worry niggled at her. The baby had its umbilical cord wrapped around its neck and its position made it impossible to reach in and free it. On the positive side, it wasn't so tight that it was causing the baby's heart rate to plummet with each contraction, but that could change at any time. Not that there was any point scaring the understandably anxious parents with that detail.

The door opened just as she was checking the clock. It was the midwife she'd assigned to Naomi Fox, beckoning her. Grace dipped her head in acknowledgement and returned her focus back to her current patient. Half an hour longer for the delivery to progress, all the while monitoring the baby, and if Kate hadn't delivered by then, they might have to consider other intervention methods.

Quietly, she relayed the information to the midwives assigned to the couple, and told them to find her if anything changed, then she slipped out of the door into the pristine hallway of the Jansen wing, where her other colleague was waiting for her.

'Where are we with Naomi?' Grace asked quietly. 'Is the OR free yet?'

'Yes, they're prepping it now and we're ready to start taking her through.'

A combination of relief and unease washed over Grace.

'Is anyone on the way?'

Naomi and Bas had been utterly discreet through the pregnancy so far—with Bas following Naomi's request for him to keep away whilst she went for her weekly foetal non-stress test, even though Grace knew it had near killed him.

But given the shock results of today's test, surely Naomi had called him to alert him to what was going on.

So much for hoping for a baseline foetal heart rate of around one hundred and twenty, to one hundred and sixty—when the results had started to emerge, it had been clear that

Naomi was having contractions and that the baby was beginning to look as though it might be struggling.

If the baby went into foetal distress, she would have no choice but to deliver via caesarean section. Yet if she delivered the baby without Bas being present, he would never forgive her.

But what was she to do? Ultimately, Naomi was her patient. Not her friend.

'Her sister should be here any minute,' the midwife told her, oblivious to the turmoil in Grace's head.

Clearly the two of them must have had some kind of falling out, if Naomi was contacting her sister instead of Bas, and the knowledge affected Grace far more than it had any right to.

She'd really begun to believe in them as a couple. The idea that Bas might have been able to overcome his demons and be with the mother of his soon-to-be-born baby had been somehow buoying.

As though, if he could achieve that much, then perhaps there was hope for her, too.

And perhaps even for her and Rik.

She'd picked up the phone half a dozen times, but never placed the call.

She'd even sat in her car in the road outside his hotel. But then she'd driven away again.

There wasn't a single part of her that didn't ache to tell him how badly she yearned for him.

With a deep breath, Grace nodded briefly to her colleague, headed into the next corridor to Naomi's room, and opened the door.

'I'm in labour, Bas.' She heard Naomi's agonised voice. 'And I couldn't even feel it.'

But it was the fact that Bas was standing there, one hand enveloping Naomi's, the other stroking the hair off her forehead, that filled Grace with relief.

Whatever Naomi had done, it seemed that her sister had at least had the presence of mind to call Bas, after all. Still, he didn't even notice Grace as she made her way to the cardiotocograph to check the recent results.

'That's not uncommon,' Grace said quietly, not wanting to intrude on her friend's moment, but needing to do her job. 'With all the fluid, and the discomfort you've been feeling up to this point.'

'So, bed rest?' Bas cut in, his voice sounding so different from his usual, unflappable self. 'You can give her something to stop the contractions, Grace. Betamimetics? Try to keep the baby in just a little longer. Preferably to at least thirty-seven weeks.'

'Her cervix is already beginning to change and your little one isn't tolerating the contractions too well.' Grace shook her head as she glanced at Bas, then looked back at Naomi. 'We'll prep you for a C-section now, Naomi.'

'I'm coming in.' Bas lifted the side of the bed, clearly readying himself to move it.

As if he were the surgeon, rather than her patient's partner.

'You'll wait here,' Grace told him firmly. 'I'll take good care of her, Bas. But you're the father right now, not the surgeon. I'll make sure we call you as soon as she's prepped.'

He glowered at her, but she stood firm. This was her area of expertise, and he needed to trust. They both knew it—however much Bas might have desperately needed to feel in control at that moment.

'Go,' he grunted at last, dipping his head to kiss Naomi's forehead.

Solicitous. Loving. It was so unlike the Bas that she'd known all these years—and yet not.

Just as Rik had said.

But there was no time to dwell. With a gentle word to Bas as she ushered him into the chair—not that she thought he heard her—she instructed her team to get Naomi up and on her feet. It was better for her and the baby if she kept moving, and it was only a brief walk to the delivery OR, just down the corridor.

And then she began prepping Naomi for the C-section, all the while talking to her, and reassuring her as much as possible.

By the time one of her team had gone to get Bas gowned up and brought in, she had Naomi in the OR and in place. And before Naomi was wheeled out—cradling her magnificently strong newborn, who they'd just named Aneka, before she would be taken to NICU—Bas stepped towards Grace.

'Thank you.'

'Any time,' she told him, half choked up despite her wide smile.

Because this was the moment she'd never had the chance to experience with her own daughter. It was the reason why she'd never been able to move on.

Which meant that Rik was right about tracking her down—she needed that connection.

Or that closure.

'I was surprised to receive your call,' Rik told his brother as they stood, finally facing one another without being over a patient.

Though *surprised* didn't quite cover the shock he'd felt when—right in the middle of packing his bags for his last day in the UK—his phone had rung with an unknown number.

He'd taken the call straight away. In hindsight he'd been hoping it had been Grace. He could never have predicted it would have been his brother, ringing to ask him to meet before he left for the airport.

So now, he was here in the hospital coffee shop. Presumably, Bas didn't want to leave the grounds whilst the mother of his baby was still recovering. He'd heard the rumours, of course. How the playboy surgeon Bas Jansen had become a father a few days earlier.

It was all a far cry from the reunion he'd spent decades envisaging. But then, he'd long since given up on that. That dream had paled into significance when he'd lost Grace— the woman he'd never expected to crash his life.

He eyed his brother. A few weeks ago, the animosity had been clear in every line of his Bas's body. Every black look shot from his ice-cold eyes. Now, Rik couldn't help but notice, his brother seemed different.

Changed.

No doubt due to the baby that the entire hospital was talking about—as well as the woman who had allegedly finally tamed him.

'Let's get on with this, shall we?' Bas suggested.

But that, too, lacked the bitter heat from weeks before.

'How is fatherhood?' Rik asked, surprising even himself.

He didn't know if he'd thought his brother would answer, but then Bas's chest actually began to swell with pride before Rik's eyes and, abruptly, Rik realised that it was Naomi, and his new baby, who had somehow effected this reunion. Not Grace, as he'd initially thought.

He wasn't sure what that meant.

'Fine,' Bas began in a clipped voice, but then he clearly couldn't help himself. 'I never thought I would ever be a parent, yet I've learned how to be a father. A proper father. I've begun to understand what it is to love, and to accept love.'

'And you didn't know that before?' Rik demanded before he could swallow the words down.

His brother's face darkened.

'How could I know?' he demanded. 'I had no idea what love felt like. It's taken me until now to understand it.'

'Then I envy you,' was all Rik could manage.

'You envy me? Are you completely deluded?'

And there it was. The truth that had been hanging over Rik for so long.

'I always envied you. You got away.'

'I got away?' his brother echoed angrily. 'I was the one who envied you.'

Rik frowned. It made no sense.

'I can't imagine why,' he bit out.

And his brother erupted.

'You had it all. You were the one she wanted—the one she heaped love onto—whilst I was the one she cast aside.'

'Say that again,' Rik demanded slowly, his tone unexpectedly dangerous, but his brother didn't seem to heed it.

In the back of his mind, Rik heard Grace's voice, telling him just how wounded Bas had been by the events of that night.

He hadn't really listened to her, though, he'd been too caught up in everything he himself had lost that night.

'You were the one she wanted to keep, whilst I was the one she couldn't wait to get rid of.'

This was insane, Rik reflected darkly. His brother had completely twisted up events to suit his agenda. He couldn't possibly remember it that way.

'Have you seriously forgotten what it was like in that house when things didn't go our stepfather's way?' Rik demanded, his voice suddenly hoarse. 'Did you consider that, with you gone, I was the only punchbag left? Did you think she'd suddenly stop turning a blind eye to his tempers?'

'That was your decision. You're the one who told authorities I was lying when I'd had enough. At least she wanted to keep you. I got sent to be with a father who never wanted me around.'

'You can't really mean that?'

Things churned inside him. Dark and forbidding. He could hardly take in what he was hearing, but his brother gritted his teeth at him as though he truly believed it.

'How do you think it feels to be the son so awful that even his mother couldn't love him?' Bas rasped. 'I spent years wondering what was so wrong...so flawed about me, that wasn't you. You were always the perfect son.'

'That's...preposterous.' Rik suddenly found himself trying to control his temper from the sheer absurdity of it.

How could his brother possibly believe that, after all that had happened in the lead up to that night?

After everything he himself had done, stepping in to take the next beating because, after the night before, he'd been afraid their stepfather might actually kill Bas this time.

But his brother leaned back, folding his arms over his chest defensively.

'That's the truth. The last words she told me were that you and I might be twins, but that I lacked your compassionate side. That I was a horrid little bastard who no one could ever love.'

'Is that what you truly think?' Rik laughed, but even to his own ears it was a hollow, cold sound.

'Is that the way you remember things in your head, Basilius? That she somehow favoured me?'

'Didn't she?' his brother demanded.

'No,' Rik snapped. 'Our mother was a master of manipulation. She used to tell me that I lacked the kind of personality that you had. She told me that I was a pathetic excuse for a boy, and that no one could ever love me.'

Neither of them spoke for a moment. Hadn't he accused Grace of that—of having manipulated him—the last time they'd spoken? How could he have equated the two? He felt sick just thinking about it.

Had he really failed to appreciate just how much she'd come to mean to him, even in the short time they'd had?

But now wasn't the time for analysing his relationship with Grace.

Rik pressed on.

'Have you really forgotten what our mother was truly like? Have you forgotten how she used to play one of us against the other? Always trying to drive that wedge between us? All for attention?'

'I haven't forgotten anything,' Bas ground out. 'I remember how she more than loved attention, she *craved* it. She couldn't live without it. Attention to her was like air is to every other normal human being. Without it, she might as well be suffocating, dying. And you gave it to her.'

'I was trying to keep her sweet.' Rik shook his head. 'In a good mood. Especially when *he* came along, and it went from her manipulation to his fists.'

'You never really bore the brunt of that, did you?' Bas said, and Rik thought it might have been intended as a dig, but in reality it came out with such anguish that it might as well have reached into his chest and squeezed.

'Not as much as you did. I know that,' Rik murmured. 'You made sure of it.'

He paused, waiting for his brother to reply, but Bas didn't. His expression was strange, as though he barely even recalled that.

'Don't you remember how you would take the blame for me?' Rik demanded, confused. 'Taking responsibility for things I was supposed to have done wrong, even though you'd had nothing to do with it? If we were out of milk. If a light had been left on. Even simply if we walked down the stairs the wrong way.'

'I remember all that,' Bas began, 'but I don't remember taking the blame for you.'

And then it struck Rik—the reason that Bas didn't remember things the way that he did. How ironic that he himself had forgotten.

'Well, you did.' Rik dipped his head in a curt nod. 'Almost all the time. You were always a protector, Basilius. Even for me. The only reason you didn't try to protect me that day was because you were concussed. Not that either of us understood that at the time.'

'Say that again?'

'You got walloped the day before. Only, it was so rough that you'd actually been sick. You told me that everything had gone black. If it hadn't been for that, you would have leaped in for me again. The way you always did.'

Bas glowered at him. But there was a flickering in his eyes, as though he was desperately trying to remember. Rik wished Grace were here, though whether for himself or for his brother, he couldn't be certain.

'So why did you betray me?' Bas demanded abruptly. 'Why did you back her up, that final time, instead of me?'

Rik eyed him incredulously. Had the concussion been so bad that he'd forgotten everything?

No wonder Grace had believed he had wronged his brother. No wonder Bas hadn't wanted to make contact with him all these years, if that was what he honestly thought. But now it was finally chance to set things right.

'Because we agreed that was what I was going to do,' Rik bit out simply.

He might have known his brother wouldn't believe him.

'What are you talking about?' Bas ground out. 'Why would we ever, *ever* agree that?'

Inside, Rik felt raw. Scraped hollow. And the things that moved within him were too dark, and angry, and frustrated.

'You really don't remember?'

'Remember what?'

Rik eyed him grimly. No wonder people never wanted to rehash a bad past. It stirred up too many unwanted ghosts. And too many *what ifs*.

'We agreed that if Child Welfare took us, then they'd probably end up splitting us up. We didn't want that.'

'That conversation never happened,' Bas scorned. 'Besides, we got split up anyway.'

'How could we have foreseen that?' demanded Rik. 'We didn't know Magnus existed. We didn't even know that dead-beat wasn't our father.'

Bas shook his head, his expression thunderous.

'So that's what you're claiming? That was our plan? That we agreed I would tell the truth, only for you to back up our mother's lie? I don't think much of that so-called plan.'

'Our plan was that we would get rid of Child Welfare, and then we were going to run away and find Mrs P. And Bertie,' Rik fired back, just about controlling his temper. 'You really don't remember?'

'I don't remember because it didn't happen.'

'It must have been the concussion,' Rik pointed out.

And he could see that his brother hated that it made sense.

Hated it, and something else. Something that Rik could only hope was *welcoming it*.

'You're saying you told them that I was lying so that they would go away?'

Rik couldn't tell whether his brother was finally beginning to see it, or not. Still, he kept trying.

He had to. He hadn't been searching for decades to simply give up because his brother didn't take his word for it.

The way he shouldn't have given up on Grace.

'And we wouldn't be torn apart before we'd had chance to escape and find Mrs P.'

The two men stood in contemplative silence. And finally, *finally* it seemed that his brother was listening to him.

'I tried to find you,' Rik offered, after one silence bled into another. 'But I had no idea where to start looking or how. I asked, but she never told me anything, of course.'

'I find that harder to believe. Even back then, Magnus Jansen had made a name for himself as a surgeon.'

Rik cast him a long look, but he knew he had to be open with his brother.

Grace had shown him that much.

'Up until our mother's death, before Christmas last year, I thought my name was Henrik Magnusson. I've spent a decade looking up every Magnusson in Sweden. I had no idea you were even in the UK, let alone that I should really be looking for the name Jansen. The only thing I ever gleaned from her, growing up, was that he was a surgeon. It was the one nugget I held onto. So damned tightly. My one connection to you.'

'So much so that you became a surgeon?' Bas rasped.

'Yes.'

So simple. So frank. It clearly rattled Bas—the idea that he might have got it all wrong, all these years.

'You expect me to believe that you only found out the truth when our mother told you…what, on her deathbed?'

'I can't tell you what to believe, Basilius. I can only tell you the facts as I know them to be. And she didn't tell me anything, whether on her deathbed or otherwise. Finally telling the truth would have been too kind an ending for her, Basilius. She was bitter and vengeful until the end.'

'Then how?' Bas bit out.

'When she died, Mrs P saw the obituary in the paper and made contact. When I told her what had happened all those years ago, she was able to fill in some of the gaps. Once I pieced it together with what I knew, I was able to find you.'

Bas looked as if he'd just taken a body blow. And Rik felt as if he'd just landed one.

'Mrs P is still out there?' he whispered.

'She is.'

'And Bertie?'

A sadness shot through Rik.

'He died. About a decade ago. Apparently, they'd both been waiting. Hoping we would one day seek them out.'

'They didn't seek us out,' Bas gritted out, as though he didn't care.

But Rik knew better. He was beginning to recognise

the brother he'd once known. The brother he'd missed, all these years.

'They didn't know where we'd gone, Basilius. And they didn't want to risk causing problems for us when we were younger. They'd hoped that with them out of the picture, our mother's jealousy would have dissipated. And when we never got in touch, they let themselves believe it.'

Bas grunted but didn't speak.

'She would love to know about you and Naomi. I can only imagine how much joy it would bring her to hear about your new baby girl.'

With a start, his brother jerked his hand up for Rik to stop, clearly needing a moment to try to make sense of it all.

But Rik couldn't afford to let him. He still had to leave for his flight, and he couldn't risk his brother shutting down again. This was his one chance.

'You seem to think you have the monopoly on being rejected, *bror*. On being mistreated, and wronged. But, from my perspective, you got the better deal. You got away from her. And maybe Magnus wasn't any more welcoming, or loving, I can't speak to that,' Henrik rasped, 'but at least his fists were never the answer.'

Bas glowered at him as though he thought it was his own fault.

'How long did you stay?'

'I got away when I was fifteen,' Rik told him bleakly. 'Then, as soon as I could, I joined the army and I got my education that way.'

He couldn't bring himself to say any more. Not yet. Not when he hadn't even told Grace any of it.

And he'd had the gall to accuse her of not being open and honest with him.

'What about him?' Bas asked abruptly. 'Where is he now?'

Rik scoffed.

He shrugged. 'Who knows? Without you or me there as

a punchbag, he turned his attention onto her. She saw her chance to take him to court for compensation and she divorced him.'

His brother's face said it all.

Erin Sundberg had been prepared to stay with the man even when he'd hurt her kids, but it had been different when she herself had become the target. He couldn't imagine caring that little for his kids—it was why he'd never planned on having any. But now, looking at his brother—a new father himself—he couldn't imagine Bas ever letting anyone lay a finger on his child.

Did that mean there was hope, after all? For him and for Grace? He'd let her go because he'd thought he couldn't love anyone. He'd thought he wasn't capable.

Now he knew that he was.

Perhaps he ought to fight for Grace with half the drive that he'd fought for his brother all these years.

'*Bror*, I need your help with something.'

CHAPTER FOURTEEN

'WHERE ARE WE GOING?' Grace asked Rik, as they strode along the busy pavement in the tourist-popular side of town.

'Think of it as my last gift to you, before I leave for Sweden,' Rik answered, which she couldn't help thinking was no answer at all. 'My apology, and my goodbye, all wrapped into one. You look perfect by the way. Beautiful.'

Self-consciously, she smoothed her hands over her caramel fitted trousers, and cream fine-knit jumper. He hadn't said where their date—not that this was a date—was going to be, so she'd thought it the safest option. Smart but casual.

As if what she wore could change the fact that he was leaving. That he'd invited her to join him. Or that, despite every fibre in her body wanting to, Grace couldn't quite break that one final, probably imagined tie to Thorncroft.

Lost in her own head, Grace almost stumbled when Rik stopped abruptly outside a little café and ushered her inside. Then, after a brief glance around, he led them both to a table.

And Grace couldn't have said why her heart kicked up a beat as she sat down, her eyes darting everywhere whilst she waited for him to speak—which he clearly didn't intend to do until after they'd ordered their drinks.

The wait seemed interminably long. And then, at last, Rik began.

'I spoke with my brother the other day.'

'I heard.' Grace nodded, taking a careful sip of her hot drink. 'Though that's all I know. He and Naomi, and their baby, have been in their own private bubble ever since the birth. It's lovely to see.'

'I think they'll be fine. I saw more of the brother I used to know.'

'So you reconciled?' A kind of happiness swelled in her

chest, though she couldn't have said if it was for Rik, or for her friend. Or both.

'I think it's safe to say that we've started to. It will take time, but I believe we're on our way.'

'I'm happy for you.'

'I know that you are,' Rik agreed, without hesitation.

'So, does that mean you'll be staying after all?'

And what did it say that her chest tightened at the idea, almost willing him to say *yes*? Where did she think anything could possibly lead, whilst she was so paralysed in Thorncroft?

'The invitation to join me is still there.'

'Thank you,' she whispered, wishing more than anything that she had the courage to do just that. 'I wish I could.'

Unexpectedly, Rik laid his hand over hers.

'It's down to you,' he told her softly.

And Grace wished it were that easy.

'Rik…' she began, then faltered.

But he made her feel stronger when he reached out and lifted her chin with his finger. Making her look at him. Holding her gaze with his own.

'At some point in the next ten minutes, your daughter will walk through that door.'

Something walloped into Grace's body—so hard that it stole the breath from her very lungs.

'Don't panic.' He squeezed her hand tightly. 'This isn't an engineered meeting. You aren't here to meet her. I'm giving you the chance to leave now, if that's what you want.'

'Why would you…?'

'I'm just showing you that you were right coming back to Thorncroft—she has been here all along.'

And everything was too tight in Grace's body, in her head, to speak. But it didn't matter, because Rik was answering all those clamouring, unspoken questions.

'She reached out to the adoption agency a few years ago,

along with her adopted mother's approval. So she wants to know who you are. This is their family café. It's amazing what my wealth, and my brother's contacts in this city, can unearth.'

'You told your brother?'

It was probably the least important question right now, but it was all she could voice. Emotions were bombarding her. Too many of them, and too heavy-hitting for her to identify.

'You once told me that you wished other people knew about your daughter. That you hated her being kept like some dirty secret, but that you just didn't know how to tell anyone.'

Grace nodded, not trusting herself to speak.

'Do you want us to go?' he checked, after a while.

Her head swam. She wasn't ready to meet her daughter, but she didn't want to leave, either.

'She doesn't know I'm here?'

'She doesn't have the slightest clue about you. I brought you here to try to help you the way that you helped me with my own brother. To give you the nudge you need to either go home and sign that register, or to walk away for good. Because you can't go on as you are now, with your life in limbo. Believe me, I know how it feels.'

It was as if his every word was lodging in her head. And it was everything she'd wanted to tell herself but hadn't had the courage to do in the past. Not alone.

But this time, she wasn't alone. Rik was right here with her. So Grace waited, not even sure if she kept remembering to breathe. Every second ticking loudly in her head, echoing its countdown.

And then, suddenly, the door opened and there was no doubting that the young girl who walked through that door was the daughter she'd given birth to. It was like looking into a mirror straight back to her past.

The girl was a carbon copy of the fourteen-year-old Grace herself had been.

'That's…her…?' she managed to whisper, to no one in particular, though she gripped Rik's hand tighter.

'That's her,' he confirmed quietly.

Tears burned her eyes, her throat constricting, and Grace watched, transfixed, as the girl bounced across the room, dropped a kiss on the cheek of the woman who had served them, and then slid behind the counter to make herself a drink. A thick, frothy, strawberry milkshake by the look of it. And all the while, the girl chatted non-stop to the woman who was obviously her adopted mother.

Her real mum, Grace reminded herself.

Because that woman was the one who had raised her to be such a joyous, fun, secure young person.

'She looks…happy,' Grace managed to choke out, as something lifted off her chest.

It felt suspiciously like relief, though she'd never realised it had been squatting there all these years. Heavy and suffocating.

And it was impossible to stop the hot tears from breaking free and tracking down her face. She dashed at them impatiently.

'She's beautiful.'

'Do you want to know her name?'

'Her name?'

Grace flickered her eyes to Rik for a scant second, then back at the girl.

'They called her Amelia. Mellie for short.'

'Mellie.' Grace rolled the name around her mouth. 'It suits her.'

Everything suited her. She was the most beautiful girl Grace thought she'd ever seen in her life. And what was more, she was happy and healthy.

Surely there was nothing more perfect, more…*right* than that?

'We need to leave.' She snatched her hand out of Rik's

abruptly, her heart pounding so loudly in her chest that it felt like the longest, most ominous roll of thunder. *'Now.'*

Snatching her bag up, and her coat, Grace stood as quickly as she could. She could barely keep from running as she headed for the door. But once she was outside on the pavement, amongst the bustle of the city traffic and the jostling of pedestrians, she turned and scurried, dodging people and flying across junctions.

And when Rik finally caught up with her—finally made her stop and catch a breath—she couldn't have said where she was or how far she'd gone.

Looking up into his concerned expression, Grace choked back a racking sob.

'I got it all wrong.'

'Got what wrong?' he asked gently. Steadyingly.

Doubling over, her hands braced against her knees, she fought to steady her breathing.

'I got it wrong, and my parents got it right.' She shook her head. 'All these years, I've hated them for taking my daughter away from me. But look at her. She's happy. And loved. And perfect.'

'All the things you've always wanted for her,' Rik pointed out. 'I know you better than you think, Grace.'

Slowly, she craned her neck to look up at him.

'All the things I've wanted for her,' she agreed. 'And more. So much more.'

'Surely that's good?'

Grace sucked in a breath.

'More than I could have given her,' she managed. Breathing heavily into the silence for several seconds. 'That love she had with her mother, that affection. I couldn't have given her that.'

'Of course you could, though that isn't what today is meant to be about.'

'No.' She shook her head. 'I couldn't. I told you, my parents loved me in their own way, but they didn't show affection. There were no dropped kisses. No spontaneous hugs. I'd forgotten how sterile it was until I saw Mellie in there with her mother. Her *real* mother. Not me. I'm just the kid who gave birth to her.'

'Grace—'

'My childhood wasn't full of affection.' She cut him off, finally standing up and drawing in lungfuls of fresh air. 'It was a little cold, and I would have been a cold mother, too. It was really only during my career that I started to see how loving couples could be. How close families could be. Mellie is exactly where she needed to be, and my parents knew that.'

'Grace…'

'I don't know who I am any more, Rik,' she blurted out suddenly, as a huge wave of regret crashed over her. 'I don't know what I believe.'

'This was supposed to help you,' he told her, his confusion clear. 'It was about making you feel better about the choices that were made on your behalf. It wasn't supposed to make you feel worse.'

'And it does make me feel better,' she told him. 'In one way. I'm glad that she has such a loving family…'

'There's a *but*?' he demanded, as though he couldn't quite believe it.

A profound sadness opened up inside her.

'Not for her,' Grace tried to explain. 'But for me. For just how wrong I had it in my mind. For the fact that I hated my parents for taking her from me, yet that was what has given her a better life than I ever could.'

'You were sixteen,' Rik pointed out. 'And perhaps if they had handled it differently…talked to you, allowed you to talk about her…it might have been different.'

'Perhaps,' she conceded. 'But I'll never know. What I *do* know is that I'm not sure who I am any more. And maybe that sounds crazy to you—'

'It doesn't,' he cut in instantly. And she was grateful for it. 'I understand better than most how family, separations, losses, are all inextricably linked with who we are. They're some of the things that give us our sense of self.'

He was so kind and understanding. More than she thought she deserved.

'I feel like I've lost all of that,' Grace confessed. 'Like I don't know what to do next.'

'Don't rush it,' he advised. 'Take some time to think things through. I'm here with you, whenever you need me.'

Rik had intended it to give her the nudge she needed to decide one way or another but, suddenly, she felt more paralysed than ever.

'What I need…' Grace tailed off, willing the pain in her chest, and in her head, to subside. Hardly surprised when it didn't.

Every fibre of her was screaming out in protest, but she forced herself on, all the same.

'What I need,' she tried again, 'is to do this for myself. On my own.'

The look that Rik cast her was pure torture.

'You need to get some space, and clear your head,' he ground out, his arms reaching for her.

She nodded wordlessly, wishing that her body didn't melt so easily at his mere touch.

'So come with me to Sweden. You said you were ready to leave Thorncroft, and there's nothing but space and fresh air at my cabin.'

'And you,' she pointed out quietly.

'Does that matter?'

It did, because Rik was now crowding her head as much as anyone. She'd thought she'd loved him. It turned out she didn't really know how to love. Because wasn't love about doing the thing that was best for the other person? And it turned out that her cold, affectionless parents had a better idea of doing the right thing for someone else—for that little girl who had been her baby—than she herself had ever had.

It made Grace feel useless. And rejected. And then, because she felt that she ought to be happy that her daughter didn't need her, and hadn't missed her, it made her feel guilty.

'I need to work out who I am,' she managed. 'And I have to do it alone.'

For an agonisingly long moment, Rik watched her, and she lost count of the number of times words leapt into her mouth and she nearly opened her mouth and took it all back.

But she didn't. And then, with an abrupt nod, Rik conveyed his acceptance.

And Grace didn't know how she felt about the fact that he found it so easy to let her go.

Rik finally closed up on his patient after a long operation to re-excise and widen the tumour bed on a man who had previously had an unplanned excision.

The full-contrast MRI had offered him a clear image of the tumour bed and surrounding tissues, and his choice of contralateral micro-anastomosis had been the optimal decision.

But the simple truth was that these days he was grateful for every surgery that helped him to take his mind off *her*.

Grace.

It had been three months since he'd come back to Sweden, and it felt like the longest three months of his life. The need to fight for her that final day had been almost overwhelming. Rik still didn't know how he'd managed to restrain himself.

He'd only known that he'd *had* to.

He who had grown accustomed to having to fight for everything that he wanted. He was used to hunting it down with the kind of dogged determination that his years in the army had taught him. That his decades of searching for his brother had taught him.

To never give up.

So taking that step back to afford Grace the time, and space, that she'd told him she needed had probably been the hardest thing he'd ever had to do. A part of him had needed to fight, more than anything, so that the woman he'd come to realise he loved didn't have to do it alone.

But things hadn't been about what he needed. They had been about what Grace needed. And having him fight for her, or chase her down, wasn't what she'd needed at all.

So he'd sat back and waited for her—was still waiting for her—and all he could do was hope that she would, ultimately, return to him.

And though he and Bas had talked twice, over video call, their conversations had focussed mainly on his beautiful new daughter. They hadn't spoken much about Grace, but one thing his brother had said had been to remind Rik of the adage that Mrs P had once taught them—the one that said *If you love someone set them free...*

It had never been Rik's way, but somehow—even though it had damned near killed him—he'd managed to be patient. To give Grace time.

So, when he scrubbed out and headed for his consultation room, the last person he expected to see waiting inside was Grace.

For a moment, he thought perhaps he was hallucinating. And then, closing the door quietly behind him, he prowled slowly across the room, pretending to himself that he wasn't drinking her in.

She wore a pair of inky-blue jeans, which clung oh-so-lovingly to her curves, and a V-neck tee, which flattered her torso perfectly. It wasn't the usual polished version of her that he had grown accustomed to.

This Grace was somehow different. Softer. He might even have said more comfortable in her own skin.

Although one thing hadn't changed. The sight of her still

made his hands itch to lift the hemline of her tee and reacquaint himself with the glorious body that lay beneath. As if he were some kind of untried kid.

He almost gave in to it. Instead, he schooled himself to hold his nerve.

'You're here,' he observed, his voice more controlled than he felt inside.

'I'm here,' she agreed, her husky voice abrading him as she edged closer.

It was like being caught in a rip tide, dragging him under no matter how hard he fought to try to reach the surface.

Although he wasn't sure he tried that hard.

He wanted her with such an intensity that he thought he might drown in that need alone. But he had to know. He had to understand exactly why she was here.

For now? Or for good?

'I finally met Amelia,' she told him, her eyes shining. So bright that he thought it might be enough to blind him. 'She's incredible.'

'She's your daughter.'

'No.' Grace shook her head, but this time there wasn't the same sadness as back in Thorncroft. 'Not really. She is her mum and dad's daughter. They're the people who raised her. But she wanted to know me—apparently her mother was adopted as a child, too, but she found out when she was eighteen and it had been a shock to her. So she's always been up front with Mellie about being adopted, and she encouraged her daughter to reach out to her birth mother—to me.'

'So meeting her was...the right thing?' he checked.

'It was.' Grace bobbed her head. 'She has a wonderful life, and a supportive family. She doesn't need a second mum. But she does want to know me. They all do. And I want to be as much a part of her life as she will let me.'

Which meant that Grace was only here for *now*, Rik realised abruptly. And something cracked in his chest.

He smiled—and who cared if it was tight?

'You seem different,' he managed, at length.

'Do I?' She offered a light shrug. 'I've been on a bit of a round-the-world trip—someone once told me that I should take the time to discover myself more—and I've visited so many of the places I always dreamed of seeing.'

That caught him by surprise.

'You've been around the world?'

'Well, not exactly.' She gave a rueful laugh. 'My neighbour has Cooper for the moment, and I've only been to about fifteen countries so far, in sixty days.'

'You've been travelling like you always wanted,' he realised. So was that what her neighbour had meant when she'd said Grace had gone away. One of the few things that his brother *had* told him. 'But you didn't give notice at the hospital?'

'I came to an agreement. Magnus had me work in various places he knew as part of a Jansen ambassadorial project that he's apparently been wanting to set up for a while. I've been working in a mobile hospital in India, an orphanage in Cambodia, a women's clinic on Vietnam. I have quite the résumé if you need to see it.'

She was teasing him, and he wasn't sure how he felt about that.

'So you've been travelling the world? On your own?'

'I needed to work out who I am again. Like you said...' she exhaled '... Amelia is happy, but she doesn't need me. It's time for me to finally move on and live the life I want to. And that isn't in Thorncroft. So I put together my list of places to go, and I went.'

'And now you're here,' he growled, trying to decide what to make of it.

'I am.'

'How long for?'

'I was walking over the Golden Bridge in Vietnam when

I suddenly realised I had no one to share it with. And when I thought about it, I realised that the only person I wanted to share it with is you.'

'No,' he bit out, 'you don't.'

Grace simply smiled.

'I promise you, Rik, I know what I want. I've taken the time to realise who I am now—just like you said I should.'

'Grace—'

'And guess what?' She refused to let him interrupt her. 'I found the place I most wanted to see was some log cabin in the Tyresta National Park. Do you know anyone who can be my guide?'

Rik wasn't sure he was still breathing. He kept telling himself to get a grip. Because if he lost himself in those hooded eyes, and that sensuous mouth, he wasn't sure any map or compass could help him navigate his way out.

And he didn't want to deal with losing her all over again when she left.

'Why are you really here, Grace?'

'I came here for you, of course.'

So direct, and so uncomplicated. Something deep within Rik cleaved in two.

He wanted fervently to believe her but, after the childhood he'd endured, it felt almost too good to be true.

He had to be sure.

She looked up at him, and the sincerity in her expression moved right through him. Shaking him, like tectonic plates shifting. Emotions jumbled and rose within him, before dropping into a dark abyss and disappearing. And then, suddenly, something else began to rise up. Something new. *Hope.*

'I don't know if I can give you everything you deserve. I don't know if I'm capable of real love.'

'You are,' she assured him quietly. 'You had it for your brother. It's what made you sacrifice the one person you held dearest all those years ago. And it's what drove you on to find him, for all those years. You're more capable of love than you think. So, I've begun to learn, am I.'

Grace eyed him steadily. That sparkle in her eyes doing things to him and making that ache in his chest press in on him even harder.

'And since we're on the subject of love, I don't want it from anybody else. I never have done. Before you came along, I thought the only thing that really mattered was my career. You changed all that. You alone.'

Rik reached out and took her shoulders, pulling her into him. His voice so gruff that he barely recognised himself.

'I should caution you that if we start this thing, I don't know that I'll ever want to let you go.'

'I think that, by definition, is real love,' Grace returned.

So sure. So confident. And it was that light shining from her beautiful eyes, that *love*, that began to find its way to convince him.

'How long are you planning on staying?' he asked harshly.

Because he didn't know if he could bear to hear the answer. He needn't have worried.

'As long as you want me,' she told him, without a hint of uncertainty.

'What if I want you for ever?'

'Then I'd have to make sure you'd want Cooper for ever, too. I've no plans on leaving him with my neighbour for good.'

'I have a back yard perfect for twenty Coopers,' he assured her. 'Because I think, with you to guide me, *älskling*, there may be hope for me, after all.'

'There is if you want it.'

He shook his head in disbelief.

'You make it sound so easy.'

'It is so easy,' she stated with certainty. 'But also…it isn't. It's hard. Sometimes we'll disagree, maybe row. Things definitely won't always go smoothly. Sometimes things will be tough. The trick will be to hold on, and to work through it. Together. It will take a certain kind of strength, but I know you have that, because it's what brought you to this point.'

'You aren't selling this,' he teased.

But Grace continued as if she hadn't heard.

'The most important point is that it will be worth it. *We* will be worth it. And I want you to hold onto that, Rik. Because as long as you love me, it will all be worthwhile.'

'I want to be able to,' he told her sincerely. 'I want all of that.'

'Then that's all there is.'

And a thousand things moved through him at that.

'Not *all* there is,' he managed, hoarsely.

'No?'

She looked confused and he loved the idea of catching her unawares. His clever, kind, beautiful Grace.

'No,' he told her, his voice sincere. 'I think I also need to show you every day just how much I love you. How much I intend to keep loving you.'

She looked at him, her eyes raking his for meaning. He knew the precise moment she realised, and that pretty flush began to stain her smooth face.

'How much, for that matter,' he continued, 'I intend to worship you.'

'I think I would like that.' Her voice cracked, and it was like a lick of heat against his very sex. 'Very much.'

And with that, Rik cupped her face in his hands, lowered his head to claim hers—and proceeded to show her exactly how much he intended to worship her.

Every single day.

* * * * *

COMING SOON!

We really hope you enjoyed reading this book. If you're looking for more romance, be sure to head to the shops when new books are available on

Thursday 26th May

To see which titles are coming soon, please visit

millsandboon.co.uk/nextmonth

MILLS & BOON